1

BERLIN, AUGUST 1930

The day Archie met Esme he was in a bad mood.

Sadly – for Archie as much as for everyone else – he was often in a bad mood. This one had not been helped by the disaster that had befallen him at Liverpool Street Station at the very beginning of his two-month trip to Berlin. A disaster that he hoped his cousin Duncan would sort out.

As promised, Duncan was waiting for him in the lobby of the Adlon Hotel as Archie emerged from the lift. Tall and gawky, with a spattering of acne above his diplomat's stiff collar, he greeted Archie with a smile of wary welcome.

Too many people were wary when they saw Archie. Archie knew it was his fault, but it still irritated him.

The lobby of the Adlon was splendid – reminiscent of the pre-war grandeur of the Kaiser's Empire rather than the clear lines and curves of contemporary Berlin. A dozen solid square pillars of yellow clouded marble held up a painted ceiling, in which electric lights were subtly embedded. A broad grand staircase led up from the lobby to the ballroom above. Staff in pale blue tunics and white gloves drifted among the well-dressed guests. A grand piano murmured beguilingly in a corner. The Adlon was an island of elegance, order and calm in the very centre of the most modern city in Europe.

'Hello, Archie,' said Duncan, holding out his hand. 'When did you get in?'

Archie shook his cousin's hand and, despite his mood, forced a grin, which actually wasn't that difficult. Archie had always liked Duncan. Sixteen years Archie's junior, Duncan was the youngest of his aunt's three children. Archie had enjoyed playing with the boy as he had grown up – there had always been something wholesome and innocent about Duncan, and the boy had idolised his older cousin. Theirs was one of the few of Archie's relationships that had survived the Great War unscathed.

'About an hour ago,' Archie replied. 'Lister is unpacking upstairs.'

'You brought the old crook with you?'

'Safer here where I can keep an eye on him than back in Yorkshire where he could do untold damage.'

'Oh, there is plenty of trouble he can get into in Berlin.'

'That's probably true,' Archie agreed. But he needed his manservant with him, just in case – Duncan didn't have to know that.

'Any luck with a secretary?' Archie asked. 'I know I gave you precious little notice.' Fortescue, the Oxford research student Archie had engaged to help him with research for the biography of Field Marshal Blücher that he was working on, had arrived at Liverpool Street Station fifteen minutes before the train was due to depart, with the news that he was awfully sorry, but he wouldn't be able to accompany Archie to Berlin after all. He had just become engaged to the most ripping girl and she didn't want him to leave her for two months – he was sure Archie would understand.

Archie *had* understood: that getting engaged was no excuse for not doing something you had agreed to do, that Archie had been relying on Fortescue and that in any case informing him of his failure to meet his obligation just as Archie was about to depart for Germany was bad form. Very bad form.

Fortescue ran. And Archie cabled Duncan from Harwich asking him if he could find a replacement.

Archie was still furious with Fortescue, but he was also relieved. He was pretty certain the man would have got on his nerves sooner rather than later in Germany. Fortescue, no doubt, felt the same way.

'As a matter of fact, I have,' said Duncan with a quiet grin. 'Never underestimate the resourcefulness of His Majesty's Diplomatic Corps.'

'Well done. Who is he?'

'*She* is American. A foreign correspondent. Just starting out, so she needs some extra cash. She speaks good German and is frightfully keen. I think you'll like her. She's from Kalamazoo.'

A woman? American? 'Does she have any background in military history?'

'I very much doubt it,' said Duncan. 'There's only so much I can do with eighteen hours' notice.'

'Of course,' Archie admitted. 'When can I meet her?'

'Now, if you like. She's waiting for you out on the terrace.'

A slim, dark-haired woman was sitting at a table on the terrace, smoking a cigarette, next to two cups of coffee. The terrace overlooked a formal garden of squares and rectangles at the back of the hotel, in the middle of which stood a tall cast-iron fountain, supporting half a dozen black elephants. The woman smiled as she saw Archie and Duncan approaching.

'Harriet Dryden, this is Archie Laverick.'

'How do you do, Mr Laverick,' the woman said, holding out a gloved hand for Archie to shake. 'How was your journey?'

As was his habit with people he met, especially women, Archie checked Harriet's eyes for a flinch or a flicker towards the left side of his face, but there was nothing. Her dark eyes were friendly with a hint of mischief, or even wickedness. Her full lips melted as her smile broadened. The whole effect was rather pleasing.

'It was very good,' Archie said with uncharacteristic optimism. 'Apart from my secretary scarpering. But I hope Duncan has sorted that out.'

'Duncan is very resourceful,' Harriet said, with a sidelong glance at the young diplomat who went ever so slightly pink.

'He is. And thank you for agreeing to help me out, Miss Dryden.'

Duncan coughed and Harriet laughed. 'I'm sorry, Mr Laverick, it won't be me helping you out.'

Archie frowned and glanced at Duncan.

'It'll be me.'

Archie turned to see a smaller woman approaching. Her hair, although cut short, was a mess of honey, and freckles sprinkled her short snub nose. Her smile was bright but nervous above a pointed chin.

'I'm sorry, Sir Laverick, I was in the bathroom.' She stuck out her hand. 'I'm Esme Carmichael.'

'How do you do,' said Archie. And while he hadn't corrected Harriet, this woman was so far out with his name that he thought he ought to do something, especially if she was going to end up employed by him. 'And it's Sir Archibald.'

Esme frowned. 'Oh. I was so sure it would be Sir Laverick. I've been practising. Mind you, I think I prefer Sir Laverick.'

'You do?'

'Yes. Sounds dashing. Like Sir Lancelot. Don't you think? Whereas Sir Archibald?' She shook her head. 'Sounds a bit stuffy. You look dashing rather than stuffy, don't you, Sir Archibald?'

Esme was examining the scars on the left side of Archie's face with interest as she said this.

Archie suppressed a smile. 'I suppose I used to be dashing. Once.'

'Still dashing,' said Esme. 'How about Sir Archi*bald*? Can we settle on that?'

'I don't think so. Let's go for Sir Archie, shall we?'

'Sure thing. So you have a job for me, Sir Archie?'

'Perhaps,' said Archie. They sat around the table and Duncan and Archie ordered coffee from the waitress. From the lounge inside, an orchestra was tuning up.

'They all start dancing at five o'clock,' said Harriet. 'It's quieter out here.'

The table was shaded from the late-afternoon late-August sun and the temperature was pleasantly warm. The elephant fountain tinkled merrily in front of them in its square enclosure of bright scarlet and white begonias.

'I remember the five o'clock dances from my time in Munich before the war,' said Archie. 'I spent a year there just after school.'

'Do you like dancing?' said Esme.

'I used to,' said Archie, with a glance down towards his right leg.

'Say, they got your leg as well as your face?' said Esme. 'I guess that's what comes of being too dashing.'

Archie felt Duncan flinch next to him, but he smiled. It was refreshing to have his scars accepted rather than denied by a new acquaintance.

The two wounds had been acquired at different times. He had been injured in the face by shrapnel from an errant *minenwerfer* while he was returning from patrol in No Man's Land in 1916 near Ypres. The metal had just missed his eye, but the exhausted doctor who had too swiftly stitched him up had created a livid scar that reached from the eye down to the corner of his mouth. From the right, he looked normal, as did his smile. Not so from the left.

The wound in his thigh was more serious, inflicted as it was during the German offensive of March 1918, a day he would like to forget but never would. His leg had never been the same since. Neither had his mind.

'Yes. The leg plays up sometimes, which is why I need someone who can drive.'

'Oh, I can drive. I learned when I was ten. My pa taught me on the ranch.'

'The ranch in Kalamazoo?' Archie glanced at Duncan, suddenly unsure whether his cousin was having him on. Was there really a place called Kalamazoo?

'There aren't many ranches in Kalamazoo.'

'I see. I'm afraid I have no idea where Kalamazoo is.'

'It's in Michigan between Detroit and Chicago. My parents are separated. My father owns a ranch in Montana, but when I was fourteen my mother had had enough of the isolation – and the cows – and took me back to Kalamazoo, which is where she originally came from.'

'My parents are separated too. Or divorced.' Archie was surprised to hear himself volunteering the information. 'As am I, for that matter.'

'I'm sorry,' said Esme. 'On both counts. It's kind of tough on a kid.'

'It is,' Archie nodded. 'What are you doing in Berlin? Fed up with Kalamazoo?'

'Fed up with the States. I went to college in Chicago—'

'That's where we met,' Harriet interrupted.

'Yeah. After college, I got a job for a Chicago newspaper. And then something happened and I decided to become a foreign correspondent in Europe.'

'You were a reporter for the paper?'

Esme reddened. 'Not exactly.' Archie looked at her doubtfully. 'I mean, not at all. I worked as a secretary. But my plan is to send stories to the editor from here.'

'Have you written any?'

'Yes.' Some of the fizz had gone out of Esme. 'And they haven't been published yet. But I'm working on it. That's why I need some extra cash.'

'I see. To pay the rent?'

'Esme is staying with us,' Harriet interrupted. 'Father is Counselor at the US embassy here, so we have a nice house with plenty of room.'

Esme smiled at her friend gratefully. 'What do you need me to do? Duncan mentioned you're writing a biography of a Prussian general?'

'That's right. Field Marshal Blücher. Came to Wellington's rescue at the Battle of Waterloo. Have you heard of him?'

'I have now.' Esme saw the doubt on Archie's face. 'Look, Mr... I mean Sir Archie. I'm not a trained historian and I know nothing about dead German generals. But I speak and read the language, I know how libraries are organised, and I can work hard. I'll be a help to you, I promise.'

'Esme is really smart,' said Harriet. 'I know, I studied with her for four years. She won't disappoint you.'

'I won't,' Esme agreed. 'But if you can find someone more qualified, I'd understand.'

Archie had no other options. He suspected Esme had guessed that. He also suspected that travelling around Germany with Esme would be more amusing than travelling around with Fortescue.

'And you're confident you can read German historical documents?' Archie asked, in German.

'*Die Weltgeschichte ist das Weltgericht*,' Esme replied.

The world's history is the world's judgement. 'Hegel?' Archie asked.

'Schiller, originally. Hegel was quoting him.'

That was impressive. 'All right,' he said. He didn't have much choice. He would probably get more done with Esme's help than without it.

'What's the pay?' Esme asked.

'I can give you a pound a day,' said Archie. 'Plus all expenses.'

'What's that in dollars?'

'About five,' Duncan said.

'That sounds acceptable,' said Esme, carefully, but Archie suspected she would have accepted anything.

'I can pay you in marks,' Archie said. 'If you prefer?'

'No, no. Pounds sterling suits me.' That was understandable: the Reichsmark was not the most stable of currencies in 1930.

'Can you start right away? I'm planning to go to Blücher's family seat in Silesia early next week, and I'd like to leave on Sunday. I'll hire us a car. I'd like to visit a couple of battlefields as well, and a car will be more practical than going by train.'

Esme winced and glanced at her friend. 'Harriet and I have been invited to a castle in Saxony over the weekend, as has Duncan. I've already accepted. I'm sure you wouldn't appreciate an employee who didn't come through on their commitments?'

Did Esme know about Fortescue, Archie wondered. She gave him a quick cheeky grin. She did know – Duncan would have told her. But she was absolutely right: in his current mood, Archie was not sympathetic to people reneging on their obligations.

Archie took his leave. As he made his way back inside across the lobby to the lift, he couldn't resist turning. Duncan was speaking with shy diffidence to the two women. He was clearly smitten with one or other of them, possibly both. Harriet Dryden glanced quickly in Archie's direction, caught his eye for the tiniest of moments and returned her gaze to the young diplomat.

Archie reflected that he may have made a mistake in employing Esme, but it was probably not a serious one. It might be fun.

And he would have an opportunity to meet her intriguing friend again.

But Archie never did get that opportunity. Because, three days later, Harriet Dryden was dead.

2

Archie checked his watch. Again. Five-and-twenty past ten. This was not a good start. What a fool!

He was the fool. He had been momentarily beguiled by Esme Carmichael's vivacity and her friend's beauty to employ a secretary with no experience and no references. Two questions remained. Was she simply late or would she not appear at all? And should he give her the heave-ho immediately or drag her around Silesia for a few days and then get rid of her?

The car was waiting outside. If Esme Carmichael didn't show up, Archie wasn't sure what he would do. On some days he could easily drive hundreds of miles, but his leg was throbbing, and he knew Silesia was too far. He certainly wouldn't trust Lister to drive a fast car on the wrong side of the road in a foreign country: they would be lucky to make it to the bottom of Unter den Linden without a smash and then probably a fight.

A plump woman with a tiny hat perched on her large head drifted past Archie's seat in the lobby, a smaller man sporting a cane and a monocle in tow. They were speaking a Slavic language of some kind. Her perfume and his cologne did battle in Archie's nostrils, with the cologne winning the day. A dachshund, trotting alongside the shapely calves of a tall young blonde, was clearly as put out by the smell as Archie was, and gave the plump woman's ankle a nip, causing her to skip into the air and utter a dachshund-like yelp. Her beau turned in fury, which was quickly melted by an apologetic smile and a pout from the young lady. The hall porter touched his hat and shepherded the couple out into the streets of Berlin.

The dachshund wagged his short tail in triumph. Good lad, Archie said to himself.

A boy, immaculately dressed in the hotel's light blue livery with white gloves, scurried over to Archie's chair and bowed stiffly. 'Sir Archibald? A message for you.'

He presented Archie with an envelope resting upon a small silver tray. A telegram.

Archie snatched it from him. 'Bloody girl,' he muttered to himself. It would be from Esme Carmichael and it would contain some excuse for why she was unable to meet him as arranged. He expected the excuse to be creative. The real reason would be a hangover, or perhaps, like Fortescue, she had suddenly been smitten by a member of the opposite sex.

He tore open the envelope and read the wire.

V SORRY DREADFUL NEWS FRIEND HARRIET SHOT AND KILLED AT CASTLE STOP POLICE NEED TO INTERVIEW US STOP IF STILL HAVE JOB CAN MEET YOU TOMORROW SAME TIME STOP RGRDS E CARMICHAEL

Archie blinked and read the telegram through again. His irritation drained away, leaving him numb. The memory of Harriet

Dryden glancing at him as he crossed the lobby of the hotel leaped to his mind. And now she was dead. Shot. Shot!

Was it an accident? Some kind of hunting accident? Or was it intentional?

'Sir?'

'Sorry,' Archie said. 'I'll need to reply. Thank you.'

'You may do so at the front desk,' the boy said, and left him.

But Archie didn't move. He had seen so much death in the trenches, but that was many years ago now, and this news shocked him profoundly. Questions began to swirl around his brain, and then his mind just froze.

'Are you all right, sir?' It was the hall porter. Archie had no idea how long he had been sitting there, just staring ahead.

'Yes, yes, of course,' he said, taking a deep breath. 'Just some bad news, that's all.'

He put his weight on his stick, pulled himself to his feet and made his way over to the front desk.

'I would like to reply to this telegram,' he said. He noticed that it had been sent from a place called Adlerstein in Saxony.

The clerk behind the desk handed him a form. Archie paused to think, and then wrote:

> CONDOLENCES STOP YOU STILL HAVE JOB IF YOU WANT IT STOP SEE YOU ADLON LOBBY 10AM TUES STOP RGRDS LAVERICK

* * *

Esme showed up the following day, only five minutes late. She was wearing a smart blue summer dress in a wavy white pattern and a yellow cloche hat. Make-up around her eyes had not succeeded in completely hiding traces of redness, and her smile, which had been so bright the week before, was now brittle.

She brushed aside Archie's brief expression of sympathy and together they left the hotel on to the Pariser Platz to find their hired car. The immaculately scrubbed square was surrounded by grand façades, including those of the Adlon Hotel and, opposite it, the French embassy. On one side of the square stood the twelve tall columns of the Brandenburg Gate topped by the bronze sculpture of the quadriga, a woman holding aloft an olive wreath while driving a chariot. On the other, Unter den Linden, lined with its famous linden trees, cut a straight line through two obedient ranks of splendid imperial buildings and monuments towards the dome of the kaiser's former palace.

The car was a cream-coloured Horch convertible, which had been procured by the hotel. A squat mechanic with a large moustache explained to Esme how everything worked in a strong Berliner accent. Esme seemed to understand most of what he said. Her German wasn't bad, Archie was relieved to see. Although she didn't seem to know the German words for gear stick or accelerator, neither did Archie, and, for that matter, neither had Field Marshal Blücher.

The hotel porters stowed Archie's and Esme's bags in the boot, and they set off down Unter den Linden with Esme driving competently and Archie navigating with a map, once again provided by the hotel.

There were plenty of cars buzzing past the famous linden trees, driven with speed and aggression but, this being Germany, by and large their drivers stuck to the rules. There were all kinds of other vehicles on the streets – white trams, cream double-decker buses, green taxis, motorcycles, bicycles, barrows pushed by street vendors and delivery boys, and even the odd stolid nag pulling a cart through the hurly-burly. Horns honked, trams rang their bells, wheels of all sizes clattered and petrol motors chuntered and roared. Esme negotiated it all with skill.

Eventually, they extricated themselves from the city, and hit the open road, top down, sun shining out of the blue Brandenburg sky.

Their conversation was restricted to directions. Archie decided to take Esme's lead with conversation, at least at the beginning of the trip. She must be upset about her friend's death. If she wanted to talk, that was fine. If she didn't, that was fine too. There was no need for her to embarrass herself – or him for that matter – if she didn't want to. Archie hadn't heard anything from Duncan, but the murder had been all over the Berlin newspapers, so Archie knew the bare bones of what had happened; he didn't need to know the details unless Esme wanted to tell him.

As she drove, a touch of anxiety crept into Esme's features and she bit her lip. At last, as they were driving alongside a pretty tree-lined lake, a couple of rowing boats crossing its blue sparkling waters, she spoke.

'I'm not sure how to put this, Sir Laverick,' she started. 'Harriet told me to say this at the beginning of this trip, and Harriet knew what she was talking about in these matters.'

What matters? Archie wondered. 'Go on,' he said, curious.

Esme swallowed. 'I'm a single woman and we are going to be alone together for several days, and I'd appreciate it if you didn't... you didn't... well, make a pass at me.'

Archie was tempted to laugh, but Esme was deadly serious.

'I won't,' he said. 'I promise.'

Esme turned to him with a quick smile of relief and then reddened. 'Of course you wouldn't, why should you? I'm sure you are a perfectly respectable gentleman who would never do anything like that. You probably wouldn't even *want* to jump on me, would you?'

The corner of Archie's lip twitched. 'That's one of those questions with no right answer. I believe I was always considered "safe in taxis".'

'Oh, Lordy, I'm sure you are! Forget I ever suggested it. I mean, suggested the opposite of it, if you see what I mean.' She took a deep breath. 'It's just Harriet was insistent that I make that crystal clear.' She let out a sad chuckle. 'It was actually her last request.'

'Then it's good you honoured it.'

She sniffed and dabbed her eye, looking resolutely ahead.

'Men were always making passes at Harriet,' she said.

Archie remembered that fine figure and those mischievous eyes. 'I'm sure they were.'

'So she became an expert at fending them off. Sometimes. When she wanted to.'

Archie kept quiet. A wave of profound sadness washed over him. It was such a waste. Whenever a young person like that died it was such a waste. He had seen so much waste.

'Men always fluttered around Harriet when we were at college,' Esme said. 'She was an expert at batting them away. She looked different then. Still real pretty, but she wore glasses – she's as blind as a bat – and though she liked to date boys, it never amounted to much more than a kiss. Unlike some of the girls in our sorority – my goodness! And then it all changed. When I came to Berlin a couple of weeks ago, she was different.'

'With men?'

'Yes. It's her mother, I'm sure. She died of cancer last year, in Washington. Then Mr Dryden was posted to the Berlin embassy as Counselor and Harriet decided to come along to help him – to act as a hostess. I think she did a good job. But Berlin's a wild place with a lot to tempt anyone. There are plenty of young diplomats who are interested in Harriet and, unlike at college, she seems pretty interested in them too.' Esme took a deep breath. 'Seemed. It kind of shocked me when I got here. There are going to be a lot of broken-hearted young men in this city.'

'Including Duncan Mandeville?'

'Yes. Including Duncan, poor guy. But I don't think he ever stood much of a chance.'

'Her father must be devastated.'

'He is. First his wife and then his daughter. There is a brother working for a stockbroker on Wall Street who is on his way over here, but Harriet never thought he was much use. I'm doing the best I can.'

'I-I'm sorry I've taken you away from the poor man.'

'He has friends and colleagues here. And I needed to get away.' She nodded to herself. 'This is good.'

But a tear leaked out of her right eye and slid down her cheek. She left it untouched, pretending it wasn't there.

Archie did the same.

They drove in silence for a few miles. For some reason, Harriet reminded Archie of a young lieutenant in his company at the beginning of the war, Dowling. He was several years younger than Archie, but he was an intelligent man – boy, really – and in the oh-so-long periods of waiting, he and Archie had had conversations which ranged far and wide.

The top of Lieutenant Dowling's head had been taken off by machine-gun bullets at Loos in 1915. A waste.

And now another waste.

'W-w-we...' Archie took a breath and concentrated. 'We just stick on this road to Kottbus. We could have a spot of lunch around there.'

'Are you feeling all right, Sir Laverick?' Esme asked.

'Y-yes,' replied Archie. 'I get a stammer every now and then. And it's Sir Archie.'

Esme struck her forehead with the flat of her hand. 'Oh, I'm sorry, Sir Archie.'

'Let's just go with Archie, shall we, Miss Carmichael?'

Esme grinned. 'I think that would be a good idea. And you can call me Esme.' She reddened again. 'If you want.'

'Certainly, Esme.'

Archie could understand how Harriet's death would affect Esme, but he didn't understand how badly it affected him. He had only spent half an hour in her company. It worried him.

The stammering worried him.

He had noticed it that morning when Lister brought him his cup of tea and his copy of yesterday's *Times*.

'Th-thank you, Lister.'

Lister's bright blue eye darted towards his employer. 'I'll pack while you are at breakfast, sir. The forecast for Breslau is warm for the next three days. Although I very much doubt that the Hun forecasters are any better than our daft lot.'

Lister had a broad Yorkshire accent, which he could temper slightly when necessary – he didn't consider speaking to Archie as necessary. A wiry man with red hair and a lively, wrinkled face, he could be mistaken for a decade older than his forty-two years. He was exactly the same age as Archie – one of many things they shared.

'P-pack the P-Panama, then,' Archie said.

Lister stood up straight and stared at him. The only time both of Lister's eyes pointed in the same direction was when he stared straight ahead. One was a slightly darker shade of blue, immobile and made of glass.

Archie fought to get the words out. 'All right, Lister. I stammered. What of it?'

'You know what of it, sir. Was it that poor girl that got shot?'

'I don't know. I think so. It must be.'

'Did Lieutenant Dowling visit last night?'

Archie nodded.

His manservant continued to stare at him. 'Do you want me to come with you? In case...'

Archie knew very well what 'in case' meant. 'No,' Archie snapped. 'I'll be quite all right without you. It's only a few days.' He was about to add 'you're not my nursemaid', but caught himself in time. 'It's just a stammer and a bad dream, Lister. I'll be fine.'

'Right you are, sir.' Doubt dripped from every syllable. 'I'm sure I'll find some way to pass the time in Berlin while you are away.'

'I bet you will. But whatever you get up to, I don't want to hear anything about it. Not like that night I left you alone in Cannes a couple of years ago. It cost me a fortune to square away the owner of that bar.'

'I don't recall anything about that, sir,' said Lister, pulling together a semblance of injured dignity from somewhere.

'My point precisely.' If Cannes had its temptations for Lister, it would have nothing on Berlin.

Lister began to lay out Archie's clothes for the day.

'Lister?'

'Yes, sir.'

'Perhaps a game of chess?'

Lister broke out the board and they played a game on the bed. Archie took the white pieces and Lister the black. Archie won the game in seventeen moves. He felt better.

And he didn't feel too bad now, in the car, speeding past the mysterious lakes and swamps of the Spree Forest, with the roof down. But the stammering worried him. Perhaps he should have brought Lister after all. Because, truth be told, Lister *was* his nursemaid. Archie didn't like admitting it to Lister and certainly not to himself.

'Esme?'

'Yes?'

'If something happens. With me. Don't be too worried. Just get me to a bed somewhere. I'll be all right.'

Esme's eyebrows shot up in alarm.

'What do you mean? What kind of something? Are you sick? Are you going to have a heart attack?'

Archie immediately regretted saying anything. He'd be fine. Probably.

'Oh, nothing. Forget it.'

'What do you mean forget it?' Esme protested. 'You can't say something like that and ask me to forget it!'

'I said, forget it,' Archie growled.

'All right.' Esme nodded. But Archie could see she was upset rather than calmed down.

He resolved to keep firmer control of himself.

They stopped for lunch at an old half-timbered inn ten miles past Kottbus. They sat in the garden surrounded by scarlet geraniums – the Germans seemed to like their geraniums – drank beer and ate cold tongue, sausage and salad, with some Ziegenkäse cheese and rye bread. Archie told Esme a little about Field Marshal Blücher and the kind of things Archie was planning to do during his stay in Germany.

Blücher had been one of Prussia's foremost generals during the Napoleonic Wars before coming to Wellington's aid on the afternoon of the Battle of Waterloo. The King of Prussia had granted him an estate at Krieblowitz in Silesia, which they were on their way to visit, followed by the battlefield beside the Katzbach river, the scene of one of Blücher's most important victories. Later,

Archie planned to gather information from libraries in Berlin and Jena and to visit various battlefields throughout Germany, as well as the town of Blücher's birth, Rostock on the Baltic coast.

Archie was pleased to see that Esme was listening closely – she even jotted things down in a small green leather-bound notebook, and she asked intelligent questions.

After lunch, they drove on in silence for ten minutes, and then Esme spoke.

'You know she was riding right next to me when she was shot,' Esme said. 'I saw her die.'

Esme was staring at the road ahead, her jaw clenched.

Archie realised she wanted to talk. 'What happened?'

3

Since Esme's arrival in Berlin three weeks before, Harriet had introduced her to a group of young diplomats, civil servants and foreign correspondents who met up regularly. Ostensibly they were making contacts and gathering information. Actually, they were having fun.

Harriet's father, Walter Dryden, was the number two to the Ambassador at the American embassy. Since he was now a widower, Harriet accompanied him to diplomatic functions or acted as hostess when he entertained at their residence near the Tiergarten. She was good at it, charming old and young alike. As a result, young diplomats at other embassies and foreign correspondents in Berlin had an excuse to cultivate her acquaintance. The journalists were the driving force: they liked to talk, they liked to drink and they needed information. They would meet up at the bar in the Adlon Hotel or for a late dinner at the Taverne on Kurfürstenstrasse, an Italian restaurant run by a Belgian couple where a number of the senior foreign correspondents had a regular table.

Harriet brought Esme along to these gatherings; if Esme was

going to become a foreign correspondent, then these were the people she should get to know. She was readily accepted. It wasn't just that any friend of Harriet's was a friend of everybody's, but also the foreign correspondents had all started out as cub reporters or stringers hustling for stories in the hotel bars of Europe. They understood what Esme was up to and wished her well. They were a competitive bunch, but she was no threat.

One of the young Germans in the core group of Harriet's friends was Baron Otto von Adlerstein, an up-and-coming civil servant in the Foreign Ministry. His family owned a castle in 'Saxon Switzerland', an area of dark forest, rocky outcrops and gorges just to the south-east of Dresden, which had been given its name by romantically inspired artists of the previous century. Otto had invited the group for a long weekend; they had all got drunk together in Berlin many times and now they were going to get drunk together in a castle in the Saxon woods.

On Friday morning, Harriet and Esme took the express from the Anhalter Station to Dresden and then a tiny train on a narrow-gauge railway that puffed along the bank of the broad Elbe before climbing slowly and steadily through rocks and trees, stopping at a series of medieval villages, until it reached Adlerstein.

Otto was waiting for them on the platform. He was tall and pale, with narrow shoulders and wispy, thinning dark hair brushed back from his forehead; a tiny duelling scar nicked his chin. He smiled broadly when he saw them, and directed a tubby porter to gather their luggage.

They emerged from the station entrance, which was on the edge of the village. A rocky crag overlooked the gabled roofs and on this crag perched a tall stone tower and a high wall.

Esme let out a low whistle. 'Is that your schloss, Otto?'

'It certainly is. And it's actually a *Burg*. A *Schloss* is more of a stately home or a palace. A *Burg* is a proper fortress.'

'That sure is a proper fortress,' said Harriet. 'I like the tower.'

'Good. Because that's where you are staying tonight.'

'You're kidding me,' said Harriet.

'It looks kind of fun,' said Esme.

'It is,' said Otto, with a grin. 'I hope you don't mind sharing. It's the oldest part of the castle, built in 1240. And there is a magnificent view.'

'I'll bet,' said Harriet. 'Are you going to lock us in?'

'You can lock the door if you wish. I'll give you the key. It's almost as magnificent as the view.'

The porter loaded the luggage into an old steam car, and they rattled through the cobbled streets of the village and up the hill to the castle.

'Most of the castle was rebuilt in the eighteenth century,' said Otto. 'They kept the tower and some of the old walls.' They drove through a gate into a courtyard surrounded on three sides by elegant yellow baroque buildings, and on the fourth by the tower.

Otto showed them their room in the tower, which was reached by a stone spiral staircase. There were two comfortable beds, rich oak panelling on the internal walls, an iron bathtub behind a screen, and mullioned windows built into the curved stone external wall. Three von Adlerstein ancestors watched over them benignly, flanked by tapestries of hunting scenes.

'I love it!' said Esme. 'You are right – that's quite some view!'

Beneath them lay the tight cluster of medieval buildings that was the village of Adlerstein, thick stork nests clinging to chimneys. On one side, a dark forest reared and plunged towards what looked like a gorge, presumably channelling the River Elbe.

But on the other, a gentle slope of parkland dropped to a little valley through which a smaller river meandered.

'It's beautiful,' said Harriet.

Otto smiled happily. 'When you're ready, come and join us out on the lawn. Here's the key I was talking about.'

He handed Esme a large, intricately wrought iron key at least eight inches long.

'Oh, I like that,' she said. 'We will be like two princesses locked in a tower.'

Otto laughed and left them.

'I think one of the princesses will make her escape tonight,' said Harriet with a wicked smile.

And she did.

* * *

There were ten of them at dinner. In addition to Harriet and Esme, Otto had invited three journalists – two Americans and an Italian, a German friend from university who was secretary to President Hindenburg, and Duncan. Otto's widowed mother and his younger sister, who lived in Berlin, acted as hostesses. Otto's father had died the year before, and although Otto had inherited the title of Baron Adlerstein, he had kept his job at the Foreign Ministry rather than move back to the family estate.

They drank cocktails on the lawn, which overlooked a pretty sunken garden and the river valley below, and then went into the dining room. Candlelight glimmered off the highly polished table and the ornate silver. More ancestors – haughtier and more extravagantly dressed than the three in Esme's room – watched the proceedings. The company was relaxed, conversation flowed as did the wine. Esme was beginning to feel at home among these people. Although everyone there spoke German to some degree, the talk was mostly in English, the common language of the group.

Esme was seated next to Otto, who paid her close attention. He had an easy charm and lacked the stiffness of some of the Prussians she had met in Berlin. She was just beginning to appreciate the regional differences in Germany. Unsurprisingly for a civil servant in the Foreign Ministry, he had a deep knowledge of European relations. This was a subject Esme was trying to bone up on, and she questioned him closely, a process they both enjoyed.

Harriet sat between two strikingly good-looking men: one of the American journalists named Gray Trexler and Erich von Witzbach, a secretary to the President of the Republic. The somewhat less striking Duncan sat opposite her. Esme marvelled as Harriet played them off against each other expertly. All three men knew what she was about, and were enjoying the game; even Duncan was doing his best.

At about midnight, tired, slightly drunk, but excited by the evening's entertainment, Harriet and Esme made their way up the candlelit spiral staircase to their room in the tower. The door remained unlocked.

Esme fell asleep the moment her head hit the pillow. But she was awakened by the clunk of the heavy door shutting.

She sat up. They hadn't closed the curtains before getting into bed and the moonlight from the three windows illuminated the empty bed on the other side of the bedroom.

Whose room was Harriet visiting? Esme wondered.

4

When Esme woke up the following morning, Harriet was back in her own bed. Esme decided not to mention anything.

It was a glorious day, tiny puffs of white cloud drifting across the landscape. The group of guests read and chatted on the lawn that overlooked the valley; they rowed on the river and then swam in it. In the afternoon, they hiked uphill along well-groomed pathways of soft pine needles through the dark forest to a crag which gave them a view of rolling hills towards the city of Dresden. On the way back, they glimpsed a magnificent stag eyeing them from among the ancient trees. In a trice he was gone. Otto told them to watch out for wild boar but, fortunately as far as Esme was concerned, they didn't see any.

Esme was enjoying herself but in the late afternoon, while Otto's sister showed Harriet the castle's walled garden, she escaped for a walk into the village alone. She needed a break from the constant conversation.

As she descended the steep cobbled lane from the castle, she passed a woman climbing the hill in the other direction. She was small, with dark hair and olive skin. She didn't look happy.

'*Guten Tag*,' Esme said as she passed her. The woman shot her a glance, her expression suffused with pain and desperation, and mumbled something in return. Esme wondered who she was and what she was doing. Was she another guest? She didn't have luggage. Perhaps she was a woman from the village delivering something? She didn't look like a local.

Suddenly, out of nowhere, black clouds gathered. Esme continued down the hill to the village as the clouds became darker and darker. A pair of storks flapped purposefully overhead, heading for somewhere to shelter from the coming storm, no doubt. Esme allowed herself just ten minutes to explore the warren of narrow streets and steeply gabled half-timbered houses and then set off back up the hill.

Thunder rumbled over the forest behind the castle and a blade of lightning slashed down into the trees. Esme saw a figure descending from the castle gate and recognised it as the woman she had seen earlier. Fat raindrops began to fall, and within a minute, it was raining heavily. Esme spotted a large chestnut tree by the side of the lane a few yards further uphill and increased her pace until she reached it.

The woman marched steadily down towards her. Her cheeks were wet with tears, Esme realised, not rainwater, and her lips were quivering in a downward curl.

Esme ventured out into the rain. 'Excuse me,' she said in German. 'Why don't you shelter here with me for a few minutes? Maybe it will stop.'

The woman paused and looked at Esme, hesitating. Esme touched her sleeve and smiled. 'Come on,' she said.

The woman nodded and joined her under the chestnut tree's canopy. Esme broke out her cigarettes and offered the woman one. She smiled quickly and accepted Esme's light.

'My name is Esme,' Esme said, deliberately choosing the informality of only her first name. 'I'm from America.'

'Ruth,' said the woman. 'I am Austrian.'

They smoked in silence for a minute, the rain pounding down on the cobbles. Although she was thin and bedraggled, there was something about the way this woman held herself, about her large mysterious dark eyes that drew Esme towards her. It wasn't vulnerability; it was strength.

'Were you visiting someone at the castle?' Esme asked.

Ruth nodded. 'I was trying to.'

'Who was that?' Esme asked.

Ruth didn't answer for a moment. 'I think you are staying there yourself?'

Esme nodded.

'I was trying to speak to Herr Gray Trexler.'

'Ah. Well, he's there. I have spent the day with him.'

Grayson Trexler was an American journalist, one of the three admirers who had been so taken with Harriet the evening before.

'I know he's there,' Ruth said. 'But he didn't want to speak to me.'

'Oh. I see. Was he expecting you?'

Ruth shook her head.

Esme's curiosity was piqued. Other people's business often piqued Esme's curiosity, which was one of the reasons she wanted to be a journalist. But she decided to wait. She felt Ruth wanted to talk.

'You know, I came all the way from Paris to see him. I went to Berlin and heard he was staying here for the weekend.'

'Gray is based in Paris, isn't he?'

Ruth nodded. 'I must see him.'

'Why?' Esme asked, even if it wasn't any of her business.

Ruth looked straight at Esme, with an expression of desperation mixed with anger. Then she turned away.

Why would a woman be in such a hurry to travel across Europe to see a man without warning him? Esme glanced at Ruth's waist. She might be a little fat. Or...

'Does he know?' Esme asked.

'Does he know what?'

Esme nodded towards Ruth's midriff.

'Is it obvious?' Ruth said, grimacing.

'No. But I'm a girl about your age. I have friends who've gotten into trouble and whose men took no notice. Does he know?' Esme asked again.

'I don't think so,' said Ruth. 'But I wonder if that's why he refused to talk to me. Maybe he guessed? I spoke to the butler at the castle, who came back with a message that Herr Trexler was busy and didn't want to see me.'

'That's very direct.'

'Gray can be direct when he wants to be.'

'It's also not very nice.'

'No,' said Ruth.

She looked so miserable that Esme reached out her arms, pulled the girl towards her and gave her a hug. Ruth looked at her in surprise and then buried her head in Esme's shoulder and began to sob. The rain fell.

Eventually, Ruth broke away and wiped her tears. 'I'm so sorry.' She smiled tentatively. 'But thank you.'

'Did you hope he would marry you?' Esme asked.

'I see you don't know him very well. He's married already. His wife is American too. She is back in Paris.'

'He wasn't wearing a ring.'

Ruth shrugged. 'He doesn't when he's away from home.'

'What are you going to do?' Esme asked.

'My sister knows a doctor in Vienna. If I get no luck from Gray, I'll go there from here.'

Esme took a deep breath. This wasn't right. 'Are you staying in the village tonight?'

'Yes. At The Golden Bear.'

'All right. Well, come back here tomorrow morning. I'll talk to Herr Trexler tonight. At the very least, he really should agree to see you. Why don't you come up to the castle and either he'll meet you or I will? Say, nine o'clock?' She and Harriet had planned to go for an hour's ride along the river early. They should have time to get back by nine.

'Do you think you can persuade him?' Ruth asked doubtfully.

'I have no idea,' said Esme. 'But I'll try to shame him into it. It's worth a go, don't you think? You're here now, you've got nothing to lose.'

'Maybe *you* have,' Ruth said. 'Gray isn't a good man to have as an enemy.'

'Who cares?' said Esme. 'The man is a louse unless he does agree to see you.'

The rain had stopped. 'All right,' said Ruth with a weak smile. 'I'll come back tomorrow. And even if it doesn't work, thank you for trying.'

5

'I say. Pull over here,' said Archie, pointing to a garage at the side of the road. 'It'd be a good idea to fill up with petrol.'

'Sure,' said Esme. The garage was nothing more than a shed and a petrol pump on a straight stretch of road that ran beside a pond lurking in dark forest. A tall, stooped man in brown overalls emerged and limped slowly towards the Horch. He seemed about forty, Archie's age. A fellow comrade-in-arms, even if this man's trench had faced west instead of east.

'Fill her up,' Esme demanded, brightly. 'And check the oil, please.'

The man scowled, grunted and turned to the pump.

Did *he* have nightmares? Archie wondered. Probably. Of Tommies charging at him with bayonets, perhaps? But actually, the ones that maimed you were the ones you didn't see: the sniper, the machine gunner, the artilleryman.

British or German, what difference did it make? He realised that Germany, like Britain, was full of men in their thirties and forties carrying scars from the war, some visible, most invisible.

In a few minutes they were back on the road.

'Sounds like a bit of a bounder, this Gray fellow,' Archie said.

'He sure does.'

'Did you know him?'

'I'd met him two or three times at the Adlon with Harriet, although he paid Harriet a lot more attention than me. He's a bit older than the rest of the group – probably in his mid-thirties. He's famous back home, and he's popular among the foreign correspondents. He's reported from Russia, India, China, Palestine. He's based in Paris at the moment; he writes for the *Chicago Globe*.'

'That's not the one you write for?'

'No. That's the *Mercury*. The *Globe* is bigger – it's the biggest in town.'

'Did you talk to him? About Ruth?'

'I tried.'

* * *

Esme was late dressing for dinner and didn't get a chance to catch Gray on his own beforehand.

At dinner, Otto's mother, Baroness Adlerstein, an elegant, somewhat haughty lady in her fifties who spoke excellent English, asked the table about the forthcoming election. 'It's an honour for me to have so many well-informed foreigners here tonight. I would be fascinated to hear what all of you think about what's happening in Germany. How will those horrible Nazis do next month? They surprised me by how many votes they gained in the local elections here in Saxony in June.'

'I saw Herr Hitler speak at the Sportspalast last week,' said Gray. 'There were sixteen thousand people there listening to him. It was quite a performance. He's hard to take seriously – he looks like such a nondescript little man with that ridiculous moustache – but then he starts to talk. And he talks and he talks and he waves his arms about and they love it. They just love it.'

'But that's just a few hotheads in Berlin.'

'It's everywhere, baroness. You saw they got 14 per cent of the vote in Saxony? They are superbly organised and they've been holding rallies all around the country.'

'I was in the Harz mountains on holiday a couple of weeks ago,' said Duncan. 'There were posters advertising Nazi meetings even in the small towns.'

'You are not suggesting they will win a majority?' asked the baroness.

'Oh, no,' said Gray. 'They only have twelve seats in the Reichstag now. Their total might go up to forty or maybe even fifty. I think Brüning will still be Chancellor – it's a question of who he governs with.'

The Weimar Republic, which had been created after the fall of the Kaiser at the end of the Great War in 1918, was an unstable entity and had become more unstable as 1930 had progressed. In March, President Hindenburg had got rid of the social democratic chancellor and replaced him with the centre-right politician, Heinrich Brüning. In June, Brüning had failed to get his budget through the Reichstag – Germany's parliament – and so Hindenburg had dissolved it, invoking Article 48 of the constitution to allow Brüning to rule by decree until elections in September. These elections were coming up. Which was why Gray Trexler was in town and foreign correspondents were buzzing all over Germany talking to people.

'So, who *will* Brüning govern with?' Esme asked. 'Could he make a deal with the Nazis or the Communists?'

The Communists were the fourth-largest party in the Reichstag, with significantly more seats than the Nazis.

Everyone looked at Erich von Witzbach, Hindenburg's personal secretary.

'The President will do whatever he believes will be in the best interests of the republic at the time,' Erich replied, with a tiny smile, refusing to be drawn.

'But he would never allow the Nazis in government, would he?' said Annachiara. Although Italian, she worked for a British news agency. Out of deference to the baroness, she was wearing an elegant black dress, but no make-up. In Berlin she was normally seen in a black trouser suit with a white shirt and black tie. Even though her dark hair was cut short, she could never be mistaken for a man, even in the most androgenous corners of a Berlin nightclub. With high cheekbones, a full mouth, and a figure she couldn't hide, anyone could see she was a beautiful woman.

'Hitler is *much* more dangerous than Mussolini,' said Joe Moretti uncomfortably loudly. Like Gray, Joe was an American journalist, mostly writing for a Philadelphia paper. 'Because the Germans are much more dangerous than the Italians.'

'But only 2 per cent of Germans voted for the Nazis at the last election,' Annachiara said. 'Even if that number doubles or trebles, that's still nowhere nearly as popular as our stupid Duce is.'

'There's only one story in Europe for the 1930s,' said Joe. 'And that's fascism. It won't just be Italy and Germany that fall to it. There's France. Even Britain. *That's* what we should all be writing about. You can't fight fair with these Fascists. You have to hit them hard below the belt, and you have to hit them first. Of course, Hindenburg should have nothing to do with the Nazis! Neither should anyone else. Except to expose them!'

Joe had raised his voice to something just short of a shout. The baroness looked alarmed. 'Goodness!' she exclaimed.

Esme had met Joe Moretti a couple of times in the Adlon bar where he somehow managed to drink at twice the rate of everyone else. He seemed to be in a permanent state of semi-inebriation. In addition to writing for a Philadelphia newspaper, he had published a very popular book: *Why the People Love a Dictator* about Mussolini, Stalin and the various other strongmen who had emerged in Central and Eastern Europe since the war, which had sold surprisingly well in America. His inclusion of Stalin as a dictator rather than a servant of the proletariat had caused quite a stir among the left that had helped shift books. Esme had read it; it was beautifully but clearly written.

Annachiara looked daggers at Joe. 'I know Fascists – I'm married to one! I can tell you they are brutes; they are all brutes. What do *you* know? You Americans come to Europe, drink half a bottle of whisky at a hotel bar, talk to the barman, take a taxi to the next hotel, talk to the taxi driver, and then tell the people who actually live here what's going on.' Her hands flew up in a rapid and slightly scary chopping movement. 'You make me sick. You make yourselves sick, throwing up in the gutter after all that whisky.'

The room froze. Joe looked at the Italian and then burst into giggles. 'You are absolutely right, my beautiful *giornalista*. I'll take you to some bars in Phillie and then you can tell us Yanks what to do with our country.' He gave her a sloppy, crooked smile. 'Sorry.'

'You wouldn't catch me dead in any Philadelphia bar with you,' she replied haughtily to laughter around the table.

The baroness tactfully withdrew after dinner. Although she was polite and charming, she gave Esme the impression that she wasn't entirely happy that her castle was being overrun by the plebeian foreign friends of her son. The rest of the group gathered in the drawing room. Otto's sister Gisela wound up the gramophone and they drank brandy and danced the Charleston to Duke Ellington and Paul Whiteman. It turned out Joe was quite a good dancer, even when drunk. He was a slight man with thick dark wavy hair and long eyelashes above liquid brown eyes. Not as classically good-looking as his friend Gray, but cute, in Esme's opinion. Cute but drunk.

During a lull, Esme saw that Gray was alone at the drinks tray, helping himself to brandy.

'Do you have a moment?' she said. 'Can we go somewhere private?'

Gray raised his eyebrows. His creased, tanned face broke into a roguish smile under his thin Clark Gable moustache. Esme couldn't deny he had charm; this was a man who had conquered before and was confident he would soon conquer again.

'There is something important I need to discuss with you.'

'Sure,' said Gray. 'Let's go outside.'

As they left the room, Harriet spotted them and frowned in a mixture of puzzlement and disapproval. Esme suspected she had got the wrong end of the stick, but she could set her right later.

They slipped out of the French windows on to the lawn, which was still wet with the earlier rain. The air was cool and three-quarters of a moon was pulling itself up from behind the trees towards the night. An owl hooted from somewhere around the far side of the castle. Very romantic.

But Esme wasn't in a romantic mood.

Gray Trexler looked like he might be. Esme soon set him right on that.

'I went for a walk down to the village this evening before dinner.'

'Oh, yes?'

'I bumped into someone.' Esme hesitated – she had a momentary spasm of doubt. Was this really any of her business?

Too late now. She plunged on. 'Her name is Ruth. She says she knows you from Paris. Knows you quite well.'

In the dim moonlight, Esme could see Gray's eyebrows draw together. 'Used to. She came here to see me. I sent her away.'

'You did. Do you know what she wanted to see you about?'

'I've no idea.' Gray's voice was hard. 'As she may have told you, she and I had a brief dalliance in Paris. It meant nothing. I'm married – she knew that. It finished. I finished it. And I'm not going to restart it just because she barges in on a gathering of me and my friends.' His voice softened a bit. 'I've been in this situation before. The firmer and clearer you are with these women, the better it is all round.'

'These women? How many of them are there?'

'Don't come over all puritanical with me, Esme. This is the 1930s. People sleep with each other. Just ask your friend Harriet. If you can't handle that, you shouldn't be here.'

'But that's not what she wanted to talk to you about,' Esme said, ignoring with difficulty the slur against Harriet.

Gray's frown deepened, and then he understood. He turned on his heel and walked rapidly back towards the house. He didn't want to know.

'She's pregnant!' Esme called after him.

Gray stopped just short of the French windows and turned back to her. 'Keep your voice down!' he hissed.

Esme caught up with him. 'She's pregnant, Gray. And she thought you needed to know.'

'And what can that conceivably have to do with you?'

'Good word, "conceivably",' Esme said. Gray glared at her.

Esme knew Gray had a point, but the image of the poor bedraggled girl remained with her. 'She's coming back to the castle at nine o'clock tomorrow morning. Meet her then. No need to invite her in, just walk with her outside. Give her a chance.'

Gray took a step closer. 'I will not meet her,' he hissed. 'I will not "give her a chance".' He swallowed. 'I'll put this down to silly sentimentality on your part. But if you tell anyone,' he jabbed a finger at her for emphasis, '*anyone* about Ruth, I will make your life in Berlin very difficult. Especially your *professional* life. I can do that, you know.'

Esme swallowed. Gray was threatening to kill off her journalistic career before it had even started.

'Just see her tomorrow,' she said, but her voice sounded weaker than she intended.

Gray turned his back on her and returned to the gramophone and *Rhapsody in Blue*.

6

A maid knocked on their door at half past six the following morning to wake them.

The idea of an early-morning ride had seemed enticing when Harriet and Esme had cooked it up with Otto the day before, but at twenty-nine minutes to seven, it seemed like a much less brilliant scheme. Esme had woken up briefly sometime in the night and checked her friend's bed. Empty.

Harriet must be even more bleary than she.

But the early-morning air, made crisp and fresh by the previous day's thunderstorm, braced them as they made their way outside the castle walls to the stables where Otto was waiting for them with a groom. Esme was in a much better mood when she and Harriet were trotting down towards the river on two fine horses, a grey and a palomino.

Esme was an excellent horsewoman – she had learned to ride on the ranch in Montana soon after she had learned to walk – and she missed it. This was the first time she had been on horseback since she had arrived in Germany, and she had scarcely had the opportunity in Chicago. The saddle was different from the one she was used to on the ranch, of course, but Esme had no difficulty adjusting to it.

Harriet was much less confident on a horse than Esme, but, despite her fatigue, she seemed to be in a very good mood as they set out. As someone who had spent the best part of the night with a new man might be, Esme speculated.

Dew sparkled in the low sunlight, and a pair of swans glided gracefully a foot or so above the quiet surface of the river, before splashing down into its waters. Following Otto's instructions, the women turned left at the bank opposite the little Greek temple that had been built as a folly by one of those watchful ancestors in the dining room, and followed the river downstream.

'It's so good to be out here,' said Esme. 'I can't believe this castle. It's like a fairy tale.'

'I guess the Germans got their fairy tales from places like this,' said Harriet. 'But you're right. Otto is sweet to invite us.'

'He is,' said Esme.

'Do you like him?' said Harriet. 'I think he likes you.'

'He's just being polite.'

'I'm not so sure. Well?'

'Maybe,' Esme said. 'He is a nice fellow. But I don't know whether I actually find him attractive.'

Harriet laughed. 'You can work on that.' She sighed. 'On that subject, be careful of your new employer, Sir Archibald. You'll be spending a lot of time with him alone. Let him know right away he shouldn't try any funny stuff. Unless you want him to, of course.'

'Of course I don't want him to!' Esme protested. 'You don't really think he'd try anything? He seems such a proper English gentleman.'

'What he *seems* counts for nothing,' said Harriet. 'Believe me, I know.'

Esme was about to reply, 'I'm sure you do,' but that would have been mean. Esme had witnessed Harriet successfully fending off men in Chicago – she was an expert.

'All right,' she said. 'I'll make it clear.'

'Promise?'

'Promise.'

'Good.'

They rode along the river, then turned uphill onto a broad path through the woods.

'It *is* nice to be away from Berlin for a bit,' Harriet said.

There was something in Harriet's tone that caught Esme's sensitive ear.

'What do you mean?'

'Well. To be away from Daddy.'

'I'm sure it is. It's a bit of a responsibility you have there.'

'It's not just that.' Harriet pursed her lips. Esme could tell she was considering whether to tell her something.

'Yes?' she said, intrigued.

Harriet glanced at her. 'It's just... I've realised Daddy isn't quite the man I thought he was.'

'Your mother's death must have hit him hard. Hit both of you hard.'

'Yes. I suppose that's it. I think it's changed him; it's certainly changed me. But it's difficult to accept, that's all. Very difficult.'

'What is?' said Esme.

Harriet looked at her friend. Then she shook her head. 'Nothing.'

'Nothing? It's something, Harriet.'

'It *is* something. Quite a big something. But I don't want to talk about it. I shouldn't have mentioned it.'

Naturally, Esme's curiosity was piqued. But she had done

enough sticking her nose in where it wasn't wanted for one weekend.

'Fair enough,' she said to her friend. She had her own subject she wanted to talk to Harriet about – the poor woman she had met the evening before – and she wasn't sure how to do it.

'Have you heard anything back from your editor?' Harriet asked before Esme had had a chance to decide what to say.

'Not a squeak. I mailed him those two stories I wrote ten days ago. He hasn't cabled me to say whether he'll accept them and it'll be a few more days before I receive a reply by mail if he sent one. I guess it's possible he might even have printed one of them already in the paper.'

'I hope so,' said Harriet.

'I doubt it.' Esme sighed. She had written the two stories soon after her arrival. One was her first impressions of Berlin. The other was about an uninspiring speech she had seen Chancellor Brüning make on the need for fiscal rectitude. The first-impressions piece had been better written than the Brüning speech, but neither was exactly newsworthy. Don Finnegan, the editor of the *Chicago Mercury*, would never print something that wasn't newsworthy.

'You know you said you needed a big interview to break through?' said Harriet.

'That's right,' said Esme. 'But I don't know how I'm going to get one with all these other journalists around.'

'I'm not sure,' said Harriet with a smile, 'but I *think* I might have found something for you.'

'Really?' said Esme. 'What? Who is it?'

'I can't say yet. We'll see.'

'Did Erich fix it up?' said Esme.

As the President's personal secretary, Esme had identified Erich von Witzbach as a person who might be able to arrange an interview for her with someone important and she had been summoning up the courage to approach him. But there was really no reason why Erich should fix up an interview for her rather than Gray or Joe or Annachiara or any of the other journalists he knew and was friends with. But if Harriet asked him? Maybe.

'I don't want to get your hopes up,' said Harriet, avoiding Esme's question. 'But I'm optimistic I'll find out quite soon.'

They emerged from the wood. 'Come on! Let's see how fast these horses can gallop,' said Esme.

She squeezed her mount's flanks and gave him his head and he flew across the meadow down to the river. Esme let out a whoop. Boy, did that feel good!

She bent down to pat the palomino and turned to see Harriet's horse a long way behind in an unsteady lope. Esme hadn't realised how unconfident her friend was on horseback.

'Sorry,' she said as Harriet finally caught up with her, pale faced and breathing heavily. 'I couldn't resist it.'

'This is a big horse,' Harriet said nervously. 'It's a long way down to the ground.'

'Let's walk the rest of the way back,' said Esme and they set off towards the Greek temple by the river. A hedge and a line of trees ran down to it from the woods behind the castle.

If Esme was going to tell Harriet about Ruth, now was the time, before they reached the castle. It was juicy gossip and Esme owed Gray no duty of confidentiality if he behaved like such a heel. There was Gray's threat to ruin Esme's career, but Esme was sure she could rely on Harriet to keep a confidence.

Unless.

Unless it was Gray Trexler whom Harriet had sneaked off to see these last two nights. Harriet might tell Gray that Esme had informed her about Ruth and her pregnancy. Then again, if

Harriet *was* seeing Gray, Esme should definitely warn her what kind of man she was sleeping with.

So was it Gray whom Harriet was seeing? Or was it Erich? Esme very much doubted it was Duncan. Or Otto or Joe.

She had been hoping that Harriet would volunteer the information without being asked. But Esme was going to have to ask.

'You know, I woke up in the middle of the night last night,' Esme said.

'Oh, yes?'

'Yes. And the night before.'

Harriet turned to her friend and grinned. 'And you want to know where I was?'

Esme returned her smile. 'You said you would escape the tower and it looks like you did.'

'I sure did,' said Harriet, still smiling.

Then two things happened simultaneously. There was a loud crack from the direction of the temple and Harriet's chest erupted in crimson. Both horses reared immediately and Esme lost sight of her friend as she fought to control hers.

It took Esme a few seconds, but when she could look up, the riderless grey was galloping at full pelt back towards the castle. Harriet was crumpled on the ground, her chest a pool of blood and her brown eyes staring sightlessly at the blue sky high, high above.

7

'So who shot her?' Archie asked.

They were passing through a small village; Esme was stuck behind a cart piled with milk churns. She manoeuvred around it, dodging a small Opel driving much too fast in the opposite direction with its horn blaring. Chickens scattered, geese hissed.

'Ruth Jakubowski,' said Esme, once they were in the clear. 'At least that's what the police think.'

'Ruth?'

'Yes. I told the police about our conversation the previous evening, which made them suspicious immediately. Apparently, she hadn't announced herself at the castle at nine as I'd asked her to, although the police think she had been there. She was seen coming down the hill from the castle that morning. And the political police had been watching her while she was in Berlin.'

'Why?'

'It turns out she's a communist.'

'Isn't Berlin full of communists?'

'I guess so. But she was a known troublemaker in Vienna;

they suspect her of being a spy for the Russians. She's also Jewish, which probably doesn't help.'

'So they think *she* killed Harriet?'

'They are certain of it. The police managed to arrest her as the train from Dresden stopped at the Czech border. They're very proud of themselves.'

Archie frowned.

'And then Otto discovered that a rifle was missing from the castle.'

'Really? The same one that shot Harriet?'

'I assume so, but I'm not sure. I left on Monday before the police told us.'

'If it's the same weapon, how do the police think Ruth got hold of it?'

Esme shrugged. 'I got no idea.'

'Why do they think Ruth shot her?'

'Jealousy. I had to tell the police about Harriet disappearing in the night. They asked Gray Trexler about it, and he admitted Harriet had come to his bedroom. It was all rather awkward; the police started asking the others if they knew anything about Harriet's relationship with Gray. So, now they all know. Everyone apart from Harriet's father.'

'The police think Ruth found out about their affair and decided to kill Harriet?'

'That's about the size of it.'

They drove on. The woods gave way to flat farmland as they entered Silesia.

'What do *you* think?' Archie asked. 'Do you think Ruth shot Harriet?'

'I find that difficult to believe,' said Esme. 'She didn't look like a murderer to me, whatever a murderer looks like. But then she didn't look like a communist revolutionary either. And she seemed to me much more angry with Gray than with a lover she didn't even know about. But what do I know? I guess we just have to trust the police.'

'I suppose so,' said Archie.

Esme seemed slightly less tense at the wheel. Archie wondered whether talking about what she had experienced over the weekend had helped.

'What was she like? Harriet?' Archie coughed awkwardly. 'Of course, if you'd rather not talk about her...'

'No, no, I'd like to,' Esme replied. 'She was my best friend in college. But that was four years back, and I hadn't seen her since then till I came to Berlin. After college, she stayed with her parents in Rome and then in Washington. But we wrote each other a lot. Long letters about everything and nothing.'

'What was she like at college?'

'She was very different from me. I came from a small midwestern city and before that a ranch in Montana, and she had lived all over Europe. But we shared a dorm room in our freshman year at the University of Chicago and we got along really well.

'We were both kind of innocent, in our different ways. I hadn't seen much of the world, and Mr Dryden is a stickler for protocol, in the home as well as outside it. He kept Harriet on a tight leash. Or he did.'

'He did?'

'Sure. I think I told you Harriet's mother got sick with cancer and died last year? Harriet wrote me long letters about it. It broke her up – broke her father up as well. He began to rely on Harriet much more. Became much less strict – not strict at all, as a matter of fact. I discovered that when I arrived in Berlin. She'd become a different girl. Not just different from college, that was four years ago and people change – *I* have changed. But also different from her letters.'

'You mentioned that Harriet was different with men?' Archie said.

'Yes. I don't mean to be mean about her or anything. But you know what she did with Gray, so I may as well tell you. I had a bad time this summer in Chicago and I wrote Harriet to tell her about it. She knew how I'd always wanted to be a foreign correspondent in Europe and so she invited me to come stay with her in Berlin. She said she knew a whole lot of journalists here who could help me. She said she'd spoken with her father who was very happy to have an old friend of hers to stay with them; he said he thought it'd be good for her.

'It seemed like a great opportunity to me, so I quit my job at the *Mercury* and bought a one-way ticket on a liner to Hamburg.'

'One way?'

'Nothing like a one-way ticket to focus the mind,' Esme said with a grin.

'I suppose so.'

'Harriet met me in Hamburg, and took me to Berlin. Mr Dryden was real nice to me, as was Harriet and so have all of her friends been. But she had changed. You saw her. She always was pretty, but she ditched the glasses and she just acted differently around men. And they loved it. You saw it. You loved it too – admit it.'

Archie's instinct was to deny it, but since Esme had been honest with him, he could only be honest with her. 'Yes. She made quite an impression on me.'

Esme grinned. 'Naturally. And on Gray and Erich and Duncan and probably Otto. That girl had power over men. What I wasn't sure about was how far she used it. Until she slipped out of our room in the tower. If you see what I mean?'

She took her eyes off the road to glance at Archie.

'I do see what you mean,' he said.

'I don't want to sound disapproving,' said Esme. 'As Gray made clear to me, we're in the 1930s and you should see what goes on in the nightclubs in Berlin. But it just surprised me, that's all.'

'I understand.'

Esme winced anxiously. 'Oh, I shouldn't talk about poor Harriet like this, and to my employer as well! Please ignore everything I've said.'

'Don't worry,' said Archie. To his surprise, he felt an urge to touch Esme's arm to comfort her, but after her stern warnings about jumping on her, he thought he had better not. 'I will ignore it all.'

She turned and gave him a small smile. 'Actually, thank you for listening.'

8

Archie and Esme spent a fruitful couple of days in Silesia. They stayed in an inn in the small town of Kanth, about fifteen miles south of Breslau. The following day, they drove to Blücher's estate at nearby Krieblowitz, where they were met by a tall, striking Englishwoman in her fifties, Princess Evelyn Blücher. She had married the field marshal's great-grandson, who was in Berlin at that moment, and she proved to be an excellent source of information on the schloss and its former owner.

In the years when Europe was not at war, Blücher had been an enthusiastic farmer, and Archie was keen to see for himself the land Blücher had farmed. Archie had his own small estate in the West Riding of Yorkshire, in one of the dales, so he knew a bit about agriculture. This land was flatter than his home at Yarmer Hall – the principal crops were sugar beet and potatoes. It reminded him a little of the Vale of York.

Princess Evelyn showed them dozens of mementoes big and small, from a large portrait of Blücher at the Battle of Leipzig to a small, silver, much-used snuffbox. She led them to the family mausoleum where the general was buried, which was tucked away in a quiet spot on the estate. Archie wasn't there to learn new historical information, but rather to get a *feel* for the man. The success of the biography would ultimately rest on its author's feel for his subject.

Esme was surprisingly useful. She was an inconspicuous and assiduous notetaker and, in quiet moments when they were left alone, encouraged Archie to voice his thoughts which she diligently wrote down.

The next day they drove forty miles north-west to the site of the Battle of the Katzbach, where Field Marshal Blücher had trounced Napoleon's general Marshal MacDonald on the same day in 1813 that Napoleon himself had defeated the Austrian and Russian armies at the Battle of Dresden. Thanks to Blücher's victory that day, the Austrian–Prussian–Russian coalition had held and two months later defeated Napoleon decisively at the massive Battle of Leipzig.

Archie had pored over maps of the battlefield and had read many accounts of the struggle that day, but there was nothing like seeing the terrain for himself. Wielding his walking stick, he stomped all over the farmland and walked the banks of the River Katzbach explaining to Esme all the while what had happened and where. Driving rain had rendered muskets useless that day and flooded the river, tearing down bridges and making fords impassable. This is where Blücher's energy and fondness for the decisive attack had paid off, confirming his nickname amongst his troops of Marshal Vorwärts. The French were routed: their casualties were estimated at twelve thousand – many of whom had drowned in the rain-swollen river – with eighteen thousand soldiers captured, compared to only one thousand losses for the Prussians. Esme wrote it all down.

They spent the night in an inn in the Market Square of the nearby town of Liegnitz. Archie lay down for an hour or so to give his leg a rest, and then met Esme for dinner.

'Thanks for your help today,' Archie said. 'I think you'll make an excellent secretary.'

Esme winced. 'Not secretary, please.'

'What's wrong with secretary?'

'I was a secretary back in Chicago. That meant I couldn't be a reporter. I don't want to be a secretary any more.'

'What shall I call you, then? Assistant? That's worse, isn't it?'

'How about research assistant?'

'Very good. I think you'll make an excellent research assistant.' Archie raised his glass of hock.

'Thank you.'

Archie was pleased to see that there was pike on the menu, while Esme chose the traditional sauerbraten – braised beef marinated in vinegar.

'I've just read your book on General Moltke,' she said. 'It was in Mr Dryden's library. He recommended it. I enjoyed it.'

'Good. But you sound surprised.'

'I *am* surprised. Very. Wars and battles bore me to tears, usually. But you made this boring old German general an interesting man.'

'He *was* an interesting man.'

'I even enjoyed learning about the military strategy. Now, that was a surprise!'

Archie grinned. 'I think it surprised my publishers too. They had to do several reprints. And that's why they asked me for another.'

'Bluey.'

Archie frowned. 'Do you mean Field Marshal Gebhard Leberecht von Blücher, Prince of Wahlstatt?'

'You can call him that. I'm calling him Bluey.'

'Well, I like old Bluey. And I hope eventually my readers will like him too.'

'Why did you do it? Write that biography of Moltke?'

Archie paused before answering. His instinct was to brush off Esme's question with a platitude – that's what he normally did to people who asked him that kind of thing. But her direct question requested a direct answer, and he found himself inclined to give it. The better she understood him, the more help she would be.

'I had some... difficulties after the war. I spent nearly four years in and out of the trenches, and it rather took it out of me. I was a beast to myself. I was a beast to my wife. My way of dealing with the war was to banish it from my mind. Not talk about it. Not think about it. Deny it ever happened.'

'And that didn't work?'

'No. My father died in 1920 and I inherited the estate in Yorkshire. There was a very unpleasant episode with my wife and we divorced. I liked living in Yorkshire, it was calming, but my mind kept on coming back to the war. I realised pretending it never happened wasn't going to work.

'I come from a military family: my grandfather was a general, my father was a major, and my elder brother was a soldier too. When I was a boy, I loved talking about military strategy with my grandfather, who frankly was a much better soldier than my father. He was also the first person to translate Clausewitz's *On War* into English. My brother Fred joined the army straight from school, going into the family regiment, the Yorkshire Fusiliers. I went to Oxford, where I read history, and then I got a job in the City.

'Then the war came and I joined up right away. It was horrible – but you know that. After a couple of months of glorious cavalry charges against machine guns, we all got bogged down in the trenches. It was a new kind of warfare, and although I was only a lieutenant, I tried to work out new ways of fighting it. A friend of mine, Dowling, and I would spend hours discussing tactics, and we did come up with some good ideas. I won't bore you with what they were – something to do with pinning down enemy machine guns by running a line of string towards where they were firing from – but they worked.

'Which is a long way of saying that I was – I am – fascinated with military strategy and tactics. I remembered my grandfather had always admired General Moltke, whom he called the father of modern warfare. So I decided to read up on him. Like my grandfather, I know German, and so I read everything about Prussia's wars with Denmark and Austria and France in the 1860s and 70s, and how Moltke won them. It totally absorbed me, and I began to feel better.'

Archie frowned. 'I don't know why, exactly. It may have been because I was thinking about war, but from a tangent, if you see what I mean, rather than directly. I still can't bear to think about it directly. That, and it anchored my mind in a project. So, I decided to write a book about him. I started working on it about five years ago. It was published last year. And ever since then, I've been better.' Archie paused. 'Mostly.'

'I see,' said Esme. 'And so when you had finished with Moltke, you looked for another Prussian general to obsess over?'

'That's about right,' said Archie. 'I thought about Moltke's nephew, the chap who planned the invasion of France and Belgium in 1914, but I just didn't like him as much.'

'So you chose Bluey?'

'I chose Bluey.'

'You could just have seen a psychotherapist,' Esme said.

Archie shuddered.

'Have you read any Freud?'

'Certainly not. I think I prefer Bluey to Freud. The last thing I need is to discover I had sexual longings for my mother.'

'You might have had,' said Esme. 'In your subconscious. You never know.'

'*I* know,' said Archie. 'I didn't. Although she's still an attractive woman,' he admitted grudgingly.

'See! My, you have a big ego,' said Esme. 'Psychologically speaking.'

'Why, thank you.'

'You're welcome.'

Their food came. The restaurant was filling up with the solid burghers of Liegnitz. Outside, the cathedral bell tolled the hour. The setting sun illuminated the elaborately gabled baroque buildings around the square in their pastel shades – green, yellow, pink and orange.

'Have you written any articles since you've been in Berlin?' Archie asked.

'A couple,' said Esme. 'I've mailed them off to my editor.'

'At the *Chicago Mercury*?'

'You have been paying attention.'

'And you are their correspondent in Berlin?'

'Yes,' said Esme, looking down at her sauerbraten.

'Well, I'm glad you've got the time to help me.'

Esme put down her fork and sighed. 'I'm not their foreign correspondent in Berlin. I'd like to be. Back in Chicago, I only worked as a secretary in the advertising department; they wouldn't let me near the newsroom. But I offered to write articles for the paper before I left for Europe.'

'Well, that should do the trick, shouldn't it?'

'The editor said no.'

'Oh.'

'But I came anyway.'

'Oh.'

'I have sent him a couple of articles, but I haven't heard back.'

'Nothing wrong with optimism,' said Archie.

'I'm not sure that's right,' said Esme. 'I'm not feeling too optimistic now.'

'Maybe some other paper will take them?'

'Maybe. I've got to find a good article to write first. What I need is a good interview. That's how Susan Abchurch did it.'

'Who's she?'

'Haven't you heard of Susan Abchurch?'

Archie shook his head.

'She's a big deal in America. One of our top foreign correspondents. When I was still in college, she came to Chicago to give a lecture. I was fascinated. Now she can write for any major newspaper she chooses, but when she started out, she bought a one-way ticket to Europe, just like me. Her big break was an interview with the Sinn Féin mayor of Cork who was on hunger strike and died a month later. Talk about luck!'

'Not for the Sinn Féin man, presumably,' said Archie.

'Probably not,' Esme conceded. 'But definitely a break for Susan Abchurch. She has reported from England, Russia, France and Germany. She's based in Berlin, but she's not there now – Gray says she's back in the States for the summer. I can't wait to meet her.'

'She does sound impressive,' said Archie.

'I tell you, after I heard her speak, I knew that's what I wanted to do. Become a foreign correspondent just like her. It was just a question of figuring out how. Step one was getting here. To Europe. Now all I need is that one interview.'

Archie chewed his pike, which was delicious. 'What about

Princess Evelyn? Couldn't you write something about her? She is an unusual woman. You heard how she spent the war in Berlin among all those German aristocrats?'

'Perhaps,' said Esme. 'I did have an idea. But I'm not sure it would be proper.'

'What's that?'

'I could write about Harriet's murder. Not in a crime-reporter way. But in a kind of Agatha Christie who-is-the-killer way. Have you read Agatha Christie?'

'Can't say I have.'

'Well, I have, and I think she's brilliant. And I think readers would love an article like that.'

'Possibly,' said Archie. He raised an eyebrow. 'But you would be writing about your friend. What would her father have to say about that?'

'Annachiara and Gray filed the story right away. And it's in all the Berlin papers – you must have seen them?'

'I have. They haven't mentioned an arrest yet, as far as I have seen. The article you're talking about would be more intrusive, wouldn't it?'

Esme sighed. 'You're right, of course. Although, I can imagine Harriet encouraging me to do it. And Susan Abchurch was very firm about how you couldn't have too many scruples as a journalist.'

'By and large, I'm in favour of scruples,' said Archie, dryly. 'Anyway. Didn't you say the police know who did it? That Austrian woman?'

'Yes,' Esme admitted, reluctantly. 'I guess you're right.'

* * *

Archie had a bad night. He had gone to sleep thinking about Esme's description of Harriet's murder, and the German police's eagerness to arrest the Austrian woman. It didn't add up.

Then he fell asleep. Lieutenant Dowling came to see him. At first it was a pleasant dream, warm with comradeship. They chatted over mugs of tea about how to pin down the Hun machine guns. The sentries furthest away from the German position on either flank would stake out a few yards of string pointing towards the machine gun as soon as it started to fire. Then, the instant the enemy machine gun opened up again, the sentries would fire five rounds each rapid along the string, a sudden concentration of fire that put the wind up the machine gunner.

Dowling put down his mug of tea, smiled, climbed out of the trench and ambled across No Man's Land towards the enemy machine-gun position. Archie tried to call him back, but Dowling took no notice. Archie tried to climb out of the trench to grab Dowling, but his legs were too heavy and he couldn't make it over the parapet.

Dowling kept walking and walking. Archie knew he would get cut down eventually, but there was not a damn thing he could do about it.

Then it started properly. The traditional nightmare. March 1918 and the Germans attacking. His company was outnumbered, the company in the trenches on their right had slipped away. The shells, the bullets, the flying mud, the blood, the bone, the screams and then the running. Running, running, running.

His own scream woke him up. He was sweating.

Damn! He hadn't had that dream for months. What had set it off? It must have been that tiny mention of the stratagem to pin down machine guns at dinner the night before. Or Harriet's murder. Harriet's murder had shaken him more than he had realised.

He lay awake, staring at the ceiling, for ten minutes? An hour? Two hours?

Too scared to go to sleep, he got out his chess set and played a game against himself. He won in seventeen moves. He felt very slightly better.

So he played another game.

9

They set off immediately after breakfast – it was a long drive back to Berlin.

'Did you sleep all right?' Esme asked.

'Do I look that bad?'

'You don't look great.'

Archie sighed. 'No, I didn't sleep very well.'

'What was the trouble?'

None of your business, Archie thought. He was not going to tell her about his nightmares or Lieutenant Dowling. He didn't answer for a few seconds, then, in a grudging nod to politeness, came up with an answer that was partly true.

'I was thinking about the Austrian woman, Ruth. I can't believe she really did shoot Harriet.'

'Neither can I. I was thinking about that too. But why do you doubt she did it?'

'Lots of reasons. As you say, why should she kill her? Jealousy doesn't really stack up – did she even know Harriet was Trexler's lover? You didn't know, and you were Harriet's best friend and were living with her.'

'Perhaps she found out in Berlin? Someone could have told her there.'

'All right. Even if she did know, and she wanted to kill Harriet, how did she know you and Harriet were going for a ride that morning?'

Esme paused. 'Good question.'

'Then there is the missing rifle. It must have been the gun that shot Harriet. It's too much of a coincidence that a rifle should go missing the very day that a person is shot with one.'

'I guess so.'

'In which case, how did Ruth get hold of it? Did she break into the castle in the middle of the night? It sounds as if that would be difficult?'

'Very difficult. High walls. Locked gates.'

'Right. And how did she know where the rifle was kept?'

'You got me there.'

'And finally, what was the distance from the temple where you think the shot was fired to you and Harriet?'

'I don't know,' said Esme, frowning. 'Maybe a thousand feet? Maybe further than that. Quite a distance.'

'Three or four hundred yards. And Harriet was shot directly in the chest, first time. One shot. Whoever pressed the trigger knew how to use a rifle, was a marksman, in fact.'

'And you think Ruth wasn't?'

'Do you know how to fire one?'

'Oh, yes. My elder brother taught me when I was twelve. I shot a deer once.'

'All right. You probably do know how to use a rifle. But most girls in Europe don't.'

'Ruth is supposed to be a communist revolutionary. Maybe they teach them how to fire guns?'

'Maybe. But when you add it all up, it seems very unlikely that Ruth shot Harriet.'

'It does,' said Esme. 'Poor girl. She's probably locked up in some German jail somewhere. And she's pregnant!'

'I doubt they will have given her bail.' Archie glanced at Esme. 'But you know what it means if she didn't shoot Harriet?'

'What?'

'Someone else did.'

'Obviously.'

'Someone who was staying in the castle that weekend.'

'No!' Esme's reply was instant.

'Think about it,' said Archie. 'It must be someone who was able to move about the castle to steal the gun. Someone who knew that you and Harriet were going for a morning ride. Someone who was a good shot.' Archie shook his head. 'I'm sorry, Esme, it must be someone you know.'

'That's absurd!' said Esme.

'Is it?'

Esme pursed her lips and concentrated on the road ahead. Archie let her drive.

'No,' she said, swallowing. 'It's not absurd.'

'Do you know who it might be?' Archie said.

'No. It could be any of them. Or rather none of them. Lordy, I don't know! Poor Ruth!'

'Perhaps the police have worked out she's innocent by now,' said Archie.

'They seemed pretty determined Ruth was their culprit.'

'But when they think more about it?'

Esme took a deep breath. 'Then they'll want to talk to all of us again.'

'Perhaps they'll be waiting for you in Berlin?'

They entered a small town and were driving along the high

street, when Esme suddenly stopped outside a post office. Bright red geraniums nodded at them from the post office's window boxes.

'What are you doing?' Archie asked.

'I'm going to make a telephone call,' said Esme. 'I won't be long.'

'Who are you ringing?'

But Esme didn't answer and left Archie alone in the Horch. He lit up a cigar and watched the townspeople bustle by. A tall church spire presided over the little town, announcing the hour with a clear bell. Archie wondered how the devil they kept the place so clean – no litter, not even any horse dung.

It took Esme fifteen minutes. 'I thought so!' she said. 'The police still believe Ruth murdered Harriet.'

'How do you know?'

'I telephoned the castle and spoke to the baroness. I inquired how she was and then I asked about the investigation. The police are still holding Ruth.'

'What about the rifle? Have they found it?'

'No,' said Esme. 'But...'

'But?'

'I said we'd be coming to see her tomorrow. At Burg Adlerstein. We can ask her then.'

'You what!'

'It's on the way. More or less.'

'It's not on the way!'

'Well, it's a little out of the way, but only a little. We can stop in Dresden. Have you ever visited Dresden? There is that battle you mentioned yesterday. The Battle of Dresden? You'd love to see another battlefield, wouldn't you?'

'Blücher wasn't at the Battle of Dresden,' Archie muttered. 'And besides, I haven't studied it.'

'Oh, so because Napoleon won that one, you don't want to see it? You only like the ones the Prussians win?'

'Don't be absurd! We need to get back to Berlin!'

'We'll get back there. Just a day later.'

'No, Esme.'

'We can't let that poor woman rot in jail! We *have* to help her.'

'No, we don't. It has nothing to do with us.'

'Well, it has something to do with me,' Esme said. 'Harriet was my friend. And I feel so sorry for that poor girl. And, as you say, if it wasn't Ruth who shot Harriet, who was it?'

'Y-you just want to write that article for the paper, don't you?' Archie said.

'That's not true,' Esme protested. 'Oh, come on, Archie! It's only a day.'

'You should have asked me rather than ambushing me like this,' said Archie coldly.

'I'm sorry. It's just when I was on the telephone to the baroness, it seemed like a good idea.'

'W-well, the answer is no. And... and.' Archie paused, unable to get the sentence out. He stared out of the window and waited.

'W-what I was going to say, is stop at the next post office and telephone her back.'

'My, you are angry,' said Esme.

Archie looked away.

10

Esme knew she had made a mistake. Asking to come and visit the baroness at Adlerstein had seemed like a good idea at the time. Without really thinking about it, she had assumed Archie would want to go too. After all, he had stayed up all night thinking of lots of reasons why Ruth was innocent. And they were good reasons.

Harriet. Oh, Harriet!

Another rush of grief welled up from somewhere inside her, threatening to overwhelm her – one of many over the last five days. She did her best to fight it.

They came in waves. She had cried herself to sleep the last few nights, the image of Harriet's bloody chest and her lifeless eyes slipping from wakefulness into her dreams. But she was determined to remain professional in front of Archie, to show him a 'stiff upper lip'. Wasn't that what those British called it? But it was difficult. It was *so* difficult.

She couldn't believe she would never see Harriet again. And yet she had seen her friend's chest explode right in front of her; Harriet was definitely dead all right.

Why? Who? Who had done this?

She had hoped that working with Archie would help. And there was no doubt the work had distracted her; there were whole chunks of time when she was writing down notes on military manoeuvres when she forgot about Harriet.

But that was only for minutes, an hour at most. Harriet's death wasn't going away.

She felt guilty that she was not back in Berlin, helping Harriet's poor father. Mr Dryden's upper lip had definitely trembled. But she preferred to be away in Silesia with Archie and Bluey.

She felt herself drawn to the question of who had killed Harriet if it wasn't Ruth. And if it was Ruth, why had she done it? Esme wanted to find out who had murdered her friend. She *needed* to do it. She could tell herself that it was for Harriet's sake, but it was really for herself. She had to do *something*. Or she would just fall apart. And she was determined not to let herself do that in front of the stiff Englishman.

She thought again about her idea of writing an article about Harriet's murder. A mystery about who the killer was would make it a much better story. In fact, it would be best if Esme didn't know who the killer was right away: that would keep readers on tenterhooks and set them up for another article.

She had to do *something*. Just being in Berlin and writing about what was going on there might not be enough. If she wanted to be a foreign correspondent – and she desperately wanted to be a foreign correspondent – she needed a better plan. A big interview would work, but there were dozens of real foreign correspondents with much more experience than her who were all chasing after the big interview.

She had to be creative; try something else.

Trouble was, she doubted she could go through with writing about Harriet's death. She was certain Harriet wouldn't mind –

indeed making a fuss of her murder seemed respectful towards her friend, not the opposite. But Mr Dryden probably would. As would, come to think of it, the guests at the castle on whom the finger of suspicion would be pointed.

She wasn't sure she was brave enough for that.

But, most importantly, Archie was her boss. She should have asked him first.

'Sorry, Archie,' she said glancing at the back of his head.

He muttered something she couldn't hear.

'Excuse me? What was that?'

He turned to her, his face stern. 'Sir Archibald. My name is Sir Archibald, Miss C-C-Carmichael.'

She tried not to wince, aware that he was staring at her. That hurt. She might have deserved it, but it hurt.

'Of course, Sir Archibald,' she said.

He grunted, and turned away.

She drove on, Archie muttering to himself beside her.

She was sore. She had enjoyed the previous day, she had liked working with Archie and she thought she had been a helpful, effective secretary. Make that research assistant. And then she had blown it. All right, she knew she had been in the wrong to change their plans like that without asking him, but he had no business taking it so badly. Now she would have to call him Sir Archibald, which frankly was a very silly name. Maybe she would try Sir Baldy? See how he liked that.

Maybe she would quit as soon as they got back to Berlin.

The muttering was getting louder. She couldn't follow most of it, but she thought she picked out the name 'Dowling' and the word 'wait!' Archie kept facing away from her, out towards the countryside.

'Stop!' he said, clearly this time.

'What?'

He turned to her, his face twisted in anguish, the scar down its left side livid. 'I said stop!' he shouted.

'All right, all right.' She pulled over to the side of the road. They were beside a meadow in which a small herd of black and white cows were grazing.

She turned the engine off. Silence. A car roared past, a large chauffeur-driven Maybach. Then more silence.

Archie was staring at the cows, his lips moving rapidly, nothing emerging from them but an indistinguishable murmur.

'What are we doing?' Esme asked, reasonably.

No reaction from Archie. Until he suddenly flung open the car door, leaped out and climbed over the wooden fence into the meadow.

Unsure whether to follow him, Esme stayed in the car and watched.

Archie had left his stick behind and moved at a rapid limp towards the cows. He appeared to be talking to them, and he raised his arms and began pointing in the direction of a copse of tall trees.

Two of the cows looked up. One ambled away from him, the other put her head down for more grass.

Archie stopped about twenty feet away from the cow and started haranguing it. The cow ignored him. A third beast walked towards him in curiosity.

Archie waved his arms at the animal. Then he froze. He put his hands over his head and flung himself to the ground.

'Lordy!' This wasn't right. The poor man was out of his mind.

Esme got out of the car and moved over to the fence.

Suddenly, Archie leapt to his feet and started running towards her. He flung off his jacket and then ripped at his shirt. Bare chested, he ran a few more steps and then paused to take off his shoes and then his pants.

Esme swung her legs over the fence and ran towards him. He turned towards the cows and pulled off his drawers. Then he turned back and dashed towards her. She could see his expression now, total fear. Blinding, soul-revealing terror.

Only then did he seem to see her and he flung himself onto the ground once again, grinding his face into the grass, emitting heart-rending sobs, his bare back and buttocks quivering with fear.

Esme paused a few feet away from him. She gathered up his shirt and his jacket and his pants, and placed his shirt gently on his back.

'Archie?' she said as softly as she could manage. 'Archie. It's all right. It's all right. They are only cows. There are no guns. There are no shells. It's all right.'

The sobbing stopped, but Archie's face remained buried in the grass.

Esme touched his back. She decided to sing him a song.

> Hush little baby don't say a word,
> Mamma's gonna buy you a mocking bird.
> And if that mocking bird don't sing
> Mamma's gonna buy you a diamond ring

She wasn't entirely sure it was an appropriate song to sing to an Englishman lying naked in a field in Germany, but it seemed to do the trick: Archie lay still.

She repeated the song a couple more times and then touched his arm.

'Come on, Archie. Time to get up and put some clothes on.'

Archie hauled himself to his feet. He stood naked in the field, blinking. Esme couldn't help staring for a moment. His body was criss-crossed with scars, especially his shoulder and his left leg.

And then there was the rest of it; she couldn't help looking at that too.

'Lordy.'

Esme gathered up his shirt and gently eased his arms into it. Then his pants and finally his shoes. Socks and drawers could wait till later.

'Come,' she said, and led him back to the car.

He mumbled something. Esme strained to hear. She made out the words 'blood' and 'uniform'. Perhaps that's why he had shed his clothes, trying to get rid of the blood from those dreadful battlefields?

He seemed drained, scarcely able to walk. The expression of horror had been replaced by emptiness. His eyes were unfocused.

Then Esme remembered what Archie had said as they left Berlin. About if something happened, she shouldn't worry. She should just get him to a bed somewhere.

Well, something had happened, and she was worried.

They had passed a village a few miles back with an inn, and once Esme had Archie safe in the passenger seat, she turned the car around and headed back for it. The innkeeper was unhelpful at first, but when Esme mentioned *der Krieg* and made a swirling gesture with her finger by her forehead, he suddenly became more sympathetic.

They found Archie a bed and put him in it.

11

Archie slept for two hours, Esme watching over him.

This was 'shell shock', no doubt. Esme had heard about it – dark mutterings about someone's uncle or brother or the moody advertising salesman on the paper in Chicago who had seen nasty things in the war and were never the same since.

It didn't look much fun. Esme knew how badly she felt when she had seen one friend die in front of her. Archie had seen dozens over a period of years. She couldn't imagine what that was like.

She was sipping a cup of coffee the innkeeper's wife had made her when Archie groaned and opened his eyes.

He stared at her without recognition, then blinked.

'Esme?'

'Yes.'

He pulled himself up on to his elbows. 'What am I doing here?' he said.

'"Something happened" just like you said it would, so I found you a bed.'

'Oh, Christ! What happened?'

'You decided to stop the car and get out and discuss something with some cows.'

'Did I? Then what happened?'

'You ran. And fell down. And I brought you here.'

Archie looked down at his poorly buttoned shirt and his pants. He groaned. 'Did I?'

Esme nodded. 'You did.'

'What? Entirely?'

Esme nodded again. 'Stark naked.'

'Oh, Christ! I am so sorry.'

'I was badly shocked,' Esme said. 'Really, quite overwhelmed. I nearly took off all my clothes and fell on the ground next to you.'

Archie frowned. And blinked. For a moment, Esme thought she had gone too far. Then the corner of his lip on the good side of his face twitched upwards. He began to laugh. And laugh.

Esme laughed too.

'You don't remember any of it, do you?' she said.

Archie shook his head.

'This has happened before?' she asked.

'A few times. But not for four years. I thought it was in the past now. I told you that I had been better once I started writing my biographies.'

'Do you know what set it off?'

'Partly talking about how we pinned down those machine guns. But I think it's the murder of your friend. The waste of a young life. Yes… I think it's that.'

'How do you feel now?'

'Tired. But not so bad. That laugh helped. I knew I was in trouble when I started stammering. Always a bad sign.'

'I'll look out for it.'

'Thank you, Esme.' Archie smiled. 'God knows what would have happened if you hadn't been there.'

'You're welcome. And don't you mean Miss Carmichael, Sir Archibald?'

Archie winced. 'I do remember that bit. No, I mean Esme. And you should call me Archie.'

'Not Sir Baldy?'

'No, Esme. Not Sir Baldy.' Archie raised his eyebrows. 'You know, sometimes I think you don't take my baronetcy seriously. My ancestor paid good money to King Charles I for it.'

'Baronetcy? What on earth is a baronetcy? I thought you were a bold knight. Or perhaps a bald knight?'

'I'm afraid not. Knights have to earn their honour. Or, sad to say in these days of Lloyd George, pay for it themselves. Baronets get their ancestors to do it. Less effort.'

'I see. A baronet is like a baby baron? In the same way a cigarette is a baby cigar?'

Archie smiled. 'By God, you've got it, Esme!'

With a twist of guilt, the concept of a 'baby baron' reminded Esme of the lullaby she had sung Archie that morning. Fortunately, Archie was oblivious.

'Shall we set off for Berlin now?' she said. 'Or do you need some more rest?'

'Let's have some lunch. I'm starving. Just give me a moment to get properly dressed.'

'Certainly. The rest of your clothes are folded on the chair over there.'

'Oh, and Esme?'

'Yes.'

'Let's go to Dresden, not Berlin.'

Esme grinned. 'You can't keep away from those battlefields.'

'The Saxon State Library there has one of the finest collection of incunabula in Europe.'

'Inclubbablah?'

'Incunabula. The first printed books, dating from before 1500. I collect them.'

'Of course you do.'

'And tell Baroness von Adlerstein we will see her tomorrow, if it is convenient for her.'

12

Dresden was a wonder. A baroque jewel, or rather a box of jewels. Row upon row, square upon square of splendid buildings, nestling in a curve of the River Elbe.

They were expected at Adlerstein for coffee at four o'clock, so they had the morning to explore Dresden. They had an early breakfast in their hotel, the Savoy, before grabbing a taxi to take them up the slope on the far bank of the river to the site of the battlefield.

Archie had stayed up the night before reading his trusty *Die Schlachten der Napoleonischen Kriege* by Ernst von Odeleben. Russian and Austrian troops had threatened Dresden, which was defended by French and Saxon armies. Napoleon had arrived from the north in the nick of time to relieve the city and win the day. There was a good vantage point above the city marked by a granite monument at the spot where a French turncoat general had been killed while fighting for the Russians. From there, Archie and Esme had a magnificent view of Dresden and its surroundings. The Elbe wound its broad lazy path down from wooded crags in the distance, through vine-draped slopes to the city itself.

Esme listened politely to Archie's explanation of the battle, but didn't take notes. Since Blücher had not been present, they were not necessary.

'You said the big battle was a couple of months later, didn't you?'

'Yes,' Archie replied. 'The Battle of Nations. Around Leipzig.'

'And Bluey was at that one? I take it we'll be going to Leipzig later, then?'

'Definitely,' Archie said. 'If you are still willing to work for me?'

Esme glanced at him.

'I'd understand if you didn't, after yesterday,' Archie continued. 'That wasn't what you were employed to do.'

'No, it wasn't,' said Esme. 'I hope you can guarantee it won't happen again.'

'Well, that's the hell of it,' said Archie. 'I can't guarantee it. That's why I brought my man Lister with me to Berlin. He knows what to do – he's seen it before. I should have taken him with me on this trip, but I suppose I was overconfident. I haven't had an episode for years; I assumed they were in the past now. Turns out I was wrong.'

Esme's gaze was frank, appraising. Then she seemed to make up her mind. 'Well, I guess I've seen it all now. And I'm desperate for the cash. So, yes, I will trudge around the battlefield of Leipzig with you.'

Archie smiled. 'Jolly good,' he said. 'Now. To the library!'

As they made their way down the hill to the waiting taxi, Archie thought it *was* jolly good. In most respects Lister and Esme were totally different, but they had a similar disrespect for him which he found strangely stimulating – comforting, even.

Before the war, he had led a sociable, gay life, much of it spent in London with plenty of friends, even more acquaintances. He laughed, he made other people laugh, his friends mocked him, he mocked his friends. But after the war, that had changed. There was something forbidding about him. What, was obvious. His face, for one. His occasional flashes of temper for another. Despite himself he had become solemn, serious, *dignified*.

Archie smiled, recalling how Esme had mocked his baronetcy. He couldn't agree with her more, it *was* ridiculous. His father had treasured it, as had Fred. By rights, it should have been Fred who had inherited the title, but Fred had died in Jerusalem in 1917 and was resting in a graveyard on the Mount of Olives. Archie felt like a fraud, a usurper.

Mind you – Sir Frederick Laverick. That *would* have been ridiculous. How had his father not realised that Frederick was not the best name for a Laverick, especially if he would have to stick a 'sir' in front of it for most of his life? Archie suspected his more intelligent mother had realised the problem immediately and found it amusing.

So, all in all, Archie was glad he had not quite succeeded in scaring Esme away. He would be more careful next time he caught himself stammering.

The Saxon State Library took up most of what was known as 'The Japanese Palace', a magnificent building on the New Town side of the Elbe. It housed half a million volumes, including many illuminated manuscripts and two thousand incunabula, books printed between 1455 and 1500. It was these that Archie had come to see.

'The paper is remarkably white for books that are so old,' Esme observed.

'It is. At the beginning, the paper was very well made, very expensive. Newer printed books were usually made with lower-quality paper so they actually look older today than these do. The covers are robust too. You don't need to be careful handling them.'

'And how many of these do you have in your collection?'

'Eighty-six. I inherited my grandfather's collection of seventy-two and I have been slowly adding to them over the last three years. Look! This is the Gutenberg Bible.'

Archie stopped in front of a large book in a dark brown leather cover, lying open in a glass vitrine.

'What's so special about this?' Esme asked.

'Not only is it the first book ever printed using moveable type – in 1455 – but it is also one of the most beautiful. The quality of the ink and the paper is superb. The ink is still black and glossy and the paper spotless white. You see how neat and carefully spaced the print is?'

They admired the four columns of Gothic type on the open page.

'It's funny how just printed words alone can be beautiful,' said Esme. 'But they are.'

'I *want* one of those,' said Archie.

'Sir Archibald!' said Esme. 'You do know that lust is a deadly sin?'

Archie grinned at her. 'I can't help it.'

'Are there many of them? Or is this the only one?'

'There are forty-three. But they hardly ever come up for sale. And when they do, they are really expensive.'

Esme whistled. 'Sounds like unrequited love, I'm afraid, Archie.'

'I know. But one can dream.'

'Dream away,' said Esme.

Archie checked his wristwatch. 'I think we have time to find a book dealer. I rather fancy seeing if I can buy something printed in Dresden.'

A librarian directed them to a shop in the Italian Village in the Old Town, just behind the cathedral: the neighbourhood where the stonemasons from Italy who had built the glorious church had settled several hundred years before.

They found the sign *Antiquariat Garfinkel* down a narrow alley. As Archie and Esme entered the shop, an aroma of old leather enveloped them. Sunlight squeezed in through small windows to illuminate a room lined with caged bookcases, behind which rows of red and brown spines hinted at rich, ancient knowledge. Behind a high counter of solid dark wood a large young man with dark curly hair was reading a book, gently rocking back and forth and moving his lips.

'Good morning!' said Archie in German.

The man took no notice.

Archie and Esme stood at the counter and waited.

'Good morning!' Archie repeated. And then, 'Excuse me!'

Nothing.

'I think he might be praying,' Esme whispered in English to Archie. 'Perhaps he's Jewish? It could be the torah he's reading.'

This, at least, elicited a response. '*Onkel!*' the young man shouted.

They heard some movement in a back room, and a few seconds later an older, smaller man with thinning grey hair wearing a brown coat emerged. He peered at his customers over his half-rimmed spectacles and smiled somewhat unctuously, Archie thought.

'Ah, good morning, sir, madam. I apologise for my nephew, Moses. He's not good with customers. My name is Garfinkel. How can I help you?'

'What's he reading?' asked Esme.

'It'll be a catalogue of some kind,' said the man.

'Hain,' the young man Moses said.

'Ah. That will be Friedrich Hain's list of incunabula,' Herr Garfinkel said. 'It's his favourite.'

'Does it have an exciting ending?' Esme asked the young man.

Moses took no notice. The bookseller looked at her with a frown.

'Ignore her,' Archie said. 'Although it's actually incunabula we've come to see you about.'

'Oh, yes?'

'Yes. You see, I collect them. I'm building up a collection from as many towns and cities across Europe as I can. One from each. So I wondered if you had any incunabula printed here in Dresden?'

The man smiled. 'That's a very interesting approach. But I'm afraid nothing was printed here before 1500. The city didn't really flourish until later on. But of course there were other towns in Saxony which printed books in the fifteenth century.'

'Such as?'

'We could ask Moses.'

They turned to the young man who was now staring at Archie with an expression of rapt attention.

'Leipzig,' he said. 'Lots of books printed in Leipzig. Meissen. Freiberg in Sachsen.'

'I don't have any of those in stock,' said his uncle. 'But I can try to track some down. If you come back tomorrow, I might have something for you?'

Archie glanced at Esme. They were planning to stay that night in Dresden after visiting the baroness. 'Jolly good. We will look in tomorrow morning. Thank you, Herr Garfinkel.'

'Until tomorrow,' said the old man.

His nephew was still staring at them as they left the shop.

13

Archie and Esme arrived at Burg Adlerstein at four o'clock precisely. From the old village beneath it, the castle did indeed look like something out of a fairy tale – high walls of old stone and the tall wrinkled tower rising above the rocks and trees. Archie could imagine a princess with long tresses waving from the highest window to a rescuing knight.

But neither Esme nor Harriet had had long tresses and Archie was, as Esme had established, not a dashing knight but merely a baby baron with a gammy leg and a mangled face.

Once through the gate and into the courtyard, the castle seemed newer, more elegant. The inward-facing windows were large, framed with ornamental white stone against pale yellow walls.

The baroness received them in a small, pretty sitting room overlooking the lawn at the back of the castle, which led down to the valley Esme had described.

The baroness was no crusty dowager, but a tall woman in her fifties, with fashionably cut short dark hair, shrewd blue eyes and a dress that reached down no further than mid-calf.

Archie kissed the baroness's hand in the formal German manner and uttered some words of greeting in that language.

'English, if you don't mind, Sir Archibald,' said the baroness. 'I insisted that my children learned to speak English and French so I need to keep in practice myself.' Her voice was rich, low and authoritative; her English was slow and clear with a pronounced accent. Archie found it compellingly attractive. 'This is my daughter, Gisela. She has been staying with me since the awful tragedy of last weekend.'

Gisela was a big woman, with short blonde hair tightly waved around a side parting, a powerful jaw and friendly blue eyes. 'How do you do, Sir Archibald.'

Archie shook her hand, the baroness indicated that they be seated and a maid brought in coffee and cakes.

'I'm so sorry about what happened,' said Archie. 'It must be dreadful to have a murder take place in your house.'

'Oh, it was frightful. I had never met Harriet before, she seemed such a charming woman, but it must be much worse for you, my dear,' she said to Esme.

To Archie's surprise, Esme looked as if she was about to burst into tears. Then Archie was surprised at his surprise: of course she wanted to cry.

There was a moment of awkwardness while the baroness watched Esme impassively and her daughter studied a spot on the carpet six inches in front of Archie's right foot.

Then a spark of warmth glowed in the baroness's blue eyes. 'Come here, child,' she said, as she stood up to put an arm around Esme. 'Cry if you want to.'

And Esme did, leaning into the older woman.

Archie watched, moved. Impressed. Regretful. Why couldn't he do that, he asked himself.

Eventually, Esme broke away. 'I'll just go and—'

'No, you won't,' said the baroness. 'You will stay here and have a large slice of cake.' She handed Esme a clean handkerchief.

Esme blew her nose. 'Thank you.'

Esme glanced at Archie and took a deep breath. 'We actually wanted to ask you some questions about Harriet's murder.'

'Oh, really?'

'Yes. You see, we think it's very unlikely that Ruth Jakubowski shot her.'

'Oh.' The baroness frowned. 'The police seemed certain, didn't they, Gisela?'

Her daughter nodded. 'Yes. Quite certain. They think she stole a rifle from the gun room, hid in the temple and shot her.'

'You never met Ruth, did you?' Esme said.

'No,' said the baroness. 'But I understand she was a communist revolutionary. A real Bolshevik.'

'She may well have been a communist,' Esme said. 'I never asked her. But she looked to me like a scared girl who was pregnant and had been let down by a man. It's true she was desperate – and angry with Gray – but she didn't look as if she was going to shoot anyone, let alone Gray's lover.'

'I understand she might not have looked like that when you met her. But the police do seem quite convinced.'

'How do they think she got hold of the gun?' Archie asked. 'This place looks difficult to break into.' The castle actually looked impregnable on three sides, but on the fourth, the side opening out on to the garden and the valley, it may have been possible to get in somehow.

'Yes, I wondered that,' said the baroness. 'There was no sign of a broken window or lock anywhere that we could see.'

'Was the gun room locked?'

'No. No need.'

stone room next to a door opening out on to the courtyard. A dozen rifles and shotguns were lined up in two racks. Ammunition was stored in an unlocked cupboard.

'Did any of your guests know where this was?' Archie asked.

Gisela frowned. 'I don't see how they would know.'

'Some of them did,' Esme said. 'On the Saturday, Otto was talking to Gray and Erich about guns. He said that his grandfather had owned a fine pair of shotguns made for him by Purdey in London. Must be those ones there.' Esme pointed to a pair of shotguns with intricately decorated barrels. 'He said he would show them to Gray and Erich.'

'Interesting. And anyone else?'

Esme scrunched up her face, trying to think. Her snub nosed twitched under its freckles. 'We were on the lawn. They went off into the house. I think Annachiara may have gone with them, but I'm not sure.'

'Not Joe?'

'No.'

'What about Duncan Mandeville?'

'Yes! He went too.'

'I missed all that,' said Gisela.

'That's interesting,' said Archie. 'Now, I'd like to see where Harriet was shot, if I may. You can stay here, Esme, if you think you might find it upsetting.'

'That's all right,' said Esme. 'I was the one who insisted you come here, and you'll need me to show you the spot.'

They went through the castle to a door which let out onto the lawn, and walked down the slope towards the river. Esme needn't have come: it was clear where Harriet had been shot – a broad circle of grass had been churned up by many feet.

Archie looked along the riverbank to the temple. 'Yes, that's about three hundred yards, I'd say. Was there much wind?'

Esme frowned. 'I'm not sure. I don't think so.'

'No, it was a lovely day,' said Gisela. 'Nothing more than a gentle breeze, if that.'

'And how fast were you moving?' Archie asked.

'Just a slow walk,' Esme said.

'Even so, whoever killed Harriet must have known what they were doing. Fired once, hit her in the chest first time. The man must be a good shot. Probably fought in the war.'

'Women can be good shots too,' said Esme.

Archie nodded. 'I suppose so. But not many are, can we agree on that?'

'There has been a lot of violence in Germany since the war,' said Gisela. 'Women have been involved as well as men. Especially communist women.'

'All right,' Archie said. 'It is possible Ruth is a markswoman. Can we go over to the temple? I'd like to know where she, or whoever, went after they had shot Harriet.'

They walked along the edge of the river to the temple, which was raised on a slight mound about twenty yards back from the bank. A short distance behind it, a hedge ran up towards the castle and its surrounding woods.

'The killer must have run along behind the hedge,' Archie said. 'Is it possible to get into the forest from here?' he asked Gisela.

'Yes. There's a gate that is unlocked. It would be easy to escape this way.'

'And get back down to the village without being seen?'

'Certainly.' She paused. 'Or to join the road back up to the castle.'

'You mean if he or she was a guest?' Archie asked.

'That was what you were suggesting,' Gisela said. 'Are you serious?'

'I don't know, Esme, are we serious? Ruth *could* know how to handle a rifle.'

Esme looked at Gisela. 'Archie has this theory that girls don't know how to shoot. Do *you* know how to fire a rifle?'

'Actually, my mother taught me,' Gisela admitted.

'See?' said Esme to Archie. But then she shook her head. 'No, I don't think it was Ruth.'

'No. I don't think so either. We should try to find out what she was up to that morning. Where was she staying? When did she get a train?'

'We can go down into the village and ask,' Esme said.

'I'll come with you, if you like,' said Gisela. 'They are more likely to answer me than you. But let's say goodbye to my mother first.'

The baroness was noticeably cooler when Archie and Esme met her in the hallway to say goodbye.

'I'm just going to show Sir Archibald and Esme round the village, Mama,' said Gisela.

'All right, dear,' said the baroness. 'But before you go, Esme, I've been thinking you are too quick to dismiss the police and the likelihood that that Bolshevik girl shot your friend. I know I said I was concerned about the Nazis earlier, but there was nearly a communist revolution here in Saxony in 1923. That's only seven years ago. And there was almost another one in Berlin on May Day last year.

'These people believe in changing the world through violent means. And when they talk about struggling for "the people", I don't think they mean fighting for people like me living in castles, or people like you and your friends staying in them as our guests, I think they mean fighting against us. It can be difficult for foreigners who don't know Germany well to understand that, but the police do.'

She fixed Archie and Esme with a powerful stare. 'I come from Posen, myself. My family inhabited our manor house there for a hundred and twenty years until it was given away to Poland after the war. It killed my father; he died two years later. And now my husband has died too. I will not let some communists take Burg Adlerstein away from this family.'

Her gaze softened as she looked at Archie. 'I'm sure you understand, Sir Archibald. I imagine your own home has been in your family a while?'

'A good long while.' Since 1672 was indeed a good long while. And he did understand; he would put up a fight for Yarmer Hall. It would be a brave communist indeed who tried to take the castle from the baroness.

She nodded. She seemed comforted by Archie's presence. She understood that like her he had roots in the land going back centuries; the fact that the land was the pasture of the Yorkshire Dales rather than the forested crags of Saxony didn't matter.

'Thank you for indulging us and answering our questions,' said Esme. 'Harriet was my best friend, and I do want to know what happened to her. And *why* it happened.'

The baroness turned to her and smiled. 'Of course. My advice is to have confidence in the police. They know what they are doing in these matters.'

14

Archie, Esme and Gisela walked down the hill to the village, an undulating sea of ancient red roofs dotted with stork nests made of great bundles of sticks, a church spire rising out of its midst.

'It must be difficult for your mother,' said Esme. 'A murder in the castle. She seems to be handling it well.'

'It is. Mama is good in a crisis. Father died last year and left the castle in a difficult situation. We knew there were problems, but we didn't appreciate quite how great they were. She and Otto have had their work cut out keeping things afloat.' Gisela sighed. 'Poor Mama hasn't got over my other two brothers falling in the war. Manfred should be the one running the estate now. But he didn't even make it past Christmas in 1914.'

Just like his own older brother Fred, Archie thought.

'And now there's this. But she will cope. She always copes. She's a strong woman.'

'It's understandable that she doesn't like the idea of one of her guests murdering someone,' said Archie.

'Neither do I,' said Gisela. 'And she makes some good points.

I know the communists have seats in the Reichstag, but there are many radicals who want to overthrow the republic by violence.'

'That's as maybe,' said Esme. 'But why does that involve killing Harriet?'

'It's a good question,' said Archie. 'Do you know where Ruth was staying, Esme?'

'Yes. She said The Golden Bear.'

'It's the only inn in the village,' said Gisela. 'I'll take you there.'

The Golden Bear seemed to wobble beneath its steeply angled roof, a patchwork of diagonal timbers barely keeping the medieval structure together. The innkeeper's wife, a round woman with buck teeth and a strong Saxon nasal twang that Archie and Esme struggled to understand, was very happy to gossip with the daughter of the castle about the big news of the week. She and her husband had been interviewed by the police. Fräulein Jakubowski had indeed stayed at their inn for the night. She had had an early breakfast and left the inn at about half past seven. She had returned just after nine, gathered her suitcase and walked off towards the station.

She had conversed little with the innkeeper or his wife or the other guests at the inn: a couple from the Rhineland and a travelling salesman from Berlin. What little she did have to say she said in an Austrian accent. She neither said nor did anything to suggest she was a communist, but the innkeeper's wife wasn't surprised to hear she was, and suspected her of being Jewish as well. She was glad she had been arrested.

Gisela then took Esme and Archie to the railway station on the edge of town. Once again, the porter knew Gisela and was forthcoming. Ruth had arrived on the train from Berlin on the Saturday afternoon, and departed on the Sunday morning on the 9.42 train to Dresden.

Archie, Esme and Gisela left the station and stood on the pavement outside.

Archie summed up what they had heard. 'Not much time to do everything Ruth was supposed to have done,' he said. 'If she left the inn at seven-thirty, she would have to climb the hill to the castle, break in, steal the rifle and creep down to the temple by eight-twenty. Then rush back to the inn by nine.'

'It would take twenty minutes to get up to the castle from the village,' Esme said. 'A bit quicker coming back downhill.'

'And then she would have had to break into the castle and creep about in the forest.' Archie shook his head. 'It doesn't work, does it? Ruth wouldn't know exactly when you and Harriet would be riding along the river. I suspect the murderer was there well in advance. This was slowly and carefully planned, not done at a sprint.'

'But wouldn't the police have considered all of this?' Esme said.

'Shall we ask them?' said Archie. 'There must be a village policeman.'

'There certainly is,' Gisela said. 'Old Dümmler has been the policeman in the village for as long as I've been alive and probably many years before that.'

'Can you point us to him?' Archie asked.

'I can. In fact, I'll come with you.'

* * *

Old Dümmler had a similar twang to the innkeeper's wife, but fortunately he spoke much more slowly. He was a stubby man with a bristling Hindenburg moustache and a uniform a size too small for him. The police house wasn't far from the railway station, and Constable Dümmler was rolling up on his bicycle just as Archie, Esme and Gisela reached it.

'Ah, Fräulein Adlerstein!' he exclaimed with what was obviously genuine pleasure. 'You are looking very well! I hope you are not here to report a crime at the castle? There have been enough of those for one year.'

Gisela grinned broadly. 'No, Dümmler, don't worry. You remember my friend Esme Carmichael? And this is her friend, Sir Archie Laverick.'

'Of course I remember Fräulein Carmichael. I was the first one to the scene. That must have been a terrible shock for you, Fräulein.' His voice was kind, comforting. 'Not something you can recover from quickly.'

'No,' said Esme. 'You are dead right there. I do remember your face, but it's all a bit of a blur.'

'I'm sure it is. Come in, come in! Have a cup of coffee with me.'

They followed the constable into the police house and he led them into a small, official-looking room with a filing cabinet and a picture of President Hindenburg. Archie noticed that the police constable's moustache was if anything even bigger than the President's. Frau Dümmler made an appearance to greet Gisela and then disappeared again to make the coffee. After asking Gisela's permission, the policeman lit up a Meerschaum pipe.

'How can I help you, Fräulein?' he asked, taking the first puffs to get it going.

'We'd like to talk to you about the murder, Dümmi. Unofficially.'

'Phew. I much prefer unofficial,' said the policeman, ignoring the slightly disrespectful nickname. 'No writing things down.'

'You see, my friends here don't believe that Ruth Jakubowski did shoot Miss Dryden.'

The policeman frowned, and looked with a keen eye at Archie and Esme. 'And why is that?'

Archie cleared his throat. 'Several reasons. We don't see how Ruth could have known where the rifle was stored. We don't see how she could have broken in to steal it. We don't think she would have had time to get to the castle, steal the rifle, shoot Harriet and return to the inn. We can't see why she would want to kill Harriet anyway.'

The constable was silent for a while, drawing on his pipe. Gisela, Archie and Esme let him think. His wife brought in three cups of coffee and withdrew.

'She was seen by two witnesses walking up to the castle that morning, you know, even though she never actually knocked on the door,' the policeman said. 'So she was there at the time Fräulein Dryden was shot. Dresden CID would claim she might have had help locating and stealing the rifle; that would have saved her time at the castle. She shot Harriet because she was jealous – Herr Trexler was her former lover.'

Esme piped up. 'I spoke to her the night before, constable. Ruth was not a murderer. And if she was going to murder anyone, it would have been Gray, not Harriet. But I very much doubt she would shoot him. Or anyone.'

A smile creased old Dümmler's face. 'This is between us, Fräulein Adlerstein?'

'Of course, Dümmi. And I can vouch for my friends.' Gisela looked pointedly at Archie and Esme.

'Absolutely,' said Archie.

'You have my word,' said Esme.

With a quick glance at Gisela and a puff of his pipe, the constable leaned forward. 'You are absolutely right. I haven't met the woman – they arrested her on the train at the Czech border and took her straight to Dresden – but it is obvious to me she is innocent. I am not involved in the investigation, but I have done a lot of standing around in the company of those who are, and she is not guilty. She can't possibly have stolen the rifle and shot the victim in time.'

'If you think that, why don't the policemen who are investigating?'

'As with all these things, it's political. The investigation is being run by CID in Dresden, but Department 1A from Berlin is involved – that's the political police. You see, they had information Jakubowski was leaving Paris for Berlin and they followed her as soon as she arrived at Friedrichstrasse station. They saw her go to the Soviet embassy where they believe she met a Soviet diplomat named Yevgeny Barsukov. So, they think she is some kind of spy for the Russians.'

'I know Yevgeny!' said Esme. 'I've seen him at the Adlon bar with Harriet and the others.'

Constable Dümmler frowned at this information.

'Do the Dresden police agree with their colleagues in Berlin?' Archie asked him.

'At a senior level, yes, they do. Once again, it's political.'

'Are these policemen from one of the right-wing parties?' Esme asked. 'The German Nationals?'

The constable smiled. 'Oh, no, they are all good *sozis*. The police departments in Berlin and in Saxony are run by SPD men.' The SPD was the Social Democratic Party, the largest party in the national parliament. 'And there is no one the SPD hates more than the communists. You heard about the street battles in Berlin last May Day when all those people were shot?'

'Yes.'

'The Berlin Police Commissioner provoked them. He sent armed police into Wedding and Neukölln with orders to shoot if there was any trouble. And here in Saxony they are still shaken by the October Plot in 1923 when the commies planned to overthrow the government. They think the Soviets were behind that.'

'Do they believe that Ruth Jakubowski is involved in some kind of plot to overthrow the government?' Archie asked.

'In which case, why would she kill the daughter of an American diplomat?' Esme added.

'Oh, I don't know. This politics is way over my head. Maybe they see this as a good reason to arrest her? Or to get Barsukov into trouble?'

'I see,' Archie said. 'Do you think the detectives from Dresden know Ruth is innocent?'

'If you asked them, they would say no.' Dümmler jabbed his pipe at Archie. 'But don't ask them, in case you were thinking of it. And if they asked themselves, which they won't, they would probably also deny it. But deep in their souls, they know she didn't shoot anyone.'

'That's terrible!' protested Esme. 'The poor girl is pregnant in a foreign country and locked up for a crime she didn't commit!'

'I'm not sure anyone will care,' the constable said.

'I care!' said Esme. 'Not only that, but if Ruth didn't kill poor Harriet, someone else did.'

Dümmler nodded sagely. 'That's true.' He glanced at Gisela. 'I like your friend. She has a good sense of justice.' He puffed his pipe. 'And for what it's worth, Fräulein Carmichael, which is less than two pfennigs, I think it's wrong too. Even if she is a commie.'

'Where is she being held?' Esme asked.

'At police headquarters in Dresden. She was charged with murder this morning.'

'Is there any chance we could get to see her?'

'Perhaps bail her out?' added Archie.

'There's no chance of bail,' said Dümmler. 'You could try to see her, if she wants to see you. But remember. If you do talk to the police in Dresden, don't mention anything I've just told you.'

* * *

'It looks as if you were right,' said Gisela to Archie and Esme as they climbed into the Horch back in the castle courtyard. 'Old Dümmi is a wise man.'

'Thank you for your help,' Esme said.

'Not at all. Listen. I'll be going back to Berlin this weekend. I'm living in Kreuzberg. If you need any more help from me, just get in touch.' She rummaged in her bag and produced a calling card and handed it to Esme.

'Thanks,' said Esme. 'Although I'm not sure what we can do: things are looking tough for poor Ruth.'

15

Ruth Jakubowski did not look to Archie like a dangerous communist terrorist. She looked small, scared and miserable. Her dark eyes were rimmed with red, her black curly hair was tangled and her cheeks were sunken.

They were in an interview room deep in the bowels of Dresden police headquarters. Two policemen in blue uniforms and black shakos ignored them from beside the door.

Archie and Esme had spent another night at the Savoy Hotel in Dresden and after breakfast that morning – where they had read the news of Ruth's charging in the *Deutsche Allgemeine Zeitung* – had tried their luck at the police station. Esme had received a cordial reception from a lanky assistant detective who had interviewed her at the castle. He confirmed that Ruth had been charged with the murder of Harriet Dryden and added that they were considering espionage and conspiracy charges as well. He was surprised by Esme's request to see Ruth, and even more surprised that Ruth agreed to see her, given Esme's friendship with the woman she had murdered.

But here they were.

Ruth spoke first. 'I'm so sorry,' she said. 'They tell me that the woman who was killed was a friend of yours and you were right there when it happened?'

Esme nodded.

'I don't mean I'm sorry because I shot her. I didn't do that, I promise you. I'm just sorry because it must be so awful for you.'

'I know you didn't shoot her,' Esme said.

The effect of these words on Ruth was startling. A tear crept out of one eye. And then another. She made no effort to wipe them away.

'You were so kind to me that evening,' she said. 'As I was locked away here wondering what on earth was happening, I kept thinking about your kindness. And then, when they told me it was your friend that I was supposed to have shot, I felt terrible. That's why I wanted to see you now – to explain. But how do you know I didn't kill her when everyone else seems to believe I did?'

'You are not a killer,' Esme said, her voice faltering. 'I know that. You are a woman who is in a dreadful situation and it's not your fault.'

Archie was going to add the more concrete reasons why they thought Ruth was innocent, but he held his tongue. For Esme, that was the heart of it.

Esme cleared her throat. 'We would like to help you,' she said. 'Archie and I. We understand that the police have political reasons to blame you for what happened. But we'd like to show them that it wasn't you. And we'd like to find out who did kill my friend.'

'And who are you?' Ruth asked Archie.

'Archie Laverick. I'm a... a friend of Esme's. And I agree with her. I don't think you did kill poor Harriet. But it would help us if you could answer some questions. I'm sure the police will have asked you most of these, but you can understand they haven't told us your answers.'

'And we haven't told them about our doubts,' said Esme.

Although they just had, thought Archie, aware of the two police constables watching them impassively.

'All right.' Ruth nodded.

'What happened that morning?' Archie asked.

'I had spent all night stewing over whether I should go up to the castle. You had urged me to, Esme, and you had promised you would speak to Gray, but I wasn't sure you'd actually do it, and even if you did, I doubted very much that he would agree to see me.

'But I decided to go anyway. I left the inn about half past seven. But when I got to the castle gate I lost my nerve. I was feeling pretty low – I couldn't believe anything would go right for me. So I sat on a wall along the lane to the castle and then made my way back down to the inn. Did you talk to Gray?'

'I did,' said Esme. 'And I told him you were pregnant.'

'Oh. And did he say he would see me that morning?'

'No. He was very firm on that point.'

Ruth nodded. 'I'm not surprised. In a way I'm relieved. If he had been willing to see me and I didn't show up at the castle I would feel even more of a fool.'

'He has no intention of helping you at all,' said Esme bitterly.

Despite everything else that had happened to her, this further bit of news seemed to crush Ruth.

Esme reached out a hand towards her over the desk in the interview room, but one of the constables stopped her. 'Fräulein!'

Esme withdrew her hand.

'How long have you known Trexler?' Archie asked.

'Two years. And four months. We met in Vienna where he was a correspondent for the *Chicago Globe*. Then, when he moved to Paris last year, I followed him. I was never anything more than his mistress, but he told me his wife had lovers too. I believed him – but who knows? Maybe he was lying to me. I only met her a couple of times in Vienna. She was beautiful but she didn't seem to like him very much.'

Archie wondered how this thin, scared woman could be the lover of the man of the world that Esme had described Gray Trexler to be. But Archie glimpsed something about her, the way she held herself, a flash of the eye, something that in different circumstances a man might find alluring.

'Then a couple of months ago, he ended it,' she said. 'He didn't tell me why, but I think I know.'

She hesitated.

'Why?' Esme prompted her.

'I was becoming too fond of him. Too demanding. Stepping outside my proper role of mistress and recreational sex provider.' Bitterness laced her words. 'It's my fault. Gray was never really serious about me, nor claimed he ever would be. I think he almost ended it when I moved to Paris, but I talked him out of it. I pretended indifference. But eventually I couldn't keep up the pretence.'

She shrugged. 'Then I realised I was pregnant. I tried to get in touch with him in Paris, but I learned he had gone to Berlin for a few weeks to cover the election. So I came to Berlin, found out he was in Saxony and came here.' She sighed. 'It's on the way to Vienna where my sister knows a doctor who can help me. I know Gray. In my heart of hearts, I knew he would leave me to deal with this by myself, but I hoped I was wrong. I wasn't.'

'No, you weren't,' said Esme.

'Can you tell us a little about Yevgeny Barsukov?' Archie asked. 'I understand that the Berlin police followed you to the Soviet embassy last week?'

'He's a friend of Gray's. He used to be stationed in the Russians' Vienna embassy. I met him there through Gray. I knew he had been posted to Berlin, so I thought he might tell me where Gray was.'

'And did he?'

'No. But he gave me a couple of other names of journalists in Berlin who might. An American called Joe Moretti and an Englishman called Claude Tazewell. I tried telephoning Joe, but his landlady said he was away. Mr Tazewell told me Gray was staying at Burg Adlerstein.'

'The police seem to think Barsukov is a spy.'

'They do,' said Ruth.

'Is he?'

Ruth's shoulders slumped. 'I don't know. Possibly. He is a Russian diplomat, after all. I never noticed any signs that he was a spy in Vienna, and Gray and I saw quite a lot of him there. But then if he was a spy, he would hardly tell me, would he?'

And if you were a spy, you would hardly tell us, would you, thought Archie, but he didn't say it. He was quite sure that was a point the police had made to her. Forcefully. Whatever Ruth's real relationship with Barsukov was, talking about it in the police station would not help her.

One of the constables looked at his watch. 'Your time is up,' he said.

'All right,' said Archie. 'Do you have a lawyer, Miss Jakubowski?'

'Yes. The police found me one. He is a nice man, but I'm not sure how much help he can be. His name is Schrör.'

'Thank you for letting us see you,' said Esme. 'And we *will* help you. We *will* prove you are innocent.'

'I am not sure you will. But Esme, thank you for trying. And for believing in me.'

* * *

The assistant detective gave them the lawyer's address. Herr Schrör's office was on the third floor of a scruffy building just off Christianstrasse. A secretary in a tiny office waved them through to a slightly bigger inner office, in which a clean-shaven, dark-haired young man peered over a teetering wall of papers through wire-rimmed glasses.

He leaped to his feet and shook Archie's and Esme's hands with a warm smile.

'Good morning! Schrör. How can I help you?'

'My name is Esme Carmichael and this is Sir Archibald Laverick,' said Esme. 'We have come here from police headquarters. We'd like to talk to you about one of your clients, Ruth Jakubowski.'

'Ah.' The lawyer regained his seat. 'Esme Carmichael? You were the witness to Harriet Dryden's death?'

'Yes,' said Esme. 'I was her friend.'

'Right – um – I'm not sure I can be of any assistance. You see, Fräulein Jakubowski is my client...'

'Oh, no. I think you have the wrong end of the stick. I am not angry with Fräulein Jakubowski. We think she is innocent!'

The young lawyer's eyebrows shot up behind his glasses.

'In fact, we are pretty certain she is innocent.'

'Oh. I see. And why do you think she's innocent?'

Esme glanced at Archie who repeated his litany of reasons, omitting the views of Constable Dümmler.

'We think her arrest may be political. Because she is a communist and has been in touch with a Soviet diplomat,' Esme said.

'You are very well informed,' Schrör said.

'I don't know whether you have read it in the files, or whether

Ruth told you, but I saw her the night before Harriet was shot. She made a profound impression on me then and she did again just now. I feel sorry for her and I can't bear the idea that she may go to prison for something she didn't do.'

Schrör nodded. 'She is my client so of course I believe she is innocent,' he said. 'But I must say I am beginning to agree with you. I think she may actually *be* innocent, something that's rare for my other clients. And, what's more, I think the detectives investigating the case know it.'

'Do you think you can defend her?' Archie asked.

'If she really is innocent, in theory I should be able to. But, as you say, this smells very political. And to be frank, I'm a bit out of my depth here. I've never defended a murder case before. While I know who they are, I don't know any of the bigwigs in this city personally.'

'I assume your fees are being paid by the state?' said Archie.

'That's correct.'

'Well, if you require any expert help or extra legal advice, I'd be happy to pay for that. I'll be staying at the Adlon Hotel in Berlin for the next couple of months.'

The lawyer's face brightened, but then a cloud of suspicion drifted across his brow. 'Why would you do that?' he said.

Good question, thought Archie.

'Because my friend believes that your client is innocent. And the identity of Harriet's murderer is important to her.'

Esme threw a surprised glance at Archie, and then turned to the lawyer.

'Yes. It's very important to me.'

16

After leaving the lawyer's office, Archie and Esme walked through the town and up some broad steps from the Schlossplatz by the Frederick Augustus Bridge to the tree-lined Brühl's Terrace which ran along the old city fortifications on the left bank of the river. They stopped at a restaurant called The Belvedere, ordered an early lunch and a bottle of local white wine and admired the view of the wide blue Elbe and the magnificent buildings of the New Town on its far side.

'So. What do you think?' Esme asked.

'I don't think Ruth murdered anyone,' said Archie.

'Good. Neither do I.'

'But she may be spying for the Russians. She contacted that diplomat in Berlin; we don't know what else she may have said to him apart from asking if he knew where Trexler was.'

'Does it matter?'

'Whether she's a Soviet spy? I don't know. I suppose what the Russians and the Germans get up to is their business. But if she is genuinely trying to start a revolution, I can quite understand why the German police might want to stop her. They probably couldn't believe their luck when she turned up as a suspect for a murder.'

'We don't know that's what she was doing,' said Esme. 'Spying for the Russians.'

'We could hardly ask her about it in the police station with those two policemen watching over us,' Archie pointed out.

'Politics aside, the poor girl is in a load of trouble and, apart from her lawyer, we seem to be the only people who can help her out.'

Archie nodded. 'That's true. I do feel sorry for her.'

Esme opened her mouth to say something and hesitated.

Archie waited.

Esme shook her head. 'It reminds me of Blanche.'

'Blanche?'

'Yes. She was a friend of mine at college – a friend of Harriet's as well, actually. She ran around with men. A lot – it shocked Harriet and me a bit, to be honest; she had seemed to us like a nice girl. She *was* a nice girl. Anyway, in her sophomore year she got pregnant. The man in question didn't want to know; his father owned a department store and for some reason he seemed to think that because his father was a big businessman, the scandal would be worse for him. He said he would claim he had never slept with her, and he didn't like her much anyway.

'She found a doctor. It's pretty easy to find a doctor who'll help in that way in Chicago. But she needed money to pay for it and she didn't have any. So she decided to charge rich students for sex.'

Esme shook her head. '*Such* a dumb idea. It worked – she was an attractive girl and there were boys who would pay. But one of them talked and before long everyone knew. They called her a whore.

'I say everyone knew. The boys knew, but we didn't. She never told us about any of it. We could have helped her somehow but she was too humiliated. And by the time we found out, it was too late. She dropped out at the end of the year. The whole business scared the hell out of Harriet and me. But somehow the whole thing was all her fault, and not the dirty so-and-so who got her pregnant. He got a nice job in a bank.'

Esme's eyes were determined. Angry. 'So, yes, I want to help Ruth.'

'I understand,' said Archie. 'But then we're back to the same question. If Ruth didn't shoot Harriet...'

'Who did?'

'Precisely.'

The waiter poured them both a glass of wine. A barge powered down the centre of the river outside, its gunwales barely above the water it was so heavily laden, perhaps heading all the way to Hamburg and the North Sea.

'Well, let's think it through,' Esme said. 'You must be correct; it's got to be someone who was staying at the castle.'

'Let's go through them,' said Archie. 'We asked the baroness where everyone was when Harriet was shot. She said that Joe, Annachiara and Gisela were all at breakfast together. They have alibis.'

'Alibis? So you have read Agatha Christie!'

'Sherlock Holmes when I was a boy,' admitted Archie. 'Then she said Otto was in the estate office and Erich and Gray were going for a walk in the forest. So Otto doesn't have an alibi.'

'I'm betting on Gray,' said Esme.

'You don't like him, do you?'

'No, I do not. He's arrogant and he was beastly to Ruth. I don't know what Harriet saw in him.' Esme corrected himself. 'All right, I do. He's handsome and he's charming. But I don't trust him an inch. And there's his moustache.'

'His moustache?'

'What do you think about men with pencil moustaches? I don't trust them myself.'

'I think they're a dab hand with a razor,' said Archie. 'Those things are the very devil to shave around. You have to scrape half your upper lip in a straight line. I tried it myself for a couple of months, but gave up.'

Esme frowned. 'You would look terrible with a pencil moustache.'

'Thank you, Esme. More to the point, Gray and Erich were together in the forest.'

'Says Erich. Perhaps he's covering for Gray?'

'Why would he do that?'

'I don't know,' Esme admitted.

'And why would Gray kill Harriet?'

'Why would anyone kill Harriet?' Esme said.

Archie sipped his wine thoughtfully. 'We don't know. And we can't even guess. But *someone* had a reason. You said that Gray, Erich and Duncan were all flirting with Harriet. Had she seen any of them in Berlin?'

'She saw all of them together at the Adlon frequently.'

'But none of them alone?'

'Not that I know of. Not regularly anyhow.'

'Not even Gray?'

'Maybe she saw him without telling me. We didn't do everything together.'

'What about the Russian diplomat, Barsukov? You said you've met him. What's he like? Did Harriet know him well?'

'I met him once, at the Adlon with the others. He's very friendly, likes to talk and to drink. Boy, does he like to drink! I think he's a second secretary at the embassy, or something. But people like him. He seemed like a good friend of Gray's.'

'Could he be a spy?'

'I don't know! He must be a communist – he's a Russian diplomat, after all. I guess he could be a spy.'

'And was he chasing after Harriet?'

'Probably – they all were. He has a wife back in Moscow, I think he said. Not that that would necessarily mean anything. But Harriet never mentioned him: I don't think they spent any time alone together.'

'Was she interested in communism?'

'No, I'd say not. She *was* interested in politics at Chicago, we both were, and we were both on the left by American standards. But she wasn't a communist. And she seemed less political here in Berlin. But of course, as the ambassador's deputy at the American embassy, her father might be of interest to the Soviets.'

'You didn't get the impression Harriet was caught up with a ring of communists?'

'No. Definitely not.'

'What about Otto?'

'Well, Harriet knew him, of course. But I have no idea why on earth he would want to kill her. And you've forgotten Duncan.'

'I think we can safely forget Duncan,' Archie said.

'Is that because he's your cousin?' Esme asked. 'Or because he's British?'

'Neither,' said Archie. 'He's so young – he still has acne.'

'What does that have to do with anything? He's not that young. And he may have acne, but he doesn't have an alibi. He was in the bath.'

'You're right, it doesn't mean anything. It's just I've known him since he was a boy. A baby, actually. Does he seem like a killer to you?'

'No,' Esme admitted. 'But if we are going to do this properly, we can't rule people out just because we like them. Or because they have pimples.'

'I suppose not. The truth is we just don't know who killed her, do we?'

'No,' said Esme. 'We don't.'

Their food was taking its time. Archie reined in his impatience.

'So now what?' Esme said.

'What do you mean?'

'What do we do now?'

Archie narrowed his eyes. 'What do you mean *we*?'

'I mean you and me.'

'Do you expect me to help you?'

'It would be nice. And you did offer to pay for Ruth's legal expenses; that was generous of you. Doesn't that mean you want to help?'

Esme was looking at Archie closely.

Did he want to?

Harriet's murder had nothing to do with him. And while it clearly did have a lot to do with Esme, finding the murderer was not her responsibility.

And yet Archie was touched by the concern Esme showed for Ruth and was also touched by the Austrian woman's plight. Unless somebody did something, she would be convicted for murder and, presumably, be executed. That was profoundly wrong. Archie was concerned that Ruth was involved in some kind of Soviet-backed communist plot that they didn't know about, but that the German police did. But it was still wrong.

Archie continued to admire Esme's sense of justice. He found himself sharing it. In fact, he found the idea of helping her intriguing. He *wanted* to do it.

He had stopped stammering. He had had no more visits from

Lieutenant Dowling in the night. He was feeling – not exactly happy. But *alive.* And actually, yes, happy to be alive.

That was not a normal feeling for Archie.

'All right,' he said. 'Yes. I'll help you.'

Esme's face broke into a broad grin, that elicited a smile from Archie in return. 'Swell. I knew you would. And I'm *so* pleased. Now. Where's our food?'

17

After lunch, they dropped into Garfinkel's antiquarian bookshop to see what incunabula Herr Garfinkel had turned up.

The owner was out, so they had to deal with his assistant, Moses.

In contrast to their entrance the previous day, the big young man leaped up from his book the moment Archie and Esme came in.

He stood behind the counter expectantly, but didn't actually say anything. Nor did he look at them.

'Good afternoon. Did Herr Garfinkel find anything for me?' Archie asked in German.

Moses still didn't say anything, but he took two leather volumes – one brown and one red – down from a bookshelf and laid them on the counter in front of Archie. He avoided Archie's eye, but stared at the books.

'What are these?' Archie asked, opening the cover of one of them.

'A Latin vocabulary textbook from Leipzig and a breviary

from Meissen,' said Moses. 'They are in excellent condition. They both come from the collection of a monastery near Zwickau. Do you have Leipzig and Meissen in your collection?'

'I have something from Leipzig already, but nothing from Meissen,' Archie said.

'That's not surprising: there are over a thousand different incunabula printed in Leipzig, but only two from Meissen. This breviary, and Andreas Escobar's *Confessions*. The cover is the original pigskin; since it has been in the monastery's possession for centuries, it was never re-bound.'

'Interesting.' Archie ran his fingers over the red cover, feeling the rougher follicles of the pigskin as opposed to smooth sheepskin. He preferred buying incunabula in their original covers if he could get them. He opened the book: inside, like all incunabula printed in Germany, the text was in neat black Gothic type. 'How much is this one?'

'Herr Garfinkel said I should ask you for sixteen hundred marks.'

'Very well,' said Archie with a grin. 'I like it. Will you accept traveller's cheques?'

'Yes, certainly. Herr Garfinkel was expecting that.'

'You think that sixteen hundred marks is too much, don't you, Moses?' Esme said.

Moses looked at her in surprise.

'Well?'

Moses's big face reddened. 'Yes,' he said. 'Sixteen hundred marks *is* too much. Of course, my uncle should make a profit, but I think he is taking advantage of Herr Laverick's lack of knowledge.'

Archie raised his eyebrows.

'It is clear that you know very little about incunabula, Herr Laverick.' Moses still wasn't meeting Archie's eye.

Esme let out a tiny giggle.

Archie nodded his agreement. 'Yes, that's pretty clear to me too. So what would be a fair price?'

'Herr Garfinkel is paying seven hundred and eighty marks. So, maybe one thousand?'

'You're not a great salesman, are you, Moses?' Esme said.

'No,' Moses agreed. 'That's what Herr Garfinkel always tells me. That's why I usually don't deal with customers. But I do know a lot about books.'

Esme studied the man. 'Go ahead,' she said to him. 'Ask him.'

'Ask him?' Moses said, confused. But he was at least prepared to look at Esme.

'Ask Herr Laverick about his old books. I know you are dying to.'

Moses frowned. He inhaled deeply. And then he did look at Archie. 'I was very interested yesterday when you told me about your collection. I think that is an excellent idea to buy a book from each town in which incunabula were printed. You say you have eighty-six books?'

'Soon to be eighty-seven.' Archie laid his palm on the Meissen breviary. 'It was my grandfather who started it and I'm continuing with his idea.'

'I see. And from which towns, please?'

'Do you want all eighty-six?' said Archie.

'Of course he does,' said Esme. 'Go on. Tell him.'

Archie pulled out a notebook. For the next hour or so he read out the various towns and cities around Europe from which his collection came, while Moses tried to guess which book he owned from each printer. They had to pause twice while customers interrupted them, but Moses's glare soon got rid of them. Archie rather enjoyed it. Moses's eyes glinted with pleasure. Esme went outside and smoked several cigarettes.

They were discussing what incunabula Archie might find when he visited Rostock, when Herr Garfinkel returned. Moses instantly shut up.

'Ah, Herr Laverick! I see Moses showed you the two incunabula we have been able to dig up. Do either of them interest you?'

'Yes. The breviary from Meissen.'

'Oh, good. That will be sixteen hundred marks.'

'Yes. That was what your assistant told me. I thought twelve hundred would be more like it.'

'Twelve hundred? You would be very lucky to get this for sixteen hundred! You will never find another one, you know? This was the only title printed in Meissen before 1500, isn't that right, Moses?'

Moses stared at his uncle with something close to horror at this outright misrepresentation of the truth.

'Oh, that's a shame,' said Archie quickly, to save the poor young man from embarrassment. 'But there are another one hundred and seventy-six towns for me to choose from.'

'One hundred and seventy-five,' said Moses. 'Two hundred and sixty-two, less the eighty-six you own, less Meissen. You can't include Meissen, because you have just said you won't buy a book from there.'

Herr Garfinkel and Archie paused to look at Moses.

'He's right, you know,' said Archie. 'It's one hundred and seventy-five.'

Esme sniggered.

Archie ended up paying thirteen hundred marks for the book. He didn't want to take too much advantage of Moses's honesty. As he left, he asked Herr Garfinkel to get in touch with him at the Adlon Hotel in Berlin if anything else of interest turned up, glancing pointedly at Moses as he said it.

Moses stared at them both as they left the shop.

'I think you've made yourself a little friend, there,' said Esme.

'A jolly decent chap,' said Archie. 'You do meet such interesting people in the antiquarian book business.'

Esme just laughed.

18

They didn't get to Berlin until eight o'clock that evening. Archie dropped Esme at the Drydens' house in the Hohenzollernstrasse just south of the Tiergarten. It was an imposing villa behind a wrought-iron fence, one of a row of imposing villas. Archie guessed that Walter Dryden had recourse to more than a diplomat's salary to pay the rent.

Esme urged Archie to come in for a few minutes to meet Harriet's father. A young butler with an English accent stepped back to allow Esme to sweep into the hallway, calling out Mr Dryden's name. A moment later, a tall, handsome, silver-haired man with a grey moustache appeared and Esme flung herself at him and kissed him on the cheek. Mr Dryden beamed.

'Mr Dryden, this is Sir Archie Laverick, my new boss. Archie, Mr Dryden.'

The diplomat stiffened, the beam became a restrained smile and Dryden held out his hand.

'Good to meet you, Sir Archibald. Will you stay for a drink?'

'Just a quick one,' said Archie.

He followed Dryden and Esme into a library. 'Will you take a Scotch?'

Archie nodded and winced inwardly as the English butler dropped ice cubes into the amber liquid, with a tiny sympathetic twitch of an eyebrow in Archie's direction. Esme got nothing.

She flopped on to a sofa and Dryden took his place in a winged leather armchair next to a large old fireplace above which hung a rather dramatic primeval landscape of mountains sweeping down to a lake – somewhere in America, no doubt. The room was a proper library, filled with books that had obviously been read, not just heavy leather-bound tomes but also plenty of novels. Rich, dark wooden panels glimmered between the bookshelves.

'A fruitful trip, I trust?' Dryden asked. His accent was such a patrician American that it sounded almost English, the soft 'r's being all that gave him away. His suit, stiff collar and tie were immaculate.

'Very fruitful,' Archie said. 'Esme was a great help.'

'I'm sure she was.' Dryden smiled at Esme with something like pride. 'You'll find you are lucky to have hired her.'

'Thankfully, Archie is very patient,' said Esme.

'I read your book on Moltke,' said Dryden. 'I thought it was excellent. I never realised he was such a fascinating man.'

'He was,' said Archie.

'You wait till you read about Bluey,' said Esme. 'Archie will knock your socks off with that one.'

Archie was pleased by Esme's faith in him, even if it as yet had no justification.

'I'm sure you will,' said Dryden with a stiff smile.

'We went back to the Adlerstein castle,' said Esme. 'I wanted to show it to Archie.'

'Oh.' Dryden's face was impassive. A diplomat's mask.

'Yes. You see, I – that is we.' Esme nodded at Archie. 'We're not sure that the girl the police have arrested is the one who shot Harriet.'

'Really? Why?' Dryden still seemed unperturbed.

'She didn't have the time to steal the rifle from the castle, shoot Harriet and disappear,' said Esme.

'Oh. And what do the police think?'

'The police are convinced that the girl did do it,' said Esme. 'They think she's a communist spy.'

'But you don't?'

'What do you think, Mr Dryden?' Archie asked.

Dryden's face didn't move. 'I think you should leave it to the police.' He sighed. 'They came here demanding to go through Harriet's things. I wouldn't let them; I couldn't bear it. Diplomatic immunity, you know. They tried to kick up a fuss, but if there is one thing I've learned in my time in Berlin, it's how to deal with an officious German.'

'Do *you* know anyone who might want to kill her?' said Esme. 'I don't.'

'I can't think why anyone would want to do that,' said Dryden. His face was frozen, his blue eyes cold, his moustache stiff.

His lower lip wobbled. Then steadied. Then wobbled again.

Esme's expression changed. 'Oh, Mr Dryden! I am sorry.' She stood up from the sofa, moved over to him and put her hand on his sleeve. 'I should never have mentioned it!'

Archie rather agreed.

Dryden didn't move for several seconds. Then he slowly placed his hand on hers. A tear slid out of his left eye; he left it for a moment and then dabbed it with a fingertip. A proud, wounded man. His glance flicked upwards over Archie's shoulder.

Archie turned to see Harriet staring back at him with those amused dark eyes. Except it wasn't Harriet. It was a version of her, ten years older, perhaps, painted in oils. The same eyes, the same chin, the hair styled slightly differently, the same figure. A spectacular emerald necklace nestled above her cleavage.

Harriet's mother. Walter Dryden's late wife.

The poor man had lost so much.

Archie put his whisky down on a side table. 'I must be going, Dryden. Don't get up. I'll see myself out. Good night, Esme.'

19

Archie drove the Horch the short distance back to the Adlon Hotel, feeling very sorry for Dryden. It was clear it was important for Esme to find out what had really happened to Harriet; it was less clear that Harriet's father felt the same way.

There was a message waiting for Archie at the front desk.

Call Mr Mandeville. Urgently.

'What's up, Duncan?'

'Thank God you're back,' said Duncan. 'It's your man Lister. He's in the clink.'

'Dash it all! He needs me to bail him out, I take it?'

'It's more serious than that. There was a fight and he put the other chap in hospital. The other chap is a minor aristocrat and is kicking up a bit of a fuss. I think I've squared it with the police through a contact at the Foreign Ministry, but they'll charge him tonight unless you vouch for him this evening. If you do that, they say they'll let him go.'

'Christ! Bloody Lister.' Archie was tired. Seriously tired. His leg was throbbing and he was hungry.

'You could just let them charge him,' Duncan said. 'But if he's found guilty he might end up in a German jail for a couple of years. Maybe longer.'

Serve him bloody well right, thought Archie. 'No, no. I'll get him out. Where is he?'

'At the police station in Alexanderplatz. I'd better come with you. I'll be there in twenty minutes.'

* * *

Archie was waiting outside the hotel when Duncan rolled up in a taxi.

'Thank you, old man,' said Archie. 'I'm very grateful for what you've done and I'm sorry Lister has caused you all this trouble.'

'It's all part of the job,' said Duncan.

'No, it's not. Who did you call?'

'Chap called Adlerstein. He's a good friend. He managed to persuade the fellow Lister hit not to press charges.'

'When did this happen?'

'Three o'clock this morning. In a seedy nightclub near the Nollendorfplatz, the details of which are embarrassing to all concerned. Which is how Otto got the fellow to drop charges. But, as I say, the police want you to vouch for Lister as his employer.'

'Right-oh. But vouching for Lister is a fool's errand.'

'You brought him to Berlin, Archie. I can't guarantee that I'll get him out next time.'

There was a hint of impatience in the younger man's tone. Understandable.

'Absolutely,' said Archie. 'Otto von Adlerstein is the chap who invited you to his castle over the weekend, isn't he? Where Harriet Dryden was shot?'

'Yes, poor blighter. Did Esme tell you about it?'

'She did. In fact, we visited Otto's mother and sister at Burg Adlerstein.'

'Why did you do that?'

'Esme wanted me to see it. You see, she thinks the girl the police have arrested couldn't possibly have shot Harriet.'

'Really?' Duncan raised his eyebrows. 'Why not?'

'Lots of reasons. Quite convincing reasons. Or she convinced me anyway. I think she wants me to help her find out who *did* kill Harriet.'

'That's best left to the police, in my opinion.'

'The police seem pretty set on blaming Ruth Jakubowski.'

'Because they think she did it, no doubt.'

'Or because they think she's a communist spy.'

'Maybe she is?'

The taxi approached Alexanderplatz and drew up outside a large, forbidding red-brick building that sprawled along one side of the square. Lights illuminated a domed tower at one corner and piles of earth and machinery all around it.

'This is it,' said Duncan, paying the taxi driver. 'They call it the Red Castle. You can see why.'

'Are they building a moat?'

'An underground line. Come on. Let's spring your crook.'

A constable at the front desk led Duncan and Archie through a warren of hallways and stairs until they arrived at a seating area behind a frosted glass door. It was past ten o'clock in the evening and the building was quiet. A uniformed constable appeared and asked them to wait.

'So you have no idea who may have killed Harriet Dryden?' Archie asked Duncan.

'No. Unless it's the Russian spy the police have arrested.'

'All right. But if it isn't her? Who else might it be? Which of the guests at the castle might have wanted her dead?'

Duncan held up his hands. 'I don't know.' He saw Archie wasn't going to let him get away that easily. He paused, considered and shook his head. 'There really is no one I can think of. Everyone liked her – you saw yourself how likeable she was.'

Archie nodded. 'She was likeable.'

Duncan blushed slightly. 'It's not just she was good-looking. She was a decent girl too. Damned decent.' He pursed his lips. 'She had no enemies.'

'What about the opposite? Lovers? You know she spent the night with Gray at the castle? Two nights, according to Esme.'

'That's what I heard. I was aware Gray was chasing her, but so were lots of men.' Duncan frowned.

'Including you?'

Duncan smiled. 'Not really. I never stood a chance. But she *was* jolly to talk to. It's an awful shame.'

'It is.'

'You know, my impression was that Erich was doing better with her than Gray. Oh. Did Esme tell you about Erich?'

'Yes, she did. That's Erich von Witzbach, Hindenburg's secretary, I believe?'

'That's him. Mind you, that night in the castle, I got up to go to the lavatory and on the landing I saw Joe Moretti leaving Erich's room.'

'The drunken American journalist? Good Lord! Your schloss had all the bed hopping of an English country house weekend!'

'It did, rather, didn't it?'

'Did Moretti know you had seen him?'

'He saw me. He grinned, put his finger to his lips and winked.'

'Have you told anyone? Did you tell the police?'

'No. I didn't think it was relevant, or any of their business.'

'I suppose it wasn't,' said Archie. 'I can't see why that would have anything to do with Harriet's death.'

'Neither can I,' said Duncan. 'Dashed confusing, I'd say. You thought it reminded you of an English country house weekend. Reminded me a little of school.'

'I see what you mean,' said Archie. 'You never can tell, can you?'

The door opened and a sergeant appeared with Lister, looking tired and bedraggled, his suit rumpled and torn, his red hair tousled, a bruise on his cheek and his bottom lip split. He avoided his boss's eye.

'Sir Archibald Laverick? Is this man in your employment?'

'He is,' said Archie.

'Fortunately for him, the gentleman he assaulted has decided not to press charges. I have been instructed to release him without charge today but only if you give me your word he will not break the peace again while you are in Berlin. Can you do that, sir?'

Archie turned to Lister and spoke to him in English. 'Will you give me your word you won't get yourself into any more fights? Or any other trouble?'

As he spoke the words, Archie realised how pointless what he was asking was.

Lister looked up at Archie. 'Yes, sir. Sorry sir.' But only the glass eye seemed suitably contrite, the other one twinkled. Lister had enjoyed his evening.

'Very well. Thank you, sergeant,' Archie said in German. 'I will vouch for Herr Lister.'

'Good. Don't let me see you again, Herr Lister,' the policeman said in slow German that Lister didn't understand. 'Because next time you will be going to jail.'

* * *

Half an hour later, they were in Archie's suite at the Adlon. Archie poured himself a brandy, hesitated, and then poured his manservant one too.

'What happened?'

'Well, I was in this club. I met this girl. She was a real looker and she spoke English.' Lister's Yorkshire accent had broadened with his fatigue and the late hour. 'So I bought her a drink, and then another drink and then we got friendly and...'

Lister winced.

'And?'

'Turned out he was a bloke.'

Archie couldn't help smiling. 'So, you hit him?'

'Actually no. I was a bit angry for a moment or two. But then I thought it was pretty funny. He was a good bloke. So I bought him another drink and we had a natter.'

Archie raised his eyebrows.

'It wasn't like that, sir. His name was Vicki. Or Gunther. You take your pick. He was telling me about the kind of men he picked up when one of them lurched over to the table.'

'Oh dear.'

'Yes. He and Gunther had a little chat. It looked like the man wanted Gunther to go off with him, but Gunther said no. The man glared at me and then started trying to pull Gunther away. Gunther said no again.

'Then the man put his face right in front of Gunther's and threatened him. I don't know what with, but Gunther looked scared and kind of brave at the same time.'

'So *then* you hit this man.'

'Aye. Then I hit him. And he hit me. And I knocked him to the ground. And then he reached out to hold on to a table with his arm outstretched and I realised if I hit down hard on his elbow I would hurt his arm pretty bad.'

'You broke it?'

'It did make a cracking sound. And the bloke yelped.'

'I bet he did.' Archie closed his eyes. He was tired. Then he opened them again. 'This has got to stop, Lister. Do you understand? Mr Mandeville had to pull strings to get you out tonight. That won't happen next time.'

'There won't be a next time, sir.'

'There had better not be. Right. Get yourself to bed.'

'Yes, sir.' Lister knocked back the rest of the brandy. 'Usual time in the morning, sir?'

'Yes, Lister.'

Lister turned. 'Oh. Were you all right on your trip, sir? It's just you were stammering before you went. Did anything happen?'

'Yes. Something did happen.'

'Oh. Was it bad?'

Archie nodded. 'It was bad, Lister. Very bad.'

'As bad as that time when you ran into the churchyard at Yarmer? After you had that tiff with Lord Scotton about whether conchies should be shot. And you swore at him?'

'That bad.'

'You didn't...'

Archie took a deep breath. 'I did. Fortunately, Miss Carmichael dealt with it... well.'

'Ah, I see. Happen we'll not be seeing Miss Carmichael again then, sir?'

'You mean have I scared her off?'

Lister winced. 'It is a frightening sight, sir.'

'No, I haven't scared her off, I'm glad to say.'

'She's a brave lass, then, sir,' Lister said as he retired to his own room under the eaves at the top of the hotel.

20

Esme made sure she was up in time to join Mr Dryden for breakfast. Not that he said much: he ate his toast, drank his coffee and scanned the *Berliner Tageblatt* and the *Vossische Zeitung*. But something about the sad smile and the, 'Good morning, my dear,' with which he greeted her told her that he appreciated her company.

She recalled Harriet's comment about her father while they were out riding, just before she was shot. Something about how he was not the man she thought he was. Esme wondered what Harriet had meant. She hoped they hadn't argued right before her death – that would have made things even harder for poor Mr Dryden.

After he had left the house for the embassy in his morning coat and top hat, Esme drifted upstairs and lingered outside Harriet's bedroom. As far as she knew, no one had been in there since Harriet's death. Mr Dryden had given instructions that the room should be dusted, but otherwise left as it was, and he had forbidden the Berlin police from entering.

Esme knew that the English butler and the maid, Ida, were downstairs. She slowly turned the doorhandle and entered.

The room was instantly familiar: she had spent plenty of time in there with Harriet since her arrival in Berlin. The German furniture had come with the house, apart from an old Dryden family rocking chair that Harriet had said belonged to her grandmother. Shaker, it was, from Ohio.

Esme sniffed the air. Could she smell just a hint of the *Shalimar* that Harriet wore, or was she just imagining it? Had Harriet's smell dissipated along with the rest of her?

On Harriet's bedside table stood a photograph of her mother, looking an awful lot like Harriet, smiling happily. It was a portrait photograph, but the smile was spontaneous and warm. A good picture to wake up to.

There were several shelves of books. Esme recognised most of them – she had looked over those spines many times over the years. There was a battered copy of *Madame Bovary* in French – Harriet's favourite novel – and three Agatha Christies, two of which had originally belonged to Esme. A new novel by Dashiell Hammett: *The Maltese Falcon*. Esme picked that one out to read.

There was also the copy of *The Communist Manifesto* that Esme had bought Harriet as a joke at a bookshop in Chicago. She opened the flyleaf: *To Comrade Harriet from Esme*. She wasn't sure that Harriet had even read it, but she did know that it would ignite excessive excitement in the Berlin police if Mr Dryden ever did give them access to Harriet's bedroom.

She slipped that volume out of the bookshelf too.

Esme scanned the room. A writing desk fit snugly under the window, which overlooked the back garden. The time had come for Esme to rummage through her friend's things, through her secrets.

Esme had been hoping for a journal or a diary of some kind

containing Harriet's innermost thoughts. There was nothing like that, but she did find a small photograph album with pictures from their time together at the University of Chicago. They had been taken with Harriet's camera, so Esme featured prominently: carefree, innocent, happy, a little insecure. There were quite a few, more than Esme would have expected, of a senior called Chet – Harriet must have had a crush on him that she had not disclosed to Esme. There were also family photos and pictures of Rome, where Harriet had lived with her parents at the time.

She found an old copy of the *Maroon*, the University of Chicago's student paper, which contained Esme's first article, an account of a lecture given by a visiting poet from New York. It was sweet of Harriet to keep that.

Two drawers contained bundles of letters, tied up neatly in green ribbon.

Esme hesitated a moment – reading her friend's letters seemed wrong – but she overcame her scruples and pulled them out.

The first bundle was from her. She opened a couple and smiled at the reminders of their simple friendship, the way Esme was happy to share her triumphs and disasters with Harriet, and the little things in everyday life that tickled her.

The next bundle was from Harriet's mother. Esme read a couple of these too. At first glance they seemed stiff and formal, but affection glimmered between the lines. Then Esme opened a letter which must have been sent a few weeks before Mrs Dryden's death. The poor woman was trying to be brave in her letters to her daughter, but not really succeeding. Esme's eyes stung.

Terribly, terribly sad.

She opened another drawer. This one was a mess of papers

and pencils. Two envelopes were addressed to Harriet in an unfamiliar hand; they had clearly been opened several times.

They were from Gray Trexler. His tone was friendly, charming, light, affectionate. But there were a couple of paragraphs in each that made Esme blush.

She nabbed those two letters. It would not be a good idea for Mr Dryden to see those!

There were a couple of other loose letters floating around. One from Harriet's stockbroker brother addressed to their father. This piqued Esme's interest: why would Harriet possess her father's correspondence? But it was boring stuff about the stock market and how it was a bad time to sell.

Then there was a note from Duncan asking Harriet to join him at a diplomatic event at the Polish embassy. Harriet had scribbled a 'No' on it. Esme smiled wryly. Nice try, Duncan, but no cigar. Another from Gisela saying it was nice to bump into Harriet and her father that afternoon, and yes, she would meet her for coffee at Kranzler's the next day.

And there was one more that was unsigned, or signed only with an initial.

L'amor che muove il sole e l'altre stelle. A.

Esme didn't understand Italian, but she knew Harriet did, having lived in Rome. 'A' must be Annachiara. Unless it was some Italian diplomat unknown to Esme. She couldn't discount the possibility.

She heard movement in the corridor outside. She waited a few seconds, shut the drawers, shoved Gray's letters in *The Communist Manifesto*, and left Harriet's room.

'Good morning, Fräulein,' said the maid as she walked past, carrying an armful of linens.

21

Luncheon was just finishing as Esme made her way through the lobby of the Adlon out onto the terrace. She ordered a cup of coffee and waited for Archie.

She placed a folder on the table beside her: a sheaf of notes she had typed up for him from their trip to Silesia. He had left a message for her at the front desk that he would be a quarter of an hour late and she should wait for him.

It was the first day of September, but the afternoon was still hot and the elephant fountain tinkled away merrily. She had worked furiously hard all morning and through lunch to get the notes typed up on time and she felt pleased with what she had done. Not just that, but the distraction was welcome.

She was glad she had decided to work for Archie. She had no interest in military history, and she wasn't sure that she even liked him, but it made her feel useful – after what had happened in the cow field, more than useful.

She felt that in some way he needed her, and it was good to be needed. But also, she needed him. Despite his coldness and his grumpiness and despite even his tendency to lecture cows without any clothes on, there was something steady about him. Something safe.

It wasn't that she found him attractive – it was true he was good-looking from one angle but definitely not from the other. Despite Harriet's fears, she was pretty certain he wasn't about to jump on her. Nor was he some kind of father figure. He certainly wasn't a friend. He was her employer, he was older than her and he was from a snootier background than she, but he treated her almost like an equal. She rather liked that.

She hoped he would help her figure out who on earth had shot Harriet. And she hoped she might help him write his book.

Maybe that was wishful thinking. But she would give it a shot and see what happened.

Besides, the money would come in useful. Mr Dryden had shown no sign of turfing her out, and she was sure she could stay with him for a while, but she had no idea whether that would be a short while or a long while. It would be smart to build up a cushion until she got her first article published.

Who knew how long *that* would be. If ever.

Chin up. Esme recalled Susan Abchurch saying how important determination was in a journalist, not just to chase a story but also to get a job. Esme wasn't about to give up. Who knew, perhaps one of those articles she had sent to her editor had been printed in the *Mercury* that very day? If she let herself assume the worst she would get nowhere, that was for sure.

A striking couple emerged from the hotel out on to the terrace. The woman led the way. She was slim with short dark hair and was wearing a beautifully cut, deceptively simple blue dress, above which nestled a string of pearls. Esme coveted her elegant white hat which dipped down over her right ear. At first Esme thought the woman was in her thirties, but as she came closer, she realised she must be closer to fifty.

An older man with a small pointed grey beard followed her, just as well dressed, carrying a black cane and sporting white spats.

Esme realised she was staring, but before she could avert her gaze, the woman spotted her and headed her way, leaving her consort behind.

'Miss Carmichael?'

'Yes?'

'Oh, hello. I'm Zena de Mancoux. I was looking for Archie. The front desk said that you were waiting for him out here.' The woman spoke with an American accent.

'Yes, that's right. I'm his secretary, Esme Carmichael.' The moment she had said that, Esme kicked herself. How could she expect Archie not to call her 'his secretary', when that was how she referred to herself? 'Would you like to join me?' Esme gestured to the empty chairs around her table.

'Oh, no, we just stopped in on our way to a gallery on the off-chance he might be here. We're staying at the Bristol, just down the street. How long have you worked for him?'

'Less than a week.'

'Grumpy bugger, isn't he?'

Esme was shocked. She knew what the English word 'bugger' meant and she was a taken aback that one American lady should use it when speaking to another.

The woman was grinning, clearly happy to shock.

'Yes, he is,' said Esme. 'But I rather like him.'

'Even with that mangled face?'

'Even with that mangled face.'

'Good for you,' said the woman. 'He can be exasperating, but he's a good man really. I should know. I used to be Lady Laverick.'

'Oh,' said Esme. 'Was that before you met Monsieur Mancoux?'

Zena laughed. 'Oh, a long time before. And he is a *comte*.' Zena looked back towards the gentleman puffing away at a large cigar. He had a pleasant, if self-satisfied expression on his face. He smiled at Esme and raised his hat. 'Husbands come and husbands go, but I rather like this one.'

'That must be nice for you,' said Esme more archly than she intended. 'That is a very large cigar.'

'Oh, it's *very* large,' said Zena with a wicked grin.

Esme felt her cheeks go hot.

'You're blushing, dear,' said Zena. 'It is warm out here.'

This woman couldn't possibly mean what Esme thought she meant, could she? If it was Harriet who had said that... But it wasn't Harriet. Of course she hadn't meant it! Esme was now embarrassed that she had got the wrong end of that particular stick.

'No, what I intended to say was...'

'Was what, dear?'

'...was that your latest husband must be very rich to smoke such large cigars,' was what Esme had started to say, but that sounded ridiculous.

She opened her mouth. Closed it. 'I'm glad he makes you happy,' she settled on.

Zena de Mancoux laughed. 'He certainly does make me happy! Never had a French husband before; I'd recommend it.' She touched Esme's sleeve. 'You'll be very good for Archie! Tell him I said hello. And do look after him. I am very fond of him despite everything.'

'I'll tell him,' said Esme.

'Tell him about the hello. Not about the being fond of him. That will just distress the poor lamb.'

With that, she was gone.

So that was Archie's wife? Esme recalled that he had said that he was divorced, although he had never mentioned that his wife was American. Esme wasn't certain of Archie's age – she would put him at about forty. This woman was definitely older. She couldn't imagine Archie married to her at all. No wonder they had divorced. And although Archie had implied that he had been the cause of the split, Esme didn't believe that for one moment. She hoped the Zena woman hadn't mistreated Archie too much in the process.

Archie appeared, limping, his walking stick in one hand and a battered briefcase in the other. He nodded to her curtly as he sat down. He noticed the thick sheaf of paper.

'Sorry you had to wait. I had an appointment with the librarian at the Stabi.'

'The Stabi?'

'The Staatsbibliothek. It's the Prussian state library on Unter den Linden. They've got masses of useful stuff on Blücher – letters, memoirs, articles in military journals, campaign histories written by generals, even some doctoral dissertations that might be useful. I'll need your help sifting through it all.'

'Sure.'

'You've been working hard,' he said, picking up Esme's sheaf of papers and leafing through them.

'I have.'

He grunted. 'This looks very good.'

He almost smiled, Esme thought. But he didn't.

'I just saw your ex-wife.'

That caught his attention. He scanned the half-empty terrace. 'Really? Where?'

'Right here. She left five minutes ago. She asked me to say

hello to you.' Esme decided not to mention the husband with the big cigar.

'Oh, Christ, she's not staying at the Adlon, is she?'

'No. The Bristol.'

'That's close enough! Well, if you see her again, tell her I'm in the Stabi and I won't be out until midnight.'

'Right you are.'

'How's Dryden?'

'He put on a brave face this morning at breakfast. But you saw what he was like last night. He's in a bad way. He can't wait for Wally to get here – that's Walter Dryden the third, his son – but the sap is only sailing from New York at the weekend, so he won't arrive until the end of next week.'

Esme turned up her small nose in disgust. 'Wally said he couldn't leave his important stockbroking firm right away. Of course he could! Harriet thought the world of her little brother, but I always knew he was a phoney.'

'Dryden is clearly comforted by you staying with him.'

'I hope so. But Harriet's death has hit him hard. Real hard. You saw it.' She finished her coffee. 'I must be going. Say, would you like to meet the people who were at the castle last weekend? They'll be at the bar here later on this evening: Joe, Gray, Erich, Otto, Gisela. Maybe Annachiara. I think the plan is to meet here and go on to a nightclub later.'

'Oh, I don't know,' said Archie.

'Aren't you curious? I might ask them what they know about who shot Harriet.'

Esme's teasing half smile was becoming familiar to Archie. Yes, he *was* curious.

'All right,' he said. 'I'll see you in the bar later.'

22

The Adlon bar was discreetly situated off the lobby, up some stairs and through a pair of leather-clad doors. Inside, it was buzzing, but the loudest buzz came from the far corner where a group of men and women were sitting around a couple of small tables.

Archie recognised Duncan and Esme, who smiled and waved and extricated herself to greet him. Everyone else looked up in curiosity.

'Archie! I knew you'd come. Everyone, this is my new boss, Sir Archie Laverick. You know Duncan and Gisela, Archie, but let me introduce you to the others.'

Archie nodded to his cousin and Esme ran through the crowd as Archie was able to put faces to the names Esme had mentioned. Joe Moretti was small with unruly dark hair and a friendly smile. Erich von Witzbach was tall, blond and aloof, although there was definitely something about him: even on first introduction his cool reserve seemed to attract rather than repel. His friend Otto was blander, thinner and friendlier. And

Annachiara was dressed as Esme had promised, in a dark man's suit with a black tie, wielding a fearsomely long cigarette holder.

There were two people present whom Esme had not mentioned as guests at the castle. A tall woman with short silver-blonde hair and ridiculously high cheekbones sat next to Annachiara, and acknowledged Archie with scarcely a nod; her name was Ute Starr and she was a film actress. A small, rumpled Englishman with a greying moustache and thinning hair brushed back over his scalp stood up and shook Archie's hand – Claude Tazewell of *The Times*. He was the only one of the group not dressed in evening clothes.

Archie took the only vacant chair between Esme and Claude Tazewell and ordered a Scotch and soda.

'Everyone is here but Gray?' Archie asked Esme.

'That's right. I guess he didn't have the guts to show his face, although Joe says he will meet us later at the nightclub.'

Erich cleared his throat and stood up. The conversation died as everyone looked up to him. 'This is the first time we have all been together since the tragedy,' he said in good clear English. 'I didn't know Harriet long, but she made a great impression on me.' He smiled at Esme. 'She made a great impression on all of us. Here's to Harriet!'

Everyone around the table rose and raised their glasses, as did Archie. Everyone that is, he noticed, apart from Ute, who, although standing, stared impassively ahead, her glass at her side.

'Do the police still believe that Ruth Jakubowski shot her?' Claude Tazewell, the English journalist, asked, when they had all sat down again.

'Yes,' said Gisela. 'I came back to Berlin from Adlerstein this afternoon. I know the local policeman well, and he tells me they haven't changed their minds. They are looking for evidence of spying.'

'I can't believe it's her,' said Esme.

'Why not?' said Erich. 'She used to be Gray's girl; she was jealous of Harriet. And the police say she's a communist.'

'Apparently they have been following her,' said Gisela. 'She met Yevgeny at the embassy when she was in Berlin.'

'I know he's a Russian diplomat, but I find it difficult to take Yevgeny seriously as a spy,' said Joe.

'He probably is,' said Annachiara, her dark eyes flashing wickedly. 'All diplomats are spies, is that not true, Duncan?'

'That is certainly not true!' Duncan protested.

'No? And I was sure you were the master spy of the famed British secret service. I have always found that desperately intriguing about you.' Annachiara's voice was low and husky and her full sensual lips parted seductively. Archie was surprised by how sexy a woman wearing man's clothes could be.

But Duncan was made of stern stuff. 'Only on Tuesday and Wednesday afternoons,' he said primly.

Annachiara laughed, a raucous cackle.

Archie knew Duncan was joking. It had never occurred to him that his cousin could be a spy, but now he did consider it, he thought it highly unlikely. From what he knew of the British Diplomatic Service they tried to distance themselves from that sort of thing. Probably not so true of the Soviets' equivalent.

'Does anyone know Ruth?' Esme asked. 'Apart from Yevgeny?'

A clever question, Archie thought, remembering what Ruth had told them about her trip to Berlin.

'I met her once or twice when I was in Vienna covering for our man there,' said Claude. 'And she telephoned me the other day, asking where Gray was. Yevgeny had sent her my way. I told her you were all at Adlerstein.'

'Do *you* think she's a murderer, Claude?' Esme asked.

Claude puffed at his pipe thoughtfully. In his rumpled tweed suit he looked so dreadfully English, Archie thought. The younger men and women around the table waited patiently for what he had to say. 'She didn't strike me as one, although she was certainly upset about something – I didn't know what. Afterwards, the police told me about her pregnancy as I'm sure they told you. I can't be certain whether she is a murderer or not, but I very much doubt that she is a spy.'

'Why?'

'The police told me she met Yevgeny in the Soviet embassy. Or rather they said they saw her go into the Soviet embassy – I was the one who told them she said she had met Yevgeny. I've read my spy novels; I know that's not how spies meet their agents. It's far too blatant.'

'Well, if Ruth didn't shoot Harriet, then who did?' Esme asked.

It was a bold question.

'You know what you are implying, Esme?' asked Annachiara, her brow furrowed. 'That one of us shot her? Or at least that someone who was staying at the castle did.'

'Someone else could have snuck into that temple,' said Joe. 'It could have been anyone.'

'That someone would have to have known where the gun that shot Harriet was kept,' Archie said. 'They would have had to break into the castle to steal it. And they would have had to know that Harriet and Esme were planning to go for a ride that morning.'

There was an uncomfortable silence around the table.

'What has this got to do with you, Sir Archie?' Erich asked, bluntly.

'I've asked Archie help me figure out who did shoot Harriet,' Esme said.

'And how are you doing that?'

'Just asking questions,' Archie said. 'With Esme.'

'Look, we all liked Harriet,' Esme said. 'We should all want to know who shot her.'

'Even if it's one of us?' said Annachiara.

Another silence.

'It isn't one of us,' said Erich. 'It was the communist woman. Esme, I know how upsetting Harriet's death is to you, but just leave it to the police.'

'I think Erich's right,' said Duncan.

The group were all looking at Esme expectantly. She stared right back at them.

'Shall we head off?' said Otto in a more-or-less successful attempt to deflate the tension. 'The Blaue Fuchs awaits.'

'I'll leave you to it,' Claude said to Archie as they made their way out of the bar. 'I'm much too old for these places. I hope you enjoy yourself.'

'I'll do my best,' said Archie.

'Esme's quite right, you know,' Claude said, with a twinkle in his eye. 'I wasn't there, but it seems highly unlikely to me that Ruth Jakubowski did shoot poor Harriet. In which case...'

'I know.'

'Let me know if I can be of assistance,' Claude said, handing Archie his card. 'And if at any time you'd like to talk to someone about that other murder, I'd be happy to listen.'

Archie's blood ran cold. Of course the dratted man knew about 'that other murder'! He was a journalist, after all. A journalist with a good memory, evidently.

'I think that's very unlikely,' Archie replied coldly.

'Quite understand, old man,' said Claude with a friendly smile. 'I won't mention it to anyone here. But I am a reporter, you know, I have to ask. If you ever change your mind, you've got my card. Good night.'

23

The Blaue Fuchs was situated on a small street just off the Kurfürstendamm. They spilled out of their taxis and climbed some steps under the knowing glance of a blue neon fox wearing top hat and tails. The club was busy as they plunged in. Cigarette smoke fought with cigar smoke and lost. Excited conversation tried to drown out the jazz band and failed. Bodies lounged and milled about and danced, the skimpy dresses of the women fluttering around the dark evening suits of the men.

They spread out around a group of three tables and Erich ordered champagne. Archie looked around. The other patrons of the club were a mixed crowd: some tourists, some older men with younger women, some groups of young Berliners. Archie realised that not all those present were customers. Many of the more attractive young men were *Eintänzer* – professional dancers – and many of the more attractive young women were hostesses, both happy to talk or dance with people of the opposite sex for a drink and a tip.

Or people of the same sex.

Two men came over to join them. One, an American with a

pencil-thin moustache and gleaming white teeth, greeted the others, although ignoring Esme and Archie sitting next to her. Gray Trexler, presumably. The other was darker, smaller, with a rubbery, creased face and a ready smile showing chaotic teeth. There was something more genuine about the warmth of his greeting. He kissed Esme on the cheek three times and shook Archie's hand heartily.

'This is Yevgeny,' Esme said. 'Yevgeny Barsukov – Sir Archie Laverick, my new employer.'

'Esme, I am so sorry about Harriet!' said the Russian. 'I know you have been friends for so many years. My heart goes out to you. And her poor father!' The words came out in a jumble that was difficult to understand, given the Russian's strong accent.

Yevgeny held Esme's arms and looked at her with a sympathy that was so genuine and so profound that it seemed to knock Esme back. Archie felt it.

'Thank you, Yevgeny. It has been a horrible week.'

'Did you know her, Archie?'

'I just met her once,' said Archie, aware as usual how cold he sounded and how he could do nothing about it. He wanted to explain to this stranger that he too had been affected by Harriet's death, but that would just be ridiculous, so he didn't.

They drank. They danced – Esme with Erich and Joe and Otto and Duncan; Annachiara with Ute; Gisela with Yevgeny and Erich; Archie with no one. It was impossible to converse generally, but Archie spoke to Joe and Otto.

Joe was already drunk. He muttered some alarmingly persuasive observations about how in his mind the Weimar Republic's days were numbered, before lapsing into an incoherent moan about how difficult he was finding writing his follow-up book about fascism in Europe.

Otto was friendly and seemed to be genuinely interested in

Archie's field marshals. Ute Starr sat opposite him between dances and said nothing at all. Archie doubted her chances in the new world of the talkies and reflected that what was presumably her stage name was a touch optimistic.

They were all becoming more intoxicated. Joe was dancing with a thin-hipped *Eintänzer*. Esme and Yevgeny flopped down into chairs next to Archie.

'Do they dance the Black Bottom in Chicago?' Yevgeny asked her.

'You bet. Although I guess it's a little out of fashion now.'

'It's all the craze here. Not in Moscow, unfortunately.'

'I guess not,' said Esme. 'I assume you dance *Swan Lake* together?'

'Certainly!' Yevgeny giggled. 'You should see my pas de deux! You don't dance, Archie?'

'My leg,' said Archie.

'I understand,' said Yevgeny, his eyes hovering over Archie's torn face.

'Oh, come on, Archie!' said Annachiara. 'They've slowed the music down. You can shuffle. I can shuffle. We can shuffle together.'

It was true: the music had slowed with the customers' energy as the night wore on past midnight.

It was odd but strangely stimulating dancing with Annachiara. Her hair was cut short and brilliantined in the manner of a man, but Archie noticed her ears were pierced. She wasn't wearing any scent or perfume that Archie could smell. Her eyes watched Archie with amusement at the effect she could tell she was having on him.

Next to them, Erich was dancing with Gisela. Archie noticed Joe leaning back in his chair, a glass of whisky in his hand, staring at them – staring at Erich, that is – lips open. It was lust.

Drunken lust. At one point Archie caught Erich returning Joe's stare with a frown of disapproval.

Ute tapped Archie on the shoulder and he excused himself, leaving Annachiara with the tall actress. He took a seat next to Esme and Yevgeny.

Esme glanced at Archie to make sure he was listening and then turned to Yevgeny. 'You heard that they have arrested a woman called Ruth Jakubowski for Harriet's murder?'

Yevgeny nodded slightly.

'Do you know her?'

'Yes. Or rather I knew her in Vienna when she was Gray's girl. I hadn't seen her since she followed him to Paris.'

'Until she came to Berlin a couple of weeks ago?'

'That's right.'

'Do you think she could have killed Harriet?'

'I have absolutely no idea.'

'The police think she is a spy. For you. For the Russians.'

'I know they think that. She came to see me at the embassy and apparently they were following her. She was looking for Gray. I didn't know where he was, but I thought Joe or Claude might, so I gave her their numbers. And Esme?'

'Yes?'

'I know nothing about spying. I am a diplomat.'

'You have to say that, I understand. But the police think Ruth killed Harriet and I'm certain she didn't. So can you help me? *Was* she a spy?'

Yevgeny glanced at Archie and at Esme. 'No,' he said, firmly. 'Now, if you'll excuse me.' He wandered over to where Gray and Joe were sitting.

'Do you believe him?' Esme asked Archie.

'Maybe. Do you?'

'Maybe.'

'Gray seems to be ignoring you.'

'I know,' said Esme. 'And I'm ignoring him. But I'd like to talk to him about Ruth and Harriet.'

'I suspect now isn't the time.'

'No. What about tomorrow? We can ambush him in the *Globe*'s office. Do you want to come with me?'

'I've ordered some books from the stacks at the Stabi tomorrow morning.'

'Oh, Archie! You disappoint me. You know what Old Bluey would say, don't you?'

'What's that?'

'*Vorwärts*!'

Archie grinned. 'Yes, Old Bluey would say that. What time shall I meet you?'

24

Archie didn't meet Esme until eleven o'clock the following morning – she said journalists worked later hours than everyone else and she wanted to give Gray time to get into the office after his late night.

He bought a cigar from the street vendor who positioned himself outside the Adlon every morning. As he paused to light it, he glanced up at the columns of the Brandenburg Gate glowing yellow in the sunshine. Together, he and Esme walked around the corner and down Wilhelmstrasse, passing the British embassy and Hindenburg's elegant presidential palace right next to it, where presumably Erich von Witzbach was toiling away.

'Tell me some more about Gray,' Archie said.

'Have you heard of him in England?'

'I can't say I have.'

'You would have done if you were American. His columns are syndicated all over the States. He and Susan Abchurch are the two most famous foreign correspondents.'

'You say he writes for a Chicago paper?'

'Yes. The *Globe*. It's the biggest in the city. I guess he started writing for them about ten years ago in London and since then he's been everywhere: Rome, Jerusalem, Vienna, Paris, here in Berlin. He's based in Paris now, but he goes all over Europe wherever the news is. Right now it's Germany with the election. Next month he could be in Madrid or Moscow – who knows?'

'Is he good at his job?'

'I'll say. He has a network of contacts and he's good at making new ones. He's very competitive – he's always the first to get the big interview, if Susan doesn't get it, that is. He's a smart guy – he understands European politics as well as anyone. Oh, and he doesn't like the British much.'

'Had a bad time in London?'

'Palestine. He blames the British for the problems there and it gets him riled up.'

'I went to Jerusalem once. I never did understand what we are doing there,' said Archie. 'You said he's married?'

'Yes. His wife is slightly less famous. American too, but she writes for a British newspaper in Paris. I've never met her.'

They turned off Wilhelmstrasse and into Kochstrasse, where many of the German newspaper offices were located. They ducked down a small side street between an advertising column plastered with SPD posters and a gaily coloured barrow hung with rows of sausages.

'It's here, I think,' said Esme, opening a door right next to a barber's shop. They climbed some stairs to a frosted glass door bearing the name *Chicago Globe*. Inside, a young woman was sitting behind a desk, which was fortified with a typewriter, a speaker and an adding machine.

'Can I help you?' she asked in brusque German-accented English.

'Is Mr Trexler in? My name is Esme Carmichael and this is Sir Archibald Laverick.'

'Do you have an appointment?'

'No,' said Esme. 'But we would like to see him now.'

The woman's eyebrows skilfully flickered in a gesture that managed to convey extreme disapproval, and she pressed a switch on the console in front of her and announced them into the speaker.

'Jesus Christ!' the console replied. 'All right, send them in.'

They passed through a door into an office containing three large desks – only one of which was occupied – by a man Archie recognised from the night before as Grayson Trexler. He was reading the *Vossische Zeitung*, and a mess of other Berlin newspapers covered the desktop in front of him, a cigarette hanging from his lips. Archie surmised foreign correspondents had to read all the local stories before they started to write their own.

He did not look happy to see them, but roused himself to shake Archie's hand and indicated that Archie and Esme sit in two chairs in front of his desk.

'All right, Esme, what do you want?'

'To talk about Ruth,' Esme said.

'Well, I don't want to talk about Ruth. I'm done talking about Ruth.'

'She's still pregnant, you know. With your child. Don't you feel any responsibility for that?'

'No. I was careful. I did all a man can do, if you catch my meaning. She was unlucky.'

'You mean you both were unlucky.'

'No, I mean *she* was unlucky.' Gray looked steadily at Esme, his eyes twinkling provocatively. He shot her a sly grin. 'Maybe it isn't even mine?'

Esme fought visibly to control her anger. 'We think Ruth didn't shoot Harriet.'

'I know you do. Joe told me last night. But I don't really care what you think.' He turned to Archie. 'And I certainly don't care what *you* think. This has nothing to do with you.'

Archie watched him impassively. Archie could do impassive rather well.

Esme was less comfortable with Gray's attitude. 'Look, wise guy. You got Ruth pregnant. You refused to talk to her about it. As a result she is in jail for a murder she didn't commit. So you darn well should care about her!'

'What can I say? The police interviewed me. They asked me about Ruth and I told them all I knew.'

'You don't believe Ruth shot Harriet, do you?'

Gray shrugged. 'I don't know.'

'Do you believe she's a spy?'

Gray relented. 'No. I don't believe she's a spy. Sure, she is a communist, her whole damn family are communists, and she's all for the downfall of the bourgeoise and the triumph of the proletariat, but she isn't a spy.'

Gray pulled on his cigarette, as he contemplated Esme. 'Yevgeny and I became good friends in Vienna – I find diplomats make good contacts, even Russian ones. Also, I like the guy. But I doubt Ruth ever spoke to him outside my presence. He was my friend, not hers. I told the police that, but they were not really listening. The Prussian police are run by SPD men – they hate the commies and they are embarrassed by the murder of the daughter of an American diplomat, so they like the idea that the commies are responsible.'

'So you don't think Ruth shot Harriet?'

'I didn't say that,' said Gray. 'Ruth is a very passionate woman. I got to admit that's one of the things I liked about her.' He shook his head. 'I should've known that would lead to trouble eventually. That's also why I had to end it; she was taking everything much too seriously. Maybe she *was* jealous of Harriet.'

'How would she have found out about you and Harriet?' Archie asked. 'Did anyone know about your affair?'

Gray frowned, debating with himself whether to answer the question. 'What's it to you?'

'Esme is assisting me. I'm assisting her,' Archie said calmly.

Gray grudgingly decided to answer Archie's question. 'I don't know how she found out. That night was only the third time we had slept together – the first was in my apartment one afternoon the week before. The only person who might have known is you, Esme.'

'She never told me,' said Esme. 'And I never guessed.'

'There you are, then.'

'Aren't you curious how Ruth found out?' asked Esme. 'Don't you care whether it was she who shot Harriet?'

'Nope,' said Gray. 'It's not my problem.'

'But you're a reporter! You're paid to be curious about this kind of stuff.'

Gray smiled, flashing white teeth beneath his moustache. 'You have a point there, Esme. I am a reporter and you are not. I filed the story that Harriet had been murdered, I wrote a couple of paragraphs when they charged Ruth. If I'm still in Berlin for the trial, I'll cover that, although it will probably be Pete, our permanent man here.' Gray nodded towards one of the empty desks, Pete's presumably. 'I saw the *Mercury* ran a couple of paragraphs on the story last week. Did they get those from you?'

'No,' said Esme.

'Thought not. They probably got them from a wire agency, perhaps Annachiara's. So, you see, it really has nothing to do with you, little girl. Or you.' Gray glanced at Archie. 'What are you even doing here?'

Esme was about to speak, but Archie raised his hand to halt her.

He held Gray's eyes with his, waiting. Gray stared back.

'Mr Trexler. I am concerned that a woman who I am certain is innocent is about to be convicted for a crime she did not commit. She may hang. This is a woman whom you have wronged. You know she is innocent as well as we do. It is your duty to do everything in your power to persuade the police of that fact.'

Gray held Archie's stare. Then he leaned forward to tap ash from his cigarette into his ashtray. 'The thing is, I'm not convinced she is innocent. Ruth could get mad and she could get jealous. Look, I don't know how she could have found out about me and Harriet. I'll leave that to the cops.'

He shook his head. For the first time, his mask of glib indifference slipped an inch. 'I am sorry about what happened to Harriet. She was a swell girl. And if Ruth did murder her, she deserves what's coming to her.'

'And if she didn't?' Archie asked.

Gray didn't respond.

'If she didn't,' Archie repeated, 'who else might have shot Harriet?'

'I don't know.'

'Think.'

Gray blinked. 'I truly don't know.'

'Did she have any other relationships that you are aware of?'

'Plenty of men were chasing her.'

'Did any of them catch her? Apart from you?'

'How should I know?'

'She might have told you.'

'Well, she didn't.' An unpleasant grin spread across Gray's face. 'It wasn't just men who chased her. And it wasn't just men who caught her.'

Archie was taken aback by this comment. As was Esme. They

were both silent for a moment. 'What do you mean by that?' Esme said, anger rising in her voice.

Gray shrugged.

Esme frowned. 'Are you suggesting that she and I…?'

Gray held up his hands. 'Hey. I don't know. You asked me to speculate. I'm speculating.'

Esme pursed her lips. 'Let's go, Archie.'

'What *do* you mean by that, Mr Trexler?' Archie asked.

Before Gray had a chance to respond, if indeed he was going to respond, Esme had grabbed Archie's arm. 'I said, let's go.'

25

Esme fumed as she walked back towards the Drydens' house from Kochstrasse. Boy, she hated Gray! The man was a louse of the highest order.

His smooth charm, his unpleasant grin. His condescension. And the suggestion that she and Harriet were lovers! When Harriet was dead barely a week! And in front of Archie.

Archie and she had parted outside the *Globe*'s office after barely a couple of words discussion of what Gray had said. To be fair to Archie, she didn't think he believed Gray; she guessed he was merely trying to spare her embarrassment. He was going to the Stabi to look through the books he had ordered up from the stacks; he had asked her to meet him in the afternoon back at the Adlon to discuss their research plans.

She knew Gray was just trying to provoke her. Well, he had succeeded! Could he really have the gall to insinuate that she and Harriet were having an affair?

No. That's not what he was insinuating. He was insinuating something else that Esme didn't want to contemplate.

She came to the Potsdamer Platz, and gingerly made her

way through the honking, clanking, roaring traffic, only just evading a Framo three-wheeler motorcycle whose driver saw her but didn't care. There were traffic lights in Chicago, of course, but the first traffic lights on the continent of Europe had been placed on a spindly tower in the centre of the Potsdamer Platz in an attempt to tame Berlin's car-crazy citizens at the point where five busy streets collided. Improbably, the manic drivers managed to avoid the tower and each other.

Who was it who had called Berlin Chicago on the Spree? Henry James? No. Mark Twain? Must have been Mark Twain. And Esme could see what he meant. Despite its lack of skyscrapers and the stolid imperial buildings along Unter den Linden, here in the West End, Berlin was a modern, bustling, hustling city whose inhabitants could crack as wise as any wise guy on the South Side.

She decided to stop at the Café Josty on the Platz and get herself a coffee. She lit a cigarette and tried to forget Gray and lose herself in the hurly-burly of late morning in Berlin. The Potsdamer Platz was surrounded by the modern buildings of a great city – Wertheim's palatial sandstone department store, the domed and colonnaded Haus Vaterland with its warren of themed restaurants from all parts of Europe, and a massive, half-built, steel-framed office building – what was to become the new Europahaus.

But she couldn't forget Gray. It wasn't just his dig at her and Harriet. It was his dig about her not being a proper reporter.

She reached into her bag for the airmail letter she had received postmarked Chicago that morning. It was very short.

Dear Miss Carmichael,

Thank you for the articles you sent me from Berlin. They

are not of sufficient interest to our readership for publication in the paper.

Yours sincerely
Donald A. Finnegan
Editor

Well, that had all the hallmarks of well-written journalism: clear, concise and packing an emotional punch. Boy, did it pack an emotional punch!

Of course, Gray was right: Esme was not a foreign correspondent. She knew that. What worried her was that she was not sure she would ever become one.

She was about twelve when the idea had first lodged in her head. She liked to read – books, newspapers, magazines, anything – but especially the supposedly weekly copy of the *Saturday Evening Post* that arrived at the ranch in Montana with erratic frequency, rarely on Saturdays. She read it cover to cover and then reread it, especially those articles written by Americans in far-flung places. It suddenly occurred to her: could *she* be one of those Americans writing from London or Paris or even Peking or Tokyo?

Why not?

Although her mother had been relieved to return to the relative civilisation of Kalamazoo when compared to the ranch, Esme had found it stultifying. She needed to go further than Michigan. She needed to go to Europe.

So at university in Chicago, she had studied French and German and a bit of Spanish, and she had devoured Zola and Balzac, Goethe and Schiller, as well as Tolstoy and Dostoyevsky translated into English. She had written as many articles as they would let her for the college paper, the *Daily Maroon*. But it was only when, in her senior year, she had gone to that lecture where

Susan Abchurch described how she had interviewed a leading Irish Republican in 1922, days before he was murdered, that Esme knew with absolute certainty she was going to become a foreign correspondent.

Somehow.

Her job in the advertising department of the *Mercury* hadn't given her the opening she had hoped for and the string of letters she had written to British publications had mostly been unanswered, although occasionally they had garnered terse rejections. Which was why she had made her way to Europe on a one-way ticket.

That was one reason. There was also what had happened to poor Henry. Goddamned Henry!

She didn't want to think about Henry. She had sailed across a whole ocean not to think about Henry.

So now what?

Frankly, Esme wasn't really surprised the two articles she had sent to Don Finnegan hadn't made the grade. What she needed now was a big interview, like Susan Abchurch's with the Irishman.

But how could she get it?

Harriet had tried to help. She had introduced Esme to some useful contacts in Berlin over the three weeks Esme had been staying with her. Esme should make more of those. She should be more pushy. Susan Abchurch wouldn't let shyness or a fear of rejection stop her, and neither would Gray Trexler.

Who should she approach?

Erich von Witzbach was the obvious contact. He wasn't exactly a friend, but he knew who she was. Although he was much less interested in her than he had been in Harriet, he was always polite to her.

She could ask him for an interview with the President. That

would make Don Finnegan sit up – an interview with President Hindenburg! She should just go right ahead and do it.

He'd say no. Of course he'd say no. If President Hindenburg wanted to give an interview to a foreign journalist, he would pick one of the dozens of more experienced reporters in the city.

But she absolutely couldn't go back to Chicago – or even worse Kalamazoo – with her tail between her legs. She had to do *something*.

Maybe she should write up the story of Harriet's murder, after all? She was sure Harriet would be happy with that, indeed she could imagine her friend encouraging her. But Mr Dryden? And Otto, whose hospitality she was abusing? And the others, her 'suspects'? How would they feel about the implication that one of them had killed a woman, a friend?

She made a decision. She would draft the article. Then, when she had finished it, she would decide whether to send it off to Finnegan.

It would be a different article to the ones Gray had described that he had written for the *Globe*. More newsworthy. More of a puzzle. More interesting to readers.

The image of his sly grin came back to her. And his accusation.

She knew why Gray's accusation was bothering her. It wasn't really implying there had been anything improper between Harriet and her. He was implying something between Harriet and someone else.

And Esme knew who.

She recalled the note she had found in Esme's desk. The one that was written in Italian and signed 'A'.

Esme didn't know Italian and couldn't remember what the note said. Except for one word. *Amor*. She knew what that meant.

And she knew who 'A' was.

Annachiara.

26

Esme went up to Archie's suite at the Adlon to discuss research plans. The sitting room was large and furnished with a round table covered with notes and books. But as they sat down to work, Archie wasn't sure how to deal with Gray Trexler's insinuation that there had been something between Harriet and another woman.

Was that other woman Esme? Gray hadn't said that explicitly, but Esme's reaction suggested it might be.

Archie's instinct was to steer well clear of the subject, unless Esme brought it up. It had nothing to do with him, after all.

But if it had anything at all to do with Harriet's murder then he couldn't ignore it, for Ruth's sake. He'd play it by ear.

'Would you like some tea?' Archie asked her.

'I take it that's part of the job description, working for an English biographer?'

'Absolutely. It's Assam – I brought it from England. Most refreshing. The only question is whether you would like one lump or two. And don't even think of drinking it without milk.'

'Well, in that case, one lump, please.'

Lister poured them both a cup from a teapot.

Esme sipped hers. 'It's actually not bad.'

Archie had thought through carefully how Esme could help him in the library. He wanted to read through the most relevant documents himself, but he gave Esme a list of papers, books and journals held by the Staatsbibliothek which were only tangentially related to Blücher. Esme's job was to scour them for references to the general and make a note of any that might be of interest to Archie.

Archie planned to see a couple of history professors at the Friedrich Wilhelm University in Berlin and at the University of Jena in Thuringia, and he wanted Esme to accompany him to those meetings. There were also battlefields to visit: Leipzig, Auerstedt which was near Jena, Waterloo and Ligny in Belgium and Lübeck in the north. But first, Archie wanted to visit the town of Rostock, on the Baltic near Lübeck, where Blücher was born in 1742.

Oddly, the young Blücher had started his military career at the age of sixteen as a hussar in the Swedish army and fought for Sweden against the Prussians in the Seven Years' War. He had been captured and persuaded to switch sides to fight for a Prussian regiment of hussars. He had been a loyal Prussian soldier ever since.

Esme was bemused by the plethora of mini-states that made up much of Germany in the eighteenth century. Tiny principalities, duchies, grand duchies and electorates.

'Have you got a map?' she said, eventually. 'An old one. Because I'm confused.'

Archie got out his grandfather's old *Times Atlas*, which he had brought with him from Yarmer Hall, and opened it on a multi-coloured page for Germany.

Esme bent over it. 'So Rostock is in the Duchy of Mecklenburg-Schwerin? And it's right next to Swedish Pomerania. What are the Swedes doing in Germany? Where or what is Thuringia? Does anyone really care about…' she squinted at a yellow blob on the atlas, '…Schwarzburg-Sondershausen? And why did so many European monarchs seem to come from Saxe-Coburg Gotha when it's so tiny?'

Archie tried to explain.

They were poring over the atlas when a bellboy knocked on their door with a calling card. Gisela von Adlerstein was in the lobby. Archie asked the boy to send her up.

She was dressed in a sober grey suit. Archie was struck again by how tall she was, almost as tall as him.

'I am sorry to interrupt you both,' she said, in English. 'I see you are doing serious work.'

'I bet you can't point out Schwarzburg-Rudolstadt on a map,' Esme asked. 'It's supposed to be some kind of country.'

'Of course I can,' said Gisela, looking at Esme as if she were a fool. Unhesitatingly she stabbed the *Times Atlas* with her finger on a tiny patch of orange. 'And it's a principality, not a country. Friedrich is the current prince after old Sizzo died. He's a bit of a bore, but Otto likes him.'

Esme looked slightly stunned. 'Sizzo?'

'Prince Sizzo of Schwarzburg-Rudolstadt.'

'Don't worry, Esme,' Archie said. 'I have no idea where Kalamazoo is. In fact, I'm not entirely convinced it's a real place.'

Esme shuffled the pages and found a map of the Great Lakes. 'There!' she said in triumph, pointing to a spot just to the right of Lake Michigan. 'See?'

Gisela craned her neck. 'Looks real to me.'

'I apologise, Esme,' said Archie. 'Would you like a cup of tea, Fräulein Adlerstein?'

'Yes, please.'

Lister appeared with another cup and Archie poured her one from the teapot.

'So. Are you still interested in proving poor Ruth Jakubowski's innocence?' Gisela stared directly at Archie and Esme in turn.

Archie glanced at Esme. 'Yes,' he said. 'We are. Nothing we have heard so far suggests she is guilty. Quite the opposite, in fact.'

'I'm still convinced Ruth is innocent and I'm determined to prove it,' Esme said. 'We visited her in the Dresden police station – she was persuasive.'

'Good,' said Gisela. 'I have been thinking about what we learned in Adlerstein and I agree with you. At the very least, there must be some doubt as to her guilt. And the poor girl is pregnant too! I can't help feeling sorry for her.'

She leaned forward, her expression earnest. 'I work as a secretary for a judge at the Moabit Criminal Court. I wanted to be a lawyer myself, but my father wouldn't let me go to university, so that was the next best thing. I was lucky he let me work at all. The law is important to me and I respect it, but that respect makes me all the more angry when it's unjust. So, if you need any assistance, I am happy to offer it.'

'Thank you,' said Archie. He appreciated someone taking their doubts seriously. And Gisela seemed serious.

'I telephoned old Dümmi this morning. They are still holding Ruth, although they have had no luck pinning any espionage charges on her. But they are not considering anyone else for the murder.'

'She's not a spy,' said Esme. 'No one thinks so. Not Yevgeny, not Gray.'

'And not Claude Tazewell,' said Archie. 'He was quite adamant on the subject. And he seems to know what he's talking about. I suppose they could all be wrong, but I rather doubt it.'

'They are not wrong,' said Esme. 'Ruth is no spy.'

'And you don't think it's possible she killed Harriet out of jealousy?' Gisela asked.

'We spoke to Gray this morning,' said Esme. 'He seems to think she could be jealous enough to murder a rival. She is quite a passionate woman, apparently. But we still don't see how she could have done it.'

'I see,' said Gisela. 'In which case who did kill her?'

Archie and Esme exchanged glances.

'We don't know,' Esme admitted. 'It was clearly a question the others didn't like last night. I probably shouldn't have raised it.'

'Probably not,' said Gisela. 'Once they realised the implication – that one of them – or one of us – had shot her – I'm not surprised they were offended. Especially Erich. He is a bit of a Prussian about that kind of thing.'

Archie had to remind himself that while to him they were all just Germans, to Gisela there was a world of difference between a Saxon and a Prussian.

'Please don't tell any of them that we are still asking questions,' said Esme. 'It will only make them more upset. Even your brother.'

'All right, I won't.'

'Do you know what Otto thinks?' Archie asked.

'No. I did mention to him that you doubted Ruth was guilty, but he just dismissed the idea. He is a loyal government official; he has faith in the police.'

'Do *you* have any idea who may have killed her?'

Gisela shook her head.

'Did you see anything from the dining room? It does look down over the river.'

'But not over the spot where Harriet was killed. We heard the shot. Which was odd on a Sunday – there is no shooting on Sundays. I thought about poachers, although we don't have a problem with those at Adlerstein. So I got up to look out of the window. When I saw Esme running up the lawn towards the castle, I knew something was badly wrong.'

'Any idea why someone could have wanted to kill Harriet?'

'No,' said Gisela. 'As you have seen, everyone liked her.'

Archie glanced at Esme. He was about to tread on difficult ground. 'We know Harriet was having an affair with Gray. Could she also have been having an affair with someone else?'

'Like who?'

'Erich, perhaps?' Esme said.

Gisela seemed put out by the suggestion. 'Erich is an old friend of Otto's. I have known him for a long time. It's true that he is capable of having a fling with a woman, and I got the impression he found Harriet attractive, but I don't think there was anything between them.' Gisela shrugged. 'But the truth is, I just don't know.'

'Anyone else?' said Archie. 'Yevgeny perhaps? Or Duncan?'

'I haven't seen anything.'

'Any other male?' Archie asked. Then, with a quick glance at Esme. 'Or female?'

Archie noticed Esme flinch. Too bad.

'What do you mean?' Gisela was frowning.

'Did Harriet have any relationship with another woman?'

Gisela raised her eyebrows.

'We are in Berlin,' said Archie. 'These things happen, don't they?'

'Occasionally. Between people of that persuasion. But I think sometimes foreigners get the wrong idea about Berlin. The whole city isn't the cesspit of perversion that you sometimes think it is.' Gisela's blue eyes glittered with anger.

'No, of course,' said Archie, chastened. 'I didn't mean to offend you. I'm just trying to think of all the possibilities.'

'All right,' said Gisela, only partially mollified. 'What other possibilities are there? What else have you found out?'

Archie gave her a brief summary of their visit to Ruth in prison, of their meeting with Ruth's lawyer Schrör in Dresden, and of seeing Gray Trexler that morning.

'As you can see, it doesn't add up to much. Doubts, certainly, but proof? I'm afraid not.'

'I see that,' said Gisela.

'You said you were happy to help us?'

Gisela nodded. 'I am.'

'Perhaps Otto knows something?'

'I will never believe he shot Harriet!'

'No, no, I'm not suggesting that. In fact, that's why I think he might be useful. He knows everyone who was at the castle that weekend. And he seems like a decent sort of chap. He may have spotted something. I understand that he thinks it's the police's problem, but he may tell you, if you ask him in the right way.'

'As I said, my brother is a conscientious civil servant; he likes things to be done properly.' Gisela sipped her tea thoughtfully. 'But I'll have a go. And I'll let you know if he tells me anything useful.'

'Maybe find a subtle way of asking Erich too?' said Esme. 'More subtle than me. I blew it.'

'Erich will be harder,' said Gisela. 'But I can try.' She put down her cup. 'I'm sorry if I was a bit sensitive before. I do wish you luck.'

'Let's keep in touch,' said Archie. 'I'll be here at the Adlon for the next two months or so.'

* * *

'Sorry about that,' said Archie to Esme after Gisela had left. 'Asking her about Harriet.'

'No. You were right to do it. It did seem to offend her, didn't it?'

'You see, I don't think Gray was implying that there was anything untoward between you and Harriet.'

'No,' said Esme. She sighed. 'I don't think he was, either.'

'What do you mean?'

Esme stared at her empty teacup. Then she looked up at Archie. 'I took a quick look through Harriet's writing desk, to see if there was anything that might shed light on her death. I know it's dreadful, but...'

'I understand. Was there?'

'Not really. A couple of steamy notes from Gray that I nabbed so her father wouldn't find them. But there was also one line in Italian that was signed "A".'

'What did it say?'

'I don't know. I don't speak Italian. But I do remember one word. *Amor.*'

'You think it was a love note from Annachiara?'

'I didn't at the time. In fact, I wondered whether "A" was some unknown Italian diplomat. But now I think it was from Annachiara, yes.'

'Interesting.' Archie rubbed his chin. 'It's hardly conclusive proof.'

'No,' Esme admitted. 'But it raises suspicions, doesn't it?'

'So you think Annachiara might have shot Harriet because *she* was jealous? Of Harriet and Gray?'

'I don't know,' said Esme. 'But she doesn't look like much of a markswoman to me.'

'No, she doesn't. Perhaps Gray was jealous of Harriet and Annachiara?'

'You're clutching at straws, Archie.'

'I am,' Archie admitted. 'I just don't like that man.'

Esme sighed. 'I thought I knew Harriet so well. But it turns out I didn't. In some ways, there is an honesty about people's attitude to sex here. But I'm a well brought-up girl from Kalamazoo. It's been hard enough for me to accept Harriet's changed attitude to men – it's even harder to accept her attitude to women. Yet I refuse to feel ashamed of her. She was my friend. And now she's dead.'

'You shouldn't be ashamed of her,' Archie said.

He felt so sorry for Esme, even if he also felt unable to express that sentiment to her. It must have been difficult for her to tell him about Harriet, but she had been right to do it. In which case...

'What is it, Archie? Spit it out.'

Archie hesitated, and then answered her. 'Duncan told me something the night we got back to Berlin. About his stay in the castle.'

'Oh, yes?'

'He got up in the night to go to the lavatory, and saw someone leaving Erich's room.'

'Harriet?'

'No. Joe.'

'Joe!' Esme shook her head in wonder. 'Harriet and I had guessed about Joe but I never realised Erich was that way inclined. He always seems so interested in women.'

Archie shrugged. 'It looks like he is interested in both. It seems to me that despite Gisela's objections, this sort of thing does go on in Berlin. And the more open-minded we are about it, the better chance we will have of understanding why Harriet died.'

27

As Esme stepped out of the front door of the Adlon, she noticed a small crowd gathered on the corner of Wilhelmstrasse, held back by a couple of policemen.

She wandered over, curious, and saw a black Mercedes heading up the street towards her. The automobile was unmistakeable: it had been modified by raising its roof a foot or so to accommodate the tall frame and top hat of its occupant. It also bore the licence plate A1-1. It belonged to Field Marshal Paul von Hindenburg, President of the Weimar Republic.

Esme stayed to watch as the car passed slowly by, the great man himself sitting bolt upright in the back, eyes forward, neck enclosed by the stiffest of stiff collars, top hat on head, massive moustache with its waxed tips curled upwards unwavering in its duty.

And he *was* a great man. He had managed to emerge from defeat in the war as a hero, remembered for his whipping of the Russians at the Battle of Tannenberg and the successful German offensives on the Western Front in early 1918. He had retained the respect of many Germans, not just the veterans who yearned for the return of pre-war Kaiser's Germany, but also of the ordinary citizens who were concerned by the instability of Weimar politics and were comforted by someone they could trust being in charge, even if he was now eighty-three years old.

The President in the Weimar Republic took no part in the running of the government. In an ideal, stable world, he would be nothing more than a ceremonial figurehead. But the Weimar Republic was not stable.

In March 1930, as a way of breaking a political deadlock, Hindenburg had installed the centre-right politician Heinrich Brüning as Chancellor. Esme had heard Gray and Claude Tazewell argue that once he had taken that fateful step, there was no turning back for the President: he was involved. When Brüning had failed to get the SPD to support a budget cutting back on payments to the unemployed in the summer, Hindenburg had suspended the Reichstag under Article 48 of the constitution. Since then, the government had been run by decree until elections called for 14 September – two weeks' time.

Hindenburg no doubt hoped the election would give him the chance to step back and leave the politicians to it, and if he was lucky and one party or the other won a comfortable majority, perhaps it would.

But it didn't look like he was going to be lucky. The SPD were unlikely to support the austerity Brüning insisted was necessary, which left coalition-forming difficult. More worryingly, the two extremist parties – the Communists and the National Socialists – looked set to win seats in parliament.

The decisions of Brüning and of the SPD leaders were vital in determining how this would play out – they hated the Nazis and the communists more than they hated each other. But it was likely that the old field marshal would have the final word on what happened next.

This was the man Esme should interview! The world wanted to know what the President thought, which way he would jump. It was possible an old man like him might let more out of the bag to a young American interviewer like her, rather than, say, a Claude Tazewell or a Gray Trexler.

The big Mercedes drove on, followed by a smaller one. Esme noticed the patrician profile of Erich von Witzbach – aquiline nose, high chiselled cheekbones, assertive chin – in the back.

Erich turned and looked straight at her. For a moment she thought he recognised her and she smiled, but he looked away.

Had he seen her?

Did it matter?

There was something about Erich that made you want to be noticed by him.

Esme turned away and headed across the Pariser Platz towards the Tiergarten. She passed a grand palace, which had originally been given to Old Bluey himself by the Prussian king but had recently been bought at an exorbitant price by the US government for their new embassy. Much to Mr Dryden's frustration it was not yet ready to move into.

It was getting late, the sun was sinking behind the Brandenburg Gate, a yellow fire behind its chariot. She walked under the arch and plunged into the park.

She loved the Tiergarten. It was dotted with small formal gardens and a grand triumphal avenue lined with statues of statesmen ran through the middle of it, but much of it felt like the old German hunting forest that it once was. The crisp Berlin air, of which Berliners were so proud, was at its crispest here, and while you could never quite get out of earshot of automobile engines, sometimes, in its depths, it was possible to forget that you were at the heart of one of the biggest cities in Europe.

She often cut through the park to get from the Dryden house

in Hohenzollernstrasse to the centre of the city. Normally, she would pass fashionably dressed women arm in arm, or diplomats in top hats or bowlers gossiping, or nannies with babies in perambulators and sailor-suited charges skipping along beside them, or soldiers in crisp uniforms on handsome horses trotting by.

But as the sun set, these people melted away and a new type of visitor to the park appeared. Thin men with pinched faces and no shirt collars, old women crushed with the cares of the world who turned out not to be so old after all when you came close, looking for an empty bench for the night. Pretty girls in cheap dresses strolled along the pathways, as did pretty boys.

Harriet had warned Esme to avoid the park after dark, and she had heeded that warning. She was tempted to turn and leave the park as soon as possible. But she didn't.

There was still some money from the booming 1920s sloshing around Berlin, in the shops on the Kurfürstendamm, or the nightclubs like the Blaue Fuchs, but unemployment had rocketed in the last few months following the stock-market crash thousands of miles away on Wall Street the year before. If the poverty and desperation of Berliners leaked into her Berlin, she wasn't going to turn away from it.

Maybe she should write about that?

Would readers in Chicago be interested in poverty five thousand miles away on a different continent? There was desperate poverty in America now too, and it was getting worse.

Probably not. But Esme wouldn't turn away from it. And she refused to be scared.

After all, her home city of Chicago was much more dangerous than Berlin. There might be some crime here, the odd murder, the regular dust-ups between communists and Nazis, but gangsters didn't ride around in cars carrying Tommy guns shooting up people.

Like Henry.

Henry had been a friend of Esme's, a thirty-five-year-old reporter for the *Globe* whom she had met in a bar with colleagues from work. He wasn't particularly attractive, he had buck teeth and was on the scrawny side of thin, but he would do anything for a story and Esme admired his determination. His single-mindedness.

His beat was the gang warfare going on in Chicago: the restaurants shot up by guys with Tommy guns, the rivals silenced with a bullet through the head.

Esme found his work scary, but *so* exciting. He had switched roles from friend to lover one afternoon that June. Then, a month later, the inevitable happened. Henry had been warned off a story, had taken no notice and been rewarded with two bullets in the chest.

Remarkably, he survived. Esme had gone to visit him in hospital unannounced, which was where she had met his pretty wife and two kids.

So, Harriet's suggestion that Esme come and stay with her in Berlin had been particularly well timed.

A sixteen-year-old girl in a skimpy dress passed her. Esme wished her a good evening. The girl looked at her in surprise, and then returned her greeting with the sweetest of smiles. Esme tried a smile with a war veteran wielding a crooked crutch. He somehow managed to raise his cap.

She heard a man's footsteps behind her. She refused to let it bother her, she kept her pace steady.

'Good evening, Fräulein.'

'Good evening.' She turned with her smile at the ready.

The man was short, only a little taller than her, probably a couple of years older, a barrel chest and thick arms straining against his workman's jacket. No collar, no tie. Under a cloth cap his hair was blond and close-cropped – the 'summer cut' of the Berlin working man. He returned her smile and she noticed that one of his top teeth was missing, the incisor on the right.

He grabbed her arm. 'Let's go into the woods.' His accent was broad Berlin.

They were walking along a wide gravel path with trees ten yards back on either side. To their right, a much smaller footpath disappeared into the bushes. There was still some daylight left, but the gloom had overwhelmed the woods.

'Oh, I think you have made a mistake,' said Esme. 'I'm not a working girl. I'm an American citizen.'

'I know you are an American citizen,' he said. He grinned. 'But why you might not be a working girl as well, I don't understand. Don't girls in America work?'

'You know what I mean,' said Esme, trying to keep her voice steady. 'I am not a prostitute.'

'Well, don't worry, I'm not planning on paying for anything. Now, follow that path on the right.'

With one hand he pulled Esme towards the woods. With the other, he showed her a short, sharp knife hidden beneath the flap of his jacket.

Esme gasped. 'What do you want?'

'I want you to come with me.'

Esme had no choice. Her heart was pounding as he steered her off the main path and in a few moments they were alone, surrounded by dark trees. The man stopped and pushed her away from him, so they were facing each other, his hand still on her arm.

'If you scream, I'll stick you.' The man drew out his knife from under his jacket.

'I've got money,' Esme said.

'I don't want your money.'

'Then what do you want?' But Esme feared she knew the answer. She began to shake.

The man smiled again. This close to him, she realised he smelled of liquorice.

'Don't worry, I'm not a rapist.'

Esme couldn't respond. She was definitely still worried. The shaking got worse.

'But I do kill people. If I have to.'

Esme's eyes widened. Was this some Berlin Jack the Ripper? How could she be so foolish as to walk alone in the Tiergarten at night? Harriet had been right, she should have listened to her.

'Now, Fräulein Carmichael, do you know why I may have to kill you?'

How did he know her name? 'N-no,' Esme answered.

She was going to have to do something. Knee him in the crotch. Run. Scream.

But this man looked young and fit and as if he had used a knife before.

'I'll kill you if you carry on asking questions about Fräulein Dryden's death.'

Esme opened her mouth, but once again, nothing came out. Instead, she nodded her head. Her main feeling being relief that she was not going to die imminently. But she was still shaking.

'Do you understand me?'

'I-I understand you.' She had a burning question for him and with an effort, she managed to get the words out. 'Who sent you?'

'I'm not going to tell you that. Just remember, next time we get this close, I'm going to kill you. Understand?'

Esme nodded her head.

'Good. Now turn around and walk slowly for ten steps into the woods. Then stop and go home.'

He spun Esme around and gave her a push in the small of her back. Slowly, ever so slowly, she stumbled along the path. She counted out ten unsteady steps. Then she took three deep breaths. And turned around.

The man was gone.

28

Archie and Lister were playing chess when Esme arrived in Archie's suite at the Adlon the following morning.

Lister got up from the table to pour Esme a cup of coffee and then returned to resume the game.

'It won't be long,' said Archie. 'Just another four moves.'

It wasn't long, although Archie did most of the thinking, with Lister making his moves a few seconds after Archie's.

Sure enough, on the fourth move, Lister pushed his castle to the far row and muttered the words 'checkmate'. With no discussion, they tidied up the set.

'How did you know it would only take another four moves?' Esme asked. 'I can play chess, and that was an amazing queen sacrifice, Lister. You're a really good player!'

Lister glanced at Archie and grinned. 'Thank you, miss. I hope you heard that, sir.'

'Get out, Lister, you old fraud.' Seemingly unconcerned by the admonition, Lister left the room.

'That was a bit mean, Archie,' Esme said once he had gone.

Archie smiled. 'Lister and I have played that game hundreds

of times before. It was played at the Paris opera in 1858, between the American master Morphy and two players, the Duke of Brunswick and the Comte de Vauvenargues. It's the most beautiful game in history – only seventeen moves. Sometimes I play white, sometimes Lister does. He was playing it this time.'

'You have both memorised the game?'

'That one and about a dozen others. But that game is my favourite.'

'Why do you take so long over each move if you know the match so well?'

'I like to think through all the different possibilities at each move. I've thought them all through hundreds of times before, but it's the familiarity of the lines of play that I find comforting. It distracts me. Sometimes I... sometimes I need distractions. And so does Lister, I think, although he'd never admit it.'

'You must have a good memory. *He* must have a good memory.'

'He does. He's an intelligent man is our Lister.'

'Duncan mentioned something to me the other night at the Blaue Fuchs. Lister had gotten himself arrested for attacking a gentleman in some other club and you and he had to get him out of the police station.'

'That's true,' Archie admitted.

'Duncan says Lister often gets himself in trouble. He says he can't understand why you still employ him. Or why you brought him with you to Berlin.'

'It's a fair question.' Archie pulled out his silver cigarette case, offered one to Esme, which she accepted and took one himself. He lit both.

'Lister and I need each other. We have both saved each other's bacon. Lister saved my life in the trenches and more than that, he saved my self-respect. He saved me. And I have done the same for him.' Archie hesitated. 'Later – after the war.' Archie smiled. 'He is in many ways a terrible valet. He's dishonest, he's disrespectful, he's unreliable. The butler at Yarmer couldn't stand him when I took over the house.'

'So the butler went?'

'That's right. In these days you don't need a butler *and* a housekeeper, and Mrs Hartley does a perfectly adequate job without him.'

'Oh, I quite understand,' said Esme. 'I do so hate being over-buttled in the modern world.'

'I'm glad you agree,' said Archie, allowing himself a smile. 'The thing is, Lister is totally loyal to me and I am totally loyal to him. We were both nearly destroyed by the war. We need each other. And everyone else just has to live with it.'

'I can live with it,' said Esme.

Archie smiled. 'Good. He's quite impressed with you.'

'Why?'

'I told him about the cow field. And how you reacted. He thought you would do a bunk. And you didn't.'

'I didn't.'

There was a knock at the door and Lister returned, carrying some folded shirts.

Archie leaned forward to stub out his cigarette. 'All right. Shall we take on the Stabi?'

'Before we go, I should tell you something,' Esme said. 'I was attacked last night. Threatened. In the Tiergarten.'

'What?' Archie's eyes opened wide. So did Lister's.

Esme explained what had happened. How she had been threatened. How convincing she felt the threat to be.

'Oh, Esme! You shouldn't have walked through the Tiergarten at night!'

'I know. Harriet would have been furious. But it wasn't quite night time. And besides, I'm sure Liquorice Man was following me. He would have found somewhere else to accost me; I just made it easy for him.'

'I wonder who put him up to it?'

'I've got no idea.'

'Was he definitely German?'

'Oh, yes. He had a strong Berlin accent.'

'I'll tell you one thing,' said Archie. 'It wasn't Ruth. She's locked up in jail in Dresden. You must have upset someone with your questions. And it was probably someone in the bar last night.'

'That's an unpleasant thought,' said Esme. 'Do you think it must have been a German who set him on to me?'

'I was wondering that. No doubt Erich or Otto could have found a thug for hire if they really tried.'

'Gray could too,' said Esme. 'He's a resourceful journalist: I'm sure he could get hold of anything in any city of Europe.'

'And if the chap was a communist, Yevgeny might have recruited him.'

'So that doesn't get us very far, does it? We can't even rule out Annachiara or even Joe. Or Duncan, the lamb.'

'Shouldn't we just drop the whole thing?' Archie said. 'I don't want this Liquorice Man sticking a knife into my secretary.'

'Your research assistant, you mean.'

'I mean my research assistant.'

'Your research assistant doesn't want that either.'

'So – do we let it go?'

'And let Ruth hang?' Esme said.

'I take your point. But I'm not sure we have much choice.'

'That's what he wants us to think,' said Esme. 'It makes me angry. I really don't want to abandon Ruth. And I refuse to be intimidated into it by that Liquorice Man. There was something *so* arrogant about him. He was so confident that I'd just do what he said.'

'Maybe that's what you have to do,' said Archie reluctantly. He hated saying it, but he really didn't want Esme to get herself killed out of pure stubbornness.

'You've faced death before, haven't you?' she said.

'I have. I wouldn't recommend it.'

'I mean you've been scared. And you've been brave.'

'Yes, I have,' said Archie carefully. 'And you don't get one without the other.'

'What do you mean?'

'Being brave is being scared and going ahead anyway.'

'I see,' said Esme. 'Maybe I should be brave?'

'Maybe we should be sensible,' Archie said. 'I take it you don't want to abandon Ruth completely?'

'No, I don't.'

'All right. We will both be careful from now on. You will be so careful you won't ask anyone any more questions, certainly not in public in the middle of a bar. I will try to be discreet. And perhaps Gisela will find something out from Erich or Otto.'

The telephone in Archie's room rang. Lister answered it. It was the front desk – a Herr Moses Garfinkel wished to speak to Sir Archibald.

Moses looked extremely uncomfortable as he entered the room. Archie greeted him, holding out his hand. There was a delay of several seconds before Moses shook it.

'Come, sit down,' said Archie in German. 'How can I help you?'

Moses didn't say anything. Nor did he look at either Archie or Esme.

'What brings you to Berlin?' Esme asked.

'I am here with my uncle,' Moses answered eventually. 'We

have been visiting a client from Saxony to value his collection – part of it is in his Berlin house. Uncle often takes me with him to help.'

'And you thought you would drop in to say hello?'

'Yes,' said Moses. 'Hello.'

'Hello,' said Archie. Silence. 'Have you found any interesting incunabula for me?'

'Yes,' said Moses. He seemed relieved that the conversation had at last come around to his purpose. He opened a shabby briefcase and took out a squat, sturdy volume, bound in ivory-coloured leather. '*Aesop's Fables*. Printed by Michael Greyff from Reutlingen, 1489. It's not the original cover: it looks like it was re-bound in the eighteenth century. I don't recall you mentioning you had any incunabula from Reutlingen in your collection?'

'I don't, no.' Reutlingen was in Bavaria, Archie knew. He opened the volume to a page bearing an image of a wolf and a lamb in green fields on either side of a river. It looked primitive – like a children's drawing coloured in – but despite that, the wolf and lamb were infused with character. The wolf appeared particularly pleased with himself.

'These are delightful, Esme! Come and see.'

Esme got up to look over his shoulder. 'They're adorable!'

'They are, aren't they? How much is it?' Archie asked.

'My uncle says eight hundred marks. But he is trying to rob you. So you should not buy it. But I thought you would like to see it.'

'I do like to see it. And I should like to buy it. How much do you think I should pay?'

'Not a pfennig over four hundred marks.'

'Can you ask your uncle if he can let me have it for four hundred and fifty marks?'

'But that is too much!'

'I know. But I would like your uncle to make some money.'

'All right,' said Moses, reluctantly. 'I will tell him.' He stood up to leave.

Archie was suddenly struck by an idea. 'Moses?'

'Yes?'

'I am planning a trip to Rostock next week, to research my book. I told you about it, I think. But I would also like to visit some antiquarian book dealers while I am there. Would your uncle release you to join us? I am sure your advice would be very useful. I would pay you, of course.'

For the first time, Moses looked straight at Archie. He even smiled. 'Yes, Sir Archibald. I would like to do that. I will ask my uncle.'

'Excellent. Let me know. And also let me know whether your uncle will accept four hundred and fifty for *Aesop's Fables*.'

* * *

After Moses had left, Archie and Esme headed off for the Stabi. The library stood not far along Unter den Linden, just before the Friedrich Wilhelm University.

'You don't mind Moses joining us on our trip to Rostock?' Archie asked.

'No, not at all,' said Esme. 'I wonder, though. He seems very innocent but perhaps he is Dresden's best salesman?'

'What do you mean?'

'You have no idea what the correct price for that book is. Perhaps it's two hundred marks?'

Archie raised his eyebrows. 'I say, you are suspicious, aren't you?'

'Just trying to look after my employer's interests,' said Esme.

'Well, I trust him,' said Archie.

'Good,' said Esme. 'Because I think I do too.'

They came to Friedrichstrasse. As they crossed the street, Esme stopped dead. A little Opel blared its horn behind her.

'What is it, Esme?'

She scurried to the kerb. 'That's him! Liquorice Man.'

Archie looked over the other side of Unter den Linden where Esme was pointing. A broad-chested young man was standing on the kerb, facing them. He grinned, lifted his cap and turned away, disappearing down Charlottenstrasse.

'He's just trying to scare you, Esme.'

'I know. And he's succeeded.'

Esme clutched Archie's arm as they continued along Unter den Linden to the library.

29

Esme almost didn't go to the Adlon bar that evening. She was frustrated that she and Archie had made so little progress in their attempt to find out who had murdered Harriet. Sure, they had established to their own satisfaction that Ruth was not a Soviet spy and that she hadn't shot Harriet. But they had uncovered no real evidence as to who had. What they had discovered was little better than gossip.

And now Esme would be unable to ask any more questions, at least directly. She would have to rely on Archie and perhaps Gisela for that. Esme knew Archie was right: it would be wise to appear to have given up on her quest.

Which was why it was important to go to the Adlon bar. She needed people to know she had stopped asking questions.

She *was* nervous. Not only was it likely that one of her friends had killed Harriet. It was also likely that one of them had threatened to kill her via Liquorice Man, that one of them might actually have her killed if she wasn't careful.

There were nasty echoes of what had happened to Henry.

By the time Esme arrived at the Adlon that evening, most of

the group who had been at the castle were there, with the exception of Gisela. There was an empty seat next to Erich, and Esme took it.

'Did you see that story in the German papers about the poor woman who jumped out of the aeroplane?' Annachiara said. She was wearing one of her black tuxedos, her friend Ute shimmering in a silver dress beside her.

'Frau Amlinger?' said Gray. 'The woman whose husband was an officer in the Reichswehr and had just died in a plane crash in Russia?'

Esme had read that story too. The pilot of a mail plane had been approached by the wife of a comrade from the war who had just learned her husband had died in Russia. She was in great distress and desperate to get to Berlin. She had asked the pilot for a lift from Frankfurt in his plane. Although it was against the rules, the pilot had agreed.

During the flight, the pilot noticed the door in the back had been opened and his passenger was no longer in the aircraft. A farmer found her body in a field. Suicide. The mail-plane pilot speculated that she was so overwhelmed by grief that she wanted to die in the same way her husband had.

'The German papers didn't pick up on the Russia angle,' said Annachiara. 'But I wondered what a German officer was doing in Russia in an aeroplane?'

'The Reichswehr said he hadn't been in a plane crash at all. He broke his neck in a horse race. He was a cavalry officer.'

'And a former airman, according to the mail-plane pilot.'

'Precisely,' said Claude. 'It doesn't sound right to me.'

'So what *was* he doing in an airplane in Russia?' Esme repeated.

'There have been rumours for years that the Germans have been secretly training tank crews and aeroplane pilots in Russia,' said Claude. 'To get round the restrictions in the Treaty of Versailles. This seems to back that up.'

'I'll say,' said Gray. 'I heard the opposition are going to ask questions in parliament.'

'What do you think, Otto?' asked Annachiara.

'I think we have said that none of our troops are being trained by the Soviets,' said Otto.

'I know you think that's what the Foreign Ministry has said, Otto,' said Annachiara. 'But what is the Reichswehr actually doing in Russia?'

Otto grinned. He was used to fencing with the journalists. It was part of the game they played. Esme had seen Otto give them information, but not often. Sometimes they gave him information. 'I assume they are doing what we say they are doing. Which is nothing.'

'Erich is the one who knows about what the Reichswehr are up to in Russia,' said Gray. 'I saw him in Moscow a couple of years ago. Right, Erich?'

'That's right,' said Erich. 'Interesting place, Moscow. But that was before I was working for the President.'

'You were working for General Schleicher?' Gray asked. Esme knew the name: Schleicher had a reputation as a backstairs fixer who had for years acted for the Reichswehr in its dealings with civilian governments. It was rumoured that it was he who had orchestrated the removal of the socialist chancellor back in March by President Hindenburg.

'That's true,' said Erich.

'Has anyone else seen Erich in Moscow?' Gray asked the group. 'Claude?'

'Never been.'

'Annachiara?'

'Not while I was there.'

'What about you, Joe? You were posted there for the *Intelligencer*, weren't you?'

Joe nodded. 'Back in twenty-seven.' His eyes were glassy. It was after dinner and Joe was drunk. 'There were a bunch of Germans who kept dropping in. I didn't know Erich then. But maybe he *was* one of them.'

'So what do you say, Erich?'

'Off the record?' Erich looked around the table.

'All right,' Gray said, grudgingly. The journalists all nodded. It was too much to hope for anything quotable, but background information would be useful to all of them. Esme was gratified to see Erich included her in his glance. She nodded too, experiencing a rush of pleasure that he considered her a reporter, or at least a potential reporter. One of the press gang.

'I have been to Moscow a number of times over the last few years, on behalf of General Schleicher and the Reichswehr. And we did talk about cooperation with the Soviets. It makes sense to have the Russians as our friends, not our enemies.'

'Yes, but have they been training your troops?' Gray said.

'I can't answer that,' said Erich.

'Doesn't it bother General Schleicher that they are communists?' asked Esme. Everyone stared at her. But why shouldn't she ask a question?

Erich smiled at her. It was not a smile of condescension; it was a smile of encouragement, briefly softening the chiselled coldness of his features. Esme was rather pleased.

'Yes, it does,' said Erich. 'But my enemy's enemy is my friend.'

'Meaning that the French and British are Germany's enemy? And Russia is their enemy too?'

'Who knows?' said Erich. 'It's hard to tell. I do know that General Schleicher hates the constraints on the Reichswehr imposed by the Treaty of Versailles in 1919. What do you think, Otto?'

'It's difficult for Germany,' said Otto. 'As Erich says, the restrictions on the Reichswehr are painful. They are also humiliating. No tanks, no aircraft, only a hundred thousand soldiers. I don't think the British and French quite understand that. We are a republic now – the Kaiser is long gone. The war has been over eleven years, nearly twelve. We have a desire to be treated like an equal, not like some child who can't be trusted with a proper army.'

'But can you be trusted with an army?' asked Annachiara.

'Yes, we can. And most importantly, if you don't trust us, you are only playing into the hands of people like the Nazis. If they do well in these elections, that will be why.'

'Otto is right,' said Erich.

Annachiara and Gray began a little squabble about whether the Germans should have a right to a larger army and an air force. Annachiara seemed to think they shouldn't; Gray that denying them that would force them into the arms of the Soviets. Esme watched as Annachiara's long black cigarette holder danced dangerously in front of the American. Claude puffed at his pipe and dropped in the odd wise word. Ute, beside Annachiara, looked bored, slightly tragic and beautiful.

The secret to her silent-screen success, Esme assumed.

'You know what "off the record" means?' Erich asked Esme quietly, so no one else could hear.

'Of course I do!' said Esme, although, truth be told she wasn't completely sure of the detailed technicalities of the term, if indeed there were any detailed technicalities.

'I apologise; I assumed you would. But I need to check. I'd get in very hot water if what I said was printed anywhere.'

'Oh, no. I completely understand.'

'How's your journalism career going? Have you had any articles published yet?'

'Not yet,' said Esme, with a sigh. 'I sent a couple off to Chicago, but the editor turned them down. It is quite dispiriting.'

'Keep at it,' said Erich. He looked around the table. 'None of these fellows ever gives up; I've watched them.'

'I know. I keep telling myself that. What I need is a really good interview.'

Erich grinned.

'Why are you smiling?'

'That's exactly what Harriet said. She was desperate for me to get you to interview the old man.'

'Really?'

'Really. She was very persuasive.'

Esme's eyes stung. Harriet had never told her that she had been trying quite so hard to help her.

Erich put his hand on her arm, sending a tiny tingle up and down it. 'I'm sorry,' he said. 'I didn't mean to upset you.' His blue eyes were full of sympathy.

Esme sniffed and wiped away a tear before it could fully form. 'She was a good friend. I was lucky to have known her.'

'I'm sure she was.'

If Harriet was willing to stick her neck out to get Esme an interview, then surely Esme should be willing to do the same on her own behalf.

'And can you?' she said. 'Can you get me an interview with President Hindenburg? Everyone is interested in what he might do after the election.'

Erich laughed and withdrew his hand. 'They certainly are. But no, I can't get you an interview. If he did want to speak to the foreign press, then there are plenty of other correspondents for more important papers available.' He nodded towards Claude and Gray.

'I know,' said Esme. 'But he might enjoy talking to me more. An ordinary young American woman. It would be a different kind of interview.'

'He might enjoy talking to you more than someone like Claude, that's true,' said Erich. 'But the President always does what he ought, rather than what he would enjoy.'

'Fair enough,' said Esme with a shrug. She decided to use Harriet's name shamelessly, sure that Harriet would have approved. 'I think Harriet had two last wishes,' she said. 'One was that I warn my new boss not to jump on me.'

'Did you actually do that?' asked Erich with a laugh.

'I did,' said Esme. 'For Harriet's sake.'

'And how did he take it?'

'Like a true gentleman. And, as you've just told me, her other last wish was that you get me an interview with President Hindenburg.'

'Nice try,' said Erich. 'But no.'

'Won't you even think about it?'

'All right, all right. I'll think about it. But no promises.'

'Thanks, Erich.' Esme was sure Erich still meant 'no', but at least she had tried. Harriet would be proud of her.

Erich raised his glass. 'To Harriet.'

'To Harriet,' said Esme, taking a sip of her cocktail. Erich really was attractive. It was more than just the high cheekbones and the blue eyes – it was the occasional tantalising hints of warmth under the ice. If Esme had been Harriet, she would never have chosen Gray over Erich.

'Oh, I owe you an apology,' said Erich. 'I was rude last night when you suggested that one of us might be her murderer. My Prussian sense of pride was wounded. I know how upset you are about her death, but actually, that's a good reason to leave it to the police. You can't possibly be objective.'

'You're right,' said Esme. 'I've decided I will leave it to them.'

'It sounds fishy to me.' It was Joe, his liquid dark eyes focusing and then unfocusing on Esme. 'Harriet's death. It sounds fishy to me. Keep asking questions, Esme. There might be a story there. Betcha there's a story there.'

'Ignore him,' said Erich. 'I do.'

Joe blinked, and turned away from them to reach for a bottle to refill his glass.

'Here comes your boss,' said Erich. 'Would you like me to make sure he keeps his hands off you?'

Esme looked up to see Archie limping towards the group. 'There's no need for that,' she said with a smile. Although you might get him to stop taking off all his clothes and running around cow fields, she could have added, but didn't.

'Good evening,' said Archie, to the table at large. 'I've just come from the dining room. Do you mind if I join you for a drink?'

'Pull up a pew, old man,' said Claude Tazewell. The others nodded their welcome.

Esme spotted her opportunity.

'Archie – I was just telling Erich,' she said loudly, 'that we've decided not to ask any more questions about Harriet's death.'

'I'm very glad to hear it,' said Otto.

'We still think Ruth is innocent,' said Archie. 'But Esme says it's the police's job, not ours, to prove that, and I respect her decision.'

30

'Archie! I *knew* I would find you here!'

Archie's eyebrows jumped in surprise. He threw a quick panicky glance at Esme and then stood up to greet Zena de Mancoux with a tentative peck on the cheek.

'Archie, I don't think you have met Gérard?'

Archie shook the Frenchman's hand stiffly. The Comte de Mancoux gave him a warm smile through his sleepy eyes. 'It's always a pleasure to meet a new stepson.'

'Er, yes,' said Archie. Esme knew him well enough to recognise that his stiff expression was an attempt to control his confusion.

'Oh, hello, Esme,' said Zena. 'I hope Archie has been treating you well?'

'Very well,' said Esme, loyally.

The count turned to her and kissed her hand. 'Enchanted,' he said. Esme was pretty sure he was overdoing it on purpose, but it turned out it was nice to have your hand kissed by a charming foreign count.

With ill-concealed reluctance, Archie turned to the group. 'This is Zena de Mancoux. My mother.'

'Mother!' Esme yelped before she could stop herself.

'I'm pretty sure that's what the guy just said,' said Joe with a grin.

Archie looked from Esme to Zena to Esme again. 'Was this who you meant when you said you had seen my ex-wife?'

'Er, yes,' said Esme. 'You see, she said she was the former Lady Laverick and so I naturally assumed...'

'Mother!' Archie turned in frustration to the lady. 'You did that on purpose, didn't you? Trying to pass yourself off as my wife!'

'I did wonder if Miss Carmichael had gotten the wrong end of the stick, darling. I didn't want to confuse the poor lamb if she got my age wrong.'

'I know she doesn't look a day over eighty, but my mother is in fact eighty-five,' said Archie, sternly.

'Archie!' said Zena. 'You have no idea how old I am! I could be fifty-five for all you know.'

Esme had to admit, the woman did look fifty-five. Or younger. She had style, that was for sure. Her deep red dress was gorgeous, from Schiaparelli or Lanvin or one of those designers in Paris, Esme guessed.

'Mother. I'm forty-two. If you really were fifty-five, that would suggest you were thirteen when you had me and eleven when you had Fred. And you got married at ten.'

'All right, you've got me, you always were so clever at math. Please forgive me, Esme. I cruelly misled you. Now, get me a drink, Archie, and tell me how you've been.'

The count pulled up two chairs and they sat next to Archie and Esme.

'How is Yarmer, Archie?' Zena asked after Archie had attracted a waiter's attention. 'Have you had any sightings of the sun this year? Are those mighty draughts as invigorating as they used to be?'

'It's as beautiful as ever, Mother. The heather is in full bloom now, so the moors are looking magnificent.'

'Have you been there, Esme?'

'No,' said Esme. 'In fact, I have never been to England.'

'Don't go,' said Zena. 'It's cold and it's grey and it's full of Englishmen. Come to think of it, they are cold and grey too. I much prefer Gérard's Saône to the River Nidd.'

'I think you prefer the Seine,' said the count.

'I think I do,' Zena admitted. 'So the estate isn't bankrupt yet?'

'No. But agricultural prices are taking a hammering.'

'Did you get my letter last year?'

'I did, Mother. Actually, I should genuinely thank you for that.'

'Did you sell?'

'I sold.'

'I am so pleased, darling.' Once again Zena turned to Esme. 'I don't write my son often, but I sent him a letter three years ago telling him to buy a whole heap of American stocks, and then I sent him another one last summer telling him to sell them all. I have a good friend in New York whose lover is a big man on Wall Street. He likes to show off how smart he is to her and she tells me what he is buying and selling. I thought it only fair to tell my son.'

'Who appreciates it,' Archie said. 'The money will come in very useful on the estate. I fear there are tough times ahead.'

'What does your friend say now, countess?' Otto asked. 'I bought some American stocks too a few years ago, but I've hung on to them. The market looked like it was bouncing, but it's started going down again.'

Otto looked concerned. Esme was surprised. What was a German bureaucrat doing dabbling in American stocks? But then everyone in Chicago had been dabbling in them so why not in Berlin? The twenties had no doubt roared as loudly here as back in the States.

'Do you know, I have no idea, baron,' Zena said. 'I do know she has a new dog. A Pekinese called Yum-Yum.'

Otto looked abashed.

'You know, she never told me anything,' said the count to Otto.

'It would go quite against the grain to tell *you*, Gérard,' said Zena dismissively. 'I have to keep my friend's confidences. And you are quite capable of making your own money. Gérard is very clever at buying and selling paintings,' Zena confided. 'There's an artist called Fernand Léger whom he likes at the moment.'

'A man for our times,' said the count. 'I think he shows what the twentieth century is all about. Automation. The machine.'

'What paintings do you buy?' Annachiara asked. 'Apart from Léger. Do you own any of the Italian Futurists?'

As the count discussed his art collection with Annachiara and Otto, with occasional interjections from Zena, Esme murmured to Archie, 'You're half American! You never told me that.'

'Am I?' said Archie. 'I suppose I am. I don't really *feel* half American.'

'Hmm. You don't really act half American either. Maybe I can help you come to terms with that.'

'Must you?'

'I must.'

'You see, I haven't seen much of my mother over the years.

She scarpered when I was two for a man with much more money than Father. Which she spent. And now she is married to a French count, poor man.'

'He looks happy enough,' said Esme, remembering her conversation with Zena about cigars. Probably not a good idea to mention *that* to Archie. But Esme couldn't help wondering.

She noticed Ute getting up wordlessly from her position next to Annachiara. 'Just a moment, Archie. Time for the bathroom.'

'If you say so.'

Esme followed the tall actress to the ladies' room.

Ute was applying lipstick to her Cupid's bow. Esme stood at the mirror next to her, and touched up her own, thinner lips. She waited until a third woman in the room, a girl in a revealing black dress, sneezed, blew her nose repeatedly and left. Was that cocaine, Esme wondered? Despite her years in Chicago, she still felt too innocent for Berlin.

Esme took her chance: she might not have much time until someone else came in. 'Ute?'

'Yes?'

'Did you know Harriet?'

'I met her.'

'Did you like her?' Esme remembered how Ute had been the only one not to raise her glass to Harriet the other night at the bar.

Ute turned from the mirror and looked directly at Esme. 'Not really,' she said.

That was a bit blunt. Esme had to remind herself that Germans could be blunt.

Esme could be blunt too, if she tried. 'Did Annachiara like Harriet?'

The two women were staring at each other, Esme trying to match Ute's cool expression.

Ute slowly nodded. 'Yes, I think she did.'

'I see,' said Esme. 'Did she like her in the way I think she liked her?'

Ute nodded.

'Did you mind that?'

Esme was shocked to see a tear forming in Ute's left eye. Slowly, she raised a handkerchief and dabbed it.

'No. I do not mind it. Annachiara likes to have sex with other women. Harriet was no different from the others. Annachiara always comes back to me.'

Esme didn't believe her. 'Is she upset about what happened to Harriet?'

'Yes, she is. Very. I think they all are.'

'Apart from you?'

'I wish Annachiara would stop doing this.' A hint of anger crept into Ute's voice, and with it a slight lisp.

Esme nodded. 'I understand.'

Ute appraised Esme with her cool stare, one blue eye glittering through a drop of moisture.

'Esme?'

'Yes?'

'Some women, when they get to Berlin, become excited by all the new things they can do. Sexually. They want to try out new experiences.'

'I see.'

'You won't do that, will you?' There was something in Ute's emotionless voice that spoke of deep pain that touched Esme.

'No,' she said with an attempt at a reassuring smile. 'I won't.'

31

Jealous. Ute is jealous, Esme thought as she returned to the bar. She had made a half-hearted attempt to hide it, but Esme was in no doubt.

The question was, was she jealous enough to kill Harriet?

Maybe.

There was a new arrival – a big man in a nicely cut suit, black hair flopping over his eyes, who seemed to be talking to everyone at once. He noticed Esme as she took her seat.

'You must be Esme!' he said, in what Esme took at first to be an American accent. 'Harriet told me so much about you! Putzi Hanfstaengl at your service.' He pressed a card into her hand.

Esme realised that the man was, in fact, German, but he spoke good American.

'Oh, you were a friend of Harriet's?'

'I wouldn't say a friend, exactly. I only met her a couple of times. But she did tell me about you. It must be dreadful for you. The poor girl! Such a loss to all of us. She said you were staying with her?'

'That's right,' said Esme. 'With just her father now.'

'He must be devastated.'

'He is.'

'Please pass on my condolences.' Then the big man turned away to Gray to ask him about Paris.

'Who is that?' Esme asked Erich.

'That's Putzi. Ernst is his real name. The rumours are that Hitler has just taken him on as his press officer.'

'He sounds American.'

'He went to Harvard. He's very proud of being in something called the Pudding Club. Wrote all their football team chants. He likes to play the piano. Quite a performer, is Putzi.'

'Hanfstaengl?' said the count. 'Do his family publish art books?'

'That's right.'

'Sounds like an unlikely Nazi,' said Esme. 'I thought they were all street thugs.'

'Not all of them,' said Erich. 'The rumour is that Putzi saved Hitler's life after the Munich Beer Hall Putsch in 1923.' Erich grinned. 'Putzi explained to a bunch of communist red guards who were looking for him that Hitler was his valet. Not sure Hitler liked that very much.'

Esme laughed. 'You don't trust him, do you?'

'No, I don't. But he is amusing.'

Esme turned to Archie and his mother, where things were getting tense.

'Oh, come on Archie, you know your father was a little simple! He used to try to write me letters. They were very sweet, but his spelling was atrocious. And his heartfelt expressions of love were just too funny. Do you know he called me a ewe once? In an unironic way. I think he was genuinely trying to flatter me.'

'He was a good soldier, Mother,' said Archie stiffly. 'Everyone respected him.'

'But did they, darling? I'm sure they liked him. Even I liked him for a couple of years. But respected him? Didn't they call him "Privy" Laverick? That's hardly a term of respect, is it? It is quite funny, though.' She leaned forward towards Esme and gave her a lopsided smile. 'You know. Lav? Lavatory? Laverick?'

Archie winced. 'It was a term of affection, Mother.'

'Was it? I bet they never called you Privy?'

'No, they didn't.'

'What about poor Fred? Did they call him Privy? He wasn't too smart either, was he?'

Archie's lips tightened. He didn't answer.

Zena giggled sloppily. 'You know I don't think your father ever realised what a silly name Frederick Laverick was? I thought it was quite a joke. It's a shame he never made it to Sir Frederick Laverick.'

'Yes, mother, it is a shame,' said Archie, his voice strangled with anger. 'Do you even care that he's dead? That he died for his country? Your simpleton son with the silly name? Which *you* gave him.'

'Of course I care, darling. I was heartbroken.'

'You barely knew him! You hardly saw him.'

'We wrote each other.'

'Once a year. You didn't even come to his memorial service, did you? Have you been to his grave on the Mount of Olives?'

'Of course not. Have you?'

'Yes. I visited Jerusalem a few years ago to see it. It's a beautiful spot.'

'And I couldn't go to the memorial service because I was in America at the time. It was the war, remember?'

'You had run away to America, you mean,' said Archie. 'September 1914 and you were gone.'

'It wasn't my war.'

'No. It was mine. And Fred's.' Muttering something unintelligible to himself, Archie grabbed his stick, pulled himself to his feet and limped towards the elevators without saying good night to anyone.

'We should probably be going too, *chérie*,' the *comte* said to his companion. He smiled at Esme. 'It's been delightful to talk to you.'

Zena was clearly rattled. And angry. She looked at Esme. 'I was sorry to hear about your friend.' Her voice was suddenly icy. 'Murdered, they say. You should ask my son about murder. And how to get away with it. The judge should have been disbarred.'

'What do you mean, murder?'

But Zena was stumbling out of the bar, clinging on to her latest husband's arm.

* * *

Mr Dryden was still up when Esme arrived back at Harriet's house.

She stuck her head in at the library, where he was sitting with a glass of whisky, staring at the painting of his wife – Harriet's mother – opposite him.

'Did you have an interesting evening, my dear?' he asked her.

'I did. I was at the Adlon bar with a bunch of journalists and some others.'

'Harriet's friends?'

'Yes. Harriet's friends.' Esme stepped into the room. 'They are all pretty broken up. They miss her.'

Except one of those friends may have killed her. Esme still found that so hard to believe. No need to share that with Harriet's father.

'That's good. I'd like to meet them. Talk to them. I'll see them at the funeral, I presume.'

'Have you decided where to bury her?' Esme asked.

'I thought about in Maryland, with her mother. But here in Berlin, I think. The problem with being a diplomat – or a diplomat's daughter for that matter – is there is nowhere that is really home. She loved Berlin, and I loved having her here with me. The funeral will be at the American Church.'

'That will be quite some occasion.'

'It will,' said Mr Dryden. 'I've started planning it.'

Mr Dryden would be good at that. He was notorious in diplomatic Berlin as a stickler for protocol; he could be relied upon to organise a good funeral.

'You know, I wish I had got Rush to do Harriet,' he said.

'Rush?'

'G. D. Rush. The artist who painted Rose.' His eyes flicked away from Esme to the portrait of the beautiful woman opposite him, the older Harriet. 'I was planning to get him to paint her next time we were in the States together.'

'Could you get him to do one from a photograph?'

'It's not the same.'

Esme went over to him and squeezed his arm. He put his hand on hers. The upper lip quivered under his moustache. 'I'm so glad you're here, Esme. You can stay a while, can't you?'

'Now I've got this job with Archie Laverick, I can,' said Esme.

'Good,' said Mr Dryden, patting her hand. 'Good.'

32

After breakfast the following morning, Esme went up to her room to write a letter to her brother at the Red Kettle Ranch in Montana, before meeting Archie at the Adlon. She wrote occasionally to her father – inconsequential stuff. But she and her brother Carl had managed to maintain a monthly correspondence since she had left Montana for Kalamazoo with their mother. It was important for both of them – it gave Esme news of the ranch, and Carl news of his mother.

There was so much to write. Where to begin? She had yet to tell him about Harriet's death. She had written to her mother immediately, telling her how she was needed by Mr Dryden in Berlin, but had yet to inform her father or her brothers.

Dear Carl, she wrote.

Should she write about her doubts that the police had the correct suspect for the murder of Harriet, or her and Archie's efforts to find out who had really killed her?

Who *had* shot Harriet?

She had learned two things the night before. That Harriet

and Annachiara had definitely had a fling, and that Ute was jealous.

Actually, Esme herself had felt a flash of jealousy that Harriet had slept with Annachiara. Which was silly. She had thought it over as she lay in bed the night before. Was it really any worse that Harriet had slept with Annachiara than that she had slept with Gray? At least with Annachiara there was no chance of her becoming pregnant like Ruth. She wasn't aware of Harriet doing anything like that with girls at college, but Esme was coming to realise that Harriet had had her little secrets.

It was clear Ute was jealous of Harriet. Possibly jealous enough to kill her.

But Ute hadn't been at the castle.

Could she have travelled to Adlerstein anyway, sneaked into the castle, stolen the rifle and shot Harriet?

Not really. With Annachiara's help, perhaps. But why would Annachiara help Ute to shoot Harriet out of jealousy?

Of course, Esme had learned something else last night. After that nasty row between Archie and his mother, Zena had said something about Archie knowing how to get away with murder, and had mentioned a judge.

What was that about? Could she be talking about the war? Or something else? A trial?

Esme was curious.

Back to the letter.

Dear Carl,

There was a gentle knock at the door.

'Come in!'

It was Ida, the Drydens' maid. She looked concerned.

'What is it, Ida?'

Ida was a squat, clumsy-looking girl, whom Esme had realised was actually very efficient. Despite Esme's efforts at friendliness, Ida had always said the bare minimum to her. Yet Esme had a feeling Ida liked her, although she was well aware that worrying about whether the servants liked you or not was not how the Dryden household was run.

'What is it?' Esme repeated.

'Fräulein, are the police still investigating the murder of Fräulein Harriet?'

'Yes, they are,' said Esme. 'In fact, I believe that they have arrested the wrong woman for it.'

'I see. And a number of Harriet's friends were at the castle in Saxony where she was shot?'

'That's correct.'

'Including the American, Herr Moretti?'

'Including Herr Moretti.'

Ida nodded to herself. Esme noticed the maid was pinching her left hand with her right. Hard.

'Is there something you want to tell me, Ida? Something you want to tell the police? About Herr Moretti?'

'I don't know. I respect the privacy of Herr Dryden. And I know he is still in pain from the death of his wife and now of poor Fräulein Harriet. So I don't know whether to go to the police. But you were a good friend of Fräulein Harriet's, and you are kind to Herr Dryden. I think I can trust you. I don't know what to do.'

'Sit down,' Esme said. The maid perched on the edge of her bed. 'Tell me.'

'It was about two weeks before Fräulein Harriet died. You were already staying with us. It was very late, after midnight. You and Harriet were asleep, or I thought you both were.

'Anyway. I don't sleep well. And I have a fear of fire. Herr

Dryden often doesn't put the fireguard in front of the fire when he goes to bed, and sometimes in the night I get up to check the grates. It's silly, I know, but occasionally they are still burning with no fireguard.

'So, that night, I came down the back stairs and into the hallway. I heard quiet footsteps running up the front stairs and some sobbing. Although I didn't see her, I knew it was Harriet.

'The door to the library was ajar.'

Ida's hands twisted on her lap and she bent down to avoid Esme's eyes. 'I looked in. Herr Dryden was there. With Herr Moretti. And they were...'

'They were...?'

The maid's hand flew to her mouth as if trying to stop herself from saying what she had seen.

'Were they kissing?' Esme asked, knowing the answer.

The maid nodded.

'Did they have all their clothes on?'

'Oh, yes.'

'That's something,' said Esme.

'You see I don't know if this has anything to do with Fräulein Harriet's murder. But if I tell the police, then it is sure to come out eventually. It will destroy Herr Dryden.'

She shook her head. 'I don't understand men. But I know his grief for his wife is genuine. Maybe he has gone a little crazy? I don't know.'

'But you think Harriet saw them?'

'I'm sure she did,' said Ida. 'Just like I did. Without them seeing her. That's why she ran up the stairs so upset. It must be that, don't you think?'

'I do,' said Esme.

'But maybe she spoke to her father about it later? Or Herr Moretti? Or someone else?'

'And maybe that was why she was murdered?'

'Perhaps.' The maid shrugged. 'I don't know. I have been trying to think about it. Maybe Harriet blackmailed Herr Moretti and he killed her to keep her quiet. But why would she do that, since it would expose her own father? It doesn't make sense to me. Maybe this has nothing to do with her murder? What do *you* think?'

'I don't know either,' said Esme.

'Should I tell the police? It will ruin Herr Dryden if it gets out.'

'I think you should tell them eventually,' said Esme. 'But not yet. I am trying to discover who did kill Harriet and this information may help me with that. And I will be discreet. Can you keep it to yourself for now?'

Ida nodded, relieved. 'If it turns out that this isn't relevant, you will tell me, won't you? Then I will keep the secret.'

'I shall,' said Esme. 'What time did Herr Moretti arrive that evening?'

'After everyone had gone to bed; Herr Dryden must have let him in himself. But as you know, Herr Dryden sometimes has late-night visitors – he doesn't go to bed until late, usually, and people run around this city all night. After nine o'clock the family are on their own, we servants go to bed, unless it's a big dinner here.'

'People do run around all night in Berlin,' Esme agreed. 'Thanks for telling me this, Ida.'

'And thank you for listening, Fräulein.'

33

'I'm sorry about that unpleasantness last night,' said Archie as the waiter poured them each some coffee. He and Esme were on the terrace at the Adlon; Archie had suggested a cup of coffee before they headed off to the Stabi. The sun was shining, but it was noticeably cooler than it had been the week before. Archie didn't much care what his mother thought of him losing his temper with her, but he regretted making a scene in front of the others, especially Esme: he was aware he was asking her to put up with a lot from him.

'You shouldn't apologise,' said Esme. 'Your mother was mean about your father and your brother.'

'She was, wasn't she? She's always wicked; when she's sober her wickedness can be entertaining, when she's drunk it just gets nasty. I shouldn't let her get to me. I always tell myself that, but she always does. It's lucky we hardly ever see each other.'

'She would get to me if I were her daughter. And I need to apologise too.'

'What for?'

'That I thought she was your ex-wife.'

Archie grinned. 'That was funny. Mother misled you on purpose. For God's sake don't tell Daphne, if you ever meet her. I'm pleased she isn't in Berlin too – you gave me a scare when you said she was.'

'Daphne is your wife?'

'My ex-wife. I don't see much of her, either. You said you have something to tell me?'

'Lots to tell you. We were right about Annachiara and Harriet.'

Esme reported what Ute had said to her in the ladies' room the night before, and her impression that Ute was jealous.

'Interesting,' said Archie. 'So do you think Ute could have shot Harriet?'

'She wasn't at the castle that weekend. I don't know where she was, but she knew Harriet was going to be there. I guess she could have travelled to Adlerstein.'

'She would still have had to get into the castle to steal the rifle. And she would need to know that you and Harriet were going for a morning ride.'

'True. Which means she would need help from a guest. Which means Annachiara.'

'But why would Annachiara help Ute kill Harriet? Not just because Ute was jealous. That doesn't make sense.'

'Hmm.' Esme scrunched up her nose in thought. 'I wondered that. But I suppose Annachiara may have been jealous of Harriet and Gray?'

'Then she would want Gray dead, not Harriet.'

'Perhaps Harriet had rejected Annachiara in favour of Gray?'

'And Annachiara was so angry that she got her girlfriend to kill a woman with whom she had had a casual affair?'

'Perhaps it was more than a casual affair? We only have Ute's word there was nothing in it.'

'True,' said Archie. But he was doubtful and he knew it showed.

'It doesn't really make sense, does it?' said Esme.

'No. But it's something. I wonder how we can find out more. Like where Ute was that weekend.'

'And whether Annachiara's affair with Harriet *was* just casual.'

They sat in silence for a few moments, the elephants tinkling away in their fountain in front of them.

'I could try to ask Annachiara,' Esme said.

'No,' said Archie. 'We decided you shouldn't ask any more questions. If Annachiara is involved, the last thing you should do is make her think you haven't given up.'

'I can ask her for help with how to write my articles. Then it would be natural to talk about Harriet. I could also ask about Ute.'

'It doesn't sound like a good idea to me.'

'Well, I doubt Ute will say anything more to me. And Annachiara is hardly likely to tell you about Harriet and her, is she?'

'That's true,' said Archie. 'But I still think it's too risky.'

'I'll be careful.'

Archie shook his head; he wasn't happy with Esme's plan at all. 'You said you had lots to tell me?'

'Oh, yes. There is something else I found out this morning. The Drydens' maid knocked on my bedroom door after breakfast. Boy, did she have a story for me!'

'Tell.'

So Esme told.

Archie shook his head. 'Berlin is certainly living up to its reputation,' he said. 'Did you suspect that Mr Dryden is... queer?'

'No. Never! But I'm hardly an expert on that kind of thing.'

'And the maid thinks that Harriet saw them too?'

'She's certain of it. In fact, come to think of it, Harriet did mention to me right before she died – when we were horseback riding by the river – that her father wasn't who she thought he was. There was something she wanted to tell me but then decided not to. Perhaps she was referring to that?'

'I can see how that would upset her.'

'Of course it would!'

'It would be very bad for Dryden if that got out.'

'Which it might do if the maid tells the police.'

'Or if Joe told anyone. Or Harriet.'

'Why would either of them do that?'

'I don't know,' said Archie.

'The maid wondered whether Harriet was blackmailing Joe and so he shot her.'

'Sounds very unlikely,' said Archie. 'Why would Joe care if Harriet told the world about him and Dryden? From what you say, he's not exactly discreet and he doesn't have a reputation for probity to protect.'

'Hardly.'

'We know Joe didn't shoot Harriet himself – he was at breakfast with Annachiara and Gisela.'

They looked at each other in silence, their brains tumbling.

Archie finished the last of his coffee. 'We're making some progress, but we don't have the answer yet. Come on. Let's go to the library.'

As they passed through the lobby, one of the desk clerks intercepted them. 'Miss Carmichael? I have a message for you from Herr Hanfstaengl. He would be honoured if you would telephone him. Right away.'

Esme glanced at Archie. 'Phone him,' Archie said. 'I'll go on ahead. Meet me in the Stabi when you've spoken to him.'

34

Archie was finding it hard to concentrate on the book open on his desk in the large octagonal reading room at the Staatsbibliothek.

It was the memoir of a captain who had served as an aide-de-camp for Blücher in 1809, a period in the general's life that particularly interested Archie. For in that year, Blücher had suffered from a frustratingly vague 'illness' which involved all kinds of delusions, such as that the floor of his bedroom was on fire and he had to walk on tiptoe to prevent his feet from getting burnt. There had been noisy struggles involving broken furniture with phantom officers in the middle of the night. These delusions were ascribed to either grief at the Prussian king's poor management of the war, or to too much 'dissipation'.

Archie knew exactly what Blücher was suffering from; Archie was, after all, suffering from the same affliction himself. It was one of the reasons Archie had chosen Blücher as his subject, and he was on the lookout for evidence to back up his theory. Yet the tedious Captain von Musweiler – who had been right there with

Blücher at the time – refused to provide any reference to the general's suffering at all.

This was exactly the sort of book that he had envisaged Esme skimming for him first. But she couldn't do that. Because she wasn't in the library with him.

Where the hell *was* she? She was supposed to be working for him; she wasn't supposed to abandon him without any explanation in the middle of the day.

He would set her straight when she did eventually show up. *If* she showed up.

He hung on to his irritation because it was a comfortable, familiar feeling and he was using it to mask another anxiety that he was trying to ignore.

What if the thug who had accosted her in the woods of the Tiergarten had carried out his threat? It was only a short distance from the Adlon Hotel to the Staatsbibliothek along the always busy Unter den Linden. Yet it was on that stretch that they had seen the man the day before.

But Archie and Esme had told everyone loudly that they had done what the man who smelled of liquorice had demanded – namely stopped asking questions.

No. Esme was safe. She was just unreliable.

At about noon, he felt a tap on his shoulder. He turned to see Esme grinning broadly at him, her blue eyes sparkling under her short honey-blonde hair.

He felt a surge of relief run through him. For a moment he let a smile crease his face, but then he banished it.

'Where the hell have you been?' he hissed, keeping his voice low. The Stabi librarians were fiercer than most in their disapproval of their readers talking.

Esme perched on his desk. 'I did it. I got my big interview.'

'Really? Hindenburg?'

'No. Hitler!'

'Hitler? Good Lord! So that's what Putzi Hanfstaengl wanted with you? How did it go?'

'Come outside and I'll tell you.'

They left the library and sat by the fountain in the peaceful courtyard, surrounded by the ivy-clad pale stone walls of the building.

'Putzi wanted me to come to the Kaiserhof Hotel right away. He told me not to tell anyone where I was, which was why I didn't send you a message.'

'You could have made some other excuse.'

'I would never lie to you, Archie. And I did come straight here afterwards.'

'Um.' That didn't sound quite right, but Archie was too curious about Hitler to quibble. 'What was he like?'

'Unimpressive. Almost shy. He has this soft pasty face. He looks so *ordinary*, even his moustache seems ordinary close up. He's the polar opposite of someone like Erich or even Otto. He speaks in a soft Austrian accent, and he is almost feminine in the way he treats you. Not at all martial, although he did go in for the hand kissing and heel clicking. The only thing remarkable about him is his eyes. They are a very dark blue and they stick out. One moment they grab you and the next they just seem kind of crazy.'

'What did he say?'

'He started off by saying how much he likes the Americans, although apparently we are decadent and dominated by Jews. Did you know we and the British – and of course the Germans – are the tip-top races in the world? Then I asked him whether there are any circumstances the National Socialists would use force to overthrow the government if they didn't gain enough votes in the election. It's what everyone wants to know.'

'What was his reply?'

'He didn't really answer the question. He went on and on about the injustice of Versailles, how the Americans and the British need to cancel the Germans' war debt, how Germany should be permitted to have a proper army and how their soldiers should be allowed back into the Rhineland.'

The Treaty of Versailles had forbidden the Germany army from going within fifty kilometres of the Rhine.

'So what did you do then?' Archie asked.

'I meant to push him on it, but I couldn't get a word in edgeways. I was worried he was going to burst a blood vessel, but fortunately an opera singer arrived and he was all over her. He ignored me.'

'Oh.'

'I did learn that the guy likes Wagner. Boy, does he like Wagner!'

'Did he say anything else to you?'

Esme nodded. 'Yeah. He asked me whether I liked Wagner.'

'And?'

'I've never seen any.'

'Oh. Then what happened?'

'He fawned over the opera singer for fifteen minutes and then a big fat guy arrived – Hermann Göring, a flying ace from the war, you may have heard of him – and we were ushered away.'

'Ah.'

'Isn't that wonderful?' said Esme. 'I'll cable the interview to the *Mercury*. The election is only one week away – I'm sure they'll publish it.'

'But what will you say? Hitler didn't really tell you anything, did he?'

'Oh, I'll manage. I'll explain the political situation here and how there is a chance that the Nazis hold the balance of power if they do well in the elections.'

Archie could see Esme was excited at meeting Hitler, but he wasn't sure that the encounter could be classed as an interview. He hoped the editor in Chicago published her article.

But most of all, he was relieved nobody had hurt her.

He considered berating her for abandoning him, but he didn't have the heart for it.

'Did Putzi say why he gave you the interview?'

'Yes.' Esme smiled. 'Harriet. Harriet asked him.'

'Good for Harriet,' Archie said.

'Say, Archie?'

'Yes?'

'Do you mind if I run off now and write the article?'

'And leave me with Captain von Musweiler? The most boring officer who ever wore a Prussian uniform.'

'I'm sure his wife loved him.'

'Possibly. He hardly mentions her, but when he does, she sounds pretty dull too.'

'There you are then. Made for each other. I'll come right back here when I've sent off the article.'

Despite the captain waiting for him, Archie was almost cheerful as he re-entered the library.

35

Gisela hurried from work at the courthouse in Moabit to lunch with her brother at the branch of Aschinger in Alexanderplatz. Cheap and cheerful – sausages, potato salad and beer. The days of oysters à la Florentine at Horcher's were long gone.

Otto didn't look good. The creases on his lean face, which had first appeared only months before, seemed to have deepened a couple of millimetres since she had last seen him. But he managed his usual warm smile – a smile that Gisela liked to think was that little bit warmer when directed at her.

'Trouble at the Ministry?'

'No more than usual,' Otto said. 'There is a bit of a fuss about this poor woman who chucked herself out of a plane. Questions about whether the Soviets are training our army. But it will blow over. Why do you ask?'

'You seem... well... distracted.'

'It's Harriet's death. It's just so shocking. And for it to happen in the castle grounds!'

'Have you heard any more about how the police investigation is going?'

'I spoke to Mama on the phone last night. The police still have that Austrian woman in custody. They say they are gathering evidence.'

Otto winced.

'And?'

'It's the castle, Gisela. I think we may have to sell it after all.'

'No! I thought the American stock market was bouncing back?'

'So did I. But it isn't – it's been falling again since April. If it goes down much more my profits will turn to losses.'

'Didn't you tell me Mama had got some money from her aunt or something?'

'She did. But it won't be enough.'

'Not enough? How much more do you need?'

'I don't know. Another hundred and fifty thousand marks at least.'

'What are you going to do?'

'What can I do? Hang on. And hope for another bounce. We can't mortgage the estate any more. And we have a loan payment due at the end of September.'

'What happens then?'

'The bank says they'll insist on us putting the castle up for sale. Or they'll take it from us and sell it themselves.'

'Oh, Otto.' Gisela reached over the table to take her brother's hand.

'Three hundred and twenty years! It's been in our family three hundred and twenty years! And I will be the one to lose it. Papa would be furious if he were still alive!'

'It was Papa who lost it! He was the one who ran the estate unprofitably for too long. Who took out the mortgages. It's not your fault you couldn't save it.'

'I wonder sometimes if that's what killed him,' said Otto. 'What gave him that heart attack.'

'Do you think so?'

'Possibly,' said Otto. He sighed. 'I came so close! If I had only sold my American shares in September last year I could have paid off some of our debts and got the interest payments under control. But I was greedy. Crowle told me the market still had another 50 per cent to go. He urged me to buy more radio stocks. I hoped to pay off all the mortgages on the estate.'

Crowle was a New York stockbroker whom Otto had met in the Adlon bar in 1928. Gisela didn't like Crowle.

'And what does Mr Crowle say now?'

'I haven't heard from him,' said Otto. 'His firm has closed down – he transferred my account to another stockbroker.' Otto shook his head. 'Maybe they'll go bust too. Maybe I should take all my money out now, before I lose it all.'

'You borrowed to make those investments, didn't you?'

Otto nodded. 'Yes. That was the only way I could earn enough of a profit to make a difference to the castle finances. And it almost worked!'

'So if the stock market goes down further we lose the castle and you have to pay off your own debt?'

Otto nodded. 'That's right. But if the market goes back to where it was in October last year, we'll be fine. Or we will at least limp on. I have to hold out for that, Gisela. Don't you see?'

Gisela wasn't sure that she did see. Like Otto, she was devastated by the prospect of losing the castle. How could any of them be von Adlersteins if they had lost their Burg Adlerstein? It was unthinkable. Which was why Papa hadn't thought hard enough about it.

Gisela definitely blamed Papa.

She felt the burden too. If only Manfred and Alex hadn't

gone off and got themselves killed in the war! Manfred would be the baron today, but he probably wouldn't have been able to do any more than Otto had. It was up to Otto, now. And her.

'Have you spoken to Mama about this?' she asked.

'Oh, yes.'

'And what does she say?'

'She's happy for me to hold on. And hope. You know how important Adlerstein is to her. She thinks she owes it to Papa to keep it going.' He sighed. 'We all do.'

'Mama is a wise woman.'

'She is,' said Otto. 'And she understands I'm trying. She's doing her best with the estate. She's probably managing it better than Papa ever did.'

'I'm sure she is.'

Gisela sipped her beer. 'So the police don't have any suspects for Harriet's murder apart from Ruth Jakubowski?'

'Not that I know of,' said Otto. 'It must be her, surely?'

'I suppose so,' said Gisela.

'Esme seems to have her doubts,' said Otto. 'But I think she's clutching at straws. She told us last night she's given up asking questions.'

'Oh, really?'

Otto took a bite of his sausage and looked up at his sister. 'Do you know if she and Archie Laverick have found any answers to those questions?'

'Not many yet. Not enough to show Ruth Jakubowski is innocent. But they seemed to me to be still trying.'

'What have they found out?'

So Gisela told him about Archie and Esme's visit to Ruth and her lawyer and Grayson Trexler. He was her brother, after all.

* * *

Esme took the tram home from the Staatsbibliothek. No more walking through the Tiergarten. She kept a careful eye out for Liquorice Man, but didn't see anything.

She was pleased with the article about her interview with Hitler that she had dashed off and cabled to the *Mercury* in plenty of time for the next day's edition. That was an advantage of being seven hours ahead of Chicago.

She was quite sure it would make a splash. The other foreign correspondents in Berlin would take notice of her now once they heard about it. She looked forward to the expression on Gray Trexler's face. This could be the big interview she was looking for. Would it be enough for the *Mercury* to consider employing her on a permanent basis in Berlin? She was getting ahead of herself.

It should be enough to allow her to call herself a foreign correspondent.

She was also pleased with the afternoon's work for Archie. She had read through interminable letters from Prussian officers, looking for any items that might shed light on Blücher. She hadn't found much, but then that was part of the point. She had saved Archie from having to wade through them all himself.

She had got quite caught up in a Captain Dieskau's love life. The man had a lot of fun and enjoyed bragging about it to his buddy Herbert, an officer in a different guards regiment. The gay captain was sleeping with his commanding officer's wife *and* her daughter. Eventually he got caught – Esme knew he would – but he managed to smooth-talk his way out of a scandal and was transferred to another regiment in another town with another officer's wife to chase after. Unfortunately, the correspondence trailed off in October 1806, a week before the Battle of Auerstedt. Either Captain Dieskau or his friend Herbert must have fallen at that one, Esme couldn't work out which. But Old Bluey had nothing to do with any of it.

She was enjoying working for Archie. But his mother's comment the other night bothered her, the one about how he had got away with murder. Was that just a figure of speech? It must be. But then why should a judge be disbarred?

Esme didn't like to ask; whatever it was, it was Archie's business, not hers. And yet, she knew what Harriet would say.

Working for a philanderer was bad enough. Working for a murderer was just plain stupid.

Of course Archie wasn't a murderer, Esme told herself – and Harriet. But she should make sure.

There was a telegram waiting for Esme at the Drydens' house. She opened it eagerly, her heart pounding. This would be her first published article! An interview with Hitler, no less!

She scanned the message and the pounding stopped.

WILL NOT PUBLISH YOUR HITLER ARTICLE STOP NOTHING NEW STOP RGRDS D FINNEGAN

'Darn it!'

36

The Romanisches Café stood right next to the Memorial Church at the end of the Kurfürstendamm: a huge, bustling establishment with high ceilings and massive windows. It took Esme a couple of minutes to find Annachiara, who was sitting alone and aloof, her cigarette holder swooping above her cup of coffee. She was wearing a necktie, a double-breasted pinstripe suit and a small bowler hat perched on top of her brilliantined hair.

The venue was Annachiara's suggestion. Esme had telephoned her asking if she could pick her brains about journalism, and Annachiara had suggested a cup of coffee.

Esme glanced around the room quickly to see if she recognised anyone. The Romanisches Café was famous for being the centre of literary life in Berlin. Perhaps the two men – one very young, one older and more crumpled – arguing at the table she passed on the way to Annachiara's were famous poets?

Esme overheard a few words of their conversation. 'I tell you, she has a face like a barn door, and a backside to go with it.'

Perhaps not.

'Thank you so much for meeting me, Annachiara,' said Esme. 'Harriet and I always meant to come here, but we never made it. Have you spotted anyone famous?'

'You just missed Bertolt Brecht. And that's Egon Kisch,' Annachiara said in a low voice, flicking her dark eyes towards the crumpled man with a thick moustache at the next table. 'Have you heard of him?'

'The travel writer? Sure.'

'And the young man with him in the sharp suit is Billy Wilder. Another Austrian.'

'Never heard of him.'

'You will. You should read his columns in *B. Z. am Mittag*. You could learn a lot.'

The young man, as if sensing that they were talking about him, looked across at Esme and winked.

She winked back. Why not?

'I heard you met Hitler,' said Annachiara. 'That was quite a coup! I don't think you need any of my advice.'

'Putzi Hanfstaengl fixed it up,' said Esme. 'Harriet asked him to. It's all down to her.'

'I wonder why Putzi chose you and not someone more experienced,' Annachiara mused.

'Harriet could be very persuasive. Even when she's dead.'

Annachiara laughed. 'No doubt about that! I expect Putzi was trying to bait the rest of us. Let us know that he's the one who calls the shots.'

'Perhaps,' said Esme.

'When are they publishing the interview?'

'I'm not sure.' Esme could feel herself blushing. But she couldn't bring herself to admit that her article was so bad the *Mercury* wasn't going to publish it at all.

The shame was difficult to bear. Just like Susan Abchurch, she had been offered her big break. Unlike Susan Abchurch, she had blown it. Blown it comprehensively. She had been awake half the night wondering what she should do next.

Perhaps she should just face up to the fact that she didn't have what it took to become a foreign correspondent. Spend her earnings from working for Archie on a passage back to America.

And then what? Chicago? Kalamazoo? She could type. She could find herself a dead-end job. Or a dead-end job would find her.

The prospect filled her with dread. The problem was, the more she saw of the other foreign correspondents in Berlin, the more she wanted that life for herself. She enjoyed being in Berlin, the beating heart of Europe, arguing about the tremors that were running through the continent. And yes, she wanted to explain them. Write about them. To people like her former self leafing through newspapers in Kalamazoo or Grand Rapids or Omaha.

Annachiara was watching her carefully.

'You know, I'd be happy to talk to you about how to be a foreign correspondent in this town. But I don't think that's the reason you want to talk to me.'

'You don't?'

'I don't. I think you want to talk about Harriet.'

Esme smiled hesitantly. 'You got me.' So much for that little attempt at deceiving the Italian journalist. She was much too sharp.

'When you and Ute returned from the ladies' room at the Adlon the other evening, I could tell you'd been talking about Harriet. And me.'

Annachiara paused, waiting for confirmation.

Esme obliged. 'Yes. Ute did tell me about you.'

'I thought so. I suspect it was no surprise to you that I like women, but I imagine it came as a considerable surprise that Harriet did?'

Esme shrugged. 'Yes. That's true.'

Annachiara nodded. 'Normally I believe that a woman's sexual preferences are her own affair, but in this case, I think you deserve to know about Harriet, since she was such a good friend of yours.'

'Do I want to know about this?' Esme asked, not at all sure she did, after all.

Annachiara drew tobacco through her holder and the cigarette glowed. 'I think maybe you do. You see, your friend was not really a lesbian. Or even bisexual. She wanted to experiment, I could tell. This happens to some people when they arrive in Berlin. I am happy to help women explore their sexual desires, especially if they are as attractive as Harriet. Sometimes I make a discovery. Often, so do they. But Harriet's heart was not in it.'

'I see.'

'We met in my apartment one afternoon, after a boozy lunch.' Annachiara looked directly at Esme. 'It didn't work. But we had a good talk afterwards. She was troubled, that woman. Very troubled. By her mother's death. By her father. She was looking for sex as a release. Sex with men wasn't working. So she tried sex with women. But that worked even less well.'

'Poor Harriet. Did she say which men she had sex with?' Esme asked. 'Apart from Gray?'

'I think this was before Gray. I'm not sure if they were anyone we know. There was an attractive French third secretary hanging about her, but he's gone back to Paris. Erich, perhaps?' Annachiara shrugged.

Yes. Perhaps Erich, thought Esme. 'What did Ute think of you and her?'

'Ute didn't like it. Ute has always known what I do – I never hide it from her – but she is getting increasingly jealous. She knows Harriet is not my type, however gorgeous she was.'

'Who is your type?' Esme asked.

Annachiara chuckled. 'Ute.'

'She is a beautiful woman.'

'Maybe Gisela,' Annachiara said, a little wistfully.

'Tall and blonde, like Ute?'

'Not quite as ravishing as Ute. But she has something, don't you think? She is intelligent. And adventurous.'

Esme hesitated.

Annachiara laughed. 'You want to know whether anything has happened between me and Gisela, don't you?'

'I *was* curious.'

'Curiosity is good in a journalist,' Annachiara said. 'But no. I haven't made any advances towards her; my instinct is she wouldn't appreciate that. My instinct is pretty good at these things.'

'I found a note from you – or I assume it was you – in Harriet's writing desk. It was a line in Italian, signed "A".'

'Ah. More curiosity, I see. *L'amor che muove il sole e l'altre stelle.* Dante. We had spoken about him together.'

'What does it mean?'

'*The love that moves the sun and the other stars.* I love that line. And I love it when foreign women like Dante. I was acknowledging a romantic afternoon rather than declaring my undying devotion.' Annachiara slowly blinked. 'I liked your friend. I shall miss her.'

The waiter came with a cup of coffee for Esme. She declined the offer of cake.

'And now you are wondering whether all this had anything to do with her death?' Annachiara said.

'Archie and I have stopped asking about that,' Esme said.

'I understand. But you can't help wondering?'

'No,' Esme admitted. 'I can't help wondering.'

'Well, it didn't. Ute was no more jealous of Harriet than she has been of many other women – women whom I saw more than once. While I liked Harriet, our fling was nothing special to me.'

Esme took a deep breath. 'I see.'

'And Ute was in Berlin when Harriet was killed. Otto hadn't invited her to the castle. I can understand that. I'm sure Otto doesn't disapprove of our relationship, but his mother might have. It would have been right in front of her nose and the baroness is no fool.'

'Do you know what Ute was doing that weekend?'

'She had a screen test on Saturday. For a talkie at the Ufa studios in Babelsberg. She didn't get it.' Annachiara sighed. 'Poor Ute hasn't had a single role in a talkie yet.'

It would be very tight for Ute to get from a screen test in Babelsberg, which was on the outskirts of Berlin, to Adlerstein by Saturday night so that she could sneak into the castle with Annachiara's help on Sunday morning. And Annachiara was convincing. It didn't seem likely.

It had been a gloomy morning, but a sudden beam of sunshine burst through the café's huge windows, prompting cigarette smoke and dust motes to twist and dance above the chattering patrons.

'You know, Harriet was very fond of you,' Annachiara said. 'And not in the way I am fond of Ute. That afternoon, she told me she was pleased you were with her in Berlin. That you were a constant from her old life, her old self, and that she really valued your friendship. *That* is what I can tell you about her.'

Despite herself, Esme felt the tears come. She dabbed her eyes.

The woman with the short hair and the black necktie smiled warmly at her.

'All right. Now that's out of the way, perhaps I can help you with your journalism. Do you have any questions for me?'

Esme pulled herself together. She had thought up some anodyne questions about being a foreign correspondent in Berlin, but she realised she needed real help. Perhaps Annachiara would be able to give it.

'Yes, I do, actually. The editor at the *Chicago Mercury* decided not to publish my interview with Hitler.'

One of Annachiara's dark eyebrows lifted. 'Really? Why?'

'He said there was nothing new in it.'

'Have you got it with you?'

'Yes.'

'Let me see.'

Esme extracted a sheet of paper from her bag and handed it over to Annachiara, who scanned it quickly.

'Your editor is right,' she said. 'There is nothing new here.'

Esme winced. 'I thought I did a good job of explaining the threat of Hitler and his ideas to the Weimar Republic and the chance that the Nazis may win a lot more seats in the Reichstag during the election.'

'There is nothing wrong with your analysis. And God knows, the American people need to be told loud and clear about the threat of fascism. But there's nothing new here to grab the reader.'

Esme felt deflated. 'What should I have written then?'

'What did you ask him? What did he say?'

Esme laughed ruefully. 'Well, it wasn't much of an interview, really. I only got to ask him the one question. About whether the

Nazis would use force to overthrow the government if they didn't get enough votes in the election. But he didn't answer it. He just launched into a rant about how the Americans and the British and the Germans are the master race and how unfair the Treaty of Versailles is.'

Esme smiled. 'It was absurd, really. This pasty-faced nonentity with wild eyes lecturing a young American girl about his idiotic ideas as if he and I would rule the world together.'

'Absurd? Or scary?'

'Both,' said Esme. 'Both at once. Then an opera singer showed up and he immediately lost all interest in me. It was Wagner, Wagner, Wagner. Then finally Göring arrived. Have you seen how fat that man is? He has bulges in all the most extraordinary places. I am not sure I have ever seen a behind that big. And you know...'

'Yes?'

'I think he was wearing make-up.'

Annachiara laughed. 'I'd heard he did that. There you are, then! Write that.'

'Write what?'

'Write about what it's like to be a young American girl in Berlin and meet a man who is either the scariest or most ridiculous man in Europe, you are not sure which. And mention the size of Göring's arse. Or is it "ass" where you come from?'

'I'm not sure it's either in the pages of the *Chicago Mercury*.' Esme laughed. 'But I see what you mean.'

'*That* would be something new for your editor. He would print it.'

'Do you think so?'

Annachiara leaned back in her chair and examined Esme. 'I do think so. And I think people would read it. And that's important. People on your continent need to know about fascism on this one.'

Annachiara was dead right about that.

'You're Italian. You must know about fascism. Do you think the Nazis could ever come to power in this country?'

'They might. Or they might not. Germany is a different country to Italy. But it's worth watching.'

'I think so,' said Esme. 'That's why I'm here.'

'Did you know my husband is a Fascist?'

'No! I didn't even know you were married.' Although now she came to think about it, Esme dimly remembered Annachiara saying something about that once.

'Oh, yes. I got married at twenty-two. I married an idealistic socialist journalist in Bologna. Now he's a high-up in the Ministry of Education in Rome and I'm here in Berlin. People change. Countries change.'

'You changed?'

'Do you mean politically? Or sexually?'

'I, er...'

Annachiara laughed. 'You meant sexually, didn't you? I haven't really changed sexually. I just discovered myself and gave myself permission to be who I am. Berlin is good like that. Not like Bologna or Rome. I hope Berlin doesn't change.' She sucked at her cigarette holder. 'Have you read Joe's book?'

'*Why the People Love a Dictator*? Yes, I have.'

'It's good, isn't it?'

'Very good. He's a good writer.'

'He is. We argue often enough, and he's drunk half the time, but I was unfair to him the other night. He's very good at talking to people. He walked all over those countries he wrote about: Italy, Hungary, Romania, Poland, Turkey, Greece and, yes, Russia. He talked to people in the bars outside factories and in the bars in village marketplaces. And he listens. He's a very good listener. I'm Italian, and I was impressed by what he picked up about how Italians feel about Mussolini.'

'Do you know him well?'

'Fairly well. We were both in Moscow together a few years ago. He was there for a Philadelphia paper and I was with my news agency.'

Esme realised she had an opportunity to ask a couple of questions about Joe. 'Is he a communist? I can't quite work it out from his book.'

'I don't think he is a card-carrying member,' said Annachiara. 'And the book *is* critical of Stalin. But he was impressed with a lot of what we saw in Russia. And he had a... a friend there who I am fairly sure was in the OGPU.'

'The OGPU?'

'The Soviet secret police.'

'And what sort of friend are we speaking about?'

'*That* sort of friend. If you were a journalist in Moscow you often came across people wanting to be your friend. Usually, they were of the opposite sex, but not necessarily in the case of Joe. Or me.'

'You?'

Annachiara laughed. 'Yes. A couple of dreadful women propositioned me. I had no difficulty in saying no.'

'But Joe said yes?'

'He did.'

'Did Joe see Erich in Moscow?' Esme asked.

'I don't think so. Gray seemed to think Erich had been in Moscow, but I don't remember him there, and Joe denied seeing him when Gray asked, didn't he?'

'Yes, I guess he did. Is there anything between them?'

The dark eyebrow rose again. 'A sexual relationship, you mean?'

'I wondered.'

Annachiara took a thoughtful drag from her holder. 'I very much doubt it. Erich is a handsome man, as I am sure Joe has noticed, but I think he prefers ladies to gentlemen.'

Esme was reluctant to spread Duncan's gossip. 'You can never really be sure, though, can you?'

'No,' Annachiara admitted. 'You can never be sure.'

37

Archie decided to take a turn around the Tiergarten before meeting Esme for another stint in the Stabi. It would be the last session for a few days – the plan was that they would travel together to Rostock and Lübeck the following Monday. It had been raining that morning, but suddenly the clouds had dispersed, leaving Berlin crisp, cool and bright.

He had discovered a little rose garden in the centre of the park. His leg was stiff and ached, but he had learned that the best thing to do in those circumstances was to exercise it. Nevertheless, he stopped for a rest on a damp bench in the rose garden beneath a thirty-foot-tall marble statue of a German empress, Augusta Victoria, wearing a flowing dress and a wide-brimmed hat. As well as being the niece of Queen Victoria, she was the daughter of the Duke of Schleswig-Hollstein-Sonderburg-Augustenburg. He smiled to himself: that was one for Esme.

He wondered where exactly in the Tiergarten Esme had been accosted. In the trees not far from where he was sitting, probably.

He was worried about her. It was all very well announcing to everyone at the Adlon that they had stopped asking questions about Harriet; Esme had seemed convincing. But they couldn't be sure that whoever had put the thug up to threatening Esme had actually been present then.

And the truth was, he and Esme were still asking questions.

And beginning to get answers.

Dryden. Joe. Annachiara. Ute. Harriet.

Some or all of them were linked. Archie and Esme didn't know exactly how yet, but Archie was beginning to feel they might get there eventually.

He was increasingly convinced that poor Ruth Jakubowski languishing in a jail in Dresden had nothing to do with any of it.

When Archie returned to the Adlon, there was a message for him to telephone Claude Tazewell at *The Times*'s office. Archie went to one of the booths off the lobby and dialled the number.

'Ah. Laverick. I might have got something for you, old man.'

'Oh, yes?'

'I know that Esme announced you were no longer investigating poor Harriet's murder.'

'She did.'

'Even so. I was out in Neukölln yesterday evening, riot check, talking to some of the communists and Nazis out there about the election and the chances of trouble, when who should I see there in a park but Erich von Witzbach?'

'That seems an unlikely place for him to go.'

'Precisely. He was with Yevgeny Barsukov.'

'But what were they doing in Neukölln when they could easily have met in a bar here in the middle of town?'

'I suspect they didn't want people like me to see them.'

'That *is* interesting. Do you see any connection with Harriet's murder?'

'No, I don't. But it occurred to me that you might.'

'I'm not sure I can. But it is food for thought. Thanks, Tazewell.'

Archie put down the phone.

Dryden. Joe. Erich. Yevgeny.

Interesting.

38

The sun was out and the sky was clear when Esme emerged from the Romanisches Café. She took the tram to the Potsdamer Platz and decided to walk to the Stabi from there. If she stuck to busy streets she should be safe.

But she saw him.

Once again he was on the other side of the street, on the corner of Friedrichstrasse and some side alley.

He was standing on the edge of the sidewalk, four-square, staring at her, waiting for her to notice him.

A surge of panic rose up in her chest. She had spoken to Gisela about Harriet's murder and who knows whom Gisela had spoken to in turn? And Esme had just had a lengthy discussion about Harriet with Annachiara.

Did Liquorice Man know that?

Esme refused to be intimidated by the man. She stood still and glared back at him.

Liquorice Man grinned and tipped his cap. Then he disappeared down a narrow side street.

Two figures followed him at a rapid walk. One was a tall,

slim, dark-haired woman with long strides wearing a loose floral dress and high heels.

The other was Lister.

They turned into the narrow road.

Curious, Esme hurried across Friedrichstrasse after them.

As she entered the small street, she heard the sounds of a scuffle around a corner a few feet ahead.

It was a narrow passageway with a high wall at its end. Liquorice Man was lying in a ball on the ground while Lister was kicking him in the back, urged on by the woman who had a noticeably deep voice.

'All right, yer Boche bugger, listen to me!' Lister said before sticking his boot into the man's back again.

The woman translated rapidly in German: 'Pig dog! Listen!'

'Stop bothering Miss Carmichael or I will rip off your balls and stuff them down your throat. Do you understand?'

The translation followed rapidly. There was no response from the man on the ground apart from a plaintive groan.

Lister landed another kick.

'Do you understand?' he repeated.

'*Ja. Ich verstehe.*'

'All right. Now sit up.'

The man sat up and leaned back against the wall. His nose was bleeding. He spotted Esme.

Lister noticed and turned to face her.

'Begging your pardon, miss. Would you like me to kill him?' He winked at Esme with his glass eye – a strange sensation.

His companion, who couldn't see his face, opened her mouth in shock.

'Translate that, Gunther.'

The woman – whose name appeared to be Gunther – did what he or she was told.

The man on the ground stiffened.

Esme paused for effect. Then she nodded. 'Go ahead, Lister.'

The thug seemed to understand. 'No. No! Please! I was only trying to scare you. I would never have actually harmed you.'

'You wouldn't?' said Esme, in German.

'I wouldn't.'

'Do you promise?'

The man looked up at Lister. 'I promise.'

'Shall I kill him anyway?' Lister said. 'I'd like to.'

'What's your name?' Esme asked.

'Fritz. Fritz Walch.'

'And who sent you to scare me, Fritz Walch?' Esme asked.

'I don't know.'

'How can you not know? Someone must have paid you. Told you who to threaten.'

'It was all in an envelope. The instructions and the money.'

'I don't believe you.'

Lister kicked Fritz Walch again, hard, in the thigh. Fritz let out a brief cry.

Esme winced. Enough was enough. 'On second thoughts, Lister, let him go.'

Lister grabbed the thug's collar, dragged him to his feet, and pushed him towards the entrance to the passageway. 'Go on! Scram!'

Fritz scrammed.

Esme grinned. 'That was impressive, Lister! How did you do that? He's much bigger than you and I'm sure he knows how to fight.'

'Three things, miss. Speed. Go for the eyes. And then the tommy rollocks.'

'Tommy rollocks? What are tommy rollocks?'

'If you don't know, miss, I'm not the man to tell you. But let's just say I have found they are most precious to even the biggest opponent.'

'And who is your friend?'

'Oh. This is Gunther,' Lister said. 'Gunther, this is Miss Carmichael, the lady I was telling you about.'

Esme held out her hand. 'Delighted to meet you, Gunther.'

'I prefer Vicki, if you don't mind,' said the person in the wig and dress. The wig – a dark bob – was awry, showing a patch of black stubble around his temple, but his make-up had been carefully and subtly applied, making the most of his delicate cheekbones and deep blue eyes. An attractive man, Esme thought. Or woman, for that matter. 'Arthur brought me along to do some translation for him.' His English was clear but heavily accented.

'Well, my heartfelt thanks to both of you. Have you been following me, Lister?'

'Aye, I have, miss. I overheard you telling Sir Archibald how that bloke had accosted you in the park, so I thought I should keep an eye on you. I realised that I needed to make myself clear to him, so I asked Gunther to come along with me. To translate, like.'

'It sounded exciting,' said Gunther. 'I enjoy watching Arthur, how do you say, attack people. He is very good at it.'

'He seems to be,' said Esme. 'Well, if you don't mind, I have some work to do for your employer.' She paused and looked Lister directly in his one twinkling eye. 'Thank you, Arthur.'

Lister nodded. 'It was a pleasure, miss.'

* * *

'What are "tommy rollocks", Archie?'

Archie raised his eyebrows, wondering where on earth Esme had got that expression from. They were sitting by the fountain in the courtyard outside the Stabi. 'It's cockney rhyming slang, I believe.'

'Rhyming slang? What does it rhyme with?'

'With a word a young lady shouldn't know.'

'Oh, come on Archie, you are such a prude!' Esme said. 'I didn't realise Lister was a cockney. He's not from London, is he?'

'No, he's a Yorkshireman through and through. He probably picked it up in the army. Anyway, why have you and Lister been talking about tommy rollocks?'

Esme told him.

Archie laughed. 'I wondered where the old rogue had been these last couple of days.'

'Let's hope his warning worked. It seemed to scare the bejesus out of the tough.'

'How did it go with Annachiara?'

'She wasn't fooled for a moment. She knew I wanted to talk about her and Harriet and whether Ute was jealous.'

Archie winced. 'I thought it was a risk.'

'I know. But I'm not sure it will matter, even if our Liquorice Man isn't scared off. Annachiara persuaded me that although Ute gets jealous, there was nothing particular about Annachiara's relationship with Harriet to set her off – certainly not to the extent that Ute would kill Harriet as a result.'

'Annachiara could be lying. Maybe the relationship was more serious than she made out?'

Esme shook her head. 'I really don't think so. Ute had a screen test in Babelsberg on the Saturday and it would be mighty tight to make it to Adlerstein after that. Besides, I don't see why Annachiara would help her shoot Harriet. The whole thing doesn't stack up.'

'All right,' said Archie. 'That leaves us with Joe and Dryden.'

'You think Joe shot Harriet? Didn't Gisela and the baroness say he was at breakfast at the time? And why would he do that?'

'I've been thinking,' said Archie. 'We know Joe and Dryden are connected?'

'Right.'

'And we know Joe and Erich are connected. At least according to Duncan.'

'Yes.'

'So what if Joe was getting sensitive information from Dryden and passed it on to Erich?'

'And Erich passed it on to the German government?'

'Yes. Or perhaps to the Soviet government.' Archie told Esme about his conversation with Claude Tazewell and Erich meeting Yevgeny in a park in Neukölln.

'Interesting. But what has that got to do with Harriet?'

'We know Harriet saw Joe and Dryden together. Maybe she learned that Joe was passing on American secrets to Erich. Maybe she confronted Joe or Erich – warned them to stop or threatened to expose them. Maybe they killed her. Or had her killed.'

Esme furrowed her brow. 'I see what you're getting at. But that makes Mr Dryden a spy. A traitor.'

'I know.'

Esme shook her head. 'I just don't believe it. He wouldn't do that. The embassy means everything to him!'

'Perhaps he didn't have a choice. Perhaps Joe threatened him with exposure if he didn't pass information on to him. You say he's under a lot of pressure. Perhaps he just gave Joe the information in a lapse of judgement. Because he had fallen for him.'

'I don't buy that,' said Esme. 'He's a good man. And he has just lost his daughter! He's not a traitor, Archie! He can't be.'

She was almost in tears.

'I know you like him. And I know you feel sorry for him,' said Archie softly. 'But we can't rule it out, just because you'd like to.'

Esme pursed her lips and looked away from Archie towards the ivy climbing up the pale walls of the Stabi. Eventually, she sighed. 'You're right, we can't rule it out. But we're a long way from being certain that's what happened. We need to find more evidence.' She shook her head. 'If Mr Dryden's affair with Joe came out it would destroy him. I don't think we should go to the police, not until we're sure, and maybe not even then.'

'If he's a traitor, the Americans would want to know about that. America is not my country, so it's not up to me, but at some point, you'll have to tell the ambassador.'

'The ambassador is in the States for a few weeks campaigning for his successor to his senate seat, so we can't talk to him anyway.'

'Well, someone else, then. Here or in Washington.'

'Oh, Lordy. Not yet, Archie. Surely not yet? It's all just guesswork at the moment.'

'You're right, not yet. But Ruth is still in jail. I was thinking of telephoning Herr Schrör, her lawyer. See if Ruth knew anything about a connection between Joe and Yevgeny in Vienna.'

'It's worth a try, I guess,' said Esme. 'But please don't tell Herr Schrör anything about Mr Dryden!'

39

Archie and Esme spent several hours together working in the Stabi, and then walked back to Archie's suite at the Adlon to go over what Esme had discovered about Old Bluey before they went to Rostock the following week.

Lister was waiting for them.

'Thank you for keeping an eye out for Miss Carmichael, Lister.'

'It was no trouble, sir. I'm happy to be of assistance. I think we won't be hearing any more from that particular gentleman.'

'I hope not. Now, what have you got for me, Esme?'

Esme went through the books she had looked at that afternoon. There was one memoir that she thought it worth Archie reading quickly, something written by a neighbour from Silesia.

'Before you go,' Archie said, 'I'll just ring Schrör. See how the investigation into Ruth is going.'

Schrör did not have good news. Ruth was still in custody. The Dresden police were still trying to find evidence that she was part of a communist conspiracy, but without much luck, as far as Schrör could tell.

'But surely they don't have enough evidence to prove Ruth shot Harriet?' Archie asked him.

'Perhaps not. But there is a lot of interest in this case in the local press. The Adlersteins are an important family in Saxony – they have been for generations. There will be pressure to get a conviction and not one that involves guests of the family.'

'Pressure from the baroness? Has she been talking to them?'

'She doesn't have to. Deference will do the trick.'

'Will Ruth get a fair trial?'

'I don't know,' said Schrör. 'It would help a lot if we could point them towards other suspects. Have you discovered anything that might be useful? Anything about the other guests at the castle that day?'

'Perhaps.' Archie wasn't going to tell Schrör about Joe and Dryden, at least not yet. 'There might be a communist connection, I'm afraid, but one that we don't think involves Ruth. There is an American journalist called Joe Moretti. I think Ruth tried to telephone him when she got to Berlin and was looking for Gray. She implied she didn't know him very well, but he is a good friend of Gray Trexler's. Can you ask whether she knows of any relationship between Joe Moretti and Yevgeny Barsukov when Yevgeny was in Vienna?'

'All right, I'll do that. But I'd rather downplay the communist angle if I can.'

'I understand,' said Archie. 'We have one or two more suspicions. We'll let you know if they turn into anything more concrete.'

'I'm very happy hearing about suspicions,' said Schrör. 'Anything that might help.'

'We will tell you when we can, Herr Schrör. In the meantime, have you got all Ruth's legal bills covered?'

'So far, yes. I'll let you know if I need funds for anything. And I will ask her about Moretti and Barsukov.'

Archie had no sooner replaced the phone on its cradle, when it rang.

'Archie! It's Gisela.'

'What is it, Gisela? You sound upset.' She was sobbing down the telephone.

'Oh, Archie! I've just been attacked! They warned me to stop asking questions about Harriet.'

'Who did? Who warned you?'

'I've never seen him before. A man. Young. Strong.'

'Are you all right? What did he do?'

'He hit me. I think I'm getting a black eye. He didn't do too much damage apart from that. But he certainly scared me. Can I come round and see you and Esme?'

'By all means.'

'Now?'

* * *

'Hi! Fräulein Adlerstein!'

Gisela was standing on the pavement just outside the telephone kiosk on her street in Kreuzberg when she heard the cry. She turned to see Joe Moretti striding towards her, a lopsided grin on his face. He was carrying a paper bag containing a couple of bottles.

'Fancy seeing you here!'

'I live just up there,' said Gisela, pointing to her block of flats. 'I could say the same about you.'

'I live just over the road!' Joe nodded to a four-storey building opposite.

'Really? I never knew.'

'We probably operate on different schedules,' said Joe. 'Say! What happened to your face?'

Gisela's hand flew up to her eye.

'I was attacked. They tried to take my handbag but I hung on to it.'

Joe peered at her eye. 'I've had the odd black eye in my time. That one looks recent.'

'It was. Just half an hour ago.'

'You should put ice on that. Did you report it to the police?'

'That was what I was just doing then,' said Gisela. 'But I must go out now. I have an appointment.'

'Are you sure? Can I help?'

Gisela forced a smile. 'I'll be all right, Mr Moretti. Thank you.' She turned away from him and hurried off to the U-Bahn.

40

‘What happened, Fräulein Adlerstein?’ Archie asked as she entered his hotel suite. It was nearly seven: Esme had waited for her and Lister was hovering.

‘I left work early,’ Gisela said. ‘And just as I was approaching my flat in Kreuzberg, he came up to me. He had a knife. Forced me down a side street.’

‘Didn’t anyone see?’ Esme asked.

‘No. He was discreet about it. Then once he got me into the side street, he warned me to stop asking questions about Harriet. Then he hit me.’ Gisela’s hand touched her eye.

‘I bet that hurt,’ Esme said.

‘It did. It was all over in a minute. Then he was gone.’

‘I wonder if it was the same guy who threatened me. What did he look like?’

‘Did someone threaten you?’

‘Yes. In the Tiergarten a couple of days ago. He didn’t actually strike me, but he did scare me. And he had a knife.’

‘He was quite short, but strong. A big chest, you know? And short blond hair,’ said Gisela.

'Did you happen to notice whether his breath smelled of liquorice?'

'What an extraordinary question!' She knitted her brow. 'But yes. I think it may have done.'

'That sounds like him,' said Lister. 'Fritz Walch. Wasn't that his name, miss?'

'It does sound like the same fellow,' said Esme. 'He's been following me this morning, just to show he was watching me. And then this morning Lister slugged him.'

'I thought it had an effect,' said Lister. 'But he must have decided to put the frighteners on you instead.'

'That's worrying,' said Esme. 'I had hoped we had stopped him.'

'Maybe we should listen to him,' said Gisela. 'It doesn't sound as if he's going to give up.'

They all looked at each other. 'Maybe we should,' said Archie.

'How have you been getting on?' said Gisela. 'Do you still think Ruth Jakubowski is innocent?'

Esme and Archie exchanged glances. Archie gave her a small nod. So Esme told Gisela all about what they had discovered about the maid seeing Joe and Dryden and Duncan seeing Joe leaving Erich's room and then about Harriet's brief fling with Annachiara.

Gisela was shocked. 'I find that difficult to believe!'

'Which part?'

'Any of it. Is the maid reliable?'

'I think so,' said Esme. 'Why would she make something like that up?'

'I suppose you are right.' Gisela shuddered. 'And you would know about your friend.'

'I didn't,' said Esme. 'It came as a complete surprise to me.

But I do think Annachiara is telling the truth.'

'That's as may be, but I am quite sure Duncan is mistaken. There is nothing between Erich and Joe.'

'How can you know?' Archie said.

'Because I was almost engaged to him!' Gisela said.

'To Erich? Oh.' Esme looked abashed. 'We didn't realise that.'

'It was a couple of years ago. I've known him for ages. We were courting for a few months and I was sure he was going to ask me to marry him, but then it all stopped. I never knew why.' Gisela bit her lip. 'I was upset.'

'Do you think Erich might have called it off because he is actually a homosexual?'

'No!' said Gisela. 'Absolutely not! I've seen Erich with women and not just me. He likes women very much. Too much. That was what was worrying me when I thought he might ask me to marry him. But I'm sure I would have said yes. Perhaps it's better for me that he didn't.'

'Perhaps he is bisexual. You know – likes men *and* women?'

'That's absurd,' said Gisela. 'Not Erich. I just know it's not true.'

'What are his politics?' Esme asked. 'Did you ever talk about politics?'

'Not much. But he and Otto talked about it endlessly.'

'Is he a socialist?' Esme asked. 'A communist, even? We know he's been to Russia.'

'I'm sure he isn't. Otto and he do discuss communism sometimes, and Erich talks about his time in Moscow, but it's always at an intellectual level. Besides, he's close to General Schleicher who everyone knows can't stand the commies or the *sozis*. And I know how much he admires Hindenburg. So no, Erich von Witzbach is not a communist.'

'All right,' said Archie. He realised that Gisela was upset by

Esme's theories about Erich, and she had just been beaten up, after all. 'Are you willing to continue to help us, after what just happened to you?'

'I'm not sure. What about you? Are you going to carry on with your investigations?'

Archie glanced at Esme and raised his eyebrows. At first, he had thought that Esme was safe – Lister had scared the thug off. Now he was not so sure.

'Unless we keep asking questions, Ruth Jakubowski will hang,' Esme said. 'I know it's a risk, but I can't let that happen. You can stop helping us if you like, Gisela. But I'm sticking with it. Right, Archie?'

Archie was still concerned about Esme's safety, but he knew by now he couldn't talk her out of it.

'Right, Esme.'

41

The Hotel Bristol was only a couple of hundred yards down Unter den Linden from the Adlon – not far out of Esme's way back home.

It was another grand hotel that had been built at the height of Imperial Germany's power. Whereas a couple of weeks before, Esme would have found its marbled lobby intimidating, now she just breezed in and asked at the front desk for the Comtesse de Mancoux. The desk clerk picked up his phone and then asked Esme if she would mind waiting a few minutes.

She didn't.

Ten minutes later, Zena and her equable husband appeared, she resplendent in a plunging emerald evening dress, he dapper in winged collar, white tie and tails. Now Esme felt underdressed.

Zena smiled when she saw her. 'How nice to see you, Miss Carmichael! We are just on our way out. Dinner with an art collector friend of Gérard's. A prince, no less.'

'Do you have a moment?' Esme said. 'I'd like to talk to you in private. It'll only take a minute.'

'Is this about my son?'

Esme nodded.

'Would you mind, Gérard?'

'Not at all,' said the count, and drifted off.

Zena led Esme to a quiet corner behind the grand piano, which was unattended at that moment, and they sat on two small chairs.

'I must apologise,' said Zena. 'For that fight between Archie and me the other night. We rub each other up the wrong way – always have. He takes things too personally.'

I'm not surprised, thought Esme, although she didn't say it. 'There was something you said that night that has been troubling me. Something about Archie getting away with murder?'

'Oh, that's just a figure of speech!'

'Possibly. But a judge being disbarred isn't.'

'No,' Zena admitted. 'You're right. It wasn't, exactly. But it's nothing, I promise you. Archie was found innocent. It was almost ten years ago.'

'Found innocent of murder? At a trial?'

Zena hesitated. 'Yes.'

'But you didn't think he was innocent?'

'I didn't say that.'

'But you did say he had gotten away with murder.'

Zena hesitated. 'I may have said that. But I was angry. And I'd had a little bit to drink. Look, I'm sure he *was* innocent. They found him not guilty, didn't they?'

'With the help of a judge who should have been disbarred?'

'I don't see what business this is of yours, Miss Carmichael.'

'I'm working very closely with him as his research assistant. I travelled alone with him to Silesia and we are going to Rostock together on Monday. So, yes, it is very much my business.' A thought horrified her. 'Who was he supposed to have murdered? His secretary?'

Zena reached out and clasped Esme's hand. Two things struck Esme about Zena's hand: how smooth her skin was and how big were the stones on her fingers. Rich men had given her some seriously expensive jewellery.

'Miss Carmichael. I haven't seen much of my son since he was tiny, but I do know this about him. He is a good man. He is a much better person than his mother. He may have been damaged by the war, but you are perfectly safe with him. I'm certain of it.'

Esme looked at Zena's cool blue eyes.

'You say that, but you don't *actually* know it, do you? You don't know him. You don't know how badly the war has affected him. *I* do. Or I've seen part of it.' She pursed her lips. 'I'm worried about him.'

'Are you, dear?'

Zena was staring closely at Esme.

'Yes,' Esme said. 'Yes, I am.'

Zena withdrew her hand. 'I'm glad someone is. I've spent my life trying not to worry about Archie.'

'But you're his mother!'

'I know I am.' She reached into her purse, offered Esme a cigarette, which she accepted, and lit one herself.

'I was much too young to get married. I was staying in London for the season with my cousin who had married a lord, and I met Archie's father. He was dashing but a terrible bore. I married him anyway and spent my early twenties trapped in the wilds of Yorkshire. Cold. Damp. Grey. I escaped. And I believed that the only way to truly escape was to put the whole Laverick family behind me.'

'But you had two children. Sons, right?'

'Yes. And I was too young to have them. I don't much like children, even my own.'

'That's a terrible thing to say!'

'It is, isn't it?' Zena tried a knowing grin, but it didn't work. 'But it's honest. They were better off without me. Then poor Fred – the eldest – died.'

'I heard. I am sorry.'

Zena smiled, more tentatively this time. 'I kidded myself that it didn't matter, that I didn't really care about him, that millions of mothers' children were being sacrificed in the mud of Flanders or the dirt of Palestine or wherever, but of course I did care really.' She sighed. 'I just pretended I didn't.'

'And what about Archie?'

'Archie hates me, doesn't he? I would if I were Archie. But...' She took a deep breath, and Esme was astonished to see a tear appear in her eye. 'But I've come to realise forty years too late that I love him. Gerry made me realise it. That's why I tried to look him up here in Berlin. In fact, that's why we came here. I heard he was planning a trip here to research a new book.'

'He doesn't know you came here looking for him, does he?'

'Oh, no, of course not. And please don't tell him.' She shook her head. 'Anyway, it was a dumb idea. I'm rude to him and he's resentful of me and we fight. You saw it.'

Esme had seen it.

'Here comes Gérard! We must be going. Do look after Archie, won't you?'

'How can I look after him?' Esme protested. 'I'm not his nanny. I'm not even his secretary.' *And I'm not his mother*, she felt like adding.

'Oh, you can look after him,' said Zena as she stood up to meet her husband.

'One last question,' said Esme.

'Yes?'

'When exactly was this trial?'

'Twenty-four? No, twenty-three! I remember I was in London when the verdict came out. It was Derby day. I won two hundred pounds! Papyrus was the horse's name. That was a good day.'

Was that because your son was found not guilty of murder, Esme wondered? Or was it because you won a horse race?

* * *

Gisela left the Adlon and took the tram back to Kreuzberg. Her landlady only allowed her to use her telephone in emergencies, and although this might just be classified as an emergency, Gisela definitely didn't want the old bat listening in.

Also, she didn't want to bump into Joe Moretti again.

So she went two stops past her street and found a different phone box than the one from which she had called Sir Archibald earlier.

She inserted her pfennigs and asked the operator for a number she knew well.

'Hello? It's Gisela. I'm worried. Esme and Sir Archibald are making progress. And they haven't been scared off.'

42

The next day was a Saturday, a work day for Mr Dryden. He was as immaculately dressed as usual for breakfast, his moustache freshly trimmed, the scent of his now-familiar cologne mixing with the smell of toast at the breakfast table. Yet the skin around his eyes was tight, as were his lips.

'Are you all right, Mr Dryden?' Esme asked. He clearly wasn't; he hadn't been since Harriet had died, but he seemed worse than usual this morning.

Dryden put down his newspaper. 'The police came yesterday. It was a different lot from last time. The political police. They asked me about Harriet.' He took a deep breath. 'They wanted to search her room again.'

'Did you let them?'

Dryden nodded. 'They say they are just trying to find out why that woman killed Harriet. They think there's a communist connection. They asked whether Harriet was a communist.' He snorted. 'I told them that was preposterous. They even began to ask about *my* views. I explained to them that I was a solid Republican and told them a little bit about what that meant. But I thought it was a fair request to look through Harriet's things and I knew there would be no evidence of communism in there.'

Phew, thought Esme. She was very glad she had removed *The Communist Manifesto*. And Gray's letters, come to that. If the police had found them, they might have read them out at a future trial, to Mr Dryden's embarrassment.

Mind you, that would be nothing compared to the embarrassment if his clinch with Joe Moretti became public.

Dryden had noticed Esme's reaction and misinterpreted it. 'Harriet wasn't a communist, was she? I know she was interested in politics at university, and she was always articulate on political topics, which was a godsend at diplomatic functions. I suspect she voted Democrat in the last election, but she never actually *said* that to me.'

'No, she wasn't a communist,' said Esme. 'But, yes, I do think she voted for Al Smith. And she was quite up to arguing politics with socialists. She definitely didn't like the Nazis.'

'You know her friends. Are any of them communists? The police asked me that.'

Well, there's a question, thought Esme.

'No, not really,' she said. 'She knew a Russian diplomat who is presumably a communist, but not well. Some of the foreign correspondents are what you might call "left wing".' Esme spotted her opportunity. 'Joe Moretti, for example. Have you met him?'

'Yes, I believe I have,' said Dryden. 'Nice fellow. Harriet had him round to dinner here with a man called Trexler and young Baron Adlerstein. He wrote a book about the popularity of fascism, didn't he? I've heard it's rather good – I must read it.'

Esme was impressed by how convincing a liar Dryden was, and for a moment she wondered whether Ida the maid had got the wrong end of the stick.

But only for a moment. Walter Dryden was a professional diplomat. He told half-truths for his country. He could certainly tell half-truths for himself.

'That's him. I wonder whether *he* is a communist?' she asked innocently.

Dryden raised his eyebrows. 'Is he?'

'He may be. I heard he spent some time in Moscow.'

'I expect that was just on some journalistic assignment.'

'No doubt,' said Esme, noting Mr Dryden's mild defence of Joe.

The diplomat picked up his paper again.

'Mr Dryden?'

'Yes?'

'Is there a horse race in London called the Derby? I know about the Kentucky Derby, I wondered whether there was one in England?'

'Oh, yes, there is,' said Dryden. 'It's very famous – the biggest horse race of the year. It's held just outside London – a place called Epsom. And they pronounce it *D-ah-by*.'

'Ah, that makes sense. Someone mentioned it the other day. What time of year does it take place?'

Dryden knitted his brow. 'Summer. I'm pretty sure it's in June.'

Esme smiled her thanks.

* * *

She spent the morning rewriting her interview with Hitler. She followed Annachiara's advice, deleting nearly all the background information on the state of coalition politics in the Weimar Republic and instead describing how very strange the whole thing had been.

When she read it through, she liked it, although it seemed different from the other stories she had read filed by the foreign correspondents in Berlin.

Annachiara would have said that was the point. And Esme suspected she was probably correct.

There was only one way to find out. After polishing it for an hour, Esme left the house to take it to the nearest telegraph office and send it off.

Then she headed for the Stabi.

With luck, she should avoid Archie; he had told her he planned to spend the morning getting his notes together for the trip to Rostock. She asked at the desk whether they kept old copies of the London *Times*.

They did.

She leafed through copies of the newspaper for June 1923.

The Derby was run on 6 June, and it was indeed won by Papyrus. And on 7 June the paper carried a full report of the trial of Sir Archibald Laverick for the murder of a man named Victor Radway.

The jury had found him not guilty, following detailed directions from the judge, who had highlighted Sir Archibald's exemplary war record and that Victor Radway was a conscientious objector who had avoided the war altogether.

The prosecution's case was that Archie had suspected that his wife, Lady Daphne Laverick, had been having an affair with Radway. Archie had burst in on them at a hotel at the seaside town of Blakeney in Norfolk. There had been a fight. Victor Radway had been hit over the head with a tyre iron from Archie's Bentley and had died of a fractured skull two days later.

Daphne had testified that Radway had attacked Archie, there had been a scuffle, and that Radway had fallen and hit his head on a brass firedog.

Archie had refused to take the stand.

Lordy!

Esme sat up from her paper and stared distractedly at a row of bound copies of *Le Figaro* on the Stabi's shelves.

The Times's reporter had offered no explicit opinion on whether he agreed with the judge and jury. But it was pretty clear that in the reporter's mind, although Sir Archibald Laverick might be not guilty, he certainly wasn't innocent.

What exactly had the fact that Victor Radway was a conscientious objector and Archie a war hero had to do with whether he had struck Radway? For sure, Daphne Laverick had testified that her husband was innocent, but couldn't that be just guilt that she had been caught red-handed and that Archie, whose fuse was probably even shorter then – so soon after the war – had lost his temper?

The police were convinced that it was the tyre iron that had killed Radway, what with the fact that his blood and a strand of his hair had been found on it.

No doubt the judge had thought that the coward had it coming to him.

But it seemed to Esme that Archie had quite probably beaten a man to death. And not in war. In a hotel room.

Esme was getting to know Archie much better now. She was certain that he would never murder anyone in cold blood. But in hot blood? When something had set him off?

She could believe he had killed someone in the past. And, dreadful though the thought was, she could believe he could kill someone again in the future.

She was supposed to be joining him on a train to Rostock on Monday.

Darn it! What should she do now?

* * *

Back at the Drydens' house at Hohenzollernstrasse, there was a message for Esme to call Otto.

'Oh, hello, Esme. Thanks for telephoning me back.'

'I was out for the afternoon at the Stabi. What's up?'

'The weather forecast is that it's going to be beautiful tomorrow. Would you like to come to Wannsee with me? Erich and Gisela are coming too. It might be the last chance to go for a swim this year.'

'Oh. That's very kind of you to ask me,' said Esme.

'We planned to take Harriet this summer, but we never quite got around to it and now...' Otto trailed off. 'Sorry, I don't know what that has to do with it.'

'No. No, that's all right. Yes, I'd love to come!'

'Excellent news! We will pick you up at ten o'clock.'

43

Otto, Erich and Gisela showed up outside the house in Hohenzollernstrasse in a sporty green convertible, driven by Erich.

It was indeed a beautiful day and even at ten o'clock in the morning the sun was warm. Esme crammed into the small back seat with Gisela, and they set off for the Wannsee.

They were all in a good mood, even Gisela, whose black eye was clearly visible under her straw hat, despite the thick layer of make-up she had applied. For form's sake, Esme asked her how she had got it and she had replied with a wink which the two men couldn't see, that she had been robbed in the street. Her eyes were sparkling, her cheeks were shining and her short blonde hair glowed in the sunshine. Esme had a strong feeling that the reason for that was Erich, sitting in front of her in the driver's seat.

They took the AVUS, an *autobahn* built ten years earlier that sliced straight as an arrow through the forest south-west from the city. It doubled as a racetrack, and on a sunny Sunday there were plenty of would-be racing drivers who treated it as such. Including Erich.

The trees flew by, cars sped, swerved and braked. The drive was terrifying and intoxicating. Gisela clutched her hat and let out a whoop and Esme echoed her.

Wannsee was as crowded as they should have expected on the last Sunday of summer. Despite the *-see* in its name, it wasn't really a lake, but rather a bay in a particularly broad section of the River Havel, with a one-kilometre stretch of sand, almost every centimetre of which was occupied by bodies.

There were changing rooms, and Esme put on her striped swimsuit to join the crowd. They found a patch of sand next to a group of four girls with a gramophone playing jazz. Paul Whiteman. Everyone in Berlin liked Paul Whiteman. Beyond the girls, a few yards out in the water, a group of about a dozen young men and women were enthusiastically doing group exercises together.

Esme decided she liked the crowd. Despite the slump, the unemployment, the unsettling political situation, Berlin was enjoying itself, and if Berlin was, so would she.

Erich and Otto were wearing trunks. Erich's body was a wonder to behold in its beauty. Carefully defined muscles which precisely hit that balance of strength and grace. Gisela couldn't help staring, and neither could the four girls next to them, each one of whom threw glances his way.

Erich was ostensibly oblivious to them all behind fashionable dark glasses, although he exuded a supreme self-confidence in his looks and his abilities that somehow managed not to be arrogant, but alluring. At least to Esme. A couple of boys who were in turn trying to catch the four girls' attention seemed less impressed.

Otto was skinny. Narrow shoulders, two ribs that protruded

above a concave belly, thin legs. But he too seemed carefree that morning.

The Wannsee was chock full of boats, mostly dinghies with brightly coloured sails, but also the occasional speedboat or motor yacht. The rich were playing too.

They ran into the water, which was less cold than Esme had suspected, and swam and splashed and chatted and laughed.

When they were dry, Otto suggested that they find a spot in the woods to avoid the crowd.

He knew a good place by a pond ten minutes from the beach. It wasn't entirely deserted – there were two other groups with picnic baskets – but it was a beautiful spot with the sun dappling the sandy paths and the undergrowth and sparkling off the water.

Erich had procured the picnic: quail's eggs, smoked salmon on rye bread and cold partridge washed down with sparkling Sekt.

The chatter dwindled until all four of them were lying on their backs, observing the patches of blue sky hovering high above the forest canopy.

'Come on, Gisela!' said Erich. 'Let's go for another swim.'

'Good idea!' said Gisela, stirring herself. 'Are you coming?'

It was a question that somehow demanded the answer 'no'.

'I don't think so,' said Otto.

'Neither do I,' said Esme, it only just then occurring to her that this whole thing was a set-up.

So be it.

After Erich and Gisela disappeared down the path with their towels, Esme was the first to speak.

'Gisela told me that she and Erich used to be close,' Esme said. 'Gisela seems to think that Erich almost asked her to marry him.'

'That was a near miss,' said Otto.

'Really? I would have thought your best friend marrying your sister would please you.'

'It would have been a disaster. I love Erich dearly, and I think he was genuinely fond of Gisela. Still is. But he is constitutionally incapable of being faithful. And if he ever cheated on my sister, I would be furious.'

'Ah. I see what you mean.'

'I told him that.'

'You did?'

'Yes. I think that's why he didn't ask Gisela to marry him. I don't mean that he was scared of what I might do to him. He just knew I was right.'

'So, you warned him off your sister! Does she know that?'

'No. And don't tell her! But I think she realises that's why Erich didn't marry her.'

'Erich gets his wicked way with women?'

'Oh, yes. You know he was effectively drummed out of the army? He had an affair with a senior officer's wife the year after the war ended. He was only nineteen! She was thirty-four. I met her once, a beautiful woman. Anyway, there was a scandal that had to be hushed up. His father, who is a general, was furious. He and Erich have barely spoken since. Erich had to leave.'

'But I thought Erich used to work for General Schleicher?'

'Who hates Erich's father. Employing Erich as a civilian out of law school was revenge. It was tricky getting Hindenburg to take him on, but General Schleicher is very persuasive.'

'So Erich is Schleicher's man?'

'You could say that, yes.'

'It seems to be a bit of a tradition in the German army, junior officers having affairs with their elders' wives,' Esme said. She told Otto about the antics of Captain Dieskau in the Napoleonic Wars.

Otto laughed.

'Did Erich ever get his wicked way with Harriet, do you think?' Esme asked.

'I don't believe so. He tried – you must have seen him. She didn't encourage him, but then she didn't discourage him either.'

'That was Harriet.'

'She probably saw through him.'

'Perhaps. But then she chose Gray.' Esme shuddered.

'I would have thought he was quite a catch. He has plenty of charm. And he seems a nice man.'

Esme snorted. 'The man is a louse.'

Otto laughed. 'Erich is not exactly trustworthy, at least where women are concerned. But he's not a louse.'

They lay next to each other in silence for a couple of minutes, a woodpecker drumming against a nearby tree.

'I'm sorry about Harriet, Esme. I know she was such a good friend to you. And she was a special woman. Not just beautiful but... special.'

'She was, wasn't she?' said Esme.

'And for her to be murdered like that at Adlerstein!'

'I know. That must be horrid for you and for your mother.'

'It will be a bad way to leave it.'

'Leave it?' said Esme. 'Are you leaving Adlerstein?'

Otto got up on his elbows to face her. 'I think we're going to have to sell it.'

'No! What is it? The slump?'

'Yes,' said Otto. 'It's all hitting at the same time. Food prices are falling, which hurts the farms. The stock market is sliding. The banks, who used to be generous, are calling in their loans.

And the truth is my father did a pretty bad job of managing the estate for the last twenty years.'

'So you have to sell up?'

'Unless something turns up in the next couple of weeks, yes.'

'Oh, Otto! That must be dreadful for you!'

'It is. And for Mama. We are both doing our best. It's not just that it's a beautiful place. I feel like I have the responsibility of three centuries' worth of Adlersteins on my shoulders. I can imagine them all looking down on me from somewhere up there,' he raised a finger towards the sky high above the trees, 'urging me to stop being so useless and come up with something to save the place. My brothers too.'

'And there is nothing?'

'We got something from my mother's aunt, but not nearly enough. And, as I think you know, I invested in Wall Street stocks. Borrowed to do it. At first it seemed to be working really well. Then there was the crash in October last year, but then the shares went up again, and now they just seem to go down every day. And there's nothing I can do! Except sell them. And then there would be no chance of saving the castle.'

'Oh, Otto!' Esme reached across to touch his hand. 'I'm so sorry for you!'

'Don't worry,' said Otto. 'I told myself I would stop thinking about all that today and just enjoy myself. You never know, something may turn up.'

'You never know,' said Esme. But, actually, they both knew. Something wouldn't turn up.

'Thank you for your sympathy,' Otto said.

'It's not much.'

'It helps.'

There was silence between them. Esme's hand was still on Otto's.

He leaned forward. Esme was surprised, but then she wasn't surprised. Here we go, she thought. And why not?

They kissed.

Otto's kiss was tentative. Soft. Gentle. Rather nice.

Esme grabbed him behind the head and kissed him harder. Much harder.

They heard chatter coming up through the woods.

They broke away, a shy, surprised smile on Otto's lips.

Lordy, thought Esme. Where did that come from? She grinned. 'I like to help.'

44

Esme's mind was a mess. She had had fun that day with the other three. It had been a relief to forget for a couple of hours the fraught question of who really had killed Harriet.

And it had been fun kissing Otto. A baron, no less! Even if he rarely used that title. She had no idea where that would lead – probably nowhere – but it would be amusing to find out.

Otto was the first man she had kissed since Henry back in Chicago. At least she could be fairly certain that he didn't have a wife and daughter hidden away somewhere. Couldn't she?

She felt sorry for Otto, and for his sister and mother. The expectations of all those long-dead Adlersteins weighed heavily on him. There was nothing he could do, although betting on the stock market did not seem to Esme the best idea. She had seen first-hand in Chicago the dreams of so many so-called investors being shattered by the blows of the previous October. It was amazing how many people had bet their nest eggs on the stock market. Not just her dentist, but her dentist's nurse. Not just the top ad salesman at the *Mercury*, but the janitor who overheard tips from the business desk.

She was safe: she hadn't had any money to lose.

But as she returned to the Drydens' house, her thoughts turned to her trip to Rostock the following morning and the implications of what she had read in *The Times* report the previous day sank in.

Was Archie a murderer? And if he was, should she go to Rostock alone with him?

During a sleepless night, the answer seemed to be clearly no. Then the problem became how to get out of it. Archie would be justifiably angry; he had told her about how upset he had been when the secretary he had hired to accompany him to Germany had left him high and dry on the station platform in London.

That was exactly what she was planning to do.

But, as she began unpacking her bag the following morning, she thought again. Archie had always treated her well. She had no real idea whether the accusations against him were justified. He deserved a chance to give his side of the story.

So she would join him that morning, after all. Then, at the first opportunity in Rostock, she would ask him what had really happened. And, depending on his answers, she would either stay on as his research assistant or get the first train back to Berlin.

Despite having taken that decision, she was nervous as she carried her small suitcase through Stettin Station towards the platform to Rostock. But she felt a surge of relief when she spotted Archie's dapper figure with his walking stick.

Because, standing next to him, was the large, shambling form of Moses Garfinkel.

* * *

Archie was in an uncharacteristically good mood as he waited for Esme on the platform at Stettin Station. Once again, he had decided to leave Lister in Berlin, under strict instructions that he should behave himself. He had received a letter from Moses on Saturday morning to say that his uncle would allow him to join Archie on his trip to Rostock. He was looking forward to the company of a fellow bibliophile, even one as odd as Moses.

Archie was beginning to get to know Old Bluey. But he wouldn't really feel that he understood the man until he had seen where he came from, where he was born.

Rostock.

Esme seemed subdued as they climbed on the train, almost nervous. Perhaps she wasn't convinced that Lister really had scared off Liquorice Man. But she should be safer with Archie in Rostock than she was on the streets of Berlin.

They were installed, just the three of them, in their own compartment. Miles and miles of drab houses turned into the gentle green hills and lakes of Mecklenburg. Archie was reading up on the Battle of Lübeck, Esme had her nose in a detective story by Dashiell Hammett and Moses was going through a fifteenth-century book on botany, printed in Mainz and written in Latin, translating it to himself with barely perceptible movement of his lips.

Archie liked the idea that someone was treating these old books as books – to be read and enjoyed – rather than as trophies on shelves to be counted and admired. He had tried reading some of his grandfather's collection, but it was hard work and they were, let's be honest, a trifle dull. His Latin was scarcely up to it, and the fifteenth-century German, French or English wasn't much easier.

'I spoke to Schrör,' Archie said to Esme, in English. He wasn't sure how much English Moses understood, if any, but he had decided that there was no harm in Moses overhearing anything he and Esme might discuss about Harriet's murder. It probably wouldn't make any sense to him, and even if it did, who would he tell?

'Oh, yes?'

'Joe Moretti did visit Gray in Vienna and Ruth remembers Gray introducing him to Yevgeny in a bar there.'

'Introducing him?'

'Yes. Ruth didn't think that Joe and Yevgeny knew each other before then.'

'Perhaps that's how they met?' Esme said.

'Or perhaps they were simply pretending not to know each other.'

'It doesn't get us very far, does it?'

'No,' Archie agreed.

'And you didn't mention anything about Joe and Mr Dryden to Schrör?'

'Of course not,' said Archie with a touch of irritability. 'I said I wouldn't, didn't I? But I am worried about Ruth, as is Schrör. At some point we must tell Schrör what we know.'

'I guess so.' Esme glanced at Archie and then at Moses engrossed in his book. Archie gave her a slight nod to indicate that he thought it was all right for her to talk in front of the bookseller.

'I managed to slip Joe into a conversation with Mr Dryden at breakfast the other day. To see how he would react. Apparently, the police came around to ask if Harriet was a communist.'

'Not surprising, I suppose,' said Archie. 'Given what they think about Ruth.'

'Yes. So, I floated the idea that Joe might be one.'

'Good show. Did Dryden bite?'

'No. He's a diplomat, he's good at not biting.'

'Ah, well. Worth a stab.'

'Also, I saw Otto and Erich yesterday. Gisela came too. We went for a picnic by the Wannsee.'

'Ah! Did you learn anything?'

'I spoke to Otto. He confirmed that Erich and Gisela almost got engaged. Apparently, Otto warned Erich off. Thought he couldn't be trusted to stay away from other women.'

'That's probably true enough. Nothing about other men?'

'It wasn't the kind of thing I could ask,' Esme said. 'Apparently there was a scandal when Erich was in the army. He had an affair with a senior officer's wife and got himself thrown out. He is now very much General Schleicher's man.'

'Who is General Schleicher?'

'From what I can gather he acts like the political wing of the army. He was involved in the negotiations between the army and President Ebert at the birth of the Weimar Republic right after the war. He is an old friend of President Hindenburg's son. Whenever the army gets involved in politics, you can bet Schleicher is behind it.'

'Sounds like a good man to have as your mentor?'

'Absolutely. Otto suggested to me it was Schleicher who got Erich his job with Hindenburg. Also, you've heard these rumours about links between the Reichswehr and the Soviets?'

'That the Russians are training the German army and air force?'

'That's right. The talk is General Schleicher is behind that too.'

'I see. And would this General Schleicher be interested in what Walter Dryden had to say about American policy towards Germany?'

'He might. Although from what I can make out, what the Americans seem most concerned about is the repayment of loans doled out by American banks to the Germans over the last ten years.'

'Schleicher isn't a communist, is he?'

'No,' said Esme. 'The complete opposite. But, as Otto and Erich said, he might use the Soviets if they can help him build up his army.'

'If he's the opposite, could he be a Nazi?'

Esme considered the question. 'There's no doubt that many war veterans have become Nazis, and the Nazis want to rebuild the Reich and its army and repudiate Versailles and the reparations the Allies made the Germans pay them. But Hitler is an Austrian corporal; I'm not sure how Prussian generals feel about a man like that running their country. If the election on Sunday is close, Hindenburg may have to choose between a coalition including communists and one including Nazis. All the foreign correspondents are trying to guess which way he will go.'

'And how do the Americans fit into this?'

'Hard to say. They've been heavily involved in negotiations with the German government about the final payments of reparations from the war – much of which has been financed by American banks. The Nazis are against the plan; they don't think Germany should pay anything. I expect that's where the German government, or the Nazis, would have most interest – finding out what the Americans' negotiating strategy is. But of course, I don't know what secrets the Americans have any more than you do.'

'So we don't know if Erich is passing on Dryden's secrets to his own government or to the communists,' Archie said. 'Or maybe even the Nazis?'

'That's right.'

'And our hypothesis is that Harriet found out about it and threatened to expose Joe and Erich.'

'And so they killed her. Or had someone kill her.'

'We just don't know whether that happened,' said Archie. 'We need proof. If we're going to persuade the police to let Ruth go free, we are going to need proof.' He sighed. 'We're not going to find it in Rostock. Perhaps if we put it all to one side for a few days, things will seem clearer.'

'Perhaps.' Esme didn't seem hopeful. In fact, she seemed uncharacteristically unenthusiastic about finding her friend's murderer.

45

Rostock was a major German port for the Baltic, but it was situated a few miles inland, on the banks of the broad River Warnow. The sprawling town had an ancient medieval centre. They were booked into a small hotel in the Neuer Markt which, despite its name, was an old cobbled square surrounded by multicoloured brick houses and a formidable *Rathaus*.

Esme was still subdued. Fair enough, Archie supposed. If he was allowed his moods, then why shouldn't she be? Nevertheless, it made him realise how much he looked forward to her cheerfulness.

He invited Moses to join Esme and him for dinner, but Moses outright refused. Archie understood, but Esme put up a struggle, stopping just short of dragging Moses along with them. Moses was big and stubborn and there was nothing Esme could do.

Archie and Esme walked a couple of hundred yards to the Alter Markt – presumably even older than its Neuer companion – and found a restaurant opposite a church with a dizzying spire rising high above the town. A stiff breeze whipped in from the

Baltic, only a few miles away. Esme was silent. She looked troubled. And something else... frightened.

Part of Archie wanted to fight silence with silence: grumpiness with grumpiness. He didn't like being outgrumped. But he was worried.

'Why were you so keen for Moses to come with us?' he asked.

'It was only polite that he should join us.'

'It was polite for us to ask him. It wasn't particularly polite to refuse to let him say no.'

Esme looked up, staring straight into Archie's eyes. Her own blue eyes were fierce. Archie was taken aback.

'It was because of what I read in the Stabi on Saturday.'

'About Old Bluey? Wait a moment. We didn't go to the Stabi on Saturday.'

'I did. They carry back copies of the London *Times* there. I found the edition of 7 June 1923 very interesting.'

'Why? What happened then?' Archie said. Then he realised. He swallowed.

'There was a court report. Of a trial that had finished the day before at the Old Bailey. A murder trial.'

Archie didn't reply. He couldn't reply.

'Archie! You were on trial for murder!'

'I was. How did you find out?'

'Your mother told me.'

'Bloody woman.'

'And Claude Tazewell confirmed it.'

'Bloody man.'

'He's a journalist, Archie! It's his job to read the papers as well as write them!'

'I was found not guilty.'

'After the judge more or less told the jury to let you off. The tyre iron from your car was found with blood and hair on it! I understand that the judge thought you were a war hero and that the other guy was a coward, but that didn't mean you didn't kill him.'

'Daphne said it was an accident.'

'Which was very nice of Daphne. You didn't testify, did you?'

'No,' said Archie.

'Well?'

'Well, what?'

'Well, did you kill that poor man? What was his name – Victor Radway?'

'I didn't testify at my trial and I'm not testifying now.'

'So you didn't do it?'

'I didn't say that.'

'So, you *did* do it.'

'I didn't say that either.'

Esme's eyes were on fire. 'Look, Archie. I need to know whether you are a murderer. I am here, right now, with you, alone apart from Moses. That's why I wanted him to come with us this evening. That's why I almost didn't come with you this morning. I'm scared, Archie. And I will continue to be scared until you tell me you didn't kill that man.'

She didn't look scared. She looked angry. But Archie understood her point.

'Just trust me, Esme. I am not a killer.' He winced. 'Outside war.'

'So you *didn't* kill Radway?'

Archie shook his head.

'Who did, then? What happened?'

'That's what I can't say. I won't say.'

'Oh, Archie!' The waiter arrived at their table and opened a bottle of hock. He read the atmosphere, poured the wine as quickly as he could and withdrew.

'Harriet would be furious if she knew I was travelling around Germany with a murderer. So would my mother. In fact, I'm pretty darned angry about it myself.'

'I see that,' said Archie. 'But can't you trust me? If I say I didn't kill anyone, can't you just believe me?'

'No,' said Esme. She took a gulp of wine. 'And unless you can come up with a full explanation, I will take the first train back to Berlin tomorrow morning.'

'I'm not a murderer,' said Archie. 'But even if I was, why would I harm you? Victor Radway was a friend of mine and he slept with my wife. He made me very angry. You're not going to do anything like that, are you?'

'Archie. I have seen you lose control of yourself before. If I continue to work for you, I am sure I will see you lose control of yourself again. And, frankly, I don't know what you will do next time. What you are capable of doing.'

'I-I didn't kill Victor Radway.'

'Then who did? Was it an accident?'

Archie didn't answer. He couldn't answer that question.

'Very well. Enjoy your dinner. I'm going back to the hotel now.'

'No, Esme!'

'Yes!'

'I-I'll walk you back.'

'I'd feel a helluva lot safer if you didn't.'

46

Archie had a bad night. It was his worst since Silesia.

He got out his chess set and played through the seventeen-move Paris Opera game three times. Then he played Réti versus Tartakower from 1910 and Lasker versus Thomas from 1912. Then he tried to go to sleep. Then he got up and leafed through his chess book for another game to memorise. He decided on Wilhelm Steinitz versus Curt von Bardeleben, which had been played at Hastings in 1895. The game had lasted twenty-five moves and then Bardeleben had simply walked out, not even bothering to resign. Steinitz showed later that there was an inevitable checkmate in ten moves. Plenty for Archie to get his teeth into.

Eventually, sometime after two o'clock, Archie crawled into bed and fell asleep.

And then Lieutenant Dowling visited him. Lieutenant Dowling had a lot to say.

Archie could barely keep his eyes open as he ordered coffee at breakfast the following morning in the hotel dining room. Alone.

Moses didn't join him, which wasn't surprising. Archie had hoped that Esme would look for him on her way out at least to say goodbye, but there was no sign of her.

He opened his trusty *Battles of the Napoleonic Wars* by Odeleben, more as an alibi than anything else – to show that he was happy to be breakfasting alone. He had read the section on the Lübeck campaign so many times he more or less had it by heart.

'You look terrible.'

He raised his eyes to see Esme looking down at him. 'Mind if I join you?'

'Please do,' he said, gesturing to the two empty chairs at his table.

'Playing chess last night, were you?'

'Yes. As a matter of fact, I was.' Esme seemed in a good mood as she grabbed some pumpernickel and buttered it thoroughly before laying some Westphalian ham and cheese on top of it. A good German breakfast.

'You know,' she said. 'You should trust me. You ask me to trust you, but you don't trust me.'

'I do trust you, Esme.'

'Not enough to tell me what happened when that man was killed in 1923.'

Archie could feel his shoulders tightening. Esme was right, of course.

'I can't tell you. I'm sorry, Esme, I just can't.'

'You see, that's just unfair,' Esme said, but despite her words, her tone was light. 'Because, you see, I do trust you. Poor fool that I am, I just don't think you are going to do away with me over the next three days.'

'That isn't really the plan,' Archie said.

'Glad to hear it. In that case, I will stay, and listen to your ramblings and write them all down and pretend not to be bored. And look out for Moses if you are mean to him.'

'I have no intention of being mean to Moses,' Archie protested.

'Glad to hear that too.'

Archie felt a wave of relief wash over him. He was surprised how much he had wanted Esme to stay. But he couldn't let her see that, so he kept his face frozen.

'Well?'

'Well, what?'

'Well, are you pleased I am not scuttling back to Berlin?'

'I... ah?'

Esme burst into laughter at his confusion.

He grinned broadly. He just couldn't help it. 'Yes, Esme, I am very pleased. Thank you for trusting me.'

'You promise not to whack me over the head with a stray Napoleonic cannonball?'

'I promise.'

'Do you swear on Old Bluey's pointy moustache?'

'I swear on his pointy moustache.'

'And his too-tight cavalry pants?'

'And his too-tight cavalry trousers.'

'"Pants". You have to say "pants".'

Archie sighed deeply and winced. 'And his too-tight cavalry pants.'

Esme nodded and shoved the pumpernickel into her mouth. 'That's all right then.'

Archie sipped his coffee. 'You seem in a good mood.'

Esme grinned. 'I am,' she said, reaching into her bag. 'Look at this.'

It was a telegram.

RECEIVED REWORKED HITLER INTERVIEW STOP GOOD JOB PRINTING TUES STOP NEED ARTICLE ON VOTERS IN ELECTION AS SEEN BY CHICAGO GIRL FOR NEXT MONDAY STOP RGRDS D FINNEGAN

'Tuesday! That's today!'

'Congratulations!' Archie said. 'Why did he change his mind?'

'I did what Annachiara suggested. Wrote about my impressions of Hitler as an American girl. I'd like to talk to some people on the street here in Rostock if I can. You don't mind, do you?'

'That should be possible. I plan to visit the two antiquarian bookshops here with Moses. You can do it then.'

'Swell. So what are we doing today?'

47

Gisela hurried out of the courthouse at Moabit and took a bus to Wedding. She didn't have much time – she had got Helga to cover for her while her judge was at lunch.

Wedding was an area of usually drab five-storey tenements, home to workers in Berlin's factories. Except many of its inhabitants were no longer workers; they had been thrown out by their employers cutting back or closing down. And the tenements were no longer uniformly drab. With the election less than a week away, large banners hung from windows and on every pillar or stretch of bare wall posters were plastered.

The predominant colour was red. The red and yellow of the hammer and sickle. Or, in some places, the red and black of the swastika.

The café Gisela was looking for was in Wiesenstrasse, a street that favoured workmen's tools over crooked crosses. She felt immediately self-conscious as she entered wearing the smart grey suit she wore for work; the barman and the half-dozen male patrons all stared at her. All, that is, apart from a young man with close-cropped fair hair and a barrel chest sitting alone at a small table behind a small glass of beer; his eyes flickered only briefly towards her. A red mark sat angrily on his left cheek.

'That's quite a bruise you have there, Herr Walch,' she said.

'I could say the same about you.'

Gisela's hand touched her eye. 'I did that myself,' she said. 'With a rolling pin, actually. I wanted them to think you had attacked me.'

'Did it work?'

'It seemed to. It hurt, though.'

'I bet it did. But then so do my injuries. Most of them you can't see. But I can hardly walk.'

'What happened?'

'Some crazy Tommy went for me. And his German boyfriend in a dress. He works for that American girl I was supposed to frighten. Or he's her friend: one or the other.'

'Big guy, was he?'

'No. Small and fast and mean.' Walch winced, stretched and held his back. 'Have you got the second hundred?'

'But you haven't finished yet!'

'Oh, yes, I have.' He took a tin from his pocket and popped a liquorice in his mouth without offering one to Gisela. For which she was grateful.

'You are not scared of him, are you? A big chap like you?'

'I am, a little bit, as a matter of fact. Point is, you were going to pay me two hundred marks for scaring a defenceless girl. I want a lot more than that for tussling with a vicious nutcase. Plus I didn't tell him who had sent me. So I saved your arse at the courthouse.'

'Thank you. Would you do it for more money?'

'Actually, come to think about it, no.'

'Do you know someone who would?'

'How much have you got?'

Otto could rustle up a worthless castle attached to a few hundred thousand in mortgage debt, Gisela thought. But cash?

'Three hundred?'

Walch shook his head. 'Forget it. No one is going to help you for three hundred.'

Gisela considered walking out of the café there and then. But leaving Fritz Walch empty-handed was not a wise idea, however badly beaten up he was. He was a regular customer of the Moabit Courthouse, which was how Gisela had found him, and he could easily get her fired. Or he could simply beat *her* up.

'I don't have the money with me now. It's at home. I'll give it to you here this time next week.'

'Tomorrow.'

'Next week. I don't have it now, Herr Walch.'

Fritz Walch grunted. Given the way his eyes drifted over her body, Gisela had the feeling he had a soft spot for her.

He leaned forward. Gisela could smell that disgusting liquorice. 'All right. I'll see you here. This time next week.'

* * *

As she hopped off the bus outside the courthouse, she stopped at a telephone kiosk.

'Otto? It's Gisela. I need to talk to you.'

48

Esme was the first one downstairs in the small hotel lobby. It had been a busy three days.

On the first day, they had wandered around Rostock to get a feel for the place, then taken a ferry over the river and a taxi to the village of Toitenwinkel just on the edge of the town towards the sea, where Blücher had been born. In the afternoon, they dropped in on a history professor from the university, which stood on the aptly named Blücher Platz. He droned on for an hour and a half about the general. Esme found him arrogant and boring and was pleased to learn afterwards that Archie thought the same.

The next day, they took a train to Lübeck, about seventy miles to the west along the Baltic coast, where they ate marzipan. And traipsed around fields and ditches and city walls. The Battle of Lübeck was *complicated*. Old Bluey had lost that one: one of many. Esme was beginning to suspect he might not have been such great shakes as a general after all. Moses scouted out the antiquarian book dealers in town, but came away empty-handed.

On the third day, Archie and Moses scurried off to old bookshops while Esme roamed the streets accosting innocent Rostockers and asking them how they were going to vote and why. She found the question 'Can you explain to an American girl what this election is about?' provoked some interesting answers. Far more people than she had expected thought that the election was about making Germany strong again and that Hitler was the man to do it.

Worrying, that.

There were also a surprising number of comments about cowboys. The Germans seemed to have a thing about cowboys, and enjoyed the opportunity of speaking to an American about them. Although Esme knew a lot about ranch hands from her childhood in Montana – and about Indians for that matter – they were an entirely different species from the men the Germans read about, or saw on their movie screens.

Archie had shown no inclination to murder her. But she was still angry that he hadn't told her why he was innocent, if he really was innocent. Esme needed to know.

A telegraph boy hurried into the hotel and passed an envelope to the manager behind the desk.

'It's for you, Fräulein Carmichael.'

Esme opened it. It was in English. And it was from Otto.

CAN I SEE YOU WHEN YOU GET BACK TO BERLIN TONIGHT IF POSSIBLE QUERY SOMETHING IMPORTANT TO TELL YOU STOP O

Esme wondered what that could be? It sounded like it was more than simply wanting to ask her out for the evening. If Otto had information he wanted to give her, it was probably related to Harriet's death.

And Esme definitely wanted to hear it.

She asked the boy to wait while she drafted a response. Yes, she would meet him that evening. He should leave a message where and when at the Drydens' house. She was curious how he had known where to find her. Although she had told him she was going to Rostock with Archie, she hadn't told him which hotel they were staying at, nor when they were returning to Berlin.

In the short taxi ride to the station, Esme told Archie that Otto had asked to see her back in Berlin that evening. Archie's curiosity was piqued, but they didn't have time to discuss it. Once again, they had a compartment to themselves on the train.

Moses opened up one of the two books Archie had bought in Rostock, a copy of Ovid's epic poem *Metamorphoses*, written in Latin and printed in Rostock in 1480.

'Good book?' Esme asked.

Moses's eyes flickered upward for the briefest of moments, but then returned to the page.

Esme ploughed on. 'He's pretty racy, I hear, Ovid? I've never read him. Have you read any, Archie?'

'Yes. At school.'

'Would you recommend it, Moses?'

Moses didn't reply, but the level of his concentration on the Gothic type in front of him seemed to intensify.

'Don't tease him, Esme.'

'I'm not teasing him, Archie! I think it's wonderful that someone actually reads these old books. Have you read many of them, Moses?'

Moses's eyes flicked back to Esme again and then returned to the book.

Suddenly, Esme knew how to hook him. 'How many incunabula have you read?'

Now Moses looked at her. 'Three thousand six hundred and twelve. This is the three thousand six hundred and thirteenth.'

Esme's jaw dropped. She glanced at Archie. 'That's a lot of books. Where did you read them all?'

'The Saxon State Library mostly; they have two thousand one hundred and twenty-six. I have made friends with the librarians there. And of course I read all of those that pass through my uncle's hands.'

'And you understand the Latin?'

'Yes. And Greek and English and French and Dutch and Italian and Spanish.'

'Lordy! Who taught you all these languages?'

'I left school at fourteen and went to work in my uncle's shop. I taught myself the languages.' A barely discernible but very real note of pride crept into Moses's voice. 'With dictionaries from the library.'

Esme eyed him. 'And do you have a target, Moses? For how many incunabula you want to read. How many are there out there?'

'About thirty thousand.' Moses hesitated. 'I would like to read all of them, but I know that will be impossible. Maybe ten thousand in my lifetime.'

'And you are counting?'

'Yes. I am counting. Prinz Eugen is supposed to have read the entire contents of his library in Vienna. That was fifteen thousand books.'

'And when you heard that, you wanted to do the same?' said Esme.

Moses smiled shyly.

'You mean Eugene, Prince of Savoy?' said Archie. 'The Austrian general?'

'That is correct,' said Moses. 'He was one of the greatest book collectors of the seventeenth century.'

'And a pretty good general too,' said Archie.

'There you are, Archie,' said Esme. 'A general who collects books. Tailor-made for you!'

Archie nodded. 'I don't know much about him, but he does sound interesting.'

Moses went back to his book.

'What do you think Otto wants to tell you?' Archie asked Esme.

'I don't know,' Esme replied. 'It must be about Harriet's murder.' There was absolutely no need for Archie to know about the kiss by the little lake near Wannsee. The more Esme thought about it, the less likely she believed Otto's message had anything to do with that.

It would be nice to see him again, though. She suspected he thought the same.

'Maybe he's found something out about Erich?' Archie said. 'If Erich had told the German government about American intentions, Otto might have heard about it. Put two and two together.'

'And thought it had something to do with Harriet's murder?'

'It's possible.'

'Using Joe to extract information from a supposedly friendly diplomat doesn't sound like something the Weimar government would do,' Esme said. 'Otto would know. Perhaps I'll have a chance to ask him tonight.'

'What do you mean?'

'That seems to me quite an aggressive form of spying. The kind of thing the Russians might do.'

'But not the Germans?'

'In 1916, maybe. Not in 1930, no.'

'Perhaps,' said Archie. 'If you are right, that leaves us with Erich feeding Joe's information to the communists. Yevgeny, perhaps?'

'I wonder if Otto found out something about that?'

They sat in silence, thinking it through.

Moses coughed.

They both turned to look at him. He opened his mouth and closed it again.

'Moses?' Archie said, his voice low, warm, coaxing.

The mouth opened.

'Have you understood our conversation?' Archie asked in German.

Moses immediately looked guilty and turned away.

'It's all right if you have,' said Archie. 'We trust you.'

'Do you have something helpful for us?' Esme asked. 'We would like to hear it if you do.'

Archie nodded his agreement.

Moses turned and stared at a point between the two of them.

'I have understood what you have been saying,' Moses said in German. 'I was listening on the train coming to Rostock. I told you I can read English, but I cannot speak it. You two speak clearly, so I can understand you. It is about the murder of a friend, I think?'

'Yes. That's right.'

'And you think blackmail is involved?'

'Possibly.'

'And your friend Harriet discovered it, tried to stop it and was murdered?'

'It's no more than a working hypothesis,' said Archie. 'But yes, that's about the size of it.'

'Have you considered money?'

'Money?'

'Yes. That the blackmailer wanted money. Not secrets.'

'You mean Joe and Erich wanted money?'

'Perhaps. But the more likely thing is, I should think, that someone saw Joe and Herr Dryden together and blackmailed them for money. That is what blackmailers often want, I believe. In which case, there are no American secrets involved at all.'

Archie turned to Esme. 'The Drydens' maid?'

'Ida? If she had been blackmailing Mr Dryden for money, she would never have told me what she had seen,' said Esme.

'You know Harriet was murdered by someone at the castle,' Moses continued. 'So who at the castle needed money? And who did not have an alibi when Harriet was killed?'

'It's worth a thought,' said Archie. 'We have assumed that Joe was getting information from Dryden.'

'But what if he wasn't?' said Esme. 'What if someone knew about Mr Dryden and Joe and blackmailed Mr Dryden?'

'Or Joe?'

Esme snorted. 'There would be no point in blackmailing Joe. He wouldn't care if the world knew he was homosexual.'

'You're right: Dryden, then. Harriet found out about the blackmailer, tried to put a stop to it, and was shot.'

'So who at the castle needed money badly enough to blackmail for it?' Esme asked. But as soon as the question was out of her mouth, Esme knew the answer.

But she couldn't admit it. Not to herself. Not to Archie.

'Let's go through them,' Archie said. 'I doubt Joe himself has very much money, so he's a possibility. Perhaps Gray has money problems? Or Annachiara? I don't know about Duncan's personal finances, but I do know his family are not short of a bob or two. There would be no reason for Otto to blackmail anyone, would there? He's just inherited a whole castle.'

Esme took a deep breath. 'There might be,' she said quietly.

'What do you mean?'

'Otto is going to have to sell the castle. Possibly in the next couple of weeks.'

'How do you know?'

'He told me. Last weekend. He's desperately worried about it.'

'Good Lord! Hang on a minute! Didn't he say he had invested in the American stock market? After I thanked my mother for getting me out before the crash?'

'He did. It's not just that. The Adlerstein estate has large debts: Otto's father did a bad job of managing it.'

'And he died and only then did his poor family discover how bad things were,' Archie said. 'I've heard that story a dozen times.'

'So Otto needed the money,' said Esme. 'But I can't for a minute think he was capable of blackmail, let alone of killing Harriet!'

'I know. But that's been the difficulty from the start, hasn't it? Nobody can believe that anyone at the castle was capable of shooting her. But she's dead.'

'Even so.' Esme had a sudden desire to tell Archie that she had kissed Otto, therefore she knew for certain he wasn't a murderer, but she knew that wouldn't wash with him.

And, actually, it shouldn't wash with her.

'Otto doesn't have a terribly good alibi for the morning, does he?' said Archie. 'He was in the estate office alone, I think.'

'That's right,' said Esme. 'But it doesn't prove anything. I don't think we should dismiss the idea that Joe was passing on information from Dryden to Erich and through him to someone else.'

'No, we shouldn't. But I must say I still think Otto's in the frame.' Archie turned to Moses. 'Thank you, Moses,' he said in German.

Moses shifted uncomfortably in his seat and looked down again at the book on his lap.

Esme searched around for a straw to cling to. 'If Otto was blackmailing Dryden, what information could he have to help me?'

'Perhaps he wants to shut you up too?' Archie said.

'That's ridiculous!'

'Is it? Maybe you shouldn't see him alone.'

'I'll be careful. I'll go to a public place. You know Otto. He's hardly scary. I'll be fine.'

'I'll come with you.'

'No, Archie. He would be more likely to tell me something if I'm alone.'

'Then I'll watch you.'

'He'll spot you.'

'Then *Lister* will watch you.'

Esme hesitated.

'You will be safer. And I don't think Otto has ever met Lister.'

'No, I don't think he has.' Esme still couldn't believe that Otto was a threat, but Archie clearly could and maybe he had a point. 'I'll telephone you with the place and time we are going to meet and you can send Lister along.'

49

There were two messages waiting for Esme when she got back to the Drydens' house in Hohenzollernstrasse.

The first was a wire from Otto suggesting they meet at the Herren-Club Bar at the Excelsior Hotel at 7 p.m. Esme immediately telephoned the Adlon to leave a message for Archie letting him know.

The second was from Annachiara inviting Esme to join her at the Taverne restaurant later that evening. All the foreign correspondents would be meeting there to discuss the election, which was only days away now. Annachiara would save a seat for Esme. There was no point in arriving until ten: these journalist dinners took place late, after the correspondents had had a chance to file their stories for the day.

Pleased that she should be able to keep both appointments, Esme left a message at Annachiara's office that she would see her at the Taverne later.

Mr Dryden would be out that evening, at a dinner at the British embassy. Before Esme had left for Rostock, he had asked her to accompany him. It was awkward. Esme was flattered. She was also uncomfortable that she was taking the place of Harriet as hostess and daughter. She liked Mr Dryden, she wanted to help him, but that didn't quite feel right.

This time, she had used the excuse of not knowing what time she would be getting back from Rostock to turn him down. Next time?

She didn't know what to think about Mr Dryden. She still felt so sorry for him after the loss of first his wife and then his daughter. His clinch with Joe left her perplexed; she just couldn't understand it. If Archie was right, and Mr Dryden had knowingly passed on American secrets to Joe, then he had indeed betrayed his country and that was not good at all.

But until Archie or someone else had proved that to her, Esme's instincts were to help and protect him, just as his daughter would have done.

If she had still been alive.

* * *

The Excelsior was huge – the biggest hotel in Europe. It stood opposite the massive Anhalter Station; the hotel was big and ugly on the outside, but elegant inside. It had recently been celebrated in Vicki Baum's novel *Grand Hotel*, which had been published the year before and which Harriet had recommended to Esme. Esme hadn't read it yet: it was on her bookshelf.

Esme arrived at the Herren-Club Bar at five after seven, but saw no sign of Otto. She did, however, spot Lister, who was sitting at a table, reading a copy of *The Times* and managing to look like an English gentleman rather than an English manservant.

Esme scanned the room, searching for somewhere to sit. There was an empty round-backed bar stool by the bar, next to some loud businessmen. Lister caught her eye, and stood, leaving the table vacant. Esme made a beeline for it and managed to outstare a middle-aged man with a tiny moustache who tried to grab it first.

She pulled out *The Maltese Falcon*, but her eyes couldn't focus. She wondered why Otto wanted to see her. Did he have interesting information? Did he want to threaten her? Was it a trap of some kind?

Could she trust him?

Could she trust anyone? Not just Otto, but Joe. Annachiara. Archie. Even Mr Dryden.

She hated it. She was not a naturally suspicious woman. She was trusting and she liked being that way. She had decided to trust Archie. She would give Mr Dryden the benefit of the doubt. And now she decided she would trust Otto.

She wasn't sure whether she was attracted to him. He was nowhere near as good-looking as Erich, for example. But he seemed real. His smile was real. His anxiety about his castle was real. His loyalty to the Weimar regime was real. His interest in her was real. She *liked* him. And she knew he wasn't a liar.

But where was he?

She ordered a glass of white wine and buried her nose in her book. Two men came to try their luck – one of them was the same age as her father – but she shooed them away. She noticed Lister had found himself another table at the opposite side of the bar.

Still no sign of Otto.

It was pretty rude of him to leave a girl alone in a bar for an hour. Otto didn't strike her as being rude. Perhaps he had left a message?

She stood up and checked with the barman who said there was nothing for her. Then she moved over to Lister's table. She still had a couple of hours before she was due at the Taverne.

Lister flicked his copy of *The Times*.

'Can I buy you a drink, Lister?'

'I don't think that would be appropriate, miss.'

'Wouldn't it? All the better then. Is that a whisky?'

Lister grinned. 'Yes, it is, miss.'

Esme waylaid a waiter and asked him for two large ones. She leaned forward. 'Now then. Give me the dope on your boss.'

'That I definitely can't do.'

Esme sized him up; Lister could bend most rules, but his loyalty was unimpeachable. 'All right, then, Lister. Or Arthur. It is Arthur, isn't it? Tell me about yourself.'

50

Esme walked the half hour from the Excelsior Hotel to the Taverne restaurant in Kurfürstenstrasse to try to clear her head. She was feeling slightly woozy after drinking on an empty stomach. She was still annoyed with Otto for standing her up, but she thought she had made an ally of Arthur Lister.

He had grown up in Leeds. His father had been a mailman, or postman as he called it, and Lister had followed in his father's footsteps, while 'taking advantage of other opportunities that presented themselves', which presumably meant swiping stuff. He had volunteered in 1915, had been gassed in Flanders a few months later, but had returned to the lines and become Archie's servant, responsible for bringing him a cup of tea every morning. And other things.

He had tried but failed to get a job back in Leeds after the war. The Post Office didn't want him any more and neither did anyone else. Too many demobbed soldiers and too many empty factories in the post-war slump. So, eventually, he had taken a train to the village of Kettlethwaite in Nidderdale and presented himself to Archie at Yarmer Hall.

At that time, Archie was still married and living in London, and his father was alive and presiding over the Yarmer estate. Fortunately for Lister, Archie was staying at Yarmer Hall for a week and decided to take on Lister as his valet. Not that he really needed a valet. But he did need Lister.

The old baronet, Sir Bertram, died, Archie got divorced from Daphne and Lister had found himself in charge of Yarmer Hall, having edged out the old butler.

Esme had tried to ask about Archie, but failed miserably. When she had inquired about a murder trial, Lister had said with a straight face that he knew nothing about Sir Archibald's legal affairs. Obviously, he did know all about it, but he wasn't telling.

She told him about Archie's escapade in the cow field, hoping to provoke similar stories, but Lister simply thanked her for helping him. He meant it. Lister was evidently a rogue, but a loyal rogue.

Esme liked him.

She gathered herself outside the Taverne. She was nervous. She wasn't yet a proper foreign correspondent. She had come twice before, with Harriet, when she had simply been Harriet's friend. Now, without her, she felt like an imposter. But she was grateful to Annachiara for inviting her and she was determined to make the most of the opportunity. And she had had that interview with Hitler published!

She *was* a foreign correspondent and she should darn well act like one.

The Taverne was an old wooden Italian restaurant with low ceilings and a loud clientele. She cut through the fug of cigarette smoke and beer fumes to the journalists' *Stammtisch*, a large round table in the corner, which was kept free for them. Fortunately, Annachiara was already there. She smiled and indicated the empty chair she had saved for Esme next to her.

Claude Tazewell removed his pipe and offered her a grin, Gray ignored her and Joe, who had the seat next to her on her other side, gave her a warm smile. Everyone who was anyone among the foreign correspondents in Berlin was there: Sigrid Schultz of one of the big Chicago papers, Birchell of the *New York Times* and Sefton Delmer of the London *Daily Express*.

But Esme's attention was gripped by the woman sitting opposite her, with a large round jaw, a small mouth and tiny quick eyes that darted around the table, briefly resting on Esme before moving on.

Susan Abchurch.

The talk was all about Sunday's election, which parties would get how many seats, how the communists and the Nazis would do, whether Brüning would remain Chancellor and what role President Hindenburg would play, if any. Annachiara thought there was a chance that the Nazis might attempt to take power by force if they did well in the polls and were kept out of government, but the rest of the table seemed to think this unlikely.

Gray Trexler said that a contact of his had seen Erich von Witzbach having dinner with Hermann Göring at Horcher's two days before.

'And who is Erich von Witzbach?' asked Susan Abchurch.

'Oh. He's President Hindenburg's secretary,' said Esme, quickly before anyone else could answer her.

'Do you know him?'

'Yes,' Esme said. 'That is, we all do.' She realised this was a stupid answer. 'I mean my friends and me.'

'Your friends? And who are you, my dear?'

'Esme Carmichael.' Esme smiled. 'I'm trying to become a foreign correspondent.'

Susan frowned. 'Did you write a piece for the *Mercury*? About an interview with Hitler?'

'Yes, I did,' said Esme, feeling at the same moment proud and scared, like a nervous student handing her finals paper to a professor.

'Tell me. How on earth did *you* get an interview with Hitler?'

'Through Putzi Hanfstaengl,' said Esme. 'And my friend Harriet Dryden who put in a good word for me.'

'I read your piece,' said Susan, her deep voice capturing the attention of all those seated around the table. 'It was a wasted opportunity. It was fluff. The world wants to know what Hitler is going to do next: the world *needs* to know, and instead you give them fluff.'

'Come on, Susan!' said Annachiara, her dark eyes flashing. 'I read it too. It was good. It was different. She did much more than parrot a Hitler rant. Any of us can go to the Sportspalast and hear one of those.'

'We shouldn't put up with it,' said Gray. 'Interviews like that must be given to experienced journalists. Not amateurs. Someone's got to tell Putzi.'

Esme's face stung.

Claude Tazewell puffed at his pipe. 'I expect that's the point,' he said. Everyone turned to him with respect. 'Putzi wants to show us his power. That *he* has Hitler's ear. He decides who has access. I don't think we can blame Esme for that.'

Susan frowned again at her and then turned to accept a plate piled full of spaghetti from the waitress.

'She's just jealous,' whispered Joe, pouring red wine into Esme's glass and filling it to the top. 'I read your article too. It was really very good!'

Esme smiled at Joe. 'Thanks,' she said. He offered his glass and Esme clinked it.

He didn't seem drunk to her, but perhaps that was because she was, after all that whisky she had consumed with Lister.

A middle-aged woman in a grey skirt, her long brown hair packed up in a bun, approached the table and signalled to Claude Tazewell, who excused himself and joined her on the street. A tipster, no doubt, perhaps a telephone operator, with a morsel of information for him. Private information.

'Susan Abchurch is an idol of mine,' Esme said to Joe. 'I saw her give a lecture at the University of Chicago and since then I've wanted to be a foreign correspondent. To do what you do.'

'You went to Chicago?'

'I did. Did you?'

'Yes. But only for a year. I volunteered for the war, spent a year in a German prisoner-of-war camp and then got a job on a paper in Ohio. So I never graduated. But I had a helluva good time in that one year.'

'It was fun,' said Esme. 'That's where I met Harriet.'

'Of course!' Joe sipped his wine thoughtfully. 'That must be tough for her family.'

'Yes,' said Esme. 'As you know, she lost her mother last year. But her father has taken it very badly. Do you know him?'

'Yes. Yes, I do.' To her surprise, Joe hadn't denied it, or claimed only a passing knowledge. 'You're living with him, aren't you? How is he coping?' Joe's large brown eyes were watching her intently. A lock of hair hung down over one eyebrow. Esme felt an odd desire to reach over and brush it back.

'He's wounded,' she said. 'The loss of his wife hurt him badly, and now this. He puts on a brave front. He's so correct and dapper he wouldn't want to show that he is any way debilitated by what has happened, but he is. There is a portrait of his wife in his study – she was a beautiful woman and looked a lot like Harriet. He spends hours just staring at it.'

'I know the picture,' said Joe.

'I feel so badly for him.'

Joe looked at Esme steadily. 'So do I.'

'Do you?' she said.

Joe looked around the table. 'We're not going to learn anything more here this evening and they've already humiliated you. Do you want to join me for a walk? I like walking around Berlin at night.'

'Sure,' said Esme. 'That would be nice.'

51

Esme's cheeks were burning in the restaurant, whether from the heat, the stifling atmosphere or her humiliation at the hands of Susan Abchurch, she didn't know. But the night air cooled them down.

Joe led her off the neon-dazzled Kurfürstenstrasse towards the Landwehr canal. Although it was late, this being Berlin there were plenty of people about, many of them unsavoury, but they left Esme and Joe alone.

They walked along the canal in silence, strangely comfortable in each other's company. Yellow gaslight slid across the dark water, cutting through wisps of mist. The branches of the chestnut trees on either bank stretched across the canal towards each other above their heads. A young man wearing a flat cap hissed at them; it was unclear whether he was selling himself or something else. They ignored him.

Eventually, Esme spoke.

'I know about you and Mr Dryden,' she said.

'I rather thought you might,' said Joe. 'How do you know?'

'The Drydens' maid saw you. In the library late one night. Kissing.'

'Did she? Oh dear. I remember we left the door open – that was stupid. But it was late.'

'It wasn't just the maid,' said Esme. 'Harriet saw you too.'

'Harriet?' Joe turned to Esme, wincing. 'That's not good. Did she tell you?'

'No. But the maid saw her running upstairs upset.'

'I'll bet she was upset. We shouldn't have left that door open.'

'No, you shouldn't have,' said Esme. And then, more softly: 'How did it happen?'

'How did we fall in love?'

The rephrasing of Esme's question surprised her. 'Were you in love?'

'Yes,' said Joe. 'We were. We are. I am. Men can be in love with other men, you know?'

'Er, yes,' said Esme. 'I'm sure.' Then she decided to be honest. 'Actually, I don't know. I don't understand it at all.'

'I wasn't Walter's first male lover, but I was the first since he married Rose. When she died, he needed comfort. Release. Love. I gave it to him.'

'I suppose I see that,' Esme said hesitantly. 'And what did he give you?'

'The same, I guess. And a feeling of security. I like him. I love him. He's strong, yet vulnerable at the same time. He needs me. And you've got to admit he's good-looking.'

'For an older guy perhaps.'

'We met at his house in Hohenzollernstrasse. Harriet had invited me, Gray, Otto and Otto's sister round for dinner one evening. Gray had put her up to it – Walter is stand-offish with the press and Gray wanted to develop him as a contact. I could tell right away that Walter was interested in me, probably before he could. I could also tell that he wasn't going to be easy. But I wanted him. I really wanted him.'

Joe sighed. 'And he wanted me. I invited him out to lunch one day, ostensibly to ask him questions about the book I'm supposed to be writing. It was around the corner from my place in Kreuzberg. I asked him if he'd like to come up and see my apartment; I said I had some articles about the Fascists in Rome I wanted to show him. He could easily have refused, but he agreed. And that was that.'

'Are you still seeing him?'

'No,' said Joe. 'No. A couple of weeks ago, he called it off. It was just before Harriet was killed.'

'Why?'

'He said it was because he thought it was wrong.'

'You say "he said"? Do you think that's not the real reason?'

'It may be, I guess. But I believe there was something else. After Harriet was murdered, I tried to see him again. I was worried about him. I wanted to comfort him. But he refused to meet me.'

'Do you think the reason he wanted to stop seeing you might be that he was being blackmailed?'

Joe stopped and stared at Esme. 'Blackmailed?'

'We think he was being blackmailed.'

'I'll be damned! By who? The maid?'

'No. I'm sure the maid hasn't told anyone but me.' Esme was reluctant to pass on Archie's suspicion that it might have been Otto. 'We don't know who it was.'

'By "we" who do you mean?'

'Archie and me. We are sure that the woman the Saxon police have arrested for Harriet's murder is innocent.'

'And you think it had something to do with blackmail?'

'We do,' said Esme. 'So Mr Dryden didn't give you any indication at all that anyone was putting the squeeze on him?'

Joe shook his head. 'No. But, as you say, that could be a reason why he chucked me.'

'Do you have a similar relationship with Erich von Witzbach?'

Joe laughed. 'I wish. Whatever made you think that?'

'Duncan Mandeville says he saw you leaving Erich's bedroom at the castle the night before Harriet died.'

'Oh, that! I was drunk. It was a couple of days after Walter had given me the heave-ho. I thought I would try my luck with Erich. I knew it wouldn't work – I'd tried it before. But I thought what the hell? So I knocked on his door in the middle of the night.'

'And?'

'And he told me to beat it. In the nicest possible way. So I beat it.'

'So you haven't been giving Erich information, then?'

'What kind of information?' Then Joe frowned. 'Oh, I see. You think I was pumping Walter for American state secrets and then passing them on to my lover, Erich, who was giving them to – who? President Hindenburg?'

'Or the Russians.'

Joe laughed, but it was a bitter laugh. 'Walter never gave me any information, because I never asked him for any.'

Esme felt ashamed. 'I see that now. Sorry. But that implies someone was indeed shaking him down for money.'

'Does it? Poor Walter.'

They were coming to a bridge over the canal. 'I must be getting home, now,' said Esme. 'I'll get a taxi. Thanks for telling me all this, Joe. And I'm sorry I misjudged you.'

'People do that all the time,' said Joe. 'And Esme?'

'Yes?'

'Look after Walter.'

52

Esme was surprised that there was no message from Otto for her when she arrived home that evening, nor the following morning. She was typing up her notes from the Rostock trip when the Drydens' front doorbell rang. The butler Prentiss answered it, and announced that a gentleman from the police wished to speak to her.

Mr Dryden had left for the embassy after breakfast. Esme had the butler show the policeman into the drawing room. He was a detective in plain clothes – young, thin, but with a round face and shiny red cheeks. Esme didn't recognise him from her earlier interviews regarding Harriet's murder. He perched on the sofa opposite Esme.

'Good morning, Fräulein Carmichael, my name is Assistant Detective Jungwirth. Thank you for seeing me.'

'Not at all. How can I help you?'

'Do you know Baron Adlerstein?'

'Yes, I do.' Fear gripped Esme. There was no good reason why someone as well-mannered as Otto would stand her up. There must be a bad reason. 'Has something happened to him?'

'I'm afraid so, Fräulein. He was found this morning at his apartment in Fasanenstrasse. He had been shot. Killed.'

'Oh, no!' Esme's hand flew to her mouth. For a few seconds she was stunned as her brain tried to comprehend what the young detective had said. Then tears came.

She let them. Poor Otto! Poor, poor Otto.

The policeman waited and watched patiently. Esme sniffed. 'Do you know by whom?' she asked.

'Not yet. That's what we are trying to find out.'

Esme nodded. 'I understand.'

'We found a notebook and a diary. You were supposed to meet Baron Adlerstein last night?'

'Yes,' Esme nodded. 'Yes. At the Hotel Excelsior at seven o'clock. He didn't show up.'

'We are not certain exactly when he was killed – how long it was before his housekeeper found him this morning – but he may have already been dead by the time you were supposed to meet him.'

The detective examined his notes. 'We found several phone numbers of hotels in Rostock in Baron Adlerstein's notebook; it seems he was trying to track you down there. And we found your address here.'

'He knew I was travelling to Rostock with my employer, and he did figure out which hotel we were staying in. He left a message for me: he wanted to meet me back in Berlin. There was a wire waiting for me here telling me where and when. The Excelsior at seven o'clock. But he never came.'

'Did you contact him yourself afterwards?'

'No.'

'Why not?'

'I assumed he would contact me. To apologise. But obviously, he never did.'

'Do you know what he wanted to speak to you about?'

'No.'

'Can you guess?'

Esme paused to think. If the police hadn't already linked the murder of Baron Adlerstein with a recent murder at Burg Adlerstein, they soon would. And they would discover that Esme had been asking questions about Harriet's death. Here was a chance for her to cast doubt on Ruth Jakubowski being Harriet's murderer.

But she didn't want to point the police to Mr Dryden and Joe Moretti. She wouldn't expose Mr Dryden until absolutely necessary. And it wasn't necessary. Yet.

She decided to tell the young detective everything – apart from that.

'You know that Otto owns Burg Adlerstein in Saxony? And that an American woman named Harriet Dryden was shot and killed there a couple of weeks ago?'

'Yes, we do.'

'Did you know that this is Harriet's house? She was my friend – my best friend. I have been staying here with her and her father who is Counselor at the American embassy.'

The detective scribbled furiously in his notebook. 'And do you think Baron Adlerstein wanted to speak to you about Fräulein Dryden's death?'

'Possibly. I don't know.'

'Do you know of any connection between the two murders?'

Esme told the detective how she had met Ruth Jakubowski outside the castle and how she didn't believe that Ruth was responsible for Harriet's death. She said that she had been asking questions about Harriet's murder and she had been threatened in the Tiergarten. She didn't tell him about Mr Dryden and Joe Moretti, nor about Annachiara and Harriet. But she did say that she knew that Otto had financial problems. The police would find that out for themselves pretty quickly.

The detective wrote it all down and asked questions to clarify certain points. He seemed intelligent and he had a sympathetic face.

'What was your relationship with Baron Adlerstein?'

Esme couldn't quite adjust to Otto being referred to as 'Baron'. He was just Otto. Barons were old. Otto was young. Had been young.

Otto would never be old.

Another tear slipped out of her eye.

The policeman waited patiently.

'We were friends,' Esme said. 'Harriet introduced us.'

'Anything more than that?'

'What do you mean?' Esme asked, trying to summon up indignation, but of course she knew what he meant.

'Were you his girlfriend?'

Esme looked at the kind grey eyes.

'No,' she said. 'Not yet.'

53

Archie puffed at his cigar and stared at the empty page of the notebook in front of him.

A comment Esme had made in Rostock had stuck in his head. Was Old Bluey really any good at the general game?

He was one of Prussia's most celebrated generals, but it was true he had lost a lot of battles.

Blücher was a fine leader in so many ways. He inspired loyalty, even love, in the men under his command. He was undoubtedly brave to the point of reckless: indeed, at the Battle of Ligny, the seventy-two-year-old Blücher had personally led a cavalry charge and become trapped beneath his dead horse, one of several that had been shot from underneath him during his career. Napoleon, who had beaten Blücher several times in 1814 as the Allies were marching on Paris, thought he was a rotten general, but an old rascal who was always eager to get up off his feet after a defeat and charge on to the next battle. Considering the manner in which Blücher had allowed himself to be holed up in Lübeck in 1806 by much larger French forces, there was no doubt he had made mistakes.

Yet he had won some important victories, such as Katzbach in 1813, and had played key roles in the defeat of Napoleon at Leipzig that same year and at Waterloo two years later.

Perhaps he had learned from his earlier mistakes? Archie decided to keep a look out for evidence of that, of errors Blücher had made in earlier battles that he avoided in later ones.

There was no doubt that actually seeing the sites of these battles helped Archie understand the man's military strengths. And weaknesses. He was looking forward to Leipzig. He should also find time to visit those battlefields east of Paris where Blücher had been outmanoeuvred by Napoleon in 1814.

The phone in his room rang. Lister answered. 'It's Miss Carmichael, sir. She's on her way up.'

Lister opened the door, and Esme rushed past him, flinging herself into Archie's arms.

'Oh, Archie!'

Archie stiffened with surprise and saw over her shoulder that Lister was surprised too. But a moment later, concern for Esme overwhelmed him. He wrapped his arms around her and pulled her tightly into his chest, where she sobbed.

Eventually, she stepped back. 'Come and sit down,' Archie said, drawing her to the small sofa. 'What is it?'

'It's Otto. He's dead!'

'No! Weren't you supposed to see him last night?'

'He never showed up. The police think he was already dead by then.'

'Was it an accident?'

'No. He was shot. In his apartment. The housekeeper found him in the morning.'

'Do they know who did it?'

Esme shook her head. 'No. They found some notes about how he had been trying to contact me and had fixed to meet me at the Excelsior last night. That's why the detective came to interview me. I told him everything I knew. Except about Joe and Mr Dryden.'

'Well, at least we know that Ruth wasn't responsible for killing him.'

'Yes. As do the police. And we know Otto didn't kill Harriet.'

'I suppose we do,' said Archie.

'Of course he didn't!' said Esme, her eyes ablaze. 'It's obvious whoever killed Harriet killed Otto.'

'The deaths must be connected,' Archie agreed. 'It would be too much of a coincidence otherwise. I'm sorry, Esme.' His voice was soft. 'Otto was a fine man. I know you liked him.'

Esme looked straight at Archie, her eyes moist. 'The thing is, Archie. I didn't tell you, but when we met for that picnic at Wannsee on Sunday, I kissed him. Or he kissed me. We both kissed each other.'

'Oh,' said Archie. 'I didn't realise.' He reached across to take Esme's hand and squeezed it. 'I am so sorry.'

'I need to tell Mr Dryden,' said Esme. 'To warn him before the police get to him.'

'Warn him?'

'So he's ready for them. In case they ask him about Joe.'

Archie frowned. 'Maybe they should ask about Joe. Maybe we should tell them about Joe.'

'No, Archie! It will destroy him. I'm going now.'

'I'll come with you.'

'It will be better if I see him alone.'

'I'm not so sure. If I go with you, then he'll realise that what you know, I know.'

'What do you mean?'

'Well,' said Archie. 'You said this proves that Otto didn't kill Harriet. But it doesn't quite.'

'Yes, it does.'

'What if Otto *was* blackmailing Dryden? That would give Dryden a motive to kill Otto.'

'No!'

'And if he guessed that you suspected him of that, he might kill you too.'

'You're leaping to conclusions! Anyway, he couldn't have killed Otto.'

'Why not?'

'Because he was at a dinner at the British embassy last night. I saw him before he left.'

'Perhaps he stopped at Otto's apartment on the way? Or on the way home? The police don't know at what time Otto was killed, do they?'

'I still think you're wrong.'

'Maybe I am. But in the meantime, we go and see Dryden together. That way, if he wants to get rid of one of us, he will need to get rid of both of us. And that would be tricky.'

* * *

It was less than a ten-minute walk from the Adlon to the American embassy. On the way, Esme told Archie about her conversation with Joe the night before, how he had been happy to admit to his affair with Dryden, how he had denied that Dryden had given him any American secrets, how Dryden had called the affair off just before Harriet's murder and how, in Esme's opinion, Joe was genuinely in love with the older man.

Archie was doubtful; he feared Esme was too trusting. But he didn't want to contradict her when she was still reeling under the blow of Otto's death.

The embassy was in Wilhelmplatz, right opposite the Reich

Chancellery and close by the Kaiserhof Hotel. It was an excellent location, but much too small – the American government had had to rent office space all over the town for its staff. That was the reason they had bought the magnificent Blücher Palace next to the Adlon on Pariser Platz, but that was taking ages to get ready, something that was driving Mr Dryden to distraction.

The Counselor's office was ably defended by his secretary, a fifty-year-old Texan woman, but Esme's obvious distress and the mention of the word 'murder' persuaded her to see if Mr Dryden could find ten minutes for them before he went out to lunch.

He could.

He listened with sympathy as Esme explained what had happened. 'Oh, my dear, I am so sorry. I met the baron a couple of times at diplomatic functions and Harriet had him round to dinner once. A nice man.'

'He was a nice man,' said Esme.

'Do the police think the two deaths are connected?' Dryden asked, casually.

'They do now,' said Esme. 'I told them about Harriet's murder and how I thought Ruth Jakubowski was innocent. They may wish to speak to you. I thought I had better warn you.'

'Warn me?' said Dryden, raising his eyebrows. 'Why would I need warning?'

'Oh, I didn't mean that,' said Esme in confusion. 'I just meant that if the police came to see you, you wouldn't be surprised.'

'Ah. Thank you, my dear. But I very much doubt they will have any need to speak to me. Unless there is anything you said?'

'Oh, no,' said Esme. 'Quite the contrary.'

Archie interrupted. 'Mr Dryden. You mentioned you met Otto when Harriet invited him around to your house for dinner one day. Is that the same dinner at which you met Joe Moretti?'

'I think so,' said Dryden. 'Yes, it was.'

Esme shot Archie a warning glance. Archie ignored it.

'Can *you* see any connection between Otto's murder and Harriet's?'

'Me?' Dryden raised his eyebrows. 'No. Why should I? Apart from the obvious fact that Harriet was shot in Otto's castle grounds.'

Archie nodded. 'Was anyone trying to blackmail you, Mr Dryden?'

'Archie!' Esme hissed. Archie ignored her.

'No.' Dryden looked puzzled at first and then frowned. 'Why should anyone want to do that? Are you suggesting there might be a reason why someone would blackmail me?'

'Is there?'

'No. Of course not! And I resent the suggestion that there is.'

Archie smiled, but he knew it was a smile without warmth. 'I'm sorry, Mr Dryden. There's one more thing. Something I'm sure Esme would want you to know.'

Esme shifted in her chair next to him. 'There is?'

'If she were to come across anything of a private nature relating to you, she would do her very best to keep that thing private. Her very best. She is very fond of you, Mr Dryden.'

Dryden looked from Archie to Esme, his face impassive. A diplomat's mask. Interesting that Dryden felt the need to freeze, Archie thought. If he truly had no idea what Archie meant then his face would have shown more expression: confusion, anger, indifference even. But not professional neutrality.

'I am, Mr Dryden,' said Esme.

Dryden cleared his throat. 'Look here, Laverick. I don't know what you are talking about. Esme, my dear, I am so sorry to hear about your friend. Now, I have a luncheon appointment with the Japanese chargé d'affaires.'

* * *

'Archie!' Esme said, as they emerged from the building onto Wilhelmplatz, the stern façade of the Reich Chancellery opposite staring across the Platz at them. 'What was that about?'

'It was about finding out whether Dryden had been blackmailed.'

'Well, if it was, we didn't find out anything.'

'Oh, I think we did. He *was* being blackmailed. And it was probably about Joe. I could tell from his reaction. Couldn't you?'

'Maybe,' said Esme grudgingly. 'But we can't be sure. Why mention Joe?'

'To rattle him. So he knows we know.'

'Anyway, even if he was being blackmailed, it doesn't mean it was Otto who was blackmailing him, or that he killed Otto!'

'No. But it does mean he might have done.'

'I refuse to believe that, Archie. And I definitely don't believe he killed his own daughter!'

'Just keep an open mind.'

'Look. I trust you when it looks like you are a murderer. And I trust Otto. Trusted Otto, I mean.'

Archie smiled at Esme. Her trust was dangerous. But he admired it.

'Anyway, if you think Mr Dryden did kill Otto, why let him know we suspect him?'

'Because there are two of us. I don't think Dryden will try to kill both of us. It would raise a hell of a stink. Also, I let him know we are on his side. *If* he's innocent.'

'Well, I don't think he would try to kill anyone.'

'I understand that,' said Archie. 'And I hope you're right. Let's go back to the Adlon and get a cup of coffee and decide what to do next.'

54

They decided to talk to Gisela.

Archie rang the telephone number on the calling card she had given Esme, which was answered by her landlady, who sounded upset, but also guiltily excited. Gisela was at the police station, apparently.

They decided to give her time to get home, and wait until the evening to visit her. Gisela's building was in Kreuzberg, not far from the Tempelhof Aerodrome. It had seen better days, as had her landlady, a woman in her sixties in a high-necked dress and stern features who introduced herself as Frau Lattorf. A genteel widow fallen on hard times, Archie surmised – no doubt a suitable landlady for an aristocrat's daughter.

She asked them to wait in a sitting room, while she disappeared to see if Gisela would see them, her tone suggesting she very much doubted it. The room was dark, over-furnished with heavy wood, lace and gloomy portraits of gloomy Prussian ancestors. Outside, a twin-engined aeroplane roared over them as it climbed away from the aerodrome.

A minute later, Baroness Adlerstein appeared, followed by

her daughter. As Archie stood to kiss her hand he was struck by how composed the baroness seemed, especially when compared to Gisela, who looked a wreck. The poor girl's eyes were rimmed with red, yet glittered with a blue brightness that bordered on the manic.

'I'm so sorry for what happened to Otto,' Archie said.

'And so am I,' said Esme, flinging herself at Gisela and hugging her.

Gisela froze. Esme withdrew.

'Thank you,' Gisela said, distractedly. Her eyes shifted unsteadily to Esme. 'I know you liked him, Esme. And he liked you.' The tone was wooden, but Archie could see Esme appreciated the sentiment.

He knew Gisela would be upset, but somehow he hadn't expected she would be *this* upset, although of course, he should have. And now her mother was here as well, which also made sense. She must have taken the train from Adlerstein to Berlin as soon as she had heard the news that morning. He had a list of questions he had hoped to ask Gisela, but now he wasn't sure how to do it.

Esme stepped in. 'Oh, Gisela! How did it happen? The police interviewed me this morning, and they said he had been found dead in his apartment!'

'That's right,' said Gisela. 'His housekeeper found him; she comes most mornings. He was in the living room. He had been shot.' She put her hand to her mouth and started crying.

'Do they know who did it?'

'I don't think so. They asked me some questions and I answered them.'

'Did they find any connection with Harriet's death?'

'Connection? Why would there be any connection?' Gisela asked distractedly.

'Otto wanted to see me last night,' said Esme. 'I assumed it had something to do with Harriet.'

'Who cares?' wailed Gisela. 'Otto's dead! That's all that matters!'

'It was good of you to come round, but I think Gisela needs to rest,' said the baroness, her low, clear voice tinged with anger. 'She is upset. We both are.'

The woman stood erect, composed and determined.

'Of course,' said Archie. 'We'll call again in a couple of days, Gisela.'

'Perhaps you should leave it longer than that,' said the baroness. 'I have no doubt that my daughter will be in touch when she is ready.'

They left.

'Lordy, she's fierce!'

'Can you blame her?' said Archie. 'She's protecting her young.'

'The poor woman! And poor Gisela!'

55

Otto's death hit Esme hard. Of course, she had been much closer to Harriet than him, but a second killing dismantled her reserves of cheerfulness – drained them clean away.

Mr Dryden seemed affected as well. He was withdrawn, shrunken even. He was polite to Esme, but cold. Esme wished that Archie hadn't pulled that stunt of implying that Esme and he knew that Mr Dryden had been blackmailed. That had changed her from being a friend to an enemy; an enemy in his own house.

She couldn't believe that Mr Dryden had killed Otto. But she could believe that he felt responsible.

The police visited Esme the next day for a second interview. Assistant Detective Jungwirth reappeared, this time with a detective inspector in tow, who asked all the questions. It was a Sunday morning, Mr Dryden was at church, and Germans all over the country were going to polling stations, for the election was finally upon them. Esme had intended to spend the day on the streets talking to voters, but she didn't have the heart for it.

She barely had the energy to focus on the pages of *The Maltese Falcon*, which was lying on her lap in front of her.

The police had questions about Otto and, Esme was glad to hear, about Harriet. She answered them honestly, while omitting once again anything about Joe and Mr Dryden. Then she tried to slip in some questions of her own; she did a good job of coaxing answers out of the inspector. Her journalistic skills were improving.

Otto had been shot once in the heart. The police didn't know who had shot him, or if they did, they weren't telling. But they did think they knew the time of death – 6.10 p.m. the evening before he was discovered. A resident in his building had reported hearing a gunshot at that time, but the local patrolling policeman had investigated and found nothing. He had rung the bell to Otto's apartment, but on hearing no reply had moved on.

As to Ruth Jakubowski, she was still in custody. No doubt egged on by the Saxon police, or perhaps the Berlin political police, the inspector asked Esme if she knew of any link between Ruth and Otto, or whether Otto was interested in communism, or whether Harriet and Otto had had a sexual relationship.

Esme wanted to scream at them that they were looking in the wrong direction, but she couldn't without telling them about Dryden, and that she was not yet willing to do.

At least she knew for sure where Mr Dryden was at 6.10 p.m. the evening Otto was killed. In his bedroom getting changed for dinner at the British embassy.

She would enjoy telling Archie that. She knew he thought she was too trusting – of Mr Dryden, of Otto, of Joe. And it was beginning to irritate her.

Because the person she was finding it hardest to trust was Archie.

He should darn well tell her what had really happened in Norfolk that day in 1922.

* * *

She decided to go straight round to the Adlon and have it out with him. She went upstairs to her room to get a cardigan. As she passed Harriet's closed bedroom door, she paused.

She turned the doorknob and walked in.

The drawer of loose papers was still a mess, but a different kind of mess. The police had clearly rummaged through it.

But they had left the letter from Harriet's brother to her father safely in its envelope.

Harriet must have removed it from her father's possession. Why would she do that, if it was just about stock markets? The answer was, she wouldn't. It must be about something else.

Esme sat on Harriet's bed and reread the letter. It was dated ten days before their weekend at the castle and was short and to the point.

Dear Father,

I had a chat with your broker, Teddy Henderson, and he tells me that you have sold a deal of your stocks, including Ford Motor and Westinghouse. I think this is an error. The firm believes that the market will reach a bottom here and begin to rise in the fall and perhaps reach new highs in 1931. We are particularly bullish on Ford Motor. My recommendation is to buy Ford stock back over the next few weeks. I believe it will pay you to be courageous in the current market.

What have you done with the funds you have raised? Is it just in the bank waiting for an opportunity to get back into the market? I sure hope so.

Yours
Wally

The point wasn't that Wally thought the stock market was going up again. The point was that Mr Dryden had sold shares to raise cash.

To pay a blackmailer.

That wasn't the only item she had found in the drawer which appeared differently, given what she and Archie had learned.

She grabbed the card from Gisela to Harriet. She had assumed that Gisela had bumped into Harriet and her father in the Tiergarten. But as she reread it, she realised that that was not what the note had actually said at all.

Weds 18 August 1930

Dear Harriet,

It was a pleasure to bump into your father and then you this afternoon. We mentioned meeting for a cup of coffee. How about Kranzler's tomorrow morning at eleven o'clock?

Yours truly,
Gisela von Adlerstein

She reread the first line: 'your father *and then* you'. Gisela hadn't bumped into Harriet walking with her father in the Tiergarten. Harriet had bumped into Gisela and Mr Dryden together. Four days before she had been shot.

56

'Hello, Archie, how was Rostock?'

'Illuminating,' Archie said to his cousin down the telephone. 'Bad show to catch you at the embassy on a Sunday.'

'I know. What with the election today, they decided the fort should be manned. Or partially manned. By me.'

'Just a quick question. Did Walter Dryden dine at the embassy the evening before last?'

'He did. We had the permanent secretary from the Treasury over from London to discuss the Americans' debt plan. Dryden was here with his economics people. Just a warm-up, really. The proper discussions will take place tomorrow.'

'Were you there?'

'Of course! Someone has to carry the briefcases.'

'What time did Dryden show up?'

'I don't know. A bit before seven, I think.'

'And he stayed the entire evening?'

'Yes. Until after eleven. Dryden likes a glass of port or two. The embassy is always good for a glass of port.'

'All right, thank you, Duncan.'

'Archie? This doesn't have anything to do with poor Otto, does it?'

'I'd appreciate your discretion, Duncan.'

There was a moment's silence on the other end of the line. 'Right you are,' Duncan said. 'A lot of my job turns out to be putting two and two together, getting four and keeping quiet about it.'

Archie grinned. 'I'm sure you are very good at your job.'

'I'm not bad, actually,' said Duncan. 'Look, Archie, can I ask *you* a question?'

'Of course.'

'Do you think if I asked Esme out to the theatre or dinner or something, she'd say yes?'

The suave up-and-coming diplomat suddenly sounded nervous. Archie smiled to himself. 'Give it a couple of days. I think she's a bit cut up about Otto. But, yes, I suspect she might. Certainly worth a try. I'll put in a good word for you if she asks, but I doubt she'd listen to me.'

'Thanks, Archie. I'll give it a go.'

Archie put down the receiver. It sounded as if Dryden was in the clear. Esme would be pleased.

He wondered what response Duncan would get from her. Positive, he hoped.

There was a knock at the door and a boy presented Archie with a calling card. Erich von Witzbach was downstairs and wanted to see him.

* * *

Erich looked worn as he entered Archie's room. He refused the cup of coffee Archie offered him.

'My condolences about Otto,' said Archie. 'I know you were

good friends.'

'The best of friends,' said Erich. 'We met at university in Göttingen. We fenced together. Went to law school together. I shall miss him. He was a good man.' Erich sighed. 'A much better man than me.'

'I only met him a couple of times,' said Archie. 'I know Esme liked him.'

Erich smiled sadly. 'And he liked her,' he said. 'In fact, he was very taken with her.'

'I guessed as much.' Archie let silence linger.

'I've come to apologise,' said Erich. 'To you and to Esme. Especially to Esme.'

'Apologise? What for?'

'For urging you both to stop asking questions about Harriet's death.'

'I see,' said Archie. 'And why do you apologise now?'

'Because Otto's murder must have had something to do with Harriet,' said Erich. 'It's too much of a coincidence otherwise.'

'Have the police made a connection?'

'Not yet,' said Erich. 'I've been in touch with the detective inspector leading the investigation. They think there might be some communist plot behind it all, but that makes no sense. A woman was seen leaving the apartment building soon after the shot was heard, but the police haven't identified her yet, and of course she may not have had anything to do with it. Have you and Esme made any progress? Esme announced she had stopped asking questions, but I wondered if that really was the case?'

Archie examined Erich's face. He looked harassed. Concerned. Sad.

But the connection between the two deaths could be Erich.

'The reason Esme told you and the others she had stopped asking questions was that she had been threatened. In the Tiergarten. By a man who said he would kill her unless we stopped our inquiries.'

'No!' said Erich. 'Have you told the police this?'

'No, we haven't.'

'Did she stop asking questions?'

Archie didn't answer.

Erich watched him, understanding. 'Do you think *I* have something to do with this?' he said.

'Possibly,' said Archie.

'How? How possibly?'

'You mentioned that the police are fixated on a communist connection. You were seen speaking to a Soviet diplomat in a park in Neukölln recently. And having dinner with Hermann Göring in Horcher's, for that matter.'

'You are well informed.'

'We are.'

Erich frowned. 'I was wrong to dismiss your questions before. I won't do so now. As you know, I am President Hindenburg's secretary. You probably also know I have worked for General Schleicher in the past. In both those roles I have been responsible for...' He paused. 'For lines of communication. I wanted to open a line of communication with the Nazis.'

'I understand,' said Archie. 'And that was in a public place. But a park in Neukölln? That was a pretty secret meeting. You know Yevgeny Barsukov. Why not meet him somewhere in the centre of Berlin?'

'Who saw me? A journalist?'

Archie nodded. 'Claude Tazewell. On what he calls a "riot check".'

Erich sighed. 'All right. I'll tell you. Or rather I *won't* tell you.'

'What do you mean?'

'You'll see.'

'All right. Fire away.'

'You have probably heard the untrue rumours about how the Soviet Union is helping train the German army and air force?'

'I have.'

'And I think you heard Gray Trexler accusing me of being in Moscow to arrange that cooperation?'

'I did hear that.'

'Well, it's completely untrue.'

'It is?'

'Yes. I was not in Russia to negotiate military cooperation. And I was not discussing what do about the recent rumours with Yevgeny Barsukov in a park in Neukölln. Do I make myself clear?'

'You do,' said Archie.

'What did you think I was discussing?'

'We thought you might have been giving the Russians information,' said Archie. 'Or the Nazis.'

'What kind of information?'

Archie shook his head.

Erich looked as if he was about to repeat his question when he paused. Changed tack. 'I understand you don't trust me,' he said. 'And given what happened to Otto, I understand that Esme may be concerned for her own safety. But I want to help you. How can I do that? I don't have much formal power, but I work in the President's office. I can get things done. I can find things out.'

Archie was impressed. He knew he shouldn't trust Erich. But, on the other hand, if Erich genuinely wanted to help, Archie should take advantage of that.

'You can start with Ruth Jakubowski,' Archie said.

'The suspect for Harriet's murder?'

'The very same. We know she didn't shoot Harriet. She couldn't have done. It would have been physically impossible for her to break into the castle, steal the rifle and shoot her. She has no real motive. She was not working for Yevgeny Barsukov, and although she is a communist, she is probably not a spy of any kind. It's to prove her innocence that Esme got involved in asking questions in the first place.'

'If she's so obviously innocent, why haven't the police released her?'

'That's a good question and one that you may be able to answer. We believe that the local police, or more likely the political police here in Berlin, don't like her because she is a communist and a foreigner and perhaps because she is Jewish. It's political – she is the easy suspect, the quick result. And if it's political, perhaps you can suggest that the best thing to do politically might be to let her go.'

Erich nodded. 'I can talk to some people. I'll see what I can do. But that doesn't get us closer to who killed Otto. You mentioned information?'

Archie knew Erich could be tempting him to show his hand. Equally, he could be genuinely trying to help.

Archie decided to take the risk.

'You know Joe Moretti?'

'Of course I know Joe. He's a friend of mine.'

'How well do you know him?'

Erich frowned. 'As I said, he's a friend. You know that. Esme knows that. But he's not a close friend.'

'Did you know that Duncan Mandeville saw him leaving your bedroom at the castle in the middle of the night?'

Erich laughed. 'Oh, that! That was Joe trying his luck with me. He does that every now and then. When he's drunk. When he's been jilted. It's slightly annoying. But I like Joe, and I feel sorry for him. So I just turn him down. Politely. Why? What did you think? You thought we had a relationship? A homosexual relationship?'

Archie didn't reply.

'You thought he was giving me information? That I was passing on to the communists?'

Archie still didn't answer.

'Information he got how? A homosexual liaison of some kind?'

Archie was impressed with Erich's guesswork.

'With whom? A German government official? A soldier? A general, maybe? Well, you're wrong.'

Archie suspected he probably was, but didn't say so.

'Do you have any other theories? Any that involve Otto?'

Archie felt he had said enough. 'Do *you* have any idea why Otto was murdered?'

'No. None at all. That's why I'm here.' Erich stood up to leave. 'Look, Archie. I understand why you are so wary of trusting me. But if you need help, just ask. And keep asking the questions.'

He shook Archie's hand. 'I'll see what I can do about Ruth Jakubowski.'

57

After Erich had gone, Archie decided to wander the streets for a bit; see what Berlin looked like on an election day. The Sunday paper had been full of the fights between the Nazis and the communists in the working-class districts of Neukölln and Wedding.

But as he emerged from the Adlon, the sun was shining. The Pariser Platz looked much as it always did under the triumphant gaze of the goddess driving her chariot atop the Brandenburg Gate. Archie bought a cigar from the street vendor, and lit up. An English viscount, whom Archie recognised from his club back in St James's, emerged from a taxi with a sprightly young woman who was definitely not his viscountess and skipped up the steps into the hotel. Archie pretended he hadn't seen him.

He was about to set off down Unter den Linden when he heard his name called.

'Archie!'

It was Esme. She looked grave, which was not surprising.

'Hello, Esme,' Archie said. 'Guess who just came to see me?'

Esme stopped in front of him and stared, sullenly, not answering.

'Erich von Witzbach. He claims he wants to help us. He claims he was just making contact with Göring and that he was discussing the furore over the Soviets training the German army with Yevgeny Barsukov. And he confirmed Joe was trying it on that night at the castle; there was never any homosexual relationship between them. He sounded plausible, and it fits with what Joe told you, but I'm not sure yet we should believe him.'

Esme didn't reply.

'And I spoke to Duncan on the phone. He confirms Dryden was at the British embassy all evening. Or from seven till eleven anyway. So, it all depends what time Otto was killed.'

'I know when he was killed,' said Esme. On closer inspection, her face wasn't grave. It was darker than grave.

'You do?'

'Yes, I do. But that's not what I want to talk to you about. I want to talk to you about something else.'

'What?'

'Whether *you* murdered someone.'

'We've been through that!' Archie said irritably. 'I can't tell you. I *won't* tell you. I didn't kill anyone, you have to trust me on that.'

'I *don't* "have to trust you"!' said Esme, her voice rising, anger in her cheeks. 'I *need* to trust you. Can't you see? That's different.'

'What do you mean?'

Esme's anger seemed to dissipate in front of Archie's eyes into something else. Misery.

'I'm here in a foreign country, a foreign town. The only person I know here has been murdered. I met a nice guy – he's been murdered. My friend's father, the man with whom I am living, may have killed him for all I know. I had started making friends here, but I can't trust any of them. Any one of them may be a murderer, one of them probably is. And then there's *you*!'

'Me?'

'Yes, you! You're the one person I can trust. Except I can't! And I *need* to. You *have* to tell me. Did you kill that man? And if you didn't, who did?'

Archie had promised himself he would tell no one about Radway. Ever. He liked Esme, but she was his employee. She had no connection with him, or his family or Victor Radway.

But he understood her. She needed someone right then, someone on whom she could rely. And for better or for worse, that person was him.

'Let's go for a walk, shall we?'

They turned and headed away from Unter den Linden, through the Brandenburg Gate and into the Tiergarten.

Esme waited for him to speak. Archie puffed at his cigar, putting his story into the right order, making sure he really wanted to say what he was going to say.

'I met Daphne a couple of years before the war. I fell in love instantly. She was beautiful, witty, a rule-breaker. I was a very different man then to what I am now. I was amusing – charming, even. Popular. We had lots of friends. People invited us to parties. We had a hell of a lot of fun.

'We got married and the fun didn't stop. In the odd brief moment of introspection, I realised that Daphne didn't really understand me, but she didn't care and neither did I. Her family came from Surrey. She didn't understand the countryside and she *hated* Yorkshire, but we lived in London, so that didn't matter either. I worked in the City, in a half-hearted way.

'War came and I joined the family regiment, the Yorkshire

Fusiliers. The Second Battalion, my brother was in the First. Daphne said she thought I was frightfully dashing and brave. I probably was.'

'I'm sure you were,' said Esme.

'War was hell. I came back a different man. The man you see now.' Archie hesitated. 'No. Worse, in the couple of years after the war. Much worse.

'Daphne tried. She tried really hard. But I was beastly to her. She asked me what had happened, how I felt, how the war had hurt me, what I thought about her. Good questions; questions to which she had the right to know the answers. I didn't answer any of them. I barely smiled at her for years.

'Then my father died and we moved up to Yorkshire to take over Yarmer Hall. She hated it. She tried it for one damp summer, but then she spent as much time as she could in London.

'I knew she had lovers there. It would be wrong to say I didn't care – I did care – but I couldn't blame her. People did that kind of thing then; I'm sure they still do. But then I saw her with an old friend of mine from school, Vicky Radway. And I became jealous.

'By that stage, Lister was working for me. He and I had been through a lot in the war together. So, I got Lister to follow her. He was unhappy, but I cajoled him into doing it. He discovered Daphne and Radway were going for a weekend in Norfolk together – a place by the sea called Blakeney. She had told me she was going to stay with a school friend in Suffolk.

'So we drove down from Yorkshire, Lister and I and the chauffeur. I burst in on them. There was a row. I hit Radway several times.

'I turned to shout at my wife. She looked over my shoulder and screamed. I spun around to see Radway about to bash my head in with a poker. Then I saw a flash of iron as he was struck in the side of his skull. He went down. And never got up.'

'Lister?' said Esme.

Archie nodded. 'He had heard the commotion and, despite my instructions not to disturb us, he had come up to the room with the tyre iron from the car.' Archie sighed. 'He says he thought Radway was about to kill me. I believe him.'

'So *he* killed Radway? To stop Radway from killing you?'

Archie nodded. 'Right.'

'And you took the rap for Lister?'

'Yes. I owe Lister my life from the war. And what's left of my sanity. I hoped I'd get off. I thought I'd have more chance than Lister would, especially since Daphne was willing to testify that it was an accident.'

'She was?'

'She felt as guilty about it as I did. And she thought Radway was definitely going to kill me. But the police were more diligent than we expected and I stood trial. I thought it was curtains, but I stuck with it. Lister wanted to confess, but I wouldn't let him. I suspect if I had been found guilty, he might have tried to. But I was willing to go to the gallows, if necessary.'

Archie paused, his voice halting. 'In fact, I rather hoped it would be necessary.'

'Oh, Archie!'

'I used to wish that Lister had just left me in the mud at St Quentin. I still do sometimes.' Archie pulled himself together. 'I don't want to get too maudlin over this. I stood trial. The judge took my side as a war hero in the most outrageous way and the jury let me off. So here I am. Still alive.'

'So, it's Lister who is the homicidal maniac, not you?'

'That's about the size of it. Although he won't touch you, I'm sure of that.'

'Unless I'm about to hit you over the head with a poker.'

'Unless you're about to do that,' Archie conceded. 'But that's hardly likely, is it?'

'Oh, I don't know. I don't own a poker. But if I did…' She stopped and turned to him, oblivious to the Berliners in their Sunday best clothes passing on either side. 'Thank you for telling me this, Archie. I can see why you didn't want to.'

'You believe me?'

'Yes. Yes, I do. And that helps. It helps a lot.'

'Needless to say, Daphne and I got divorced. Although I will always be grateful to her for perjuring herself to save Lister. She didn't have to do that.'

'It can't have helped the shell shock,' said Esme.

Archie didn't reply. The following couple of years had been the blackest of his life. Bleak, dark days. Dream-filled, terrified nights that would never end. The feeling of being totally alone in a world that didn't want him, that didn't need him, that he had no right to exist in. At a house party with some old and sympathetic friends, he had come down naked to breakfast in the morning and hidden under the dining table, safe from the shells that had rained down on him all through the night.

Esme didn't need to know all that.

'No,' he said simply.

Esme got the message. They walked on in silence, Archie steering them along a quieter path, through the trees.

Esme shuddered. 'I think this is near where that man threatened me.'

'Is it? We are not far from the rose garden. Shall we head for that?'

'I know where you mean,' said Esme. 'Good idea.'

'You said you knew what time Otto was murdered?' said Archie.

'Ten after six.' Esme told Archie about the visit from the detectives and the information that a gunshot had been heard in Otto's apartment building at 6.10 p.m. She also told him how she had reread the letter from Harriet's brother to their father and Gisela's note; how both messages looked very different in the light of what she knew now.

58

'It's Gisela, isn't it?'

They were sitting on a bench in the rose garden, Esme having successfully nabbed it seconds after a couple and their two small sons had vacated it. Most of the blooms had disappeared for the year, but a rosebush in front of them had erupted in late-season pink blossom. Augusta Victoria watched serenely over the garden's Sunday visitors.

'Gisela shot Harriet?'

'Well, we've ruled out Ruth. And I think we can rule out Joe and Erich. And Annachiara.'

'It does look as if Gisela was blackmailing Dryden,' Archie said.

'It does,' said Esme. 'We know he was paying out money to someone because he sold all those shares.'

'And Gisela's note to Harriet suggests that she was with Dryden in the Tiergarten.'

'Blackmailing him, no doubt.'

'How did she find out about Dryden and Joe?' said Archie.

Esme shrugged. 'No idea.'

'Harriet must have realised what Gisela was up to.'

'She knew Joe and her father were having an affair. She knew her father was raising cash. She saw Gisela with him. She must have put two and two together.'

'So she confronted Gisela at Kranzler's.'

'Or in the walled garden at the castle,' said Esme. 'I remember she and Gisela went to look around the garden together, the evening before Harriet was shot.'

'Harriet threatened to expose Gisela...'

'And so Gisela shot her,' said Esme.

They sat there, mulling that idea over.

'Except she didn't,' said Archie.

'What do you mean?'

'She was at breakfast with Joe and Annachiara when Harriet was shot. She can't have done it.'

'Yes, of course! Unless Joe and Annachiara are covering for her?'

'Why would they do that? Why would they *both* do that?'

'They wouldn't,' said Esme. 'But it does look like Gisela was blackmailing Mr Dryden. And we trusted her! She seemed so helpful. What about the black eye?'

'Probably self-inflicted,' said Archie. 'To make it look as if the threat to you was real. No doubt she was the one paying Fritz Walch to scare you. She took me in. All that guff about working for a judge and wanting justice!'

'She just wanted to see what we were up to. And then put us off.' Esme shook her head. 'All right. If Gisela didn't shoot Harriet, who did? I refuse to believe it was Otto.'

'Why not? He could be working with his sister. He was desperate to raise money to keep the castle afloat. And he was alone at the time of the murder. In the estate office.'

'Then why was *he* killed too?'

'I don't know.'

'Remember, he wanted to talk to me about something urgently. Maybe he had discovered that his sister had been blackmailing Mr Dryden.'

'You're just speculating, Esme.' But Archie saw Esme's point. He didn't really think Otto had shot Harriet either.

'Perhaps we should look at it from another angle,' said Esme. 'Remember Moses suggested we focus on who didn't have an alibi?'

'I do.' Archie pulled out his notebook and pen and opened it to a blank page. 'Let me write down everyone at the castle and where they were when Harriet was shot.'

He scribbled out a list of names and locations on the page.

Esme – with Harriet on horse
Gisela, Joe, Annachiara – breakfast
Gray, Erich – walk in the forest
Duncan – bath
Otto – estate office alone
Ruth – outside castle

He and Esme stared at the list.

'It looks like Otto to me,' he said.

'It can't be,' said Esme. 'I just don't believe it.'

She stared harder.

'Archie?'

'Yes?'

'You've missed a name out.'

59

Archie stood a couple of feet behind Esme outside Walter Dryden's open library door.

Esme knocked. Dryden looked up. 'Come in, my dear.'

Archie followed Esme into the room and shut the door behind him.

Dryden was sitting in his usual chair, opposite the portrait of his wife, the *Paris Herald* folded on the small table beside him, next to a glass of amber liquid.

The half smile that had momentarily softened his face when Esme had entered disappeared when he saw Archie.

'Laverick?' he said. He glowered at Esme, clearly disapproving of her bringing Archie into his house.

'We'd both like to talk to you for a moment,' said Esme. 'It won't take long.'

That was a lie. This was going to take a while.

Habitual politeness temporarily blunted Dryden's indignation. Esme took advantage to plop herself on the sofa. Archie sat in an armchair.

'I don't have time for this,' said Dryden. 'It's the election today. I have to keep an eye on things.'

'There's nothing to keep an eye on until the results start coming in,' said Esme.

'Laverick. I'd be grateful if you would leave now.'

Archie decided to get to the point. 'Mr Dryden. We know that you and Joe Moretti have been having an affair.'

'I beg your pardon! That's outrageous!'

'And we know that you have been blackmailed as a result. By Gisela von Adlerstein.'

'You talked about blackmail yesterday. I told you it was absurd then and it's absurd now.'

'Harriet found out about the blackmail,' Archie went on. 'She tried to put a stop to it. That's why she was killed.'

Dryden opened his mouth. And closed it again. His diplomat's mask had tumbled to the floor. His face betrayed a turmoil of emotions. Anger, still. Surprise. Shock. Shame. Fear.

Esme spoke softly. Kindly. 'Ida saw you and Joe kissing one night. In here.'

'Servants' tittle-tattle,' Dryden said, quietly, but his heart wasn't in it.

'Ida told me that Harriet saw you too.'

'Harriet saw us?' Dryden put his head in his hands. And then looked up at Esme, all attempts at denial gone.

'I found a note from Gisela in Harriet's drawer mentioning that Harriet had bumped into you and Gisela together in the Tiergarten. Gisela was blackmailing you then, wasn't she?'

Dryden stared at Esme blankly.

'And Harriet had another letter. From Wally to you, asking you why you had sold lots of your stocks. It was to raise funds to pay Gisela, wasn't it?'

'What has this got to do with Harriet's death?'

'Harriet knew about your affair with Joe. She had guessed about the blackmail. We believe she spoke to Gisela to force her to stop. And so she was shot.'

'She was trying to protect you,' said Esme.

'Oh, dear God!' said Dryden. 'You mean it's my fault she was killed?'

'No,' said Archie. 'It was the fault of whoever shot her.'

'The von Adlerstein woman?'

'You could say that,' said Archie. 'How much did Gisela ask for?'

'Fifty thousand dollars at first. And now she has asked for a further two hundred thousand.'

'And you paid her?'

'I paid the first fifty thousand. I'm trying to get hold of the next two hundred thousand, but I don't think I can.'

'How did she know about you and Joe?' Esme asked.

Dryden blinked. 'She said she had seen us coming out of his apartment building in Kreuzberg. Apparently, she and Joe live on the same street.'

'That's hardly conclusive evidence, is it?'

'Not really. I should have bluffed it out. But she was so certain! She claimed that she could tell there was something between Joe and me when we first met at dinner here. I was terrified of being exposed. Not just professionally, although that would have been bad enough. But I didn't want Harriet to find out. And you say she knew all along?'

'That's right, Mr Dryden.'

'I'm not a fairy, you know,' Dryden protested weakly. 'It was just an aberration. I don't know what came over me.'

'We are not here to judge you,' said Archie. 'We would have ignored it and told Ida to do the same if Harriet hadn't been killed and an innocent woman arrested for the crime.'

'Joe told me about you,' said Esme. 'He respects you. He told me he loves you.'

'He told you that?'

As Dryden scrambled to gather his thoughts, there was a knock at the door, and Lister appeared. 'Your guests are here, Miss Carmichael.'

'Who the devil are you?' said Dryden.

'That's my man, Lister,' said Archie. 'Send them in, Lister.'

'Where's Prentiss?' demanded Dryden.

But before anyone could answer, Baroness Adlerstein entered the room, followed by her daughter.

Dryden was speechless for a moment. Then he got to his feet. The baroness held out her hand and Dryden shook it. 'Good afternoon,' he mumbled.

'Good afternoon,' said the baroness. 'Sir Archibald. I didn't know you would be here.' The baroness smiled at Esme.

Gisela looked on, her face impassive.

'Thank you for coming, baroness,' said Archie. 'Esme thought it would be good for the two of you to meet, since you have both lost your children in such dreadful circumstances.'

Dryden looked confused, but the baroness took Archie's comment in her stride. 'Ah, yes. I am sorry about Harriet. I thought she was a delightful woman.'

Dryden, still confused, mumbled his thanks. 'And for your son,' he began, but then tailed off.

'Have a seat, baroness,' Archie said. 'Fräulein von Adlerstein.'

The baroness and her daughter took the remaining two chairs in the library.

'We were just talking to Mr Dryden about how he had been blackmailed,' said Archie. 'By you, Gisela.'

'Blackmailed?' said the baroness, frowning. 'Blackmailed about what?'

'That doesn't matter,' said Archie. 'What does matter is that Harriet found out about the blackmail and confronted Gisela about it. And that's why she was shot.'

'You think *Gisela* shot Harriet? That's ridiculous!'

'Not Gisela, baroness. She was in the dining room eating breakfast. You.'

60

'Me? That is truly ridiculous.' The baroness's voice was laden with contempt. Gisela's expression was frozen solid, every muscle in her face rigid.

'It was either you, or your son,' said Archie.

'And we don't think Otto shot Harriet,' said Esme.

'Of course he didn't!' said the baroness. 'None of us did. It was that communist Austrian girl – Gray Trexler's lover.'

'She's innocent,' said Esme. 'Of that we're certain.'

'In fact,' said Archie, 'we believe Otto found out about the blackmail payment and wanted to tell Esme about it. So you shot him as well.'

'*I* shot my son?'

The baroness's outrage was subtly different when reacting to this accusation. The incredulity was more real. The shock more genuine.

She looked at Gisela. Her expression slipped from contempt into horror. 'Gisela?'

Archie glanced from mother to daughter. 'Oh, I see. You, baroness, shot Harriet. And Gisela shot Otto. Why did you do that, Gisela? Had Otto discovered you were blackmailing Mr Dryden?'

Gisela calmly reached into her handbag and pulled out a pistol. She took a couple of steps backwards and pointed it in Archie's direction.

'Gisela!' the baroness cried in surprise – and anger.

'I didn't mean to, Mama,' said Gisela, in German. 'When you told Otto that you had raised the funds to pay off the mortgages on the estate from an aunt, he suspected the money had come from somewhere else. You don't have any aunts rich enough to give us that kind of cash. I tried to say I knew nothing about it, but there was no fooling Otto – he could tell it came from me. In the end, I told him about blackmailing Mr Dryden. I thought he would thank me: I had saved the castle. Dryden is a pervert, as is Joe. They brought it on themselves.

'Otto didn't agree. He said he was going to give the money back; he said some vile things about me. Then he started talking about Harriet's death, about how he was going to meet Esme that evening to tell her about his suspicions. Then he was going to the police.

'I didn't tell Otto that it was you who shot Harriet, Mama; I think he thought I had. I lost my temper with him. I pulled out Father's pistol and threatened him. I told him I was expecting another two hundred thousand dollars from Herr Dryden, and he should use that to pay off the mortgage and just forget where it came from.'

The rigidity in Gisela's face wobbled for a moment, and then she regained control. 'He came towards me, telling me to give him the gun. I knew if I gave it to him, it would all be over for me, for you, for Burg Adlerstein. So I panicked. I shot him! In the heart. And he died, right there, in front of me.'

'Gisela!' The baroness's self-possession had disappeared. 'Gisela, how could you? Your own brother! And with Papa's gun!'

'I wish I hadn't, but I did. And that's where we are right now.'

'Gisela,' said Archie, gently. 'Give me that gun. There's no escape from here.'

'Stop where you are!' said Gisela. 'You know what happened to the last man who tried to take this gun from me. Esme. Open the window.' She nodded towards one of the library windows opening out to the garden. 'Are you coming with me, Mama?'

'No, Gisela,' said the baroness. 'You are on your own.'

There was a knock at the door.

Dryden glanced at Gisela. 'Wait!' he commanded.

The door opened anyway and Lister's head appeared. As soon as he spotted Gisela with the gun, he flung the door fully open and launched himself at her.

She pulled the trigger. Twice. One of the bullets missed, but the other hit Lister in the upper chest. He cried out and staggered. Gisela took two steps back against the wall to avoid his falling body.

Archie saw his chance. He stepped forward, raised his walking stick and brought it down firmly on Gisela's arm. She let out a yelp and dropped the weapon.

'Stand back!' Archie yelled, raising the stick to her again.

The baroness calmly picked up the revolver from the floor and pointed it at Archie. 'No, you stand back.'

Lister was groaning on the rug. Archie ignored the baroness and dropped to his knees. Lister was wounded in the shoulder. It was bleeding, but not too badly. He had seen much worse, as had Lister. 'You're going to be all right, old chap.'

'Course I am,' Lister replied through gritted teeth.

Gisela approached her mother, but the baroness waved the gun at her. 'Get away from me!' she said in German.

They all took a step back. Prentiss, the Drydens' butler, stood opened-mouthed in the doorway.

'Get in here and shut the door,' the baroness instructed him.

He did as he was told and stood next to Esme.

'None of you move,' the baroness said, pointing her gun, her husband's gun, at each of them in turn.

But her strength and coolness were seeping away before Archie's eyes.

She looked bleakly towards Dryden. 'I'm so sorry,' she said, in English again. 'About my daughter blackmailing you, and about killing poor Harriet. I didn't find out what Gisela had been doing until Harriet threatened to expose her. Harriet had worked out that Gisela was blackmailing you and warned her in the walled garden at the castle that she would go to the police unless Gisela promised to stop. Gisela believed her: she didn't know what to do.

'I did. Gisela had got herself into an awful mess. I am her mother; I had to get her out of it. I am a good shot, and I knew no one would suspect me. And if we made sure that Gisela was at breakfast when Esme and Harriet went out for their ride, then she would never be suspected either.

'We were just lucky that that Austrian girl showed up at the castle, and a communist as well! An easy suspect for the police to blame. I'd do anything to protect my children, Mr Dryden. Anything.'

The baroness turned towards Archie. 'Sir Archibald. You must understand how important it is for us not to lose Burg Adlerstein? Three hundred and twenty years it's been in the family!'

Archie rose from Lister's side. 'No house is that important. And what do you do now that one of your children has killed the other?'

'Let's go, Mama,' said Gisela. 'Climb out of the window with me and run.'

'You won't get very far,' said Archie.

The baroness's shoulders slumped. In those seconds she aged ten years: her face lost its colour and its vigour. She looked at Dryden. She looked at Gisela. She looked at Lister on the floor. And then she closed her eyes and placed the gun against her temple.

Archie wasn't inclined to plead with her not to do it. Neither, it appeared, was Gisela.

They watched in silence, for what seemed like an age.

Then the baroness opened her eyes, brought the gun down from her temple and turned to Dryden. 'Here. You take it. And shoot me if you want to. I deserve it.'

Walter Dryden took the pistol, placed it next to the telephone on his desk and picked up the receiver. '*Polizei, bitte.*'

61

As Archie entered the ornate dining room at the Adlon he spotted Esme and Joe at a table in the corner. There was a fourth place laid, which was empty.

He shook Joe's hand. The journalist looked well, relatively speaking. His face was pale but he didn't seem to be either drunk or hungover. His longish hair had been combed once that morning, although a dark curl hung down over his eye. But he did look nervous.

'Thank you for arranging this, Archie,' he said, nodding towards the empty fourth place setting.

'Not at all. It seemed to Esme and me that you might want to see each other, and there is nowhere more discreet than the Adlon at lunch time.'

Archie grinned. The dining room was three-quarters full, and no doubt some of the other diners would recognise Joe. Or their other guest. But Archie and Esme would act as an effective smokescreen.

'And Walter was happy with the idea?'

'I think he was pleased when I suggested it,' said Esme.

'Although of course he wouldn't admit that to me. You know, sometimes, Archie, I suspect that man of being English.'

'A British spy in the heart of the American embassy? I couldn't possibly comment. Although I will admit the bod knows how to hold a knife and fork.'

'Presumably, he won't be a diplomat much longer,' said Joe. 'When it all gets out.'

'I'm not sure it will all get out,' said Archie.

'How can it not? There will be a trial, won't there? And the blackmail must come out.'

'That's true. But Erich has been remarkably helpful. The view of the German government is that it would be unfortunate if the nature of the blackmail were to become public. The plan is to suggest that the liaison was of a delicate nature, but to imply that the other party was the wife of a senior unnamed German politician.'

'But what about the baroness? And Gisela?'

'It looks as if they will go along with that. The nature of the blackmail isn't vital to the case. And they are both intending to plead guilty anyway.'

'I was wondering why the police haven't been in touch.'

'We hope you won't hear from them. And the press are playing along.'

'So Walter won't lose his job?'

'He's planning to resign,' said Esme. 'As you know, the ambassador is away, campaigning in Kentucky for his successor in the senate. When he gets back to Berlin, Mr Dryden will explain everything to him and hand in his resignation. Mr Dryden thinks the ambassador will accept it. Archie isn't so sure, are you, Archie?'

'It may be easier for the ambassador to go along with everyone else,' said Archie. 'Diplomats are rather good at sweeping things under the carpet. And Dryden never gave anyone any secrets.'

'Let's hope you're right,' said Joe. 'I would hate Walter to lose his career over me. What about the Austrian woman? Have they released her?'

'I spoke to her lawyer yesterday,' said Archie. 'She is free. She has gone straight from Dresden to Vienna.' To see a doctor, he and Esme presumed, although they didn't actually know what she would do about her baby.

'I admire you both for sticking up for her,' said Joe. 'The rest of us were happy to follow the police line. We're journalists! We should have been the ones asking questions.'

'Gray didn't want to ask any questions,' Esme said bitterly. 'And he knew some of the answers. I know he's a friend of yours, Joe, but I think the man is a louse.'

'We all have our sins,' said Joe. 'I know I do. I tend to forgive sins in other people.'

That sounded very fine, thought Archie, but it didn't really cut it. He could sense it didn't cut it for Esme either.

'What about you, Esme?' Joe said. 'Have you written up the election?'

'I've filed one story for the *Mercury*. But they seem much keener on an idea I have for a series of articles about Harriet's murder. Written like a mystery story and published over several weeks. I've sent the first one off and the editor is real excited. I've kept you out of it and changed some of the names. I checked with Mr Dryden – I thought he'd be unhappy with the idea, but actually he seemed pleased. I told him I plan to imply that his affair was with a woman, the wife of someone important. He didn't actually say so, but I think he likes that idea.' She smiled. 'He also said Harriet would be pleased.'

'She probably would,' said Joe. 'Do you know when the funeral is?'

'Next week. Wednesday. At the American Church. Wally, her brother, is finally arriving from the States tomorrow.'

'Walter won't mind if I go, will he?' Joe asked.

'You can ask him,' said Archie.

The tall, lean figure of Walter Dryden approached the table, nodding left and right to acquaintances on the way. His suit was immaculate, his moustache well-trimmed, not a grey hair out of place. He shook Joe's proffered hand with a polite smile, but for just a moment he held Joe's eyes.

It was four days after the election and that was the main topic of conversation. The Nazis had done much better than many observers had expected, their seat count had gone up from 12 to 107, and they had overtaken the communists. They were now the second-largest party in the Reichstag after the SPD. Rumours were rife of first a communist coup and then a Nazi one. Chancellor Brüning and President Hindenburg had some juggling to do. Walter Dryden seemed to think that the upshot would be that Brüning would continue to govern by presidential decree, a conclusion with which Joe didn't disagree.

Archie realised that the subject didn't matter much to the four people around the table, or only as much as it gave them a neutral topic to discuss. The conversation flowed warmly; Archie ordered a second bottle of claret to help it on its way. Dryden and Joe both lightened in front of his eyes, encouraged by Esme, who refused to take the serious political situation seriously. Of course the two murders hung over all of them, but just for an hour or two, they were going to enjoy each other's company.

Archie felt... Well, what did Archie feel?

Happy.

Odd that.

Esme checked her watch. 'Oh, is that the time? I must be going. I'm supposed to be meeting someone.' She put her napkin down on the table. 'Can you come with me, Archie? To protect me.'

'Protect you from what?'

'Rioting communists. Or Nazis. Who knows what will be going on in the streets?'

Archie was happy to leave Joe and Dryden together for a few minutes. There was no riot on the Pariser Platz. The Berlin streets were quiet.

For now.

'Who are you meeting?' he asked Esme.

'You'll have to wait and see.'

'Will I?' But Archie knew. He lit his cigar. 'I'm glad your editor liked your idea for those articles.'

'Finnegan thinks he can syndicate them to newspapers across the States.'

'That's marvellous! Are you still available for Leipzig on Monday?'

'Wouldn't miss it for the world. A battle that Bluey fought in that he actually won!'

'Helped win. He wasn't in command that day. Moses will be joining us, so we'll spend some time in antiquarian bookshops.'

They stood, watching Berlin amble by.

'Archie?'

'Yes?'

'Are you figuring on writing another biography after Old Bluey?'

'As a matter of fact, I am.'

'A German? Or someone from somewhere else?'

'I was thinking of somewhere else. Maybe Vienna.'

'Because if you are, I might find the time to help. Mr Dryden has said I can stay with him while he is still in Berlin. But I'd be willing to travel elsewhere. If you needed me. We'd have to discuss a pay increase, of course. I'm an experienced research assistant now, you know.'

Archie tried to conceal his smile. 'I'll bear it in mind.'

A car screeched to a halt at the steps of the hotel, a cream-coloured Horch convertible.

'What-ho, Archie!' Duncan called from behind the steering wheel.

Archie lifted his cigar in acknowledgement.

'I think I recognise that car,' said Esme.

'Duncan said he wanted to take you for a drive in the countryside, and I told him I knew of a good garage.'

Esme kissed Archie on the cheek, the shrapnel-ravaged one.

'Move over, Duncan,' she said, opening the car door. 'I'll drive.'

* * *

MORE FROM MICHAEL RIDPATH

AUTHOR'S NOTE

This is a work of historical fiction. All the main characters are fictional, although many of the foreign correspondents bear similarities to some of those journalists who were working in Europe in the 1930s: men and women such as Vincent Sheean, Dorothy Thompson, John Gunther and his wife Frances Fineman, Norman Ebbutt and Sefton Delmer. I was inspired by two excellent accounts of the lives of American foreign correspondents at this time: *Last Call at the Hotel Imperial* by Deborah Cohen and *Fighting Words* by Nancy F. Cott.

I have often wondered about the silent pain of the hundreds of thousands of men throughout Europe following the First World War who had suffered what was then called shell shock and is now known as Post-Traumatic Stress Disorder and the hurt they caused their families. Martin Edwards pointed me towards two authors writing detective fiction in the 1930s whose work I found illuminating: Henry Wade, who was much decorated and much wounded in Flanders, and Dorothy Sayers, whose husband was badly affected by his years in the trenches.

I should like to thank Alex Day of Bernard Quaritch, Sophie

Hardach, Janet Holmes, Jayne Guitart, Peter Morris, Richenda Todd and my agent Oli Munson. Thanks also to my editor Emma Beswetherick and her colleagues at Boldwood and Cecily Blench for copy editing the manuscript and Jacqueline Beard MBE for proof reading it. And thanks and love, as always, to Barbara.

A MESSAGE FROM MICHAEL RIDPATH

Get *Operation Lost Hours*, a free 60-page story featuring Esme and Archie.

I hope you enjoyed reading this book as much as I enjoyed writing it. Thank you for buying it.

To write a book is to communicate directly with the person who reads it. I like to build as direct a relationship as I can with my readers and so I send occasional newsletters with information about my books and any special offers. If you sign up to my mailing list I will send you a free copy of a 60-page story featuring Archie and Esme and their hunt for a stolen manuscript. To sign up to the mailing list and get your free copy of *Operation Lost Hours* scan the QR code below:

ABOUT THE AUTHOR

Michael Ridpath is the bestselling author of over 20 crime novels and thrillers. His first novel, after a career in finance, was *Free to Trade*, a No 2 bestseller about the murky world of bond trading which was translated into over thirty languages. He is currently writing the Foreign Correspondent series of murder mysteries set in the capitals of Europe in the 1930s. He splits his time between London and Massachusetts.

Download your exclusive bonus content from Michael Ridpath here:

Visit Michael's website: https://www.michaelridpath.com/

Follow Michael on social media here:

- facebook.com/michaelridpathauthor
- instagram.com/michaelridpathauthor
- bookbub.com/authors/MichaelRidpath
- bsky.app/profile/michaelridpath.bsky.social

ALSO BY MICHAEL RIDPATH

The Foreign Correspondent Series

Operation Lost Hours

Operation Berlin

Operation Vienna

Printed in Dunstable, United Kingdom

84154621R10220